PRAISE FOR

SUNK IN LOVE

"An achingly beautiful second-chance romance that will stay with me for a very long time. Every page of this novel is filled with tenderness, humor, and hope. I love this book."

—Hannah Bonam-Young, *USA Today* bestselling author of *People Watching*

"Soul-nourishing, red-hot, and fiercely intimate. *Sunk in Love* features a marriage in peril with realistic, heart-crushing obstacles and a gorgeously earned HEA—a seemingly impossible feat to pull off, and yet it feels utterly flawless. Heather McBreen has a forever fan in me."

—Rachel Lynn Solomon, *New York Times* bestselling author of *What Happens in Amsterdam*

"My absolute favorite kind of romance is second chance, and Heather McBreen delivers a delicious one with *Sunk in Love*. I rooted for Roslyn and Liam to find their way back to one another, savored every tender (and steamy!) moment between them, and then cheered out loud when they finally stepped into their beautifully earned happily ever after. Second-chance lovers like me will devour this!"

—Jessica Joyce, *USA Today* bestselling author of *The Ex Vows*

"Gorgeous . . . simmers with angst, stolen glances, laugh-out-loud comedy, and delectable steam. Roslyn and Liam don't just find their way back to each other—they earn it—and in McBreen's generous, empathetic hands, the result is a marriage-in-crisis romance that's equal parts delicious and gut-wrenching. You'll want to drown in this."

—Katie Naymon, author of *You Between the Lines*

"*Sunk in Love* will meet second-chance romance readers at the trope's altar. From the fizzing tension that grows tauter with every turn of the page to the enchanting vacation backdrop that had me desperate for a taste, I devoured every word. I can't articulate all there is to adore here, but nothing so much as Liam and Roslyn's painstakingly earned happily ever after. Everyone should be paying attention to Heather McBreen."

—Clare Gilmore, *USA Today* bestselling author of *Perfect Fit*

"Swoony, sexy, and sensitive . . . a tender portrait of two people fighting to win back their happily ever after. Complete with cruise-ship hijinks, family drama, and super-hot steam, Heather McBreen delivers on the humor, tears, tummy flutters, and angst that come with giving your heart to someone who could tear it apart—or put it back together. Readers, look no further for the perfect second-chance romance from an author at the top of her craft. I'll read anything she writes!" —London Sperry, author of *Passion Project*

"A resonant, earnest look at what comes after happily ever after, Heather McBreen's sophomore novel is both deeply felt and sharply funny. The push and pull of Roslyn and Liam's love story is absolutely dripping with angst and yearning, all underscored by the deftly handled undercurrent of Roslyn's grief. *Sunk in Love* is a poignant story of two imperfect people learning to do their best for one another—and a beautiful reminder that the bravest thing we can be is hopeful. This book aches in all the best ways and has a permanent spot on my *favorites* shelf."

—Ellen O'Clover, author of *The Heartbreak Hotel*

"Heather McBreen has set the gold standard with her sophomore novel, *Sunk in Love*. In this steamy second-chance romance, McBreen expertly explores how love can help us find ourselves again after loss, all while delivering the same witty banter and delightful hijinks that made her debut so addictive. An absolute must-read for all romance lovers!" —Amy Buchanan, author of *Let's Call a Truce*

ALSO BY HEATHER McBREEN

Wedding Dashers

Sunk in Love

HEATHER McBREEN

BERKLEY ROMANCE
NEW YORK

BERKLEY ROMANCE
Published by Berkley
An imprint of Penguin Random House LLC
1745 Broadway, New York, NY 10019
penguinrandomhouse.com

Book design by Kristin del Rosario

Library of Congress Cataloging-in-Publication Data

Names: McBreen, Heather author
Title: Sunk in love / Heather McBreen.
Description: First edition. | New York: Berkley Romance, 2026.
Identifiers: LCCN 2025021445 (print) | LCCN 2025021446 (ebook) |
ISBN 9780593817643 trade paperback | ISBN 9780593817650 ebook
Subjects: LCGFT: Romance fiction | Novels | Fiction
Classification: LCC PS3613.C2758 S86 2026 (print) | LCC PS3613.C2758 (ebook)
LC record available at https://lccn.loc.gov/2025021445
LC ebook record available at https://lccn.loc.gov/2025021446

First Edition: January 2026

Printed in the United States of America
1st Printing

The authorized representative in the EU for product safety and compliance is Penguin Random House Ireland, Morrison Chambers, 32 Nassau Street, Dublin D02 YH68, Ireland, https://eu-contact.penguin.ie.

To Mom,
for encouraging me to tell my own stories

Author's Note

This story deals with topics such as alcohol consumption, divorce, depression, an abusive romantic relationship (not on page but referred to), parental abandonment (not on page but referred to), and the death of a parent (not on page but referred to). If you are sensitive to any of these, please read with care.

Sunk in Love

- 1 -

Now

I push soggy layers of pasta and dry beef back and forth on my plate, trying to guess whether the dish in front of me is actually lasagna, or if the cook realized too late that all they had was ketchup and mozzarella and decided to just go with it.

I pick up a forkful, examine it, then set it back down again.

Just because something is *called* lasagna on a menu doesn't make it lasagna. But then again, it's hard to enjoy . . . whatever this is, when my husband—soon-to-be-ex-husband—made what I enthusiastically dubbed The World's Best Lasagna.

I used to beg him for the recipe, but he'd just smile—the one with the dimples that made my knees go weak—and tell me that if he shared it, then I wouldn't ask him to make it for me anymore. Which seemed romantic at the time. A tacit declaration that he'd always be there.

But I guess that was just another lie. One of many.

"Roslyn? You've hardly touched your food," comes Grammy's voice, drawing me out of my thoughts and back into the restaurant where I'm seated under the glare of fluorescent lighting and my grandmother's gaze.

I've been dodging family dinner for months, cycling through numerous excuses. *Not feeling well. Doing taxes. Writing deadline.* But after the fourth last-minute cancellation, I figured I couldn't stave it off much longer. Which is how I ended up at a strip mall Italian eatery sitting across from my grandparents and siblings while they pepper me with questions I don't know how to answer.

"Just not hungry," I tell her, forcing a tight smile. Which I seem to be doing a lot of this evening. I wouldn't be surprised if my jaw hurts in the morning.

"Are you sick?" my little sister, Bella, asks from across the table. "You look like one of the cadavers from the lab we did last week."

"The flu has been especially bad this year," Jonah agrees, using his most distinguished I'm-your-older-brother-I-know-best voice. "My ER has seen a big uptick in high-risk cases."

"I was reading that as well," Gramps agrees before launching into a discussion of hospital politics and this year's flu variant while Bella, Jonah, and his husband all nod along, adding in thoughtful *hmmmms* and *good points* and *how interestings*, rendering me invisible as usual.

I used to resent conversations like this. Ones that widened the already existing gap between me and my family of doctors. But tonight, I'm thankful for the excuse to fade into the background of clattering plates and Frank Sinatra warbling over the speaker.

I return to picking at my food until the conversation wraps back around to me.

"If you're showing symptoms, you need to stay home, Roslyn," Gramps says, giving me a heavy look.

"I don't have the flu," I tell him.

I'm just getting divorced.

"And thanks for telling me I look like a dead body," I tell Bella. "You sure know how to flatter."

"What?" She raises both hands above the table in a sign of surrender. "I'm just saying as a doctor, you look unwell."

"Almost-doctor," I correct. "You're still in school."

"I only have one more year left," she says, giving me a pointed look as she sweeps a curtain of long blond hair from her eyes.

Between my siblings, Bella reminds me the most of our mother—tall, waifish, and elegant, like a ballerina, with glassy skin and straight, blond hair, while I look more like my dad. We might not have gotten a single child support payment from him, but I did get his short stature and dark, unruly curls that turn into a frizzy lion's mane anytime humidity exceeds 50 percent.

"If you're not hungry, why don't you ask for a box so you can bring the rest back to Liam," Grammy suggests, nodding toward my plate of picked-over food. "I'm sure he'll be hungry when he gets home from the hospital."

My stomach does a little flop at the sound of Liam's name. Though it's anyone's guess whether that's because Liam's name still inspires a cocktail of potent emotions ranging from anger to crippling sadness, or because my family still doesn't know that I asked Liam for a divorce and I've been lying about his whereabouts for the last three months.

"Right. Good idea," I tell Grammy, forcing yet another tight smile. "He'll probably be hungry after his shift." *Lie.* I don't even know if Liam's working tonight. Though long hospital shifts are an excuse my family of doctors is used to.

"It's too bad he couldn't join us for dinner," Grammy says, casting the vacant seat beside me a lingering look. "It's been ages since we've seen him. Poor thing had that stomach bug last month."

"I thought it was a sinus infection?" Jonah asks.

"Um, yeah, he had that too," I say, playing with my napkin.

"Liam sure has been sick a lot," Bella says, pinning me with a hard look, and I mentally berate myself for not diversifying my excuses a little more. I could have said he was out of town. Or hell, faked his death. Or better yet, faked my own death so I don't have to be here right now.

"Is he feeling any better?" Grammy asks.

I corral my mouth into another strained smile. "Much better."

Grammy nods, pleased. "Good. We need him in tip-top health for the family vacation coming up. After all, we've got a full itinerary planned. Hiking in Maui. Zip-lining on Oahu. Snorkeling on the Big Island."

"Right," I say. "He's really excited for the trip." *Another lie.*

Usually, the annual family vacation is one of the highlights of the year. A time to relax and unwind, all expenses generously paid for by my wealthy grandparents. But I've been dreading this year's ten-day cruise around the Hawaiian Islands. Not just because I'll be lying through my teeth about how poor Liam came down with *insert another illness here* and couldn't make the trip. But because it'll be the first family vacation since my mother passed just over a year ago.

I glance at the restaurant door, halfway expecting her to blow through, her usual twenty to forty minutes late, the familiar jangle of jewelry announcing her presence from across the room. But she won't. Not tonight. Not ever again.

My hand absentmindedly goes to my left wrist, where her favorite silver bracelet now sits.

"Speaking of Liam," Gramps says, turning toward me. "Roslyn, you must be thrilled about Liam's research getting selected."

I frown, sitting up straighter. Selected? Selected for what?

Liam and I have hardly spoken about anything more substantial than who is paying the Netflix bill in months, so I'm totally out of the loop on his life. But based on the way everyone is looking at me, this is clearly something I'm supposed to be *ecstatic* about. Something I would know if Liam and I were still together.

I decide to play along. "Right. Yes. I'm just . . . *thrilled*."

This seems to be the correct response because everyone beams.

"I'd say I'm surprised, but I'm not," Bella says. "Liam's a total badass."

"When I read his research methods, it was like watching Michelangelo and a block of marble," Jonah chimes in.

"We couldn't be happier for him," Grammy says, her eyes crinkling as she smiles.

"Same," I say, my head bobbing up and down with as much forced enthusiasm as I can muster. "So exciting!"

While I don't know what they're talking about, it's not hard to guess. Liam's a brilliant oncologist whose star has been on the rise for years. He's probably gotten *another* publishing credit or research grant. Or maybe even a giant, flashing neon sign declaring **I'm the Best**, hand-delivered by the ghost of Johns Hopkins, which at this point isn't entirely unrealistic.

Though I'm less annoyed by Liam's never-ending supply of accomplishments—or the fact that my family all probably have sex dreams about his research papers but won't touch any of my published novels with a ten-foot pole—and more irritated by the fact that apparently Liam is still in contact with them.

I endure a brief stab of anxiety that Liam might have told them the truth, before realizing that if he had, we wouldn't be talking about Liam's news; we'd probably be talking about how I'm just like my mother, and Liam was always too good for me anyway.

"I knew as soon as you brought that boy home for Christmas nine years ago that he would go far," Gramps says, pointing his fork at me.

I school my mouth to smile. "Yeah, he's . . ." My brain supplies a million adjectives, none of which are appropriate. "Brilliant," I say instead.

My grandparents grin. "We're just so proud," Gramps says, giving Grammy's hand a quick squeeze as though Liam's accomplishments were as much theirs as his. Though I suppose in a way they are.

My grandfather, Dr. Harrold Larsen, is a renowned surgeon best known for something to do with revolutionizing heart surgery that I've never fully understood but am now too afraid to ask about. He's also been Liam's biggest advocate, doing everything from writing him letters of recommendation to helping him secure a fellowship after residency.

It used to be validating, knowing how much my family loved and admired Liam. Their support felt like a stamp of approval, declaring that I'd done a good job picking a husband. Or perhaps that I was somehow worthy because *he,* the handsome, successful doctor, had picked *me*. But now it feels like a wedge between us, a reminder that, without Liam, I'm nothing more than the family disappointment.

Which is exactly why I haven't told them about the divorce yet. It's not just that it will be painful to admit my marriage failed, that whatever Liam and I once had wasn't enough. It's the blowback that will come with it. The crushing disappointment. The accusations. The blame. Mostly I'm afraid this will be the final confirmation that I'm just as much of a fuckup as my grandfather already thinks I am.

"He's already accomplished so much for his age," Gramps continues. "I wouldn't be surprised if he gets tapped for department head before forty." Gramps gives a little laugh, then pauses, like he's not sure whether to continue before saying, "You know, Roslyn, maybe if you'd finished medical school, this could have been you."

I suppress an inward groan.

Really? We're still doing this? Then again, Gramps never tires of reminding me of my *wasted potential.*

"It's a little late for that now," I say, pushing the now-cold lasagna more aggressively across my plate.

"You could always go back," Gramps says. "I'm good friends with the director of admissions and—"

"Gramps," I say, cutting him off. "I'm not going back, okay? I have a writing career."

Another lie. I *had* a writing career. Emphasis on *had.* But I haven't written anything in almost a year, not since my mother's death. I told my agent I'd have a new manuscript for her by Christmas, but it's September, and I haven't got so much as a premise.

Gramps's eyes narrow on me. "Your writing is more of a hobby, wouldn't you say?"

I thought I'd get used to the little digs since I dropped out of medical school nine years ago. But nope. They still sting.

"No," I say tightly. "My career isn't a hobby."

I wait for Gramps to push back, to condescendingly ask how many copies I've sold, or make a comment about romance being an *unserious* genre even though he's never read any of my work. Instead, Gramps gives me a hard, unblinking stare that's worse than if he'd said anything at all.

I sigh and look down at my plate, wishing my mom were here.

If she were, she'd defend me the way she always did when Gramps made comments about her losing yet another job or getting pregnant at sixteen.

While I've always been too much of a people pleaser to stand up for myself, my mom wore Gramps's disappointment like a badge of honor, a declaration that she didn't care what he thought of her. Not Gramps. Not anyone. But now that she's gone, there's no buffer, no one to suggest we leave and get gas station Popsicles instead. No one is left to be brave for me.

The thought aches like a phantom limb whose absence I can't shake, until Grammy clinks her fork against her glass, commanding everyone's attention.

"I know it wasn't easy to get you all together this evening," she says, casting my brother a look from across the table.

"Hey, don't look at me!" Jonah says. "It was Roslyn who kept canceling."

"I was sick," I lie.

"I thought it was taxes?" Bella asks.

"That too," I mutter.

Grammy chuckles good-naturedly. "As much as we love getting the family together for dinner, I must admit that your grandfather and I had an ulterior motive in bringing you here tonight."

Everyone sits up a little straighter, brows furrowing with curiosity.

"It's been a hard year on all of us." She pauses, and my chest cramps the way it always does when my mom comes up. "Which is why your grandfather and I have decided to do something special on this family trip." Gramps takes her hand, both of them exchanging soft smiles before she says, "We're going to renew our vows in Hawaii."

There's a pause of silence before the table erupts into a chorus of cheers and excited chatter.

Despite our differences, I've always admired the kind of love my grandparents have. The kind that's rooted in true admiration for each other. The kind that used to fuel my writing, back when I believed in happily ever afters and grand gestures and the power of a great kiss. Before my own marriage imploded.

"When Gramps and I got married fifty years ago, we didn't have the money for a real wedding," Grammy goes on. "Your grandfather was just a poor med student, and I didn't have two nickels to rub together. But now, we'd like to finally have the wedding we always wanted, and it will be even more special because we'll have all the people we love most there with us."

Everyone except Mom, I think.

I glance up and down the table, surveying the faces of my siblings and grandparents, wondering if anyone else feels it too. The sharp edges of grief. The sting of her absence. But everyone looks excited, happy even, and I can't help feeling like all the air is evaporating from my lungs.

Maybe it's because I'm the one who was in the car with her when she died, or because we were always closest, but I feel like her death has hit me much harder than everyone else. Like I've lost a vital organ while everyone else is nursing a few cuts and bruises.

Grammy goes on about the trip, talking about how much it means to have us all there before assigning roles for who is in charge of flowers and food and activities (Jonah, a classic firstborn, agrees to everything while Bella whines that she's too busy with med school) before looking to me.

"Roslyn, Gramps and I were talking in the car on the way here, and we'd both love it if Liam would do the ceremony. He did such a wonderful job when he officiated Jonah and Ben's wedding." She nods toward my older brother and his husband. "Will you ask him, dear?"

Panic shoots through my chest, mouth instantly turning to sand.

Liam's not *supposed* to go on the trip. He's *supposed* to stay home while I drink mai tais and enter my coastal grandmother era.

I already had it all planned out. Twelve hours before our scheduled departure, I was going to call my grandparents and explain that poor Liam had a bad stomach bug and couldn't make it. They'd express their disappointment and wish Liam a speedy recovery, and I'd pretend to hem and haw over whether to stay behind and take care of him before finally agreeing that it was best for me to come on the trip without him. After all, it's what Liam wanted me to do. It was *for the best*. But Liam being asked to officiate a vow renewal was *not* part of the plan!

My stomach tumbles back and forth like I'm already aboard the cruise, overcome with seasickness, and I look down at my plate, wondering if I might be sick.

"Dear, are you all right?" Grammy asks me, putting a concerned hand on my knee. "You look ill."

"You're not going to puke, are you?" Bella asks.

"Maybe you caught something from Liam?" Jonah asks.

"I'm fine," I croak.

But I'm not fine.

I was hoping for a few more months before I came clean about Liam and me, at least until the dust settled and the wound wasn't so fresh. But now the circumstances have changed, Liam has become essential, and I don't know how to tell the truth without wrecking the trip.

Ever since I dropped out of med school, I've tried so hard to be *good*, unproblematic, the one who minds her own business and stays out of trouble. Like maybe if I can just do everything else right in life—marry the right man, show up to family dinners, and keep to myself—I'll somehow work my way out of family purgatory and back into their good graces. But ruining my grandparents' vow renewal with Liam's and my shitty news will just prove that Gramps is right. I *am* the family disappointment.

I rack my brain, trying to come up with a solution, something to buy us more time. But the more I think about it, the more it feels like I'm standing in front of a train barreling down the tracks with nothing I can do to stop it. I'm going to have to talk to Liam.

I look back at Grammy and Gramps. "Of course I'll ask him," I say, forcing a grin. And as if my nose isn't long enough, I add, "I'm sure he'd be delighted."

Apparently, rock bottom has a basement. And I'm in it.

- 2 -

Now

I spend the entire drive home oscillating between hope and despair.

Maybe I'm catastrophizing and my family won't be that upset about the divorce?

Doubtful. Liam is everyone's favorite golden boy. They'll be devastated, and it will be my fault for ruining the trip.

But maybe I can come up with a more elaborate excuse for why he can't come? An emergency at the hospital? Something he absolutely can't get out of?

Probably not. Gramps has too many connections at Liam's workplace. It would take about three seconds before my bluff was called.

When I get home, the house is dark and cold, like no one's been here in ages, even though I've been gone only a few hours. I turn on the lights, preemptively flinching as the front hall comes into view.

No matter how many times I set foot in here, it feels like walking through a minefield of emotional booby traps.

The foyer used to be lined with photographs. Liam and me on

our wedding day. Skiing in Tahoe with my family. Christmas at my grandparents'. But after he moved out, I couldn't stand to look at them. Now all that's left are dust shadows where the frames once hung.

I remember showing Liam the listing for this house a few months before our wedding five years ago. How he'd patiently let me gush over the white shutters and the blue trim and the spacious kitchen before kissing me on the forehead and whispering, *Sorry, baby, but it's outside our budget.*

I'd begged him to go with me and see the house anyway. *Just for fun.* But once we got inside the hundred-year-old two-bed two-bath in Seattle's Phinney Ridge neighborhood, we'd both been utterly charmed. *You could use the second bedroom as a writing office,* Liam had mused. *And the dining room is big enough that we could host your whole family for Christmas.*

A week later we'd signed the papers.

At the time our future felt indisputable. We were in love. We were getting married. We were buying our first home, where we planned to have children and build a life together.

Everything felt so certain, so sure. Like nothing could ever derail our dreams.

Now the same house that once felt like a brick-and-mortar confirmation of everything we had feels like a reminder of all the things we've lost. A future that's no longer ours.

Everything from the pair of Liam's shoes collecting dust by the front door, to the bookmark tucked into the Jonas Salk biography on his side of the bed that he's never going to finish, all echo the same thing: It's over. He's gone. And whatever life we had here is gone now, too, replaced only by ghosts and haunted memories.

I kick off my shoes and tie my unruly curls in a bun before shimmying out of my jeans, eager to get back to the same dirty pair of sweats I've been living in the last few weeks. Once I feel appropriately gremlin-like, I take a deep breath, pull out my phone, and find Liam's contact.

Our communication has been sparse, approaching nonexistent, since he moved out, and I have no idea how he'll react to hearing from me. Will he be mad? Insist on telling the truth? Screen my call? But I have no choice. We need to sort this mess out. And the sooner, the better.

Three rings later, the familiar drawn-out timbre of Liam's British accent comes through clear and deep, bringing with it the image of dark eyes and sandy hair and the lingering scent of citrus and spice. "Roslyn? What's wrong? Is everything okay?"

I'm unsure what catches me more off guard, the question, or the worry threading through his voice. Does he know why I'm calling? Did Grammy and Gramps already ask him?

Then I realize.

A couple of weeks after Liam moved out, I had a nightmare reliving the fatal car accident that killed my mom. I woke up with my chest hurting so badly, I thought I was having a heart attack, or worse. So I called the only person I could think of. I called Liam.

I can still hear the low vibrations of his voice in my ear as he'd told me to stay where I was. *I'll be right there.*

Fifteen minutes later his key was in the door, and he was stroking my hair, telling me everything was going to be all right.

I'm here. You're okay.

He'd held me until I fell asleep. When I woke up, he was gone, almost like the whole thing hadn't happened. Which, to be honest, I wish it hadn't.

"I'm fine," I say curtly. "I'm calling because we have a problem."

"What kind of problem?"

"You know how the family vacation is coming up?"

I can hear the bob of his throat as he swallows. "Yes."

"Well, my grandparents have decided to renew their vows this year and . . . they asked if you would officiate."

"Officiate?" he repeats.

"Yup. They want you to perform the ceremony and talk about enduring love and commitment."

"Fuck."

"Fuck is right," I say with a humorless laugh. "So what are we going to do?"

For a long moment he's silent, and I can practically see the way his eyes are narrowing, brows furrowing like they always do when he's thinking. It's an expression I used to find sexy. In fact, there was once a time when I found most everything about Liam sexy, from his accent to the way his forearms flexed when he washed the dishes. But the same traits that once had me dragging him to the bedroom now feel like salt in a wound—inconvenient reminders that the once bright flame of passion between us has all but fizzled out.

"I suppose we'll just have to tell them the truth," Liam says at last. "About the . . ."

My throat squeezes. Though I can't tell if that's because of what he's just suggested, or the fact that he can't quite say the word *divorce.*

"But we agreed we wouldn't tell them yet," I say. "Not until the moment was right. And trust me when I say my grandparents' vow renewal isn't the right moment."

When he sighs, he sounds tired. "I know. I'm not exactly eager to look Grammy in the eyes and tell her we're ending our marriage either . . ."

There's a beat of discomfort in his voice, and my heart rate ramps up. *This is good. If he doesn't want to tell them either, maybe we can work something out.*

". . . But what other choice do we have, Roslyn? We can't keep lying."

My chest deflates. "There has to be something we can tell them. Some believable reason why you can't come," I say, my voice stretched thin with desperation. "Like maybe you're up for a Nobel Prize? They'd *definitely* believe that."

"Yeah, definitely," Liam deadpans. "Right up until the moment they find out that's not true."

"Okay, what about you're deathly afraid of ships?" I try. "Or you get seasick?"

"I'm fairly certain they won't believe that, considering I was just fine on Gramps's sailboat last summer."

Damn. He's right.

"What if you broke your leg?"

"Cruise ships are quite accessible nowadays per ADA regulations."

I huff in frustration. "Okay, how about you hit your head, end up in an induced coma, and when you wake up, you have amnesia and can't remember anything from the last few years?"

"Isn't that the plot to that Channing Tatum and Rachel McAdams movie that always makes you cry?"

My jaw flexes, not sure what annoys me more, him remembering that I love that movie, or that he's not contributing here. Maybe both.

"So what do *you* suggest?" I ask, unable to keep the frustration from my voice.

"I don't see a way to get out of this without making things worse than they already are, Ros."

I flinch at the sound of my nickname. It used to be something only he called me. Something that was especially cute when said with his charming British accent. Now it just feels like he's mocking me.

"Besides," he continues, "we're all adults. I'm sure your family can handle hearing the truth."

I swallow back a scoff. Easy for him to say.

"I think you're underestimating how much they love you, Liam. How much this will devastate them. Grammy will definitely cry."

"So why don't *you* tell them? Since it was your decision."

I bite back the urge to remind him that he's the one who decided to leave, who didn't even try. Who muttered *fine* before walking out without even a fight. Instead, I say, "Look, I just think we need to figure out a game plan here. Something to buy us a little more time."

A sigh rattles through the receiver. After a long pause, he says, "I don't want to tell them either, but I don't see a way around this."

I move toward the sink, gripping the porcelain basin as I imagine what it will be like to tell the truth. The gasps, and crestfallen faces, and questions. Oh God, *the questions . . .*

They'll ask me *when* and *why*. And *whose fault was it?* Like the dissolution of our marriage was a car accident with an easily identifiable party at fault. Then they'll ask, *how could you let a man like Liam go?* And I won't know what to say. Or how to say it.

I won't know how to explain the pit of grief I've been trapped in since my mother's death. Or all the ways it led to the end for Liam and me. And even if I did, they wouldn't understand.

My breath stalls, throat tightening like someone's pulled a zipper up its length, and before I can stop them, tears prick the backs of my eyes.

Fuck. I hate that I'm crying over this. *Over him.*

I wish I were in the *moving on* part of my life. The scene where I'm holding a paint roller, finally going over that green kitchen wall Liam and I painted together, feeling at peace, content, self-actualized.

Woman who is going to be okay. But I haven't even been able to begin the divorce paperwork hidden upstairs, much less paint a wall. And I haven't been okay in a long time.

I wipe under my eyes, about to make an excuse to end the call when I hear the faint sound of laughter through the receiver.

"Are you out somewhere?" I ask.

"No. Kevin just has some mates over," Liam says. The laughter increases, and I hear someone shout Liam's name in the background.

I look down at my ratty hoodie and sweats—my uniform of the last several months—and instantly feel a tug of annoyance. It's 9 p.m. on a Tuesday. I'm planning to fall asleep to the lullaby of trashy TV because I can't stand the silence. Meanwhile he and Kevin—whom he's been crashing with—are having a party?

I can't even remember the last time either Liam or I went out. Liam's more of a stay-home-and-cook-dinner-on-a-Friday-night type of guy. But apparently New Single Liam hosts parties. On a Tuesday, no less.

"It sounds like a party," I say, raising my voice to be heard over the increasing din.

"It's not," he says, just as someone in the background yells, "Liam, get off the phone! Katie wants to do a shot with you!"

Katie? Who's Katie?

I open my mouth to ask when Liam says, "Listen, Ros, I've gotta go."

"Don't call me Ros—" But the call has already ended.

The fuck?

I've barely spoken to Liam in the months since he moved out, but I'd imagined (hoped?) he was at least *a little* torn up about the disintegration of our five-year marriage. That the bitten-off *fine* he'd muttered before he left was indicative of a deeper emotional wound. An inability to say how he was really feeling in the moment. But apparently, he truly is *fine*.

He's going to parties. And doing shots with girls named *Katie*. Meanwhile, I'm decidedly not *fine*.

I look around the now-dark kitchen: the green accent wall we spent a Saturday painting, the stack of dirty dishes in the sink I haven't found the willpower to wash, the pungent aroma of rotting garbage wafting from the overflowing trash can that Liam used to be the one to take out. Everything's become a reminder of him. Of the life we once had. Like some kind of perverted, unhygienic shrine to our failed marriage, with me as its patron saint.

Of course I'm frustrated by the family vacation situation. But frustration is just the tip of the iceberg. Under the jagged tip is a mammoth, frozen hunk of hurt that hasn't begun to thaw since he left.

Hurt that this clearly isn't causing Liam the same pain it is me. Hurt that our once happy home is now an emotional minefield of bad memories and broken promises. Hurt that I still wake up in the middle of the night searching for his warm body next to mine, only to find cold, empty sheets.

Mostly, it hurts to know that whatever we once had wasn't enough to save us.

- 3 -

Now

I'm on the couch, bottle of wine balanced between my knees, preparing for another night bingeing *Emily in Paris*—Emily is currently the only person whose life is messier than mine—when I see that it's ten to 9 p.m., which means it's almost midnight in New Jersey, which means Abby will definitely still be up. I can picture her on the couch with a mug of tea, engrossed in whatever omegaverse smut she's currently obsessed with.

Abby and I have been best friends since college when a random committee assigned us as roommates. I was pre-med and afraid to talk to boys, and she was undecided and in the *talking stage* with four different guys. We had absolutely nothing in common except for the fact that we shared a twelve-by-twenty-foot space. But as we navigated the woes of freshman year, from our first time getting drunk at a frat party to learning how to sneak into the cafeteria without swiping our meal cards, we formed a kind of unbreakable bond, one that can only come from driving to Walgreens at 3 a.m. to buy tampons and Flamin' Hot Cheetos.

We've been inseparable ever since. That is, until a few years ago when Abby got married and moved with her husband to

New Jersey. Now our friendship exists largely via texts and phone calls.

Abby's the only person who knows about the divorce, which means I've been relying on her emotionally a lot lately. I know she loves me and wants to be there for me, but I also know that she has a life and husband and problems of her own, and I can't help but worry that one day I'll have maxed out my social currency and she'll be sick of hearing about my troubles. Not that she would ever say that, but I still try to save the midnight phone calls for emergencies only. Which this definitely is.

"Hey," comes Abby's familiar voice as soon as I dial. "Perfect timing. Jake just went to bed, and I'm reading in the living room. I just got to the end of the chapter, and the werewolf just confessed he's an alpha and that he wants to knot her."

"Don't let me interrupt, then," I tease.

She laughs. "This is more important. How did it go at dinner with your family?"

"Really fucking bad."

"Oh no. Don't tell me they found out about you and Liam?"

"No, but they're going to now that my grandparents are renewing their vows during this year's family vacation and are expecting Liam to officiate."

"Well, shit. What did you tell them?" she asks.

"Nothing. I still need to figure it out," I sigh. "But I'm soooo fucked."

"Are you going to tell Liam?"

"I already did, *not* that he was any help."

Abby gasps theatrically. "You talked to Liam? What did he say? How did he sound? Did he sound miserable? Did he cry?"

I swallow back a snort. "Not exactly. He was at a party with some girl named Katie."

"Who the *fuck* is Katie?" she demands.

"I have no idea," I say, trying to block out thoughts of a beautiful woman with a red power lip that looks suspiciously like Meredith Blake. "But apparently she wanted to do a shot with him."

"You don't think he's like . . ." She hesitates. "Dating again, is he?"

I briefly imagine what it might be like to see Liam's hand in someone else's, his lips swollen from another woman's kiss, and I instantly feel ill.

"I don't know," I admit. "He's not exactly keeping me in the loop on his life right now."

"You want me to see if I can find her online?" Abby asks.

Abby is great at social media stalking. She can predict if a guy is cheating with 99 percent accuracy just by looking at his tagged photos. But I don't think I'm emotionally ready to find out who this Katie is. At least not tonight.

"No, that's okay," I tell her.

"You sure? I've already got it narrowed down between three potentials. Did she sound like more of a Katherine or a Kathleen?"

"I'm sure," I say before adding, "I guess I'm just hurt that he's moving on so fast. I mean, I know I'm the one who officially ended things, but still. Shouldn't there at least be a mourning period? Shouldn't this feel shitty for him too?"

There's a beat of silence before Abby asks, "How do you know it's not? I mean, do you really think Liam's moved on that fast? It's only been three months. Maybe he's trying to make you jealous because he wants to get back together?" she tries. "That totally happened to me with that guy I dated in college. Hank? Henry? He started dating this other girl, but later I found out they were never even together. It was all for show to make me jealous."

I resist the urge to roll my eyes. For as long as I've known her,

Abby's always had a gaggle of men vying for her attention. *Of course* a guy would go to the effort of faking a relationship just to make Abby jealous. But that's her life, not mine. In my life, my mom dies and my husband decides to check out of our marriage.

I think about the night I said it was over, the night Liam left. How he'd just stood there, expression blank while I silently pleaded with him to fight with me—*for* me. But he hadn't. He'd just let everything fall apart around us until we were standing in the rubble.

I'd been the one to finally nail the coffin shut, but he'd handed me the hammer.

"Yeah, he's just desperate to get me back," I deadpan. "That's why he left without a fight. Because he's still in love with me."

"I just don't believe he'd move on so fast," Abby says. "When you guys were together, he practically had heart emojis for eyes every time you walked in the room."

Heat crawls up my collar. She's right. We did *used* to be like that. But that was before. Before my mom died. Before we stopped having sex. Before grief and resentment and anger pushed us apart and ruined everything.

Or maybe things were ruined long ago; it just took the death of my mother to find out that what I thought had been a firm foundation of deep and abiding love actually wasn't. That our marriage hadn't been enough to withstand the tsunami of grief that had pinned me down and gutted me. Or maybe worse still, *I* hadn't been enough. That after my mom died, things just got too hard, too difficult, and in the end, I wasn't worth it to him.

"Well, believe it. He's moved on," I say, playing with my mom's bracelet. "Now I have to figure out what to do about this fucking vacation."

"What did Liam say when you told him?"

"He thinks we should tell the truth and get it over with," I tell her, sitting up and setting the bottle of wine on the coffee table.

"And are you okay with telling them?" Abby asks.

"I mean no, but what choice do I have? It's not like I can keep pretending we're still together."

There's a long pause before Abby replies, "Well, why not?"

I snort. "Good one. But I think they'll probably figure it out when Liam stops showing up for Thanksgiving and Christmas."

"No, I mean for the trip," she clarifies. "Hear me out, what if... you two pretend to still be together."

"Pretend?" I repeat, sure I've misheard.

"Yeah. This is the first family vacation since your mom's death and your grandparents are renewing their vows. This isn't exactly the ideal time to break the news. But if you pretend to still be together, you can buy yourselves more time and not ruin the trip."

I start to laugh, only to realize that she's not laughing back. "Wait. You're serious? You can't be serious."

"I'm serious."

I shake my head. "No way!"

"Why not?"

"Because that's ridiculous!" I tell her.

"Is it, though?" she asks. "You two were together for nine years. You know everything about each other. You could pull it off if you wanted to."

If. That's a pretty big if.

And yet she's right. We *do* know everything about each other. I know that Liam's coffee order includes seven-dollar whipped cream monstrosities, and that he can only wear Calvin Klein boxer briefs because he claims that any other brand feels *itchy*. But none of this is helpful information when it comes to pretending to still be in love.

We're not Hollywood actors. We can't just fake chemistry and adoring glances when the cameras are on. Even if that's something we once felt for real.

"We aren't exactly chummy right now," I tell her, slumping back against the couch. "We can barely get through a phone call, much less put on a big show for my family. It wouldn't work."

"It would just be for ten days," she says. "I'm sure you two can call a truce for the sake of this trip."

I've told Abby about the problems between me and Liam. But I'm not sure she fully grasps how bad things were, especially in the final months leading up to the end. How deafening the silences were, how being with him felt worse than being alone, and how there would be nothing simple about Liam and me pretending to still be together.

Besides, even if we could pull it off, I doubt Liam would go along with any such charade. Not when he's clearly busy living his best new, single life with *Katie* and fuck knows who else.

"What makes you think Liam would even agree to this?" I ask.

"Isn't he super close with your family?" Abby asks.

"Yeah but—"

"So chances are he isn't ready to tell them either," she finishes.

I want to tell her she's wrong, that his relationship with my family wouldn't be enough to convince him, but she has a point.

Liam's always been tight with my family. Not just because they are the founders of the Official Liam Woods Fan Club. But because he hasn't seen his own family in England in more than fifteen years—not since his dad kicked him out when he was eighteen. Which means my family became his family and losing them would mean losing the only one he has left.

I allow the idea to expand and inflate, steadily becoming more and more fleshed out, until it takes hold with a kind of magnetic force that leaves me feeling off-balance.

What if . . . ?

No, we can't.

But what if we could? Wouldn't that buy us more time? Or at least allow us to come clean at a better time?

"I'm not saying we're going to do it," I say after a minute. "But if we did, what would pretending entail exactly? Would we have to kiss and stuff?"

"You're the romance writer," Abby says. "Aren't you supposed to be an expert on fake dating?"

"I don't think anything I've ever read has prepared me to pretend to still be with my soon-to-be-ex-husband," I say with a hollow laugh.

"So does this mean you're going to ask him?"

"I don't know," I admit, glancing toward my half-empty bottle of wine. "I think I've had too much to drink."

"Why don't you sleep on it," Abby suggests.

"And you think sleep will make me want to pretend to still be with my ex?"

"Maybe this could be good for you two."

"Good in what way exactly?"

"Good like it would give you the opportunity to spend some time together and work through your issues," she says hopefully.

Issues are what I have of *Vogue*. What Liam and I have are massive problems. Certainly not the kind that could be solved with a little fake-dating and forced proximity.

"Not to burst any bubbles here, Abs," I say. "But we're more likely to feed each other to the sharks than work through anything on this trip."

"I'm just saying," she says, speaking slowly like she's treading carefully. "I've seen this movie, and I'm pretty sure I know how it ends."

"*Texas Chainsaw Massacre*?"

She snorts. "Come on. You and Liam, pretending to still be together for ten days at sea? Trapped in a tiny stateroom? With very limited square footage?"

"I can only assume you mean we will engage in a hostile rendition of the silent treatment?"

She sighs, clearly exasperated. "I *mean* what if you and Liam fall back in love or something?"

Now it's my turn to snort. "I think you've been reading too many romance novels. That's not going to happen."

"How do you know?" she asks.

Abby, like pretty much everyone who has ever met him, has always been a big fan of Liam. Even after things imploded with us, she maintained a fierce optimism that we'd find our way back to each other.

You guys are soulmates. It might take some time, but you two will find your way back. I just know it.

But it's easy for her to see things through rose-tinted glasses when she's married to the kind of guy who wouldn't dare come home without flowers, and has her favorite macarons flown in from Paris every year on her birthday. Meanwhile, I've only grown more cynical.

I think about how after Liam left, I spent the first few days obsessively checking my phone for texts or voicemails. How I even slept with the ringer at full volume just in case he decided our marriage was worth fighting for. That *I* was worth fighting for.

But he hadn't, and the longer I went without hearing from him, the more I felt like the disintegration of our marriage was proof of some deep personal failing. Proof that I was wrong. Not just about Liam, but about *everything*.

Before Liam, I was cautious, never letting people close enough to be able to hurt me. I'd seen my mom have her heart broken by enough asshole boyfriends to know that if love was sobbing in the driveway at 2 a.m. over a man who treated you like dirt, then I didn't want it. But then Liam came along and he made me feel safe and certain and brave all at once, and little by little I let my defenses fall, and finally so did I. *Hard.*

I allowed myself to believe that Liam was different. That I could trust him to hold up the walls while everything crashed and burned around me. But in the end, I was wrong. And I'm not sure what hurts more—being wrong, or that I so badly wanted to be right.

"Because we're done," I say after a beat. "It's over. Trust me."

She sighs. "Maybe I'm just a hopeless romantic. But I always thought you two were endgame."

I'm not sure if it's an automatic reflex, or something more intuitive, but I reach for my left hand where the ring he gave me seven years ago still sits. A princess cut diamond along with a gold wedding band that, for reasons I can't quite explain, I haven't yet taken off.

I remember the day he proposed. The day he asked me to spend forever with him. I can still feel the hot air in my chest. The sting of tears in my eyes as I screamed *yes* and leapt into his arms, dizzy with happiness. Now the memory burns, sickeningly sweet, like I've eaten too much sugar too fast.

"Me, too," I tell her, my throat feeling newly sore. "I thought we were endgame too."

Nine years earlier

The dive bar is just as dive-y as I imagined it would be. Christmas lights—which I assume serve as year-round decor and not because it's November—drape the walls, casting colorful shadows across the dimly lit array of sagging booths and mismatched tables and chairs lining the wooden walls.

It's mostly empty, save for two men wearing flannel shirts and trucker hats perched at the bar, watching us with the same morbid interest as one might watch a roadside accident. It quickly becomes apparent that the green tube top Abby coerced me into wearing definitely doesn't match the vibe.

I knew this was a bad idea.

"I think we're a little overdressed," I whisper as the men at the bar cast us dubious looks.

"Who cares," Abby says, tossing her long brown hair over her shoulder. "We look hot."

While I'm sure we do look hot—or at least we would if we were at a hip nightclub in Prague and *not* a Seattle dive bar on a Wednesday—a double date with Abby's latest situationship and his reclusive roommate is pretty much the last thing I want to be on right now.

I'd much rather be on the couch while Netflix asks if I'm still watching like I've done since dropping out of med school two weeks ago. But Abby was sick of watching me mope, so here I am, dressed like I've been cast as the mean girl in an early 2000s Disney Channel show.

I'm just hoping my date isn't as boring as Abby thinks. Apparently, he's a grad student who holes up in his room studying for days, making appearances only for food and bathroom breaks. Sounds like a real party. Lucky me.

"Look, I see them," Abby says, nudging me in the direction of a booth toward the back. Kevin waves, but Kevin's friend has his back turned to us. I crane my neck, attempting to get a better look at my company for the evening. Despite only getting a glimpse of his profile, I can tell he has broad shoulders and a sharp jawline. Okay, not bad.

Abby must be thinking the same thing because she elbows my ribs and murmurs, "See? I told you this would be fun."

I don't know about *fun*. So far Netflix is still winning.

"Do I have to?" I whisper. "Can't we say I don't feel well or something?"

"Come on, at least give him a chance," Abby says. But when I continue to make a face, she adds, "But if he sucks, text me the word *pizza*, and I'll make up an excuse so we can leave, okay?"

I agree, resigning myself to at least thirty minutes of conversation before I use our code word as Abby's forceful hand propels me toward their table.

Kevin stands to greet us at the same time his friend turns around, and I swear my breath catches in my throat because this is *not* the geeky grad student I'd prepared for. Well, to be fair, he might be that, but he's also gorgeous. The type of gorgeous that makes me want to pluck a strand of his dirty blond hair and run tests on him because surely that kind of hotness must have come from a lab. Or the cutting-room floor of a Hollywood movie.

The first thing I notice is how tall he is. My gaze has to travel *up, up, up* just to meet his eyes as he stands. The second is how put together he is. Not a hair out of place, or a wrinkle in his perfectly pressed button-down rolled meticulously up his (noticeably veiny) forearms. He looks like the kind of man who sends thank-you cards after interviews and shows up to meet your family with a perfectly curated hostess gift.

He's so shiny, I think. Like a marble statue at a museum. Something to look at, but not touch. And suddenly I hate the green tube top I'm wearing even more than I did three minutes ago.

"Roslyn, this is my roommate, Liam," Kevin says, turning to Gorgeous Man. "Liam, this is Abby's roommate, Roslyn."

Liam's eyes flash as he holds out his hand to me. "Hi, Roslyn. Nice to meet you."

And if the stubborn strand of hair draped over his brow wasn't enough of an aphrodisiac, he's got a British accent.

My knees quite literally go weak.

I take his hand, (A) to be polite, and (B) because I'm having trouble staying upright.

Kevin and Abby take drink orders then head to the bar, leaving me helplessly alone with the most stunning piece of male specimen I've ever seen. He slides back into the booth and gestures for me to take the seat opposite him.

Be cool. Be cool.

But apparently growing up on a steady diet of nineties girlboss media isn't enough to spare me from brain-crippling speechlessness at the hands of this gorgeous man.

Thankfully Liam speaks first. "So you live with Abby?" he asks.

"I do. And you live with Kevin?"

"Regrettably."

A nervous, jittery laugh bubbles out of me. "You're not really friends?"

"I'd use the term loosely," he says. "He's nice, but what really drew us together was the fact that he was subletting a decent room close to campus and wasn't a serial killer."

I nod sagely. "It's so hard to find a good non–serial killer roommate these days."

He laughs and it's a good one. All low and throaty. The kind I want to hear again.

"So, do you always go on double dates with loosely defined friends?" I ask.

"No, I can't say that I do," he says, his mouth slipping into a charming smile. "But I heard that Abby's friend was very nice and very pretty, so I figured what's the harm."

I blink. Is this gorgeous man calling me pretty? Well, technically Kevin said it, but based on the way he's looking at me, all honey-eyed and curious, I can't help thinking he might agree.

"But I think the real question here is how you got dragged into coming along," he asks.

"How do you know I was dragged?"

"Because I believe Kevin's exact words to me were, *I told Abby to drag her roommate along.*"

"He actually used the word *drag*?" I ask.

"He did. Apparently Kevin has very little faith in my ability to meet women," Liam says, shooting me a self-deprecating grin. "He believed dragging was necessary."

"I have a hard time believing that's true," I say.

His eyebrows rise toward his hairline. "Oh really? And why's that?"

My lips bunch on one side of my mouth, smothering a smirk.

Okay, so he's cocky. But with that face and that accent, I'm not surprised.

"You know," I say, propping my elbows on the sticky tabletop, "I was told you'd be boring."

Another warm, husky laugh hums in the back of his throat. "And?"

"So far that's not the case."

He shifts forward in his seat, eyes flashing with amusement. "Glad to know I'm exceeding expectations."

I chew on my bottom lip, hoping he can't see the heat working its way up my neck.

"So what else did Abby tell you about me?" he asks as a dimple emerges in the side of his cheek. "Besides that I'm boring."

"Nothing really." *She left out the part where you're gorgeous.* "Just that you're in grad school and have no friends," I tell him.

"I am a grad student," he confirms.

"I notice you didn't contest the *no friends* part."

That darn dimple pops again. "I believe that one might be true," he says. "It's a bit tricky to have a social life while in the final year of med school."

I sit back. "Med school?"

"I'm almost done. Just finishing up rotations, then I'll start residency."

Something heavy drops into my center.

Of course I end up on a date with a smart, sexy guy who just so happens to be in med school. Like the universe just couldn't stand to miss out on one more opportunity to remind me of my failure.

"Where are you doing your residency?" I ask.

"Seattle," he says. "I got lucky and got accepted at a hospital here, so I won't have to move."

"And they didn't have any programs in England?" I ask.

"How do you know I'm from England?"

"I assumed based off the BBC accent."

"Oh, like you assumed I was boring?"

I laugh, and the corners of his mouth slant up as though pulled by invisible strings.

"You can thank my parents and posh prep school for the BBC accent," he says. "But I haven't been back to England since I was eighteen."

I want to ask why not, but we've only known each other a handful of minutes and it's probably not my place to pry, so instead, I ask, "What kind of medicine do you plan to practice?"

"Gynecological oncology."

Apparently, I have the maturity of a teenage boy because at the word *gynecological,* my cheeks flare with heat.

He tilts his chin. "Something wrong with that?"

"No, that's a great profession," I say quickly. "Why did you choose that?"

"So I could do cancer research and hopefully save lives."

Right. Of course this handsome, sexy, funny, perfect man is also going to save the world. God, I'm the worst.

"And yes, I do, in fact, look at vaginas all day," he says. "For training purposes, of course."

My breath hitches, catching on a snare in my throat. "Excuse me?"

"Well, you were thinking it, weren't you?"

"No I wasn't." Okay fine, I was a little bit. But he doesn't need to know that.

His eyes catch the glare of the twinkly Christmas lights overhead, and I can tell he doesn't believe me.

"I know it's in a medical context," I say. "But is that still weird? Studying vaginas?"

He shakes his head. "It's just another day at the office really."

"You should try that line in bed," I tell him.

A grin sneaks its way across his mouth, and it feels like winning a prize. One I want to win over and over again.

"As much as I wish my area of study improved my bedroom skills, I'm afraid the med school curriculum is lacking in that department."

"Ah yes," I say, nodding along. "That's exactly why I dropped out. Not enough classes on orgasming."

He shifts back in his seat, eyes sharpening. "You were in med school?"

My stomach churns with the familiar sense of dread, and my gaze falls into my lap.

"I was," I tell him. "Until two weeks ago."

If he's judging me, it doesn't register on his expression. "Why'd you leave?" he asks.

I pick up the sticky saltshaker, then put it back down again. Telling Liam about flunking out of med school isn't really my idea of a great first date—or whatever this is—but there's something about him that feels safe, a type of magnetic energy that seems to coax the words free.

"I sort of hated it," I admit.

"What did you hate about it?"

"I hated eight a.m. labs and spending every weekend studying for classes I wasn't even interested in," I tell him, the words spilling out of me like a pent-up dam.

"If you weren't interested, why did you go in the first place?"

"It's what I was expected to do. Which is probably why I stuck out four years as a biochem major in undergrad and then months of studying for the MCATs. I didn't want to disappoint anyone," I tell him, thinking about all the times I told Gramps that classes were going great even though I was miserable and felt trapped in a career path I knew wasn't right for me, and how every time he nodded and told me how proud of me he and Grammy were, I felt even more trapped.

"But I woke up one day and I just couldn't imagine suffering through another four years of med school and then residency," I tell him. "I couldn't keep killing myself just because it was someone else's dream."

He props his elbows on the table, studying me. "Whose dream was it?"

"My grandfather's," I tell him. "He's a fancy surgeon who thinks being anything other than an MD is a waste of time. Now he thinks I'm throwing away my future." I cast a glance at the jukebox, where someone's just put on "Dream a Little Dream of Me," before adding, "And maybe he's right."

"Why do you say that?"

I shift my weight, thinking about how I've always taken pride in being similar to my mom. After all, she's my best friend—always the funniest, most interesting person in the room, the kind of person people can't help gravitating toward. But the same traits that often make her the life of every party are also the traits that make her rash and impulsive. Like the time she went to Buenos Aires with a man she'd only known a day. Or the time she quit her job because her boss wouldn't approve her PTO. And I can't help but worry that I'm making the same mistake with med school. That I've done something rash and ultimately foolish by dropping out.

"I mean, it's med school," I say, gesturing vaguely. "It's basically a golden ticket to success."

"Not if you hate it," he points out.

"Tell that to my family."

"So what are you going to do instead?" he asks.

"I don't know," I admit. "And I know that sounds bad. Like, who the hell drops out of med school with no backup plan? But I just had to get out of there." I pause, unsure how to phrase my next thought.

"I thought I was going to suffocate," I say after a beat. "Like I was being weighed down by all this pressure, and I was going to end up in this life I absolutely despised with this job I resented and I'd be stuck with no way out."

I search his face, expecting to see judgment, or confusion. After all, he clearly doesn't feel the same way about medical school or becoming a doctor. Instead, his dark eyes warm with understanding. "I get it," he says. "You have to really want it. It has to be your passion. And if it's not, it'll kill you."

His words strike across my core. Somehow this man that I hardly know has managed to understand something no one else in my family could.

"Is it for you?" I ask, suddenly curious to know. "Your passion?"

His gaze instantly brightens. "It is," he says. "I love the work, and I love knowing that what I'm doing could help people. That I'm doing something that matters."

Shiny, I think yet again. He's so self-assured. And I can't help but be drawn toward him, like maybe if I get close enough some of that shininess will rub off on me.

"I wish I had that kind of certainty," I say almost wistfully. "That I just knew what I wanted to do the way everyone else in my family does. My grandfather's a doctor and so are my brother and his boyfriend. My little sister is only in middle school, but she'll probably be one too," I tell him. "They all seem so passionate about it, so certain. But I just didn't feel that way."

"Well, there must be something you're passionate about," he says. "Something else you want to do?"

"Too bad watching Netflix isn't a career path. I'd be great at it."

I laugh at my joke, but Liam frowns. "Don't sell yourself short. You got into med school. You're clearly driven and intelligent."

"That's nice of you to say, but you don't know me."

"Maybe I just like making assumptions."

I bite the inside of my cheek, fighting back a grin.

"Well, actually, there is something I want to do," I tell him.

"What's that?"

"I'm writing a book." As soon as I say it, I'm hit with a wave of embarrassment. "I mean, I'm not a real writer," I say quickly. "I didn't do an MFA program or anything."

"I'm no expert, but I'm pretty certain if you're writing, then that makes you a writer," he says, giving me a pointed look. "Do you want to publish it someday?"

I nod, feeling my cheeks heat. God, how embarrassing to admit my dreams, and even more embarrassing to hope for them.

"It's not finished yet, but when it is I'd like to try," I tell him. "But who knows, it might be bad."

"Everything is crap before it's good," he says.

I scan Liam's handsome face, finding it hard to imagine he's ever been crap at anything.

"What's your book about?" he asks.

"It's a romance." As soon as I say it, my face heats up. It's not that I'm ashamed of the genre, but I know how it's typically received: as a silly, vapid guilty pleasure. Certainly not something to be taken seriously. But Liam's face lights up.

"I love romance," he says.

I blink, wondering how this man exists. "You do?"

"I used to read my mum's paperbacks when I didn't think she was looking. Very informative," he adds with a shy grin. "I probably learned more about human anatomy from bodice rippers than med school."

"You're kidding."

"I assure you I'm not. Just ask my first girlfriend, who was completely scandalized when I asked her how many times she orgasmed from our first kiss."

I bring my hands to my face. "Ohmygod. You didn't."

"I did."

"How old were you?"

"Fourteen." His mouth widens into a grin before he says, "While very educational, romance novels might have given me slightly unrealistic expectations for sex."

"Or maybe your kissing skills just weren't up to par," I tease.

"The braces probably didn't help."

I laugh and he chuckles too, low and warm, and it takes everything in me not to melt right on the spot.

"What made you decide to start writing?" he asks.

"My mom, actually. Growing up, we read a lot together, and when we'd get to the end, she'd ask me if I liked how it ended, and if I said no, then she'd tell me that I could write my own." I smile to myself. "So much of real life doesn't work that way. We don't get to write our own endings or guarantee everything gets tied up with a neat bow, but I love that, on the page, there can always be happily ever after."

"So you're a hopeless romantic, then?" he asks.

"I'd say more of a cautiously hopeful romantic."

He shifts his weight, and his knee grazes mine under the table. "And what does that mean?"

"It means that I love the idea of love, of romance and happy endings. But I know that real life doesn't always work out the way it does in stories."

I think of my mom, of the decades spent searching for *the one*, racking up heartbreak after heartbreak. As much as I love the idea of finding a soulmate, someone who loves you wholly and completely, I've seen enough of my mom's dating life to know that's not how real life works. The only perfect men out there are the ones written by women. The rest will hurt you and cheat on you and leave you high and dry. Even the charming ones with cute accents and dimples.

"Falling in love is scary," he agrees. "Especially when the risk of getting hurt is so high. But maybe that's what makes it worth it."

"I'm not sure anything is worth having your heart broken," I say, thinking of all the nights I heard my mom crying herself to sleep.

He sits forward, studying me. "Sure, heartbreak is awful, but isn't the risk what makes it meaningful? The possibility that it doesn't work, but you want it badly enough to find out?"

I realize we've shifted closer. Like if this table weren't between us, we'd be touching. The thought makes my pulse kick up.

"Who's the hopeless romantic now?" I tease.

A thoughtful hum vibrates in the back of his throat. "The world is shitty and people will disappoint you, but I think it's nice to have something to believe in, something to hope for," he adds, his gaze tracking mine, and I can't help the heat packing into my cheeks.

Liam must notice because he winces. "Sorry. Kevin told me to be cool, and here I am grandstanding about love on a first date. I've said too much, haven't I?"

With that accent? Never. This man could say I've bewitched him body and soul, and it still wouldn't be too much.

I shake my head, bottom lip disappearing between my teeth. "No. No, you haven't said too much at all."

For a long moment he holds my gaze, and I can feel him trying and hesitating to speak. Finally he says, "So, do you think they're coming back?"

"Who?"

"Abby and Kevin?"

My face warms once again. I've been so engrossed in our conversation—in *him*—that I didn't realize how long they'd been gone.

I look over my shoulder toward the bar, but see only the two truckers and the bartender. "Where did they go?"

"Your guess is as good as mine, but I imagine somewhere dark and private. Maybe Kevin's car? Or your flat?"

My gaze narrows. Abby's much more free-spirited than me when it comes to sex, but I can't believe she'd leave me with a stranger to go bone Kevin. Unless . . .

"Do you think they did this on purpose?" I ask.

The space between his brows crinkles. "Yes, I do believe they are having sex on purpose."

I roll my eyes. "No, I mean do you think they were trying to leave us alone? Together?"

He shrugs. "No clue. But I'm not exactly mad about it."

Well, that gets another blush out of me.

"How long ago did you see them leave?" I ask.

He checks the screen of his phone for the time. "About fifteen minutes ago."

"Why didn't you say anything?"

"Probably for the same reason you didn't notice them leaving. I was distracted."

My blush intensifies.

"Do you think I should call Abby? See if everything is okay?" I ask.

"They're fine," he says with a dismissive wave. "They're using protection."

"*I mean* if she's safe," I say, giving him a hard look. "But now I know where your mind is."

His mouth curls into a grin. "Kevin's a good bloke, I promise. And for the record, they are using protection."

"How do you know?"

"Because I gave him a handful of condoms before we left."

I lift an eyebrow. "How generous of you."

"Well, as you pointed out earlier, I'm a boring student who doesn't have any friends, so I don't suppose I have much need for them," he says, giving me a heated look that makes it clear he and I both know this isn't true.

"So what do *we* do?" I ask after a beat.

"Well, we can sit here and wait for them to come back, or . . ." His eyes light up. "We can get something to eat. Are you hungry?"

My gaze briefly flicks to the chalkboard menu announcing a limited offering of fried foods that are almost certainly from a freezer. "Here?"

That damn dimple makes a reappearance. "Actually, I was going to ask if you like lasagna."

- 5 -

Now

There's nothing quite as humbling as inviting your ex to meet you for coffee so you can ask (beg) for a favor. Move over, braces and blue eye shadow phase, we have a new personal low.

My knees jostle under the table as I weigh the wisdom of getting another coffee. Do I want to maintain this jitter, or go for a full-blown panic attack? Though it's hard to tell if the jitters are from the two iced coffees I've already had, or because I'm nervous to see Liam.

Every time the door to the coffee shop opens, my heart gives a little spasm.

Is that him?

Nope. Just another lady in yoga pants.

I sigh and sit back in my seat as the whiz of the espresso machine cuts through the chorus of the third Sabrina Carpenter song they've played in the last thirty minutes.

This place used to be *our thing*. Sunday mornings spent in search of caffeine and greasy breakfast sandwiches after drinking too much the night before, and rainy afternoons when we just needed a reason to get out of the house. A second living room, we used to call it. But now, not only have I lost the person I'd planned to spend forever with, even my local coffee shop has lost its appeal.

I check our text thread to see if he's sent an ETA, but all that's there are our last messages from three days ago.

ME: Hey, can we meet? I need to talk to you about something.

LIAM: Sure.

ME: How about 4 p.m. on Saturday at the coffee shop by the house?

LIAM: Sure.

ME: Great! See you then!!!!

I wince at my overzealous use of punctuation. Liam probably thinks I'm nuts. And maybe I am, but after my conversation with Abby, I couldn't stop thinking about what she'd suggested. As much as I hate having to ask Liam for anything, she's right. This could benefit both of us, and it's at least worth a conversation.

I take another sip of my mostly ice iced coffee and return to watching the door with almost feverish anticipation.

After getting desperate enough to check both *Yahoo Answers* and *Quora* to see if someone in 2005 also wasn't sure what to wear to see their estranged husband for the first time in months, I'd landed on the only pair of jeans that still fit me and an oversized cable-knit sweater that hopefully reads *comfy, chill,* and *totally not freaking out.*

The last time I saw him—the night of the nightmare—I'd been a mess, so today I want to at least look like I've been moisturizing and drinking celery juice. And *not* like I've been chugging wine straight from the bottle while the stack of dirty dishes in the sink climbs to mountainous heights.

But now, as I sit here, tapping my foot impatiently, eyes pinned to the door, I'm feeling increasingly silly for bothering with my appearance when it seems unlikely that he's even going to show.

I check the time. He's now twenty minutes late. Liam's not the vindictive type, so it's much more likely that he simply forgot, which hurts much, much worse.

I'm about to give up and call it a day, when the little bell over the door jingles and I look up just in time to see Liam pushing three fingers through rain-damp hair.

I'm not exactly sure what I was expecting. Maybe bags under the eyes or wrinkled clothes or a distinct air of depression. At the very least *some* kind of indicator that Liam's not doing well. Certainly not . . . well, *this*.

Liam's dirty blond hair is a tad longer than normal, and he's wearing expensive-cut jeans and a tight white T-shirt that's practically straining to break free from his chest. He's also grown a beard, which I imagine is supposed to be the male equivalent of breakup bangs, but instead of looking like a mistake that will take six to nine months to grow out, it looks painfully sexy. And it's *really* pissing me off.

How many times had I asked him to grow a beard? How many times had I gone full Regina George and brushed his hair out of his eyes, telling him he looked sexy when he didn't shave for a few days? But now, when we're broken up, is the time he decides to try facial hair?

Annoyance bubbles inside me like a chemistry experiment gone wrong. But this isn't the time to be annoyed with him, I remind myself. I have to play nice.

I give a little wave to draw his attention. His eyes land on me, and he gives a curt nod of recognition.

"Sorry I'm late," he says, sliding into the seat opposite me. "I just finished a twenty-four-hour shift at the hospital."

"Oh, no worries." It is most certainly *yes worries*, but I don't want to get us off on the wrong foot. "I got your favorite, caramel macchiato with extra whip." I gesture to the whip cream monstrosity in front of him, now mostly melted.

He barely looks at it before saying, "I've been cutting out sugar."

"Oh." My eyes dart toward the chalkboard menu behind the register. "Do you want something else? I can—"

"It's fine." He waves the suggestion away. "I can't stay long anyways."

"Do you have plans tonight? Another party at Kevin's?" I can't help but ask.

His gaze narrows as though he's trying to determine which question I'm really trying to ask before finally saying, "I've got lab reports to go over before tomorrow morning."

He checks the time—like he's already eager to leave—and the movement draws my attention to his left hand. His noticeably *bare* left hand.

The axis under my feet shifts as a series of questions I'm not brave enough to ask surface.

Where is the ring now? A sock drawer? Landfill? The bottom of the ocean next to Titanic?

When did he take it off?

I search his expression as though the answers might be hidden somewhere behind his new, sexy beard, but his face remains staunchly impassive.

I clear my throat, right hand instinctively flying to my left, covering the spot where my own wedding ring still sits. "Well, uh, thanks for meeting me," I tell him. "You look good."

"Thanks."

I notice he doesn't say it back, which irritates me, but I'm trying to take the high road, so I say, "I'm glad you're doing well."

Liam crosses his arms over his noticeably firm chest. "Why did you want to meet, Roslyn?"

All righty, then. Just getting to it, I see.

I take a far too long sip of my now-coffee-flavored-water, trying to buy myself a few seconds more, but his eyes narrow. He can tell I'm stalling.

"Well . . ."

You can do this. Just spit it out.

"You know how the family vacation is next week?" I begin tentatively.

He lifts one skeptical eyebrow. "Yes."

"And how neither of us is exactly thrilled to tell my family about . . ." I look over my shoulder, paranoid someone might be listening. "The divorce?"

Liam just blinks at me, and I can tell he's losing patience. Better get on with it.

"What if . . ." I pause, swallowing. "We *didn't* tell my family we're getting divorced."

His brows draw together. "What do you mean?"

"I mean . . ." I release a heavy sigh, searching for the right words. "What if we pretended to, you know, still be together. Just for the trip."

As soon as I say it, I hear how ridiculous it sounds. And so does Liam.

"You're joking, right?"

"I get that this is . . . unconventional, but—"

"'Unconventional'?" he repeats. "You can't be serious, Roslyn. You're the one who asked for the divorce, and now you want to lie to your family?"

"We've already been lying," I remind him. "Besides, this would allow us to wait until there's a better time to tell them."

"There's no good time to tell them we're ending our marriage."

"I know, but . . ."

I think back to my conversation with Abby, and what she'd said about his relationship with my family.

"Do you really want to disappoint my grandparents by not officiating their vow renewal ceremony?" I ask. "Grammy will be heartbroken."

Liam's jaw twitches, and I can tell that strikes a chord with him.

"Besides," I continue, my voice picking up steam, "this is already going to be a hard trip for everyone since . . ." I swallow hard, forcing myself to say it. "Since the accident. And while there might not be a *good* time to tell them, the first family trip without my mom isn't the right time."

Liam wets his lips but doesn't say anything, and the longer the silence lasts, the more my heart rate ramps up. I knew I shouldn't have listened to Abby. I shouldn't even be here right now. I *should* start working on my epitaph. HERE LIES ROSLYN, SHE DIED DOING WHAT SHE WAS BEST AT: DISAPPOINTING HER FAMILY. Or maybe I should just move to Antarctica. Somewhere without Wi-Fi or postal service. Maybe—

"Fine," he says.

My eyes widen. "*What?*"

"I said *fine*. I'll do it."

Hope burns hot against my chest. "Really?"

He tenses and I hold my breath, waiting for him to reconsider, but he nods and relief balloons inside me.

"Ohmygod! Thank you!"

For a brief moment I think about flinging myself across the table and into his arms for a hug, but that would be weird, right? So I clear my throat, regaining control over my facial features before I ask, "What do you want?"

His brows draw together. "What do I want?"

"In return," I clarify. "Majority equity of the house? The stainless steel pans from Williams Sonoma? I know a big favor like this doesn't come cheap," I say with a knowing look.

Twin divots form on either side of his mouth. "I don't want anything, Roslyn."

"Are you sure, because—"

"I don't want anything," he says again, his voice pulling low. "Grammy and Gramps have done a lot for me. I should be there. Besides, I already got approved for the time off, and I've always wanted to go to Hawaii."

I snort. "You don't know how to take a vacation. You'll probably spend the whole time on your computer, as usual," I say, thinking back to past family vacations spent huddled over a laptop, dealing with an ever-present work crisis.

His mouth tenses. "But maybe that's for the best this time," he offers. "Spend as little time together as possible, right?"

I nod in agreement, but my throat feels tight.

"Speaking of which." He lifts the coffee I bought him, almost brings it to his mouth, then frowns before setting it back down as though remembering just in time he doesn't drink sugary drinks anymore. "We need to figure out how we're going to convince your family we're still together."

"I just thought we'd try and act normal," I say, but as soon as the words are out, I realize that neither of us knows what that means anymore. What is normal? How are you supposed to act around someone you used to be so in love with that it hurt? Someone who's seen you naked, scars and all. Someone you've let into the most intimate parts of your life, who knows your secrets, your hopes, your fears. Who's seen you at your worst. And your best. Someone who now feels like a stranger.

He seems to be having the same thought because, after a beat, he asks, "What's normal?"

"Well . . . We could be nice to each other," I try. "Should be easy enough, right?"

He shakes his head, dark eyes going stormy. "That's not going to work."

I frown, taken aback. "Why not?"

"Nice isn't enough. You know how your family is. They're . . ." He grasps for the word. "*Intense.*"

He's right. My family has a hard time with boundaries and staying out of one another's business. Especially Bella, who can sniff out gossip better than a tabloid.

"What are you suggesting?" I ask.

"I'm suggesting a strategy. Guidelines, for what to do and not do in this"—he gestures vaguely—"*arrangement.*"

"Okay . . ." I mull this over, trying to think of every fake-dating book I've ever read, but my mind goes inconveniently blank. "Do you want to use a safe word or something?"

As soon as I say it, I'm hit with a memory of when Liam and I started experimenting more in bed. We'd landed on *in this economy* as our safe word, but neither of us took it seriously and kept using it at the most inappropriate times, sending us both into uncontrollable fits of laughter.

I wonder if he remembers, but it's been a while since we had the kind of sex that required a safe word. Or any sex at all for that matter.

"I mean like touching," he says. "We're probably going to have to touch, right?"

I scan his features, looking for hints as to how he feels about that, but his expression remains carefully blank.

"I think there will have to be some touching," I tell him.

His chin tilts, considering. "Where?"

My cheeks grow warm at the thought of me outlining where my husband can and can't touch me. In another universe this would feel like foreplay, some kind of erotic game.

"I could put together some diagrams and a PowerPoint on acceptable touching zones if you'd like," I joke, trying to crack the tension, but his face remains stony.

Okay, then. Tough audience.

"How about just holding hands?" I try. "Or an arm around the shoulders?"

His mouth tightens into a thin line. "We don't need to be all over each other in order for this to work."

It takes everything in my power not to remind him that *he's* the one who used to be all over *me*. That it was *his* fingers that would slide under my skirt beneath the dinner table. And it was *his* hand that would sit on my thigh whenever we were in the car. But apparently, either he's trying to annoy me (spoiler, it's working) or he's suffering from a bad case of amnesia. Either way, it's not worth the fight.

"Fine. We'll keep the touching to a minimum," I tell him.

"And only in front of other people," he adds.

I'm momentarily bombarded with an image of Liam and me, alone, *touching*. The thought swells inside me, awakening something hot and slippery, but I quickly shove it back down into my own personal Pandora's box, where it belongs.

"Anything else?" I ask.

He swallows, his jaw pulling tight before he says, "I don't think we should kiss."

The words come out hot and fast, like he's been holding on to them, and for a moment I'm stunned. Not that I thought he'd want to kiss me. Or that *I* want to kiss him, but did he have to say it like *that*? Like he'd rather get a prostate exam than put his lips anywhere near mine?

"Listen, I'd prefer if we didn't kiss too," I say stiffly. "But I don't think we should totally rule it out. What if we have to?"

He frowns. "Why would we *have* to?"

"I just mean what if we're in a situation where it would be expected for us to kiss?"

His frown intensifies. "Like what?"

"I don't know. I'm just asking, in case," I add.

His brows draw together. "Last time I checked, we're not attending any New Year's Eve parties. But if we happen to find ourselves in a rousing game of spin the bottle in front of your family, then I suppose kissing's fair game."

If I had any doubts as to whether he was over me or not, now I know.

"Fine," I say stiffly. "No kissing."

Liam's jaw tenses as he sits back in his seat, eyes dancing toward the door like he's hoping a meteor will hit the building and mercifully end this conversation. When it doesn't, he says, "Anything else we need to go over?"

I mentally review the itinerary Jonah emailed everyone, trying to determine if zip-lining or jungle hiking might provide any difficult situations when my mind stalls on a more pressing matter. Something I completely overlooked until just now.

"What about the bed?"

His gaze widens, understanding sifting through his features. "We could alternate who gets it each night?"

"And where does the other person sleep?"

"The floor."

My first instinct is to tell him *no*. I'm thirty-one years old. I'll probably need a hip replacement if I sleep on the floor. But this is a very delicate scenario, and I don't want to rock the boat, metaphorically or literally.

"Fine, we can alternate," I say. "Is that everything?"

He's quiet for a long moment, and I sense some kind of energy brewing behind his tautly pulled jaw muscles, a kind of energy that makes him flex his hands and purse his lips before he finally says, "If this is going to work, I think the main thing is that we're going to have to try and be cordial with one another. At least in front of your family."

The annoyance I've been trying to keep at bay finally boils over.

"*I've* been perfectly cordial this entire time. *You're* the one who showed up twenty minutes late."

"I told you," he says tightly. "I just got off a twenty-four-hour shift of clinical trials for a new treatment that could save thousands of lives. So excuse my lack of punctuality."

My inner fuse crackles. Of course *perfect* Liam has the *perfect* excuse. But I need to prove this isn't the worst idea ever, so I gather my breath, purse my lips, and say in my most diplomatic voice, "I can be cordial if you are."

He opens his mouth, then closes it before setting it into a hard line. "Fine," he says at last, and I try to ignore the Pavlovian stomach clench that comes with hearing him say that word.

We stare at each other, caught in a wordless standoff for a

handful of seconds before he gives me one last heavy look and stands to go, coffee still untouched.

"If that's everything, I'll see you at the airport," he says.

"Shouldn't we arrive at the airport together? Since we're meeting my family there?"

Liam runs his hand down the back of his neck, fingers tracing the collar of his shirt. "Right. Good idea."

"We can meet at the house," I say.

His throat shifts as he swallows. "I'll see you then." He turns to go.

"Liam?"

His eyes drag back to meet mine.

"Make sure you wear your ring."

- 6 -

Now

When Liam shows up at the house, I'm already regretting my choice in airport attire.

I'm not sure if it was a 4 a.m. delusion, or the prospect of spending a whole week with Liam and his sexy new beard, or perhaps the feminine urge to want to make my ex come in his pants when he sees me, but apparently I woke up and decided it was a good idea to cosplay as post-breakup Princess Di. Which is how I end up standing in the driveway wearing Liam's favorite dress—a *very* short LBD—feeling increasingly ridiculous.

As soon as he sees me, his gaze drops to my legs, slowly charting a path up and over my body that leaves a rash of goose bumps everywhere his eyes land.

He fixes me with a grimace. "Why are you dressed like that?"

"Like what?" I ask, feigning innocence.

"Like . . ." He swallows thickly. "*A high-end escort.*"

At least he said *high-end*.

"I think the term you're looking for is empowered, sexually liberated woman," I say, giving him a look.

I might not be either of those things, but if Liam can take off his ring and do shots with girls named Katie, then I can at least look hot.

I wonder if he remembers this dress. If he remembers the night I wore it to a hospital function, and how he took it off me later, slow and agonizing, memorizing every part of me, first with his eyes, then his hands, and finally his tongue. But if Liam remembers, his infuriatingly guarded expression doesn't show it.

There was once a time when I could tell exactly what Liam was thinking with a single glance. Like when he wanted to leave a party early. Or the way he'd sigh and say, "You choose," when I knew he really wanted me to order pizza for dinner. All the little puzzle pieces that over time had come to build one giant Liam-shaped picture. But now he feels like someone I recognize but don't know. Not anymore.

After we collect our bags from the back of the Uber, we make our way to airport security, where I scan the hordes of early morning travelers for the rest of my family.

Realistically I know that the first meeting won't be a big deal. It's not like anyone will question us on the last time we had sex or went on a date. But it doesn't stop me from worrying that they'll see Liam and me and immediately know something's wrong. That our marital instability will be a flashing neon sign hanging over our heads.

"Do you see them?" I ask.

Liam shakes head. "Come on. Let's get through security and get coffee. Then we can find them."

Coffee. My skin crawls with need, and I nod my agreement.

We take our place at the end of the security line, and Liam immediately pulls out his phone.

I notice his wedding ring is back on his left hand, which I guess

I ought to be pleased about. It shows that he's taking this seriously. And that he still has it. But knowing that it's all part of the act—nothing more than a prop for the role he's playing—feels like yet another emotional minefield I'm not prepared for.

Maybe it's just a ring. An accessory. But it's also memorized take-out orders and nights he held my hair when I had the stomach flu. It's interwoven fingers and kissing at red lights and big belly laughs from inside jokes only we know. It's everything the ring once represented. Everything it no longer does.

Twenty minutes of silence later, we make it to the front of the line, where I begin the extreme sport of shoving all my stuff into one of the bins while trying to remember where I packed the clear bag of liquids.

Meanwhile, Liam goes through TSA like he's hoping to be congratulated with a sash and a plaque for excellence in efficiency. I'm pretty sure a TSA officer even smiles at him!

I watch, annoyed, as he gently places his laptop in a bin before tugging his sweatshirt up and over his head. The hem of his T-shirt comes with it, revealing a branded boxer waistband and a thin slice of smooth, toned stomach. A stomach I know. Or at least I thought I did.

When did Liam get *those*? And by those, I mean the shelflike ladder of abs disappearing into the waistband of his boxers.

Liam's always been in good shape, but he usually doesn't have time to hit the gym between hospital shifts and work at the research center. But apparently New Single Liam does.

I've thought about how this whole trip might be easier if we were both hurting. If there was some level of solidarity between us. Some admission that, *Hey, this is hard for both of us. Let's just try and get through it for the sake of the family.*

But Liam seems to be fine without me. Not just *fine*, but good. Like the separation has drastically improved his life, and I'm some kind of baggage he had to divest himself of so he could evolve into his *best self*, movie star abs included.

I know it's unfair of me, since I'm the one who ended things. I have no right to be bothered by whatever Liam does in his new single life. But I wish he were as miserable as me.

I wish there were bags under his eyes, and stains on his clothes, and his hair didn't look so fucking good. I wish he were messy and broken and hurting the way I am. Because if he were, then I'd at least know he was feeling *something*. That there was more to the brusque *fine* he'd muttered before walking out. But apparently not.

After we get through security, I make a beeline to the nearest bench so I can reassemble my luggage, when I lose my grip on my backpack and the contents spill out, cascading all over the floor.

Fuck.

I crouch down, darting to collect my things, when Liam appears beside me to help.

"Here," he says, handing me a pen that's slipped away. "Maybe next time you should . . ." But the rest of the suggestion dies, swallowed by a full-body stiffening. "What is this?"

I pause, hand outstretched over my loose-leaf notebook, and follow his gaze to the bold, black print across the manila envelope he's holding. THE LAW OFFICES OF HAMMERSMITH AND FINCH.

Shit.

He wasn't supposed to see that. Well, he was, eventually, but not now. Not at the airport on my way to meet my family.

I snatch it back. "They're divorce papers."

For a moment he just stares at the envelope. Everything from the cut of his mouth to the narrowed stance of his eyes feels like a sharp line.

Finally, he asks, "Why did you bring those?"

"I figured we could look them over while we're here," I tell him. Which is sort of true.

When I'd shoved the papers into my bag late last night after a glass of wine (okay, two), it had seemed like a good idea. Surely a week at sea with Liam would inspire me to sign the paperwork I've been putting off for months, right? But now I'm wondering if I was wrong. If they should have stayed on my desk, continuing to collect dust the way they have for weeks.

Tense silence brews like a storm between us. After a heavy beat, he asks, "So you're really doing this?"

My first reaction is annoyance. Because of course I'm doing this. What else does he expect? He didn't come back, or ask for another chance, and neither have I. If he didn't want to see divorce papers, maybe he should have tried a little harder to save our marriage. Or tried at all.

But it doesn't matter now. It's over—a choice we've both made, whether passively or actively—and all I can do is try to move forward and pick up the pieces of my life.

"Nothing has changed over the last three months, Liam." I pause, waiting to see if he'll interject, tell me I'm wrong, this is a mistake, he doesn't actually want a divorce. But he doesn't. "So yeah, I guess I am," I say.

"Oh." His voice comes out rough like his vocal cords have been put through a cheese grater, and I search his features, looking for traces of regret or anger or annoyance—*something* that would give me a clue as to how he's taking this—but his face remains stiff, almost purposefully blank.

"Just make sure no one sees those," he says tightly.

"What do you think I'm going to do? Pass them out at dinner?"

His jaw ticks, features hardening like wet cement, and for a moment I wonder if he's upset—a fucked-up part of me hopes he is. At least that would be better than the detached apathy—but by the time I've blinked, his expression is back in place, each emotion tucked neatly away before he grabs his bag and walks off.

- 7 -

Nine years earlier

Nice place," I say, glancing around Liam's apartment. My eyes immediately go to the tall bookshelf in the corner. He's got everything. Chaucer. Faulkner. Joyce. Baldwin. Even the *Bridgerton* series and some Roxane Gay. "Have you read all these?" I ask, letting my finger drift along the spine of one of R. F. Kuang's novels.

Liam looks up from the kitchen, where he's dicing garlic. He's got one of those little towels tossed over his shoulder, and I'll be damned if it's not the sexiest sight I've ever seen.

"Most of them," he says. "Though I don't have much time for pleasure reading while I'm in school. Now most of my reading involves anatomy textbooks and absolutely no sex scenes."

"I hate when that happens," I say, reshelving Cormac McCarthy's *The Road*. "Nothing worse than popping open your biochem textbook hoping for a real spicy scene and all you get is that the mitochondria is the powerhouse of the cell."

He laughs, and I watch as his muscles flex and tighten under his skin as his knife moves back and forth, finely chopping the cloves of garlic.

When he'd asked if I liked lasagna, I imagined he meant at a restaurant, or possibly a frozen grocery store meal. Certainly not him cooking from scratch. But Liam is proving to be full of surprises.

"So is this your usual routine?" I ask, propping my elbows on the kitchen counter and leaning toward him. "Woo her with lines about being a hopeless romantic, then bring her back to your place where you show off your knife skills and wear a slutty little towel over your shoulder?"

He looks up, eyes flashing with amusement. "Oh, you like my towel, huh?"

"Do you actually use it? Or is it just for show?"

"That depends." His brow rises, mouth arching up halfway into a smile. "Is it working?"

"That depends"—I shift forward—"entirely on how good the lasagna is."

He leans in close enough for his breath to feather my jaw. "Don't worry," he whispers. "It will be worth it."

I don't think we're talking about lasagna anymore and my chest leaps, a dozen electric currents shooting under my skin.

"How long is this lasagna going to take? I'm starving."

"About three hours."

"*Three hours?*" My mouth falls open. "You couldn't have chosen to make something quicker? Like Rice-A-Roni?"

Again, he laughs, and my stomach flutters victoriously.

"Why eat Rice-A-Roni when you can have the best lasagna in the world?"

"The best in the world? That's a bit presumptuous, don't you think?"

His eyes shine, dimples popping. "Well, I'm a presumptuous man."

I should tell him that I didn't come here to sleep with him. That his little routine isn't going to work on me. That we're just going to eat lasagna and that's it. But if I'm being totally honest with myself, I'm not sure that's true.

Maybe it's the accent. Or his face—one I would quite frankly like to sit on. Or hell, maybe it's the slutty little towel, but whatever Liam is selling, I'm a curious consumer.

"And what are we going to do while we wait?" I ask, hopping up on the counter.

His eyes skip from my green tube top to the jeans hugging my curves. "I have a few ideas."

I snort. "I'm sure you do."

He presses his palm to his heart. "Roslyn, please get your mind out of the gutter. I was going to say we could talk."

"About?" I ask.

He sets his knife down and moves to the other side of the counter so he's eye level with me. "Anything you'd like. Where you grew up. Childhood pets. Siblings."

"Do you also want to know my mom's maiden name and the street I was born on?"

He laughs and the sound settles right between my legs. "I'm a gentleman, Roslyn. I wasn't planning on stealing your bank info until after dinner," he says, keeping heated eyes on mine as he reaches for a different knife.

I watch the way he moves with a chef's precision. "Where'd you learn to cook?"

"My mum. Taught me everything I know."

The timer for the oven goes off, and he pulls the roasted tomatoes out in a glorious haze of garlic and olive oil.

"Are you two close?" I ask, watching as he pours the tomatoes into a food processor.

"We used to be," he says, keeping his focus on the food. I wait for him to elaborate, but instead he asks, "What about you? Are you close with your family?"

"Honestly, things have been pretty strained since I dropped out of med school," I say, thinking to last weekend when Gramps wouldn't even talk to me at family dinner. "But I'm really close with my mom. She's the only person who supported the decision, who didn't make me feel like I was throwing my life away."

"I'm sorry your family's been so hard on you, but I'm glad you have your mum."

"Me too," I tell him. "She's my best friend. I tell her everything. Sometimes I feel like she's more my friend than my mom."

Liam's eyes crinkle as he smiles. "I'd love to meet her someday."

My skin warms at the thought of Liam meeting my family. Of seeing him beyond tonight.

"My mom would love you. But don't get cocky," I add, when his grin expands. "I'm pretty sure she loves everyone."

"She sounds lovely."

"She is," I tell him. "She's loud and funny, and she falls in love a lot. I swear every time I see her, she has a new boyfriend."

"So your parents aren't together?" Liam asks, dumping minced garlic in with the tomatoes.

I shake my head. "They broke up when I was five."

For as long as I can remember, my mom's love life has been a revolving door of interchangeably shitty men. Not all were bad, like the guy who owned the ice cream truck and gave us unlimited free ice cream. But most have ranged from cringe try-hards who tried to buy my siblings and me off with new toys, to abusive narcissists, who would cheat on my mom and tell her it was her fault.

And with every breakup came the aftermath. The moving. The

new schools. The new job. The uncertainty of whether I'd come home from school to find my mom cooking with Ella Fitzgerald at full volume, happy and hopeful, or if I'd have to hide her phone so she wouldn't text her ex.

Sometimes things felt normal. She'd take us to the movies or order pizza for dinner or get a new job with a pay increase, and I would breathe a sigh of relief, feeling like things would finally settle down, until the next man came along and our life imploded once more.

"Do you and your siblings still see your dad?" Liam asks.

I swallow and look away, pretending to be absorbed in the sauce now simmering on the stovetop. "My siblings and I all have different dads, actually."

It's not that I'm embarrassed about my mom or her past, but I've received enough pitying glances and overheard the word *slut* thrown around over the years that I feel protective over her. I hate the idea of her being judged or looked down upon, especially when the men who knocked her up and then bailed never had to face the same accusations.

But if Liam's shocked or thrown off by this admission, he doesn't show it.

"Did you know your dad?" Liam asks.

"Not really. By the time I was old enough to remember, they'd broken up and he'd moved to New Mexico. We never heard from him except for when he wanted my mom to mail him his things."

I never felt any burning desire to know my dad. Not when he clearly didn't want anything to do with us. But once, when I was a teenager, I looked him up on Facebook. Apparently, he has a wife and two sons, and they live in a stucco house with a tile roof and a swimming pool.

His real family, I thought. *The one he actually wanted.*

I never told my mom. It was better if she didn't know.

"I'm sorry," Liam says. "Sounds like that's his loss."

"That's what my mom says too," I tell him.

His mouth wavers upward into a smile before pressing a button, and the food processor whirs to life, filling the silence with the electric buzz of the machine. Within moments, the clump of tomatoes turns into a creamy red sauce.

"That smells amazing," I tell him.

"Try it." He dunks a spoon in the sauce and holds it out to me.

Blushing, I lean toward him, catching a whiff of laundry detergent and aftershave as I put the spoon in my mouth. The flavor instantly explodes across my tongue in a burst of tangy tomatoes and rich garlic.

"Wow. That's really good," I tell him, licking my lips.

"Wait until you try it with fresh béchamel and handmade pasta."

"You're making fresh pasta?"

"No, *we're* making fresh pasta," he corrects.

"We?"

He nods.

"But I've never made pasta before."

"That's okay. I'll show you," he says, beckoning me toward him. "Come here."

A tiny bolt of electricity runs the length of my spine at the way he says it, all low and commanding, and I know I'll be replaying it in my head long after tonight's over.

Liam pours a neat pile of flour out on the counter and makes a little divot in the center. "We're going to crack a few eggs in here." He uses one hand to crack an egg right into the divot.

"Okay, now you're just showing off," I tease.

He grins. "Well, clearly my knife skills and slutty little towel didn't do the trick. Now I have to bring out the big guns."

I raise one eyebrow. "These are your big guns?"

His eyes cut to mine, a pulsing heat behind them, before he begins mixing the flour and eggs.

Maybe I'm a huge pervert, but all I can think about as he kneads the dough, pushing and pulling it like taffy, equal measures rough and gentle, is whether what he's doing with his hands is a transferable skill set.

His gaze darts up to mine, mouth curling upward, like he knows the effect he's having. "You want to try?" he asks.

I nod, and he tilts his head in invitation.

I expect him to stand off to the side and watch as I do it, but instead he steps in behind me, pressing his hips to my back. My throat goes dry at the feel of him. All of him. Every soft curve and hard ridge.

"You have to put your whole body into it," he instructs, guiding my arms back and forth as he kneads the dough. "Like this." He presses his hips right against my ass, and I'm thankful he can't see the blush crawling up my neck.

"By the way." He leans in, his lips gently brushing my earlobe. "This is my big gun."

"And here I thought you were just happy to see me."

He laughs and his whole body vibrates against mine, setting off a million tiny flames across my skin.

"You know, when you invited me over, I didn't expect to do a *Ghost* reenactment," I say.

"Well, I had to make sure you didn't think I was boring."

"I think you surpassed boring when you brought out the food processor."

"Wait until you see my blender," he says. "Though I usually reserve that for second dates."

"So this is a date?"

"Isn't it?" he asks, breath hot on the side of my neck.

"I thought this was two friends, making pasta and reenacting *Ghost.*"

"And do you normally reenact *Ghost* with your friends?"

"Not unless tequila is involved."

He leans in a little closer, hips grinding against mine in a decidedly *non-friend* maneuver. "Maybe we're not friends, then," he says.

Every cell in my body heats up. He's smooth. I'll give him that. And a panicky part of my brain tells me it's always the smooth talkers, the ones who know just what to say and how to say it, who do you the worst. I saw my mom date plenty of them to know the type.

But as we continue rolling out the dough, his hips snug against mine, I wonder, would it really be so wrong to hook up with Liam? Clearly, we're attracted to each other, and it wouldn't have to mean anything. It could just be a one-time thing. For fun. Besides, the idea of letting loose for a night, of not thinking about the future, or what I'm going to do next, or Gramps's disappointment, sounds exactly like what I need.

The thought gives me a burst of confidence as I turn around to face him.

"So, what usually happens next?" I ask.

He's tall enough that he hovers over me, neck bending as his eyes find mine. "We layer the noodles with the sauce," he says.

"No, I mean after you've pulled out the big guns."

His eyes flash, a question mark hovering behind his gaze. "Well, that depends. Did the big guns work?"

"You honestly had me at the slutty towel," I admit.

He laughs and the vibrations ping across my skin. "So you're telling me we reenacted *Ghost* for nothing?"

I bite down on my bottom lip, fighting back a smile. "I wouldn't say *nothing.*"

We've shifted closer now, his hips caging me against the counter.

"In that case, I suppose I'd ask to kiss you."

His attention drops to my mouth, and somehow that single look burrows directly between my legs.

"And if I said yes?"

I can feel the heat of him, the smell of aftershave and basil, and I know that the instant he closes the final gap between us, I'm a goner.

"Then I'd lean in." He bends toward me, so close his hot breath diffuses across my cheek. "And do this."

Our gazes hold. A beat passes. My heart pounds in my throat. Then, just when I don't think I can stand the scorched tension a second longer, he angles his jaw, cupping my cheek with his palm, and kisses me.

I expect it to be no different from the dozens of other meaningless kisses I've shared with men whose names I no longer remember. But I know within seconds of his lips meeting mine, this isn't that kind of kiss. It's the kind that burns hot against my skin, branding me. The kind that will linger long after it's over.

His mouth is slow at first, working over mine with controlled precision, a master class in restraint that nearly has me crying out with want. Then he tips my chin back and he kisses me a little rougher, a little harder, like he can't quite help himself.

A moan escapes me, inviting his hands to slink lower, pulling me flush against him, showing me where he's hard.

Maybe it's that, or the ghostlike whispers of warm breath on my neck, or the way he hoists me onto the counter, parting my knees with the urgent press of his thumb, but every cell, every nerve ending hums with the same hot whoosh of need, unified in pursuit of a singular goal. *More.*

As my fingers twist in his collar, dragging him closer, I try to remind myself that this is just a hookup. A distraction. That it means absolutely nothing. Just like all the hookups that have come before, and surely all the ones that will come after. But the thought gets lost in the pressure of his hands, the swirl of his tongue, the steady rock of his hips. In the billion singing particles all demanding *more, more, more*. And I know with every shallow gasp and full-bodied moan that the rest of my life will be divided into *before* and *after*.

Everything before this kiss. And everything after.

- 8 -

Now

After we find out that our gate does indeed exist, Liam and I walk in silence to get coffee.

We're in line to order when Liam's phone buzzes from inside his pocket. He pulls it out, eyes widening.

"Everything okay?" I ask.

"I have to take this. Here. For our coffee." He tosses me his wallet and walks off without giving me a second glance.

I frown, watching him go. Who the hell is calling him at 6 a.m.?

But if it's 6 a.m. here, then it's 2 p.m. in England.

My insides curl.

Whenever Liam's sister, Felicity, calls, it usually means something bad has happened at home. Not that he ever shared the specifics with me, but there were always clues. Bad moods. Whispered phone conversations. Liam emotionally withdrawing.

In the early years of our relationship, I tried to be understanding about the fact that Liam didn't like talking about his family. After all, it was clearly a sore subject for him. But as time went on, the lack of transparency bothered me. Not just because I knew very little about my own husband's past, but because it felt like there were certain parts of Liam that he didn't want to share with me. Parts that were off-limits.

I used to think of it as this wall between us, and if only I could just knock it down, then we'd be happier, closer. But the harder I pushed, the further he withdrew, until finally I got the hint that the wall wasn't coming down.

When I make it to the front of the line, the barista asks what she can get started for me and I place our order—iced coffee for me and a black drip for him since apparently New Single Liam doesn't do sugar anymore. When she tells me the total, I open Liam's wallet in search of his black Amex. I'm flipping through the stack of cards when I see them: two silver tinfoil packets.

I frown.

Why would Liam have condoms in his wallet? We haven't used condoms in nine years—not since we became exclusive. Unless . . .

My stomach sinks, my vision blurring around the edges.

My first thought is whether or not I need to move to the nearest garbage can so I can throw up.

The second is that I should have known.

When I saw him without his ring at the coffee shop, I assumed it was symbolic of our separation. Now I feel foolish and naive for not considering the obvious: Liam's ready to see other people.

Yes, in some theoretical sense I understood that divorce would entail Liam eventually fucking other women. It's not like I thought he'd remain chaste the rest of his life. But I didn't expect it to happen this fast. Or so casually. I figured we'd both need time. Lots of time. *Years* even.

But apparently Liam doesn't. Apparently, he's ready to take off his ring and start boning someone new.

Oh God. *Is* there someone new? Or is this just more of a precautionary thing?

Though I don't know which is worse. The thought of Liam intentionally going to the store to buy condoms? Or Liam casually tossing a box of Magnums into his grocery basket along with bread and eggs, thinking, *Hey, maybe I'll fuck someone new.*

I feel sick again.

I consider calling him on it. Letting him know that I saw the condoms and I'm hurt by it. But if I do, that will imply that I'm not ready to have sex with someone else. That I haven't moved on as quickly as he has. That I'm not an *empowered, sexually liberated woman* as I told him earlier. That to some extent the idea of him sleeping with someone else bothers me. Which of course it does. But I don't want him to know that. Not when I'm the one who ended things and I have no right to care what he does, or who he does it with. Not when I'm supposed to be *fine*, just like him.

"Ma'am? That'll be $12.76."

I force my attention back to the barista, now watching me with mild levels of concern.

"Oh. Sorry," I tell her before slamming down Liam's card with enough force to earn me a suspicious look.

After I grab our coffees, I shuffle out of the coffee shop and into the bookstore next door.

I'm just skimming the cover of a tabloid, proudly declaring a recently divorced actress is *now happier than ever* and *thriving in her new life*, when out of the corner of my eye, I see a familiar UW Med baseball cap covering two blond braids.

"Aloha!" my sister cries with a wave. "I texted the group chat that we were at the food court."

"Sorry. I didn't see it," I tell her.

I was too busy finding out my soon-to-be-ex-husband is having sex with other people!

Her lips fold together, clearly annoyed. "Figured. It's not like you answer any of my texts anymore anyways."

My gut twitches.

I wish I could tell her that she's not the only one whose texts I'm not answering. That the last few months have felt like a slow IV drip of misery and most days I can barely pull myself out of bed, much less respond to the stream of unanswered texts on my phone. Especially the DMs from readers asking when there will be another book. *Yeah, I'm wondering that too.* But Bella and I have never had that type of sisterly relationship. We mostly keep things easy, breezy, surface level. So I press my mouth into an apologetic smile. "Sorry, been busy."

Bella looks me up and down, a groove forming between her brows. "It's six a.m. Why do you look hot?"

"Thank you?"

She looks past me. "So, where's Liam? Or is he sick again?"

I'm about to tell her that *actually* Liam's on his way, when he appears by my side, arm sliding around my waist, dragging my body to his.

My limbs are momentarily rendered liquid-like as all of my brainpower concentrates on the singular phenomenon of Liam's hand resting on the curve of my hip. On the way his fingers splay out, low across my hip, firm and possessive, but also relaxed, like his hand just always goes there. Like it's the most natural thing in the world. And maybe at one time it was. But right now, after months without physical touch, the sensation is jarring.

Though apparently not to Liam. "Of course I'm here. You know I would never miss a Larsen family vacation," he says, adding one of his signature smiles.

Bella grins back at him, cheeks ripening into a blush. "Hey, Liam."

Bella's always had a harmless crush on Liam, one that dates back to the first Christmas he spent with my family when she was fourteen and so nervous around him that she couldn't speak.

In the years since, Bella's relationship with Liam has morphed from teenage crush to role model—he helped her with her med school applications and has been writing her letters of rec for residency—but her teenage crush still remains a family joke.

One that was funny when we were together. Now, not so much.

"Hey, Bella," he says, leaning in for a hug. "Long time no see."

"I guess I owe Jonah twenty bucks," she says, hugging him back. "We had a bet going whether you would actually show, and I thought you would be sick. Again," she adds, shooting me a look.

My insides shift, unsure what's worse—that my siblings placed bets on us, or that Bella bet against us. I look to Liam to see how he feels about this, but his face betrays nothing. The only clue that this registers is his hand tightening around my waist.

"Are you feeling any better?" Bella asks.

Confusion sweeps across Liam's expression.

Shit. I should have warned him that in the last three months he's had a sinus infection, bronchitis, and a particularly nasty bout of stomach flu.

I tilt my chin, giving Liam a look. *Just go with it.*

"All better, actually," he says, lips forming a sturdy smile.

"Roslyn said it was pretty bad." Bella cups her mouth, though it does nothing to muffle her voice when she says, "I heard it was coming out of both ends."

Whoops. I forgot I said that.

I brace myself, waiting to see how he reacts to the fact that I basically told the family he was having explosive diarrhea, but other than the slight flinch in his jaw, Liam hardly reacts.

"It wasn't quite *that* bad." His eyes shift to mine, giving me a look like he's vaguely considering strangling me. "You know how Roslyn exaggerates."

"Well, since you're feeling better, you still owe me a coffee date," Bella says. "Remember? You promised I could pick your brain on residency?"

They launch into a discussion on residency programs Bella is thinking about applying to just as my older brother, Jonah, and his husband, Ben, appear, both carrying enough luggage for a month, rather than a ten-day cruise. Behind them are my niece and two nephews: Henleigh, who's four, and Jackson and Riley, who are both six.

"Are you trying to sink the ship?" I ask, eyeing their luggage.

Jonah rolls his eyes. "This is what life looks like with three kids, Roslyn. We can't leave the house without bringing every single thing we own," he says, giving me a withering look.

If being busy were an Olympic sport, my brother would have more gold medals than Katie Ledecky. He takes great pride in doing more than everyone else and constantly uses it to one-up everyone around him. *Oh, you're tired? Well, at least you didn't perform heart surgery last night. You have a lot going on? Well, try having three kids under seven.* As an eldest child, he sees burnout as a prize to lord over others.

"Liam! How ya been?" my brother says, pulling Liam in for a bro hug. "Bella, you owe me twenty bucks."

"But I'm a poor med student," she whines. "Twenty dollars could buy me like a month's worth of instant ramen."

"Maybe next time don't make bets you'll lose," Jonah says, giving her a look.

Bella mutters something like *fuck off* while Jonah and Liam slap backs and Jonah compliments Liam's beard. "It looks good," he says. "I don't think I've ever seen you grow one before."

Liam strokes his cheek as though surprised to find the beard there. "Just trying a new look," he says.

I search his face for a clue, a hint that the beard has to do with the breakup, but his face remains carefully blank. Almost like he's trying not to show any emotion.

"I really like it," Bella says. "It's giving John Krasinski after he left *The Office*."

"Oh, are you talking to Liam now?" Jonah teases.

She punches his arm. "Shut up, asshole! That was nine years ago. And I have a boyfriend, remember?" she says, just as said boyfriend, Chris, walks over, two Starbucks cups in hand.

She takes her coffee and gives him a kiss on the cheek, and I swear he blushes. Even though they've been together for years now, I still don't know Chris very well, other than he's also in med school and they just moved in together, but he seems to have it bad for my sister, so I've decided I like him.

My siblings go back and forth, telling Liam how good he looks, how long it's been, how much they've been looking forward to seeing him; meanwhile I stand to the side feeling more and more like I've just been picked last for dodgeball.

I've never been terribly close with either of my siblings. I used to think it was because of the age gaps—seven years between Bella and me and five between me and Jonah—but as I got older and the age gaps weren't so jarring, it became apparent we were on different wavelengths, chasing entirely different futures.

Bella and Jonah wanted the life our grandparents planned for them. They wanted med school and prestigious jobs at prestigious hospitals, while I was a dropout who had far more in common with our free-spirited mother than either of them.

Then I started dating Liam, and finally we had something in common: We all loved him. For my sister, Liam was the blueprint for the type of guy she someday wanted to be with, while for Jonah, he was the cool brother he never had. Grammy and Gramps and Mom loved him, too, and for a while he felt like this singular unifying force in our lives.

But what was once the glue holding us together now feels like one more wall separating me from the rest of my family.

"Uncle Liam!" Jackson cries, breaking free from his dad to leap into Liam's arms. His twin brother, Riley, follows suit, and they latch on to Liam like a pair of leeches.

"Hey! Wow, you're both so big!" Liam cries, hugging them back.

"I'm bigger!" Riley yells. "Daddy weighed me!"

"I lost a tooth!" Jackson says back, not willing to be outdone.

The two brothers talk over each other, updating Liam on every conceivable thing that's happened to them in the last few months while Liam patiently nods, offering an appropriately placed *wow* every few seconds.

Liam's always been good with kids, something that used to make my ovaries do somersaults, but now, seeing him with Jackson and Riley, knowing he'll never play with our children—that there won't *be* any children—feels like another stab in the chest. Another emotional land mine I'm not ready for.

While Jackson and Riley tell Liam about the new bikes they just got and how they can't wait to go on the waterslide with him, Henleigh hangs back, still clutching Ben's hand like a life raft.

"Hen, why don't you say hi to Auntie Roslyn?" Ben suggests.

I bend down to her level, expecting a hug from my usually friendly niece, but she shakes her head and hides behind Ben's legs.

Ben shoots me an apologetic look. "Sorry, she's been shy lately, especially around people she doesn't know well."

My whole body flinches. I know I've missed a lot of family gatherings lately, but surely Henleigh doesn't think of me as a stranger?

"It's fine!" I say, a little too chipper. "I'm sure she'll warm up to me soon."

Ben's mouth wavers into a rueful smile as the twins start to climb Liam like a tree.

"All right, boys, let's give Uncle Liam some space," Jonah says, pulling the boys off Liam. "You can tell him all about your new bikes later, okay?"

They whine and complain just as my grandparents appear.

They are both dressed up—he in a sport coat and khakis and she in block heels and an Hermès scarf—like the year is 1967 and they're flying Pan Am.

As soon as Grammy spots Liam, her whole face lights up.

"Liam!" She looks at him like she imagines cartoon animals help him dress in the morning. "My, my, you just get more handsome every time I see you!" She turns to me. "Doesn't he just get more handsome, Roslyn?"

I crinkle my nose. "He sure does."

Liam squeezes Grammy back. "And you get ever more lovely. Is that a new brooch?" he asks, pointing to the jewel-encrusted ladybug on the lapel of her light jacket.

Grammy blushes and pats his cheek. "You're such a dear."

Gramps steps in to shake Liam's hand like they're business colleagues. "Liam, good to see you."

"Likewise, sir."

Gramps grips his shoulder, getting as close to a smile as I think is possible for him.

They chat about hospital politics and Liam's latest research publication—the one everyone was *thrilled* about—until Jonah claps his hands together, summoning everyone's attention.

"All right, so before we board our flight, I figured now would be a good time to hand out these," Jonah says, shoving pieces of paper into our hands.

"What's this?" I ask, frowning at the laminated page of single-spaced, size eight font.

"Itineraries," he says. "I emailed them to everyone, but I figured hard copies were good too."

At the top of the page, *Larsen Family Vacation* is printed in an aggressive font. Below that, Jonah has outlined in painful detail how we'll spend every second of every day including a dress code and moment-by-moment activities.

I scan the list of activities. Snorkeling. Hiking. Polynesian Cultural Center. Kayaking. Luau. Sunrise yoga.

I wince at the last item. There's no way I'm getting up for that.

My brother is such a firstborn and absolutely nothing like our mom, who would have been content to *see where the wind takes us.* Though perhaps a chaotic childhood made up entirely of *seeing where the wind took us* and never staying in a single place more than a year is exactly why my brother finds solace in order and schedules in adulthood.

"So? What do you think?" Jonah asks excitedly.

Bella raises her hand. "When do we get shit-faced on all-inclusive mai tais?"

Jonah's mouth collects into a frown. "This is meant to be an educational, culturally enriching family vacation, Bella. Not spring break in Cancún."

"And which do you think will be more culturally enriching? mai tais? Or piña coladas?"

He glares at her, but she just rolls her eyes.

"Lighten up, Mr. Drill Sergeant. This trip is supposed to be fun and relaxing."

I swallow hard, knowing full well that *relaxing* is the last thing this trip is going to be.

- 9 -

Now

The good news: Liam and I are about ten rows away from any of my family members.

The bad news: I'm in the middle seat.

There's an older gentleman in the window seat, whom I'd love to ask to switch with, but I know that if my family walked by and saw us not sitting together, they'd definitely ask questions. Which means I'll be spending the next six hours bumping elbows with Liam. *Lovely.*

As soon as the captain says it's okay to use our electronic devices, I pull my laptop out. Maybe if I can get some writing done, the flight won't be a total disaster. But the longer I stare at the blank screen in front of me, the more I wonder if it's possible to pop a blood vessel from thinking too hard.

This is your thing, I tell myself. But the blinking cursor staring back at me says otherwise. As has the last year.

My first book, *One Night with You,* sold much better than I or my publisher expected. "The perfect dose of charm and heat," *Entertainment Weekly* called it. The second sold even better, and almost overnight I went from wondering if I'd ever have a career as an author to amassing a social media following of loyal readers begging for bonus scenes and clues about my next project.

The success felt like real proof that maybe dropping out of med school hadn't been a huge mistake. That is, until I was expected to deliver a third, equally successful manuscript.

The problem is said *manuscript* is still very much in the brainstorming stage. And by *brainstorming,* I mean hoping I come up with something a bit more fleshed out than the paltry *rooftop sex?* currently jotted in my notebook.

"How's the book coming?" Liam asks, cutting through my thoughts.

I glance down at the taunting blank screen before slamming my laptop shut. "Not great," I tell him.

"Writer's block?"

"Sort of." Though writer's block is a vast understatement for the kind of crippling creative drought I've been in since my mom died.

Romance novels were always our special thing, a kind of treasured secret just between the two of us. While Bella and Jonah had med school and the approval of Grammy and Gramps, Mom and I had sweeping kisses, tropes, and book boyfriends.

Even if my mom never got a happily ever after in her own life, she saw romance novels as a bright light in an otherwise dark world. A place where love always prevailed and there was always the soft landing of a guaranteed happy ending. And I used to feel the same way. But after her passing, all the things I used to love about the genre—lingering glances, the brush of a hand in a dimly lit corridor—felt empty and joyless, and the once gushing spout of creativity dried to a trickle, then nothing at all. Now it's been months since I've written more than a paragraph.

"I'm sure you'll figure it out," Liam says with a tight nod. "You always do."

I make a face, not sure what annoys me more—his insincere aphorism, or his apparent lack of awareness to grasp that he's part of the problem.

It's not that I blame Liam for my writer's block, but I can't exactly pretend like the implosion of our marriage didn't dilute my ability to believe in—much less write about—happily ever after.

When I don't respond, Liam says, "Maybe this trip will help get some creative juices flowing."

I shoot him a look. "When exactly? Between sunrise hula and snorkeling? I'll be lucky if my family doesn't spend the whole trip ragging on how I should have been a doctor and how it's not too late to go back to school so I can be more like *you*, the golden boy," I say, making a face.

"Come on, they're not that bad," Liam says. "They're proud of you."

"Proud of me?" I make a *pfft* noise. "They still haven't recovered from the fact that I'm writing about genitalia in a nonmedical context."

"They're doctors, not prudes."

"Oh really? Is that why Gramps told all his friends at the golf club that I'm writing a thesis on reproductive anatomy because he was too ashamed to tell them the truth?"

"Okay but that's Gramps," he points out. "Everyone else has been more supportive. Remember how Grammy bought copies of your debut for everyone in her book club?"

I roll my eyes so hard, I momentarily worry they'll get stuck in the back of my head. "First off, we all remember how that went. Judith got upset when she found out there was premarital sex in the book, and now Grammy doesn't get invited to play gin rummy at her house anymore. It's a whole thing. And second." I pause, gaze cutting his. "If you think my family is super supportive of me dropping out of medical school to write books about anal sex, then you clearly haven't been paying attention."

"Which book has anal sex in it?"

I swallow down a groan. "Not the point, perv."

Liam was one of the first people who supported my writing, who made me feel like my silly little stories about people falling in love mattered. The only problem was that support never extended to defending me in front of my family. Liam was always content to just sit there as Gramps went in for another rousing round of *Roslyn is throwing away her life to write trashy romance novels.*

I told myself it was because Liam didn't have his own family, and he was afraid to rock the boat, but I always hoped he would stand up for me. That one day he'd tell Gramps that *he* was proud of me, even if Gramps wasn't.

"I'm just saying," he replies. "I know you have your issues with them, but you should know how lucky you are to have a family who cares about you." His entire expression hardens, eyes falling on me before he adds, "It's not something everyone has."

A tightness corkscrews in my chest. I want to tell him that it's easy for him to say when he's always been on the receiving end of their praise and admiration. Meanwhile I'm the family disappointment, but I know *whose family sucks more* isn't a battle I'm going to win, nor do I want to.

I open my laptop back up, pretending to be engrossed in the nonexistent words on the screen until Liam says, "So. *Coming out of both ends*? Really?"

I place my hand over my mouth, smothering a snort. "I had to make up some reason why you were absent from every family event in the last three months."

"And you really couldn't come up with anything better than I was shitting myself?"

I put a finger to my chin in thought. "No, I really couldn't."

"Any other terrible sicknesses I need to know about? Gout? Dysentery? A limp I need to fake?"

"If you must know, in the last three months you've had a cold, bronchitis, and food poisoning. I considered a broken leg, but I learned after I told Grammy you had food poisoning and she showed up with homemade bone broth that it was better to give you something contagious so you couldn't have visitors."

"I'm shocked you didn't just kill me off and be done with it."

"Trust me, I thought about it, but then I would have had to organize a fake funeral, which honestly seemed like a lot of work."

He snorts.

"So, anything *I* should know?" I ask, thinking back to the condoms I'd seen in his wallet. "Anything that might compromise our arrangement? Or complicate things?"

If he's seeing someone, now is the time to come clean.

Liam blinks, eyes shifting away then back to me. "Actually, there is something I should tell you . . ."

Fuck. Maybe I don't want to know. Maybe ignorance truly is bliss. Maybe—

"I may have told Grammy and Gramps something," he says.

"*Something?*" I repeat. "You're going to have to be a bit more specific."

When he doesn't say anything, I prod him with my elbow. "What? Don't tell me you told them we're also renewing our vows?"

He winces. "Worse."

"Worse? What the hell is worse than that?"

His brow scrunches. "Promise you won't freak out?"

I cross my arms over my chest. "You're not making me feel better, Liam."

He swallows, eyes skittering away, before finally he says, "I may have told them that we're trying to get pregnant."

The air whooshes out of my lungs. "You *what*?"

"It wasn't my fault! They kept asking when they were getting more great-grandchildren."

My stomach nose-dives like I've just tipped over the ledge of the first big drop on a roller coaster. "You're supposed to say, *We aren't ready yet*, or even, *That's none of your damn business*," I hiss. "Is that so hard, Liam?"

He looks over both shoulders, making sure we aren't about to be overheard before he whispers, "It wasn't that simple. They kept asking all these follow-up questions—like *When will you be ready?* and *What are you waiting for?*—and didn't we know *you* aren't getting any younger. So I told them we were trying, just to get them off my back."

I groan and rub my temples. "This doesn't get them off our backs, Liam. It puts them very much *on* our backs. Now, not only will they be devastated by the end of our marriage, they'll also have to grapple with the disappointment that we won't be giving them any more great-grandchildren. So congrats, Liam, you've officially made everything worse!"

Liam opens his mouth to respond just as the older man seated on the other side of me flags the flight attendant passing our row. "Excuse me, ma'am?"

She looks in our direction. "Yes?"

"Are there any open seats available? If so, I'd like to be moved," he says, shooting both Liam and me uneasy looks.

The flight attendant looks between us, eyes narrowing, and I feel like I've been caught talking in class. "Of course, sir, I'd be happy to find you a new seat."

I turn to Liam. "Look what you did!"

"You promised you wouldn't freak out."

"How the fuck else am I supposed to respond?"

The man looks between us, shaking his head like *good riddance*, before climbing his way out into the aisle and following the flight attendant to his new, presumably more peaceful seat.

As soon as he's gone, I slump lower in my own.

Maybe this was all a terrible idea. We can't even make it through a six-hour flight without fighting. How are we going to fake being together for ten days?

Liam must be having the same thought because when another flight attendant comes by, asking if we want anything to drink, we both say, "Gin and tonic, please."

"I thought you were off sugar?" I ask.

"I'm making an exception for this trip."

"Because you need alcohol to tolerate me?"

"*Because*," he says, eyes cutting to mine. "If I'm going to have to spend ten days lying about our relationship, it's not going to be sober."

He hits me with a hard look as the flight attendant hands us each a plastic cup, a mini tonic water, and two little bottles of gin. We only briefly make eye contact before taking a drink out of our respective glasses.

Bottoms up.

After I've finished my regrettably small drink, I release a full-bodied *hmph* and go back to my laptop, hoping I can channel some of my frustration onto the screen. But I end up just staring at it until my bladder gives me an excuse to get up. I unclick my seat belt and nudge Liam's knee. "Can you move? I need the bathroom."

But he doesn't budge. Either he's a great actor or he's out cold.

Guess I'll have to do this the hard way.

I stand up and lift one leg over his thighs—so far so good—when the airplane unexpectedly lurches, sending both myself and what's left in Liam's cup right into his lap.

The first thing I notice is how hard his chest is. Like falling into a brick wall. The second is his voice, hot and sticky against my ear when he asks, "What the fuck are you doing?"

It takes me a second to realize that not only am I on top of Liam, but I'm full-on straddling him—a position my body is a little too familiar with.

Heat pools in my middle as I mutter a quick apology and scramble as far away as the ten inches of legroom will allow, which is when we both notice it: the rapidly expanding wet spot across his crotch where his drink spilled.

"Bloody hell!" Liam cries. "Look what you did!"

I cringe. He uses Britishisms only when he's *really* mad.

"It was an accident! You're the one who wouldn't move when I told you I was going to the bathroom!"

"Because I was asleep!"

My cheeks flare. *Whoops.*

"I got wet too!" I gesture to the damp spot on the front of my dress.

"Yeah, well, it doesn't look like you pissed yourself," he grumbles.

I cover my mouth, attempting to smother a laugh.

"It's not funny," he snaps.

I mean, it's definitely a *little* funny to see cool, calm, and collected Liam's feathers finally ruffled.

Liam shakes his head, forehead creasing with frustration. "I'm going to try and clean up," he mutters, unbuckling his seat belt and standing up. I trail behind him.

"Don't follow me," he snaps.

"I need to clean up too!"

But when we get to the back of the plane, there is only one lavatory open. Because of course there is.

"How about we go in together?" I suggest.

Liam stiffens. "I'm not going in there with you while you pee."

"Relax. I'm not going to pee in front of you. Wouldn't want to ruin the romance," I add dryly. "Now come on." I grab his elbow and tow him behind me. But as soon as the door is locked, I realize I've made a crucial error. Either Liam is much bigger than I remember, or these airplane bathrooms are smaller.

How do people fuck in here?

I try to step back, but there's a grand total of three inches of space, and I find myself caged between his chest and the wall.

"Can you maybe—"

"No. I can't," he says, wincing. "I have no room."

"Here, let me—"

"Leave?" he asks hopefully.

"I was going to say *help*."

"I think you've done enough already," he says, rubbing his temples in frustration.

Maybe it's feminine rage, or because I know he's got condoms in his wallet, or I'm wearing this stupid fucking dress and he doesn't even seem to care, but the composure I've been trying to hold on to finally snaps, and I reach for a wad of paper towels and drop to my knees in front of him.

He inhales sharply. "Roslyn, what the—?"

I know it's petty and immature and probably toxic, but there's a reckless part of me that's desperate to do something, *anything* to prove that behind all the stiff jaws and guarded expressions, there's some piece of him, even a small one, that's just as fucked up over this as me.

"I'm just trying to help," I tell him, putting on my most innocent voice as I dab at the stain on the front of his pants.

His body stiffens. "I told you I . . ." But his words are lost to a shudder, and I can't deny the thrill of provoking him. Of making him feel even just a fraction of the chaos I've been feeling.

I blink up at him before standing back up. "Something wrong?"

He looks like he's in pain. "Can you *please* not—" But before he can get the rest of the sentence out, the plane shifts and I stumble forward, right into him.

"Sorry—" I start to say, but the words are instantly vaporized by the sensation of his grip on my waist, the steadying wall of his chest, the way we're flattened against each other, body to body.

A moment ago, I was the one in control. Now I'm anything but.

It's honestly humbling how quickly my body reacts to his touch, how quickly my skin singes from the contact, like some primal beast being awoken from its slumber.

His grip tightens, hands molding around my hips, and a rush of awareness chases goose bumps across my skin, a reminder that my body remembers his. Every touch. Every brush of the lips. Every intimate, stolen kiss and needy caress. All of it is packed away in his palm, now resting on my hip like my skin's been branded by him, years of memories coalescing under the pads of his fingers.

I thought—*hoped*—that enough time had passed that the memories might have dulled or were at least buried so deep in the cavern in my mind that they were not readily available for extraction. But here they are bobbing to the surface, clear and unfoggy.

Our eyes meet for one shallow exhale before his gaze drops to my mouth, pinning me with a hungry stare that sends all the blood rushing to my head. But the look only lasts a moment, so brief I wonder if I imagined it, before he blinks and it's gone, each emotion carefully tucked back into place.

The speaker overhead makes a *click* sound followed by a muffled voice. “Hello, folks, this is your captain speaking. Looks like we’ve just hit some turbulence, so we suggest you please buckle up until it passes.”

Liam pulls away, flinching like the contact burned him. “We should—”

“Right.” Cheeks scalding, I turn and push open the door so fast, I don’t look where I’m going until I collide with two outstretched arms.

“Roslyn?”

Bella stumbles back, eyes growing steadily wider as her gaze shifts past me to Liam, then back to me.

“Well, well, well,” she says, a knowing smile playing on her lips. “Looks like you two were experiencing a bit of turbulence of your own.”

It takes me a moment to register her meaning, but as soon as I do, all the blood rushes to my cheeks.

She doesn’t think . . . ?

I follow her line of sight as she glances from the indents on my knees to Liam’s mussed hair all the way down to the wet spot on the front of Liam’s pants. A wet spot that suddenly doesn’t look like a spilled drink anymore.

She definitely thinks that.

I’m about to tell Bella this isn’t what it looks like when Liam’s arm snakes around my waist, giving a protective squeeze that cuts off all oxygen and, therefore, all logic from my brain.

“Sorry, Bells, we’re just on our way back to our seats,” Liam says, shooting her an apologetic grin that might as well be a written confession that, *Yes, we were just banging in the airplane bathroom.* And I don’t know whether to be deeply pissed at him or impressed that apparently Liam’s great at improv.

"Riiiiight," she says, giving us both knowing looks before moving inside the available toilet and shutting the door. As soon as she's gone, Liam extracts his hand from around my waist and takes a big step back.

"What was that?" I hiss.

"What was *what*?"

"That!" I flap my hands like I'm trying to entice buyers to a used car lot.

"I thought that's what we're supposed to be doing? *Pretending.*"

"Yes, but not like *that*!"

His brows furrow. "What's wrong with that?"

Oh God. Am I really going to have to explain this to him?

"My sister thinks we just joined the mile high club," I whisper.

"So?"

"And . . ." My attention drops to the front of his pants.

He follows my gaze. "You think she thought—?"

"That you got *excited*? Yeah. I think she did."

"*Fuck,*" Liam mutters under his breath.

I'm about to point out, *Hey, at least my sister doesn't think we're getting a divorce,* but he scowls, and I take that as my cue to shut up.

The irony is that there was once a time when Liam and I might have considered sneaking off to an airplane bathroom together.

There were plenty of nights when it was all we could do to make it through the front door without ripping each other's clothes off. Back when I swear I used to just *look* at Liam's forearms and start ovulating. But those days feel like a hazy fever dream. Almost like they belong to someone else.

After my mom died, there was a part of me that just broke. I stopped writing. I stopped answering calls and texts. I stopped seeing friends and family. I stopped wanting sex.

Grief became a kind of shadow I couldn't get out from under. A hand on my throat, slowly tightening its grip. But instead of sitting with me in my hurt, Liam gave me space. *Lots of space.* He started working longer hours and taking on more projects at work.

I'm not good at these conversations, he'd tell me every time I tried to talk, and after a while it felt less like space and more like he was avoiding me. Like maybe my grief was what he needed space from.

At first, I felt guilty. Guilty that the increasing distance between us was my fault. That we weren't having sex. Guilty that I wasn't meeting my husband's needs. Then came the shame. Shame that I couldn't be the version of myself I once was. Shame that I was in a dark place with seemingly no way out. But over time those feelings turned sour, and guilt and shame morphed into resentment and bitterness toward Liam. For not being there the way I needed him to be. For not meeting *my* emotional needs.

I've spent so much of my life orienting myself to others, trying to please and cater and accommodate. Even after I dropped out of med school, I never stopped needing the approval of my family. It's probably the reason I'm here now, about to lie to them for ten days. But Liam was always supposed to be the one person who saw me as enough. Someone whose approval I didn't have to work to earn. Who could handle the least polished, most broken version of me. So when he wasn't, when it became apparent that my grief was too much for him—that *I* was too much for him—it reinforced everything I was afraid of.

Weeks turned into months. We fought more and talked less until the space between us felt unbridgeable and there was no way to muscle back the intimacy we'd lost. Until it was too late.

I think about the night we broke up. The way he'd just looked at me, features made of stone as I stood there sobbing in the kitchen, begging him to care that our marriage was falling apart.

The click of the door as it shut behind him. The rumble of his car pulling out of the driveway. Then the silence that cut deeper than any scalpel ever could after he was gone.

It's certainly not what I envisioned when I said *I do* five years ago, full of optimism that we'd found the kind of love that lasts. But as I've learned the hard way, the stories I used to love aren't reflections of reality, of what's possible when two people love each other enough. Rather they're fantasies, no different than stories about witches and wizards and elves. But instead of magic and slaying dragons, there's happily ever after and grand gestures and men who try.

But real life doesn't work that way. Not all love is the lasting kind.

And not all princes stay charming.

- 10 -

Now

Larsen Family Vacation Day 1

PORT OF CALL: Honolulu, Oahu

ITINERARY: *family dinner on Deck 4, 5:30 p.m.*

ATTIRE: *resort casual*

For the first time in my life, I consider being the kind of person who claps when the plane lands.

Following the bathroom incident, Liam and I spend the rest of the flight in silence, each pretending the other person doesn't exist. But as soon as we land and we're back in the presence of my family, Liam transforms from quiet and brooding to charming and effervescent, like he's Mr. Potato Head swapping out his *I don't want to be here* eyes for his *caring, attentive* ones. Which is giving me major emotional whiplash. But at least he's committing to the bit, I guess.

Once we're aboard the ship, we're given leis (Bella makes an obligatory joke about getting *laid*), and Jonah instructs us to unpack and meet back for dinner at 5:30. I've never been on a cruise before, so I'm not sure what to expect. Bad comedy shows? Endless buffets? But as I soon discover, it's literally a floating city.

Take-out sushi? Check. Mexican restaurant? Check. Want a massage? Swedish or hot stone? Swimming pools? There are four.

If Liam and I play our cards right, we won't have to see each other for more than a few hours a day. Which is something I'm looking forward to until we're inside the stateroom and I realize just how small it is. How hard—*impossible*—it will be to avoid each other.

"Um, who gets the bed tonight?" I ask, eyes dancing to the bed taking up approximately 85 percent of the room.

"I'll take the floor," he says, not meeting my eye. "You can have the bed."

"Are you sure?"

He nods, scraping a palm over his beard. After a pause, he asks, "Have you been sleeping better? I mean, are you still . . . ?"

He doesn't finish the question, but I know what he's asking. He's wondering if I'm still having nightmares.

My limbs turn loose and unsteady as flashes of memory play behind my eyes. Him holding my hand. Him tucking me into bed. Him stroking my hair until I'd fallen asleep. *I'm here, it's okay. You're okay.*

I hadn't expected him to bring that night up. I figured it was an embarrassing one-time thing destined to be forever memory-holed by both of us. Though if there's anything Liam's succeeding at today, it's surprises.

"I'm fine," I say, looking away.

"That's not what I'm asking. What happened the night you called me, that was serious." Then, in a low voice I feel right in the depths of my core, he adds, "I've been worried about you."

His words—or perhaps the concern behind them—slice through me, sharp and unyielding, a machete through my chest.

"We're alone," I tell him. "You don't need to pretend to care about me."

Liam's hand rises like maybe he might reach out to me, but he thinks better of it and shoves it in his pocket. "I'm not pretending, Roslyn." He runs a frustrated hand through his hair. "What if I hadn't gotten your call? What if I hadn't been there?"

My emotional *check engine* light flashes on.

Though I'm not sure what strikes more of a chord. The flicker of something soft and vulnerable behind his eyes. Or that he's right. What if he hadn't been there? What if I hadn't called him? And worse still, what if it happens again and there's no one to call?

But I don't want Liam to know that, so instead I say, "I don't need you to take care of me."

His mouth tenses. "You've made that clear."

"Great. Then let's pretend it never happened."

"So we're just adding to the list of things we're pretending now?"

"I guess so."

Our gazes lock, caught in a silent standoff until there's a knock at the door announcing the delivery of our luggage, thus reminding me how badly I need to get out of this dress.

"I need to change, so can you turn around? Or close your eyes?" I ask, making a twirling gesture with my index finger.

Liam lifts one eyebrow. "You do know I've seen you undress probably thousands of times, right?"

My skin warms with unwanted thoughts of all the times he's seen me undress, and all the times he did the undressing.

"I'm aware," I say quickly. "But we're not together anymore, so I think we need to avoid"—I gesture vaguely—"nudity."

As much as I don't want him to see me naked, or worse, see *him* naked, it feels a bit like trying to put toothpaste back in the tube.

I can pretend I don't know about the tattoo on his left shoulder, or what he sounds like when he comes, just like he can pretend he's not capable of drawing a map of my inner thighs with a cartographer's precision. But that's all it is. Pretending. One of many things we're currently pretending.

"I'll be in the bathroom. Just tell me when it's"—he drags a hand through his hair—"*safe* to come back out." Then he spins on his heel and retreats.

As soon as he's gone, I peel myself out of the dress.

I'm tugging on another—something flowy that meets my brother's criteria of *resort casual*—when I notice Liam's phone light up on the nightstand, announcing a new notification.

I've never been through his phone before because we've always had a relationship built on mutual trust and respect, but now that we're broken up and I know he's got condoms in his wallet, I can't help the bubble of morbid interest expanding inside me.

What if it's a woman?

Katie?

There's a dusty corner of my brain that already knows I shouldn't look. That I'm simply not mature or evolved enough to handle finding out Liam has a girlfriend. But if he's seeing someone, wouldn't it be better to know about her? So I don't get blindsided later on?

I look over both shoulders before sneaking a peek at the screen.

FROM: DR. HIRAM GROSSE
RE: RESEARCH POSITION OFFER

Dr. Woods,

It was great talking to you yesterday afternoon. We're thrilled at the prospect of you joining the team in London at the Institute of Cancer Research this coming spring . . .

I stop reading.

Wait. *What?*

I blink once. Twice. I can't fucking breathe.

Liam's moving to London? As in *England*?

"Roslyn? Can I come back out?" Liam calls, his voice muffled through the door.

I jump away from the phone and rearrange my face into something normal before calling back, "All clear."

As soon as he sees me, his brows draw together. "What's wrong?"

There's a part of me that wonders if I should just keep it to myself, pretend I didn't see it. But another part of me knows that if he's moving across the world, then we need to talk about it.

"Are you taking a job in London?" I ask after a beat.

His attention drops to his phone, then back to me. Comprehension slogs through his features. "Did you look at my phone?"

"I just saw the email notification pop up," I tell him. "I didn't read any further."

His posture stiffens and I can feel him trying to figure out how to respond. Finally, he says, "I haven't accepted the position yet, but yes. I've been offered a job at the Institute of Cancer Research in London."

His words crash over me in disorienting waves.

We haven't even signed papers or told my family. Most of his stuff is still at the house. And he's already planning a whole new life in a different country?

"What about your job at the university hospital?" I ask. "I thought you were happy there."

He drags a hand over his beard. "I mean, it's a great job, but this position has more upward mobility and access to more research funding and . . ." He pauses, drawing a breath. "And as you know, I haven't got permanent residency in the US."

For years, Liam's been extending his O-1 visa, a special visa for people doing outstanding work in their field, but we never got around to getting him permanent residence. It didn't seem urgent. Now that feels like a massive oversight.

"Can't you apply for a green card?" I ask. "Or extend your visa?"

He shifts uneasily. "I could, but I think it would be best for me to move. Besides, this position is offering to pay for me to get licensed in the UK. So it's a win-win really."

A win-win.

The words scrape against my insides like nails on a chalkboard.

"So you're moving back . . ." I can't hold back the flinch. "Permanently?"

He looks away. "I'm not sure yet."

My heart lobs in my throat. I knew that divorce would mean separate lives, separate futures. But this all feels too fast, like we've taken an unexpected sharp turn, and now I'm spinning out.

"Is this about your parents?" I ask. "Did you hear from them?"

He shakes his head, jaw clenching. "No. It's about me."

"So you actually want to move to London?"

There's a brief hesitation, the tiniest of cursory breaths like he's watching to see what I'm going to do before he says, "I haven't been to England in over a decade. I think it will be good for me to go back, to start over somewhere else."

Somewhere else. He says it like that's all this is, a thirst for adventure, but I know what he really means. He means somewhere without *me*. And I don't know whether to be angry or heartbroken that this is what it's come to. That things are so unbelievably fucked up that he needs to put six thousand miles between us.

"Were you going to tell me?" I ask. "Or were you just going to call me from the airport when you were on your way?"

He sighs, exasperated. "Come on, Roslyn, don't be like this."

"Like what?" I ask, my voice ratcheting up as my heartbeat creeps into my throat. "I just found out you're moving to London, and you didn't think I should know?"

He massages his temples. "Of course I would have told you. But it's not even a done deal yet."

I can't help but note the tiny waver in his voice, the way his eyes shift downward. It's a foreign look on his usually certain expression, and part of me wants to pause, to unpack the unspoken concerns bracketed in the deep lines on either side of his mouth. But another part of me knows it's not my problem anymore. Our marriage is over, and despite whatever emotional baggage might come with him moving across the world, this isn't my business. Not anymore.

"I assume my grandparents don't know?" I ask after a beat.

He shifts his weight, clearly uncomfortable. "No. They don't."

I guess I ought to feel happy. I *finally* have some dirt on him. Something I know my grandparents will be upset about, especially given that my grandfather got him his current job at the university hospital. Instead, I feel like everything is suddenly on fire and I don't have a moment to collect my things before the flames swallow me whole.

I wish I hadn't seen the email. Or the condoms in his wallet. I wish I could go back in time, to before we had this conversation. To before everything fell apart.

"I'm gonna head to the pool," I say, reaching for my sunglasses and room key, desperate to leave, to be anywhere but this cabin with him.

"Aren't we meeting your family for dinner?"

"Not until five thirty, so you can do whatever until then, but I'll be at the pool taking advantage of the all-inclusive alcohol package," I tell him, already taking large strides toward the door.

"Don't drink too much," he calls after me. "You don't want to get sloppy in front of your family like on Thanksgiving last year," he adds, catching my eye.

He says it like he wasn't a little bit drunk too. Like we didn't go home and eat grocery store pie straight from the tin. Like he didn't kiss my forehead and carry me to bed at the end of the night. But maybe that's the point. Maybe he doesn't want to remember. And frankly, neither do I.

- 11 -

Nine years earlier

Liam's thumb skates along the outside of my arm, tracing the same spot over and over like he's trying to commit it to memory. His bare skin is warm and a little damp with sweat, and he smells like soap and citrus and that extra thing I can't quite pinpoint that's just him. But whatever it is, I like it. A lot.

"Are you sniffing me?"

"No," I say a little too quickly.

The corners of his mouth curl upward. "I mean it's okay if you are. I smell good."

I give his arm a little punch. "Does being cocky come naturally to you, or do you have to work at it?"

His gaze tracks up and down my body with unfettered desire. Then, without warning, Liam flips us over, arms caging me in against the mattress. "Funny you should ask." His lips dip to the side of my neck. "I have to." He pauses, kissing the sensitive skin. "Work." *Kiss.* "Very." *Kiss.* "Hard." *Kiss.* "At." *Kiss.* "It." *Kiss.*

I laugh, trying (not very hard) to push him away, but he only grips my hips tighter, and I can't help the little moan that escapes me.

It wasn't supposed to be like this. Liam was supposed to be an orgasm-shaped distraction from my post-dropout woes. But our one-night stand turned into nonstop texting, which turned into another hookup, which turned into me coming over almost every night. And *coming* every night.

Now we've been sleeping together for three weeks and I think I have a crush. A big, fat, all-consuming crush. Not just because the sex is good—*really* good. I like how he makes me feel.

While Liam can be tender and sweet in bed, he's also vocal and direct about what he wants and how he wants it, and I realize for the first time in my life, it feels freeing to be told what to do. So much of my life has been dictated by the plans and expectations of others, but here, with Liam—someone who understands me and gets me—I feel like I can let go. Like I don't have to be in control or worry about the future or who I'm disappointing or if I'm enough. Because when I'm with him, he makes me feel like I am.

Mostly, I genuinely like spending time with Liam. I like the way his whole face brightens when he talks about his work and how my heartbeat ramps up when he says something adorably British like *rubbish* or the *lift*, and how I always leave his apartment smelling like him.

But if I've learned anything from my mom's failed relationships or the smattering of hookups I've had, it's that good things never last and I shouldn't get attached. So I let Liam plant one more kiss on my neck before I hop out of his bed, scouring the floor for my underwear.

"Are you leaving already?" Liam asks.

I spot the tangle of lace under the bed. "I should get going."

"Oh." I hate the way my heart beats hopefully at the disappointment in his voice. "Are you sure you don't want to stay for dinner?"

I'm about to tell him I really shouldn't when tiny black spots pop behind my eyes, vision blurring as I'm hit with an unexpected wave of nausea that sends me stumbling back onto the bed.

Liam rushes to my side, his hands a steadying weight on my back. "Are you okay?" he asks, and my heartbeat jumps at the concern woven into his voice.

"Yeah. Fine." I put my head in my hands, willing the dizziness to subside. "I think I just stood up too fast."

"You don't look too good."

I push out a laugh. "Exactly what every naked woman you just had sex with wants to hear."

His brow furrows. "I'm serious. You look pale. Do you need water?"

"I'm fine. I just—" But the rest of the sentence doesn't make it out before I stand up and rush to the bathroom, barely making it to the toilet before I puke up the contents of my stomach.

A second later Liam appears behind me, hand at the base of my neck, rubbing in slow circles while he uses his other hand to pull my hair away from my sticky face.

I puke again, eyes burning, throat aching.

God. This is humiliating. Things might be going well with Liam, but I know how these casual arrangements are. He wants to see me looking sexy in bed, *not* puking my guts out in his toilet.

"I'm so sorry," I croak as hot, embarrassed tears prick my eyes.

"There's nothing to apologize for," he says, stroking my back, up and down, a calming weight that tempers my racing heart.

"I've been feeling off for a few days, but I felt okay when I came over—" I pause to retch again. "God, I'm so sorry, I probably got you sick too."

"It's okay. If I get sick, then we'll just be sick together."

Maybe he's just trying to be nice, but fuck if I don't feel the door in my chest, the one I've tried to keep shut, open just a bit wider for him.

After I've puked up everything in my stomach, I try to stand but my legs are too wobbly, so Liam picks me up and carries me back to bed, where he hands me a clean T-shirt and boxers.

He gestures for me to raise my arms and I feel like a small, helpless child as he dresses me before tucking me back into bed.

"You really don't have to do this," I tell him. "I know we're just hooking up." His eyes flash with something almost like hurt. "I can go. I promise. I—"

"Roslyn." He gives me a stern look. "You're not going anywhere." Then in a voice that soothes like cold water on a burn, he says, "I'm going to take care of you, okay?"

My bottom lip quivers between my teeth. "Are you sure?"

He almost laughs, like the idea of not taking care of me is ridiculous to him. "Yes, I'm sure. Now sit up for me so I can take your temperature."

I do as I'm told, and he places his hand on my forehead. When he pulls back, he's frowning. "You're burning up." He leaves and returns a moment later with a couple Tylenol and a glass of water. "Here. Take these for the fever."

"Yes, Doc."

His mouth rises, a small slow smile that feels handcrafted just for me.

I've come to learn that he has a few different smiles. A lazy one he offers when he's sleepy or bored or both. A big, toothy one when he's trying to be charming. And then there's the hopeful smile. The one with soft lips and even softer eyes, which feels like it's just for me. That one is my favorite.

"You know," I say, nestling back against his pillows, "this isn't exactly what I had in mind when I was imagining a sexy doctor fantasy."

"Oh?" he asks, brushing a strand of hair from my forehead. "And what usually happens in your fantasy?"

"Well, for one, I'm not puking my guts out. And second, you're usually wearing a stethoscope and nothing else."

"Sorry I'm not meeting expectations. Would it help if I took my shirt off?"

"Honestly, that might cure me."

He laughs. "Do you think you can keep any food down? I can make you some soup if you'd like?"

"That depends. Will it take three hours?"

"Homemade bone broth usually takes between twelve and forty-eight hours, but I can make you soup from a tin if you prefer," he says, looking at me like he's suggested I lick the inside of a trash can.

"Considering I might be dead before then, canned soup would be perfect."

He shakes his head, mouth flirting with a smile, and I swear my insides melt.

Fuck. I like him so much. Every time he looks at me, touches me, it feels like my heart is in my throat, like there's a band tightening over my chest, making it harder to breathe.

He turns toward the door.

"Liam?"

He pivots back to face me. "Yeah?"

"Thank you. This is really nice of you."

His eyes shift up and down, tattooing my body with his gaze. "Of course. Anytime."

"Hopefully it doesn't happen again," I say with a laugh.

"Well, if it does, I'll be there." Then he turns and slips out the door while my heart beats faster.

Don't get attached, I remind myself. *This won't last. Just like none of Mom's ever did.* But the reminder dulls against the ache in my chest, the feeling of my heart widening and stretching to make space for him. Or perhaps there was always space. Perhaps I've been holding it just for him.

Twenty minutes later, Liam returns with a bowl of classic Campbell's chicken noodle soup and a mug of hot tea because, as he puts it, *I'm English and therefore legally obligated to make you tea when you don't feel well,* before settling beside me in bed.

"How do you feel?" he asks.

"A bit better. I think throwing up helped." I wince. "Er, sorry about that."

"Roslyn, please," he says, giving me a look. "We operated on cadavers last term. I think I can handle a little vomit."

"So I haven't scared you away?" I ask, my voice unexpectedly small.

"Not even a little," he says, leaning in to plant a kiss on my forehead.

His lips linger a beat too long for two people who are just casually sleeping together when I hear footsteps followed by a door opening and shutting on the other side of Liam's bedroom wall. We both freeze.

"Does Kevin know about us sleeping together?" I whisper.

"I don't see how he couldn't. You're not exactly quiet, you know," Liam says, giving me a look.

I blush. It's hard to stay quiet when the man knows how to do things with his hands and mouth that ought to come with a warning label.

"Has he said anything?" I ask.

"No, but he did give me back the handful of condoms I gave him and said, *I think you need these more than me.*"

My cheeks sizzle and not from the fever. "Abby still doesn't know. I've been really sneaky."

Liam's fingers tangle with mine, mindlessly brushing his thumb on the inside of my palm. "And where exactly does she think you've been every night for the last few weeks?"

"At the gym. Which is perfect because if I come home all red-faced and disheveled, she'll just think I was working out."

The corners of Liam's mouth tug upward.

"What?" I ask.

"I'm just thinking about you, coming home all sweaty and disheveled."

He wiggles his eyebrows and I swat at his chest, laughing.

"Do you think you'll ever tell Abby about us?" he asks.

Ever. I don't know if he means to, but he makes it sound like this is a long-term thing. Something indefinite. That we'll always be like this. I know we won't, but it's a nice thought anyway.

"I'll tell her eventually," I say. "But I'm giving her time. She and Kevin just broke up, and I don't want to brag about having the best sex of my life with Kevin's roommate."

"The best, eh?" Liam asks, leaning in to nibble on my earlobe.

Heat blossoms against my rib cage. With other partners, sex was always a means to an end. He came, I came—sometimes on my own when he couldn't get me there. It was all very practical and utilitarian. But sex with Liam is different. It's intense. Focused. Hungry. Not just for each other, but for the moment, like it's something tenuous we're both trying to hold on to, to make last for as long as we can. And he always gets me there. Multiple times.

"You know, Kevin is going home to Colorado for Christmas

next week, so we'll have the place to ourselves," he says, curling a hand around my waist. "Which means we can make as much noise as we want."

"Does that mean you're not going home for Christmas?"

"This is home," he says.

I know he means Seattle, or even this apartment, but there's a hopeful little part of my brain that wants him to mean *me*.

"No, home to England," I clarify.

His gaze falters ever so slightly, but he slides his expression right back into place. "I'm staying here in Seattle."

"Won't your family miss you?" I ask.

"I don't think so." A shadow passes over his face, and I realize it's the first time the mask has slipped and the shiny, flirty man I've been sleeping with gives way to someone with harder edges and sharper lines. Someone decidedly less shiny.

I don't want to pry—after all, we're just hooking up and he's not obligated to tell me about his personal life—but I can't help the prick of curiosity.

"Is everything okay?" I try.

Liam looks away, suddenly engrossed in my now-empty bowl of soup.

"I don't exactly talk to my parents," he says after a long pause.

"Oh." I shift my weight, and the mattress creaks. "I'm sorry."

He shrugs like it's not a big deal, but I can tell from the clench in his jaw that, whatever it is, it's something he holds close to his chest.

"So if you're not going home for Christmas, then what are you going to do?" I ask.

"Probably pull Christmas crackers all by my lonesome."

"That's the saddest thing I've ever heard," I tell him.

His hands move down to my waist, thumb skimming across

my hip bone. "It's not so bad. Last year I watched *Die Hard* and ate enough sweets to make me sick." He says it with a smile, but the expression doesn't fully reach his eyes, which makes the whole thing even more sad.

I sit up, shaking my head. "Okay, first off, *Die Hard* isn't a Christmas movie." He opens his mouth to argue, but I press on. "And second, I can't let you do that. It's too sad."

"I'm not sure I have a choice," he says.

"Yes, you do. You can come to my family's Christmas."

As soon as I say it, I wish I could swallow back the words. I mean, geez, this is supposed to be casual, and he definitely doesn't want to meet my family. My loud, annoying, invasive family, who will ask Liam a million questions about med school and which residency program he's doing. God, they'll probably be obsessed with him.

"I mean you totally don't have to," I say quickly. "I was just thinking if you don't have—"

"I'd love to," he says, cutting me off.

"You would?"

He nods, his whole face brightening. And God, he looks so earnest right now, it makes my heart squeeze. I tell myself it's because I hate the thought of him spending Christmas alone, that I'm just being nice. That I would have offered it to anyone. But I know that's not true.

"Are you sure?" I ask. "Because my family is sort of a lot. My mom will probably bring her new boyfriend and my grandparents will complain that he has too many tattoos, and there will probably be a fight and my sister will be annoyed at my brother for bossing her around and Grammy will cry because she wants everything just perfect."

The words rush out of me, hot and fast, and I brace myself to hear him tell me no. Of course he doesn't really want to come. He was only joking. Instead, his eyes lock on mine, and he says in that charming voice of his, "I want to, Roslyn."

"Really?"

"Really," he confirms.

I smile and he smiles back, a wide one that swallows up his whole face.

"You know," I say, sinking back against his pillow, "my family will probably think you're my boyfriend."

I mean it like a joke. Like, *Isn't that so silly? Of course you're not my boyfriend.* Or even, *We should probably get our story straight before they ask.* But Liam's gaze drags to mine. "Am I?" he asks.

"Are you what?"

"Your boyfriend."

My heart races. "I . . . I don't know," I admit.

He tilts his chin, gaze tracking me up and down. "We've been seeing each other almost every day and, well . . ." He rubs the back of his neck, two splotches of color appearing in his cheeks. "I really like you, Ros."

Ros. I like the way his mouth in particular wraps around the single syllable, holding the *r* sound in the back of his throat.

"I like the way my sheets always smell like you after you leave, and how unbelievably sexy you look wearing my shirt right now." His eyes drop down the length of my body, and I blush. "I like the way my heart beats faster every time my phone goes off because I'm hoping it's you and how my favorite part of every day is when you come over."

Something soft settles against my chest at the way he's looking at me, so earnest, so sincere, and a dozen warnings go off in my head. We shouldn't. We should keep things simple, detached. I should keep my walls tall and my moats deep. After all, that's the best way not to get hurt. But my excuses fade into background noise as the truth, the one I've been trying to ignore, gets louder.

The truth is that I can feel myself falling for him. The slow, easy kind of fall, which doesn't even feel like falling at all. More like stepping into a warm bath or waking up next to someone who feels more like home than any four walls ever could.

Like maybe I could love him. Not now, not yet. But I could.

I think about what he said the night we met. *Isn't the risk what makes it meaningful? The possibility that it doesn't work, but you want it badly enough to find out?*

If I let myself, I can picture the future. How we'd collect stories and memories and favorite places and things that remind us of each other. How we'd make plans and form routines and witness each other's lives. How our hearts would grow and expand together.

Maybe I'll end up like my mom. Maybe I'll get my heart broken. But for the first time in my life, I wonder if maybe the risk might be worth it. If *he* might be worth it.

"Seeing you is my favorite part of the day too," I tell him. Then in a smaller voice, I ask, "So what does this mean?"

"I want to be with you," he says, lacing his fingers through mine. "I want you in every way I can have you. In sickness and in health," he adds with a half laugh.

My pulse strums against my ribs, throat squeezing with emotion.

He sounds so certain, so sure, and suddenly I am too.

I'm still scared—terrified, really. Of getting attached. Of getting hurt. But maybe Liam is someone worth getting attached to.

So I focus on the strong jaw that kisses me so well, and I tell him the only thing I can think to say. The only thing that makes sense. "I want to be with you too."

- 12 -

Now

Somehow I end up at the kids' table. Not literally, but it certainly feels like it when I'm at the very end, wedged beside Henleigh, Jackson, and Riley, who are happily coloring, while Chris, Ben, Jonah, Gramps, and Bella discuss (fawn over) Liam's research and I'm rendered invisible.

"What are you drawing?" I ask Jackson, sneaking a peek at what is either a fish or a penis. It's very hard to tell which.

"It's a torpedo," he says, giving me a *duh* look.

"Really?" I twist my head, trying to get a better view.

"Yeah, see, that's the head." He points to what must be the tip of the torpedo, which bears a startling resemblance to the head of a penis. Either that or the past year of celibacy must finally be catching up with me.

For the millionth time, I wish my mom were here. If she were here, I'd have someone other than a six-year-old to talk to. But she's not, so I do the next best thing: I reach for the bottle of wine.

I'm pouring a glass when I hear my name.

"Roslyn? Did you hear me?"

My gaze jerks up to see that the entire table is looking at me like they expect an answer.

"I asked how the writing's going, dear?" Grammy asks.

I swallow hard. Right. *The writing.*

"Fine," I say, hoping that will be the end of it and they'll go back to talking about how great Liam is. But it's not.

"The other day I read an article about AI taking jobs from writers," Jonah says. "Are you worried about that?"

My insides contract. Of course Jonah read one article and thinks he knows all about publishing.

"I—"

"Maybe you should write something sad where someone has cancer. Like Nicholas Sparks," Bella suggests. "Those seem to do well."

"Well, the thing is—"

"How many copies have sold this year?" Gramps asks.

Maybe everyone else's questions are born out of polite interest, an effort to be insightful or helpful—even if they're not—but I know that's not Gramps's intent. He wants to hear me admit that I fucked up. That I'm wasting my potential writing romance novels instead of becoming a doctor.

It's the same thing he used to do with my mom.

Growing up, Gramps would take any chance he could to remind my mom that she'd thrown her life away by getting pregnant at sixteen. They'd go back and forth, fighting about how she couldn't hold down a job, money problems, the shitty boyfriends she was always bringing home, and lost potential until my mom would storm out, telling my siblings it was time to go and that we were never coming back. Of course, we always did, usually because Grammy would call and smooth things over, or my mom needed money.

Over time, things mellowed out and screaming matches turned into snide comments and disappointed looks, but residual tension lingered. A tension that is apparently now being redistributed to me.

My eyes skate to Liam, wondering if perhaps our pretend marriage is where he'll finally stand up for me. But alas, he's looking at his phone under the table, not even paying attention.

"It's a good thing Liam makes enough to support you both, Roslyn," Grammy says, the corners of her mouth rising in a hopeful smile. "So you're not under pressure to earn a living from writing."

"Right. Good thing," I say, taking another sip of wine.

Grammy probably thinks she's said something helpful, a nice little reminder that it's totally okay to fail at publishing because I have a rich doctor husband who can take care of me. *Yay!* But the words fall over me like acid on skin.

While I'm lucky enough to receive royalty checks from my writing, they aren't enough to sustain me financially. More like cute little reminders that, *Hey, you published a book!* Which means that after the divorce is finalized, I'll have to get a "real" job. Maybe even two. Something with health care and benefits. But I have no idea what I'll do, or what my BS in biochem even qualifies me for.

Anxiety rises up the back of my throat, and I once again reach for my wine; however, when I lift the glass to my lips, I realize it's empty. Hmm. That was fast.

But as I reach for the bottle to pour myself another, a hand appears atop mine.

"Don't you think you've had enough, *babe*?" Liam whispers, his breath hot on my earlobe.

A shiver climbs the length of my spine, but it's undetermined if that's from the closeness, or irritation that my drinking is the thing that's finally captured Liam's attention.

"Dear, Liam's right," Grammy says, catching my eye from

across the table. "You shouldn't drink so much." Her attention shifts from side to side before she finally whispers, "It's not good for the baby."

"What ba—" But I catch myself just in time. "I mean, it's just a glass," I lie. "And I'm not even pregnant."

I look to Liam, waiting to see if he'll defend me—after all, it's his fault that they think we're *trying* in the first place—but his eyebrows knit together, jaw torqued with frustration.

"*Babe,* can I talk to you for a minute?" he asks. But Liam doesn't give me a chance to answer before his hand folds around my wrist, pulling me to my feet and away from the table. His grip is gentle enough to probably not raise suspicion, but firm enough to let me know he's serious. Which only makes me madder.

"What the fuck? Let go of me!" I hiss.

Liam waits until we're around the corner, by the restrooms and safely out of earshot, before he turns to me. "What is wrong with you?"

"Me? You're the one frog-marching me away from the table!"

"You can't be getting drunk at dinner with your family, Roslyn."

"It was one glass," I protest.

"It was four."

"Since when do you care how much I drink? Or is that new?" I challenge. "Like the beard?"

His mouth parts, eyes widening, and I think I might have tapped a nerve, but he blinks and his features slide purposefully back into place. "I care when your family thinks we're trying to have a baby."

"And whose fault is that?"

He pushes out a labored breath. "Look, I'm sorry, I shouldn't have said we were trying to get pregnant, but if we're going to pull off this lie, we have to be careful."

He's right. Logically I know that. But because, as he correctly pointed out, I did in fact have four glasses and not much else, hot, frustrated tears spring to my eyes.

Liam's gaze widens, clearly flummoxed. "Are you crying?"

"No, I just . . ." I wipe furiously at my eyes, trying to banish the tears, when Liam looks past me, muttering a hasty *shit*.

I follow his gaze to where Bella is walking right toward us. Which means she's about to see me, *crying*. Which means she's going to ask questions we don't want to answer.

Liam must realize this, too, because he grips my shoulders, shoving me backward.

"*Whatthefuck!*" I cry as a door opens and shuts, plunging us both into darkness.

"Shhh! Calm down!"

"You can't tell me to calm down when you've just shoved me into a . . ." I look around the darkness, trying to figure out where exactly we are.

"A supply closet," he finishes for me.

He pulls his hand away and my vision adjusts to the darkness, taking in the rows of cleaners and toilet paper.

"Great. And why exactly are we in our second enclosed space of the day?" I ask.

"Because I didn't want Bella to see you . . ." He frowns, gesturing vaguely to me as though trying to figure how to kindly phrase the words *looking like a hot mess*.

"And you don't think shoving me into a closet looks even more suspicious?"

"She didn't see. And I didn't *shove* you. You're being dramatic."

"*I'm* the one being dramatic right now?"

His eyes flare, catching the slice of light filtering through the slit in the door, and I realize just how close we are. Close enough that the heat pouring off his body in waves feels like phantom hands, reminders of everywhere they've been.

I try to step aside, out of his vortex.

"Ouch, that was my foot," he hisses.

"Well, can you move?"

"I can't. There's a maximum of three centimeters behind me."

"Maybe you should consider that the next time you want to pick a meeting spot!"

"Ow! That's my foot! *Again!*"

I groan. "This isn't working. Can we please get out of here?" I reach for the door, but he grabs my wrist.

"Wait," he says, his voice softening. "Can we talk for a second?"

"Do I have a choice in the matter?" I ask, my eyes flicking down to the hand curled around my wrist.

He sighs and lets go. "Sorry. I just . . ." He swallows, flexing his hand like the contact burned him. "You normally don't drink so much, and you look like you've lost weight and . . ." His voice trails off before starting again. "I just wanted to check that you're okay."

"You shoved me into this tiny closet because you're worried about me?"

His weight shifts, his hip grazing mine. I want to beg him not to stand so close.

"I just . . ." He pushes out a breath. "Just tell me, is everything all right with you?"

When his gaze rises to mine, his eyes are wide with worry. He looks genuinely concerned, and for a beat I wonder if behind all the clenched jaws and stoic eyes, he's not as apathetic as he seems. If this is more than just a routine wellness check.

But the thought is almost instantly swallowed by memories of all the nights he spent working late or sleeping on the couch. All the nights he didn't try to understand my pain. *I'm not good at talk-*

ing about that kind of stuff, he'd say before finding an excuse to leave, like my grief was some kind of communicable disease he didn't want to get too close to catch.

Maybe he is worried about me. Maybe past all my thin walls and flimsy defenses he can see how broken and hurting I am. But he didn't want my grief then, and I don't plan on burdening him with it now. So I pull myself up to my full height, my head still spinning from the wine, and tell him what he wants to hear.

"I'm fine," I say. "Totally fine."

- 13 -

Now

After dinner, Ben and Jonah leave to get the kids ready for bed, Liam and Gramps head to the bar to discuss Liam's research—because no one cares how much Liam drinks—and I go back to the cabin to grab my laptop. Apparently, I'm still just drunk enough to convince myself I might actually get words on the screen.

Back up on deck, I find an empty chair.

On either side of me, endless ocean stretches all the way to the horizon, blurring the line between where the sky and sea finally meet in a perfect crest of pink and blue and orange.

A warm breeze tangles in my hair, licking the sides of my neck, and for what feels like the first time all day—maybe even all year—I try to ground myself in the moment.

Since the accident, I've had a hard time enjoying things the way I used to. The sun never feels as warm, colors not as bright. Even music and movies and books I used to love have lost some of their flavor, as if I'm moving through a blander, less vibrant version of the world—a world without my mom in it. A world I'm no longer sure how to navigate.

If she were here she'd remind me to stop and appreciate the

small things. A gorgeous sunset. A lungful of salty air. Golden sunlight feathering across my skin. Then she'd tell me it's okay to cry, to not be *fine* like I keep pretending I am.

If my mom were here, she'd hold me close and pat my hair like when I was little. She'd tell me that I was her softest. That I wasn't like Jonah or Bella. That I was more tenderhearted, which was just a nice way of telling me I was the sensitive one. Then she'd tell me that heartbreak wasn't the worst thing that could happen to a person because it meant you'd been hopeful, and being hopeful is the bravest thing we can be.

But right now, I don't feel brave. Or hopeful.

"Hey, Roslyn."

I look up to see Bella standing over me, her eyes bright, awash in the pinkish glow of golden hour. Her blond hair is swept up in a messy updo, and she looks so much like Mom, it's like seeing a ghost.

"I was wondering where you went after dinner," she says, taking a seat beside me. "You practically ran off as soon as the bill was paid."

"Oh, just trying to get some writing done," I tell her, gesturing to the very-much-closed laptop on my lap.

The space between her brows pinches. "Is everything okay?"

The question, or perhaps the worry in her voice, catches me off guard.

Bella and I have always been friendly, but we've never been the type of sisters who hung out or shared clothes.

When we were younger, I pinned the distance on the seven years between us—she was learning fractions while I was losing my virginity to a guy with My Chemical Romance posters over his dorm bed. But when we got older, it became clear that we were very different people.

And while I was always close to Mom, Bella wasn't.

I remember the two of them getting into screaming matches when Bella was a teenager, usually about how Mom couldn't hold on to a job, or how embarrassing it was that she had a different boyfriend all the time.

After high school, Bella went to undergrad on the East Coast and only ever came home for Christmas. She never said as much, but I always had a sneaking suspicion it was because of Mom. That she was a part of my sister's identity that she wanted to shed.

And to some extent, I understood. Life with Mom wasn't easy. The endless rotation of boyfriends and jobs. The constant moving around. But it's part of why I haven't felt like I can talk to Bella about Mom's passing. Not when my grief feels like a burden she isn't carrying.

"Everything's fine," I tell her. "Why do you ask?"

Bella shifts her weight like she's trying to choose her next words carefully. "Things got sort of weird with you and Liam at dinner," she says finally.

My entire body feels like it's ensnared in live wires, one misstep from being barbecued alive. Did she see Liam and me fighting? Or does she mean the tense moment at the dinner table?

"Everything's fine," I say again, forcing back the panic in my voice. "We're doing great."

"You sure?"

"Super sure."

She pauses, taking me in like I'm a slide under a microscope, before she finally pushes out a heavy breath. "Okay, good. I'd hate it if you two were fighting."

"All couples fight," I say, the line coming clipped, rehearsed.

"Yeah, but not you and Liam." She says it like it's a fact, no different than the Law of Gravity or the Pythagorean theorem.

"Of course we fight," I tell her. "But we didn't tonight," I add when her mouth turns. "We're good."

She nods, but her eyes flash with an uncertainty that makes my chest cramp.

"Maybe this is silly," she says after a beat, "but I've always thought of you and Liam as this perfect couple."

Guilt rises in my throat, hot and furious.

I should be used to this by now. After all, I've been lying about Liam and me for months. But the lying feels worse when it's my little sister, whose list of teenage crushes included Harry Styles, one of the guys from BTS, and Liam. When he's been the only reason for my little sister to ever look up to me, and now, I'm letting her down.

"Bella, there's no such thing as a perfect couple," I say diplomatically.

She brushes the comment away. "I know, I know. But Mom always had so many shitty boyfriends. And I feel like you and Liam were the first couple to model a healthy relationship for me." She blushes before she adds, "I mean, every time Liam looks at you, it's like he's just realized what love is all over again."

My pulse scatters, tendrils of heat winding their way around my skin.

She means in the past, I tell myself. *Not anymore.*

"Yeah, well . . ." I clear my throat. "We're happy!"

God, I can practically feel my nose growing as I speak.

"Probably doesn't hurt that the poor guy gets a boner just looking at you," she jokes.

"He's thirty-six, not thirteen," I say, giving her a look.

Her mouth curls up. "Yeah, well, that's not what I saw."

"What did you see?" I ask, hating how fast the question spills out of me.

She tilts her head, dying sunlight kissing her skin. "He kept looking at you then adjusting his pants." She laughs at the memory. "You two have been together for nine years and he's still down bad. You must give incredible head."

"Bella!"

A peal of laughter spills from my sister's lips, and my heart aches. It's nice to hear her laugh. I just wish it wasn't because of a lie.

"I'm just saying. Things with Chris and me are good, but his dick doesn't twitch every time I walk by." She chuckles, her eyes filled with mirth.

My blood turns to heavy sludge in my veins. She must be seeing things. Or maybe Liam has jock itch. There's no way Liam—who is *fine*—is getting hard at the dinner table. Not over me.

When I don't respond, she pushes out a wistful sigh. "I wish Chris and I were still like that. But we're definitely not in the honeymoon stage anymore. Chris pees with the door open and we have way less sex now than when we were first dating."

"That's normal," I tell her, thinking about when Liam and I first moved in together and hot date nights turned into folding laundry together on the couch. "The honeymoon stage isn't meant to last forever."

"It seems to with you and Liam."

A cold burn of shame presses against my chest. I wish I could grip her shoulders and scream that it's all fucking fake. That we didn't have sex in the airplane. In fact, we haven't had sex in over a year, not since Mom died. That we're frauds and whatever idea of a honeymoon stage she's thinking of is in all likelihood made up by Hollywood and people like, well . . . *me*. People who write love stories and perpetuate myths like *happily ever after* and *fate*.

But not only am I a liar, I'm also a coward, so I change the subject.

"Besides him peeing with the door open, how are things with you and Chris?" I ask.

Her brow scrunches, mouth pinching into a tight line. "We're good, I guess. I just . . ." She swallows, rocking back and forth on her heels. "When did you know Liam was the one?"

I blink, surprised. My title as *older sister* has mostly been in name only. Bella never talks to me about boy troubles or anything more substantive than what to get Grammy and Gramps for Christmas.

"What do you mean?" I ask.

"I mean, like, when did you know he was it for you?"

I stiffen, thinking back to when Liam and I first started officially dating. The small moments. His arm on my waist as I fell asleep. The way he always texted me to make sure I got home okay. I fell for him in the quiet. The still. In the moments when he made me feel safe and cared for. When he started to feel like home. Like someone who would always be there to catch me.

But in the end, he hadn't. He'd just let me fall.

"I knew pretty early on," I tell her. "Why do you ask?"

"I was just curious." She says it like she doesn't really care, but I can tell something is bothering her.

"Bella, is something wrong?" I try.

"I just . . ." Bella licks her bottom lip, eyes slanting away then back to me before she finally says, "I just thought Chris would have proposed by now, you know? It's been four years."

"Have you talked to him about it?" I ask.

She shifts uneasily. "We know we want to get married, and we're both going to graduate med school this year," she says. "I just don't understand what's taking so long."

"Maybe he's already ring shopping," I try. "Or maybe he's just waiting for after graduation? Or after residency?"

She shrugs, her lips tightening into a line before she asks, "How did you get Liam to propose? Did you tell him you wanted him to? Or did it just happen?"

I instantly feel like an impostor. I am no more qualified to give relationship advice than perform brain surgery.

"We talked about getting married," I tell her. "But I had no idea he was planning to propose, and frankly neither did he."

I think about the day Liam spontaneously popped the question in my grandparents' kitchen. There hadn't been a ring, or flowers or a candlelit dinner for two, but we'd been so in love, so completely head over heels for each other, that it hadn't mattered. Now the memory feels like pressing down on an old wound to see if it still throbs.

Bella nods, clearly dissatisfied with my unhelpful answer, before she turns and walks to the deck. After a beat, she says, "It's weird being here without Mom."

My limbs stiffen, blood feeling heavy in my veins as I instinctively reach for Mom's bracelet.

"Yeah, it is," I say, wondering where this is going. If we're finally going to broach the subject.

Bella sighs, tucking an errant blond hair behind her ear. "I miss her but . . . there's a part of me that's sort of relieved she's not here, you know?"

My breath stutters unevenly. "What do you mean?"

Maybe I imagine it, but Bella's eyes drop to Mom's bracelet on my wrist. She crosses and uncrosses her arms, mouth shifting to the corner of her jaw. Finally, she says, "If Mom were here, she and Gramps would be fighting the whole time. She'd be pissed that Chris got to come when she wasn't allowed to invite whatever flavor-of-the-week boyfriend she had. I'd try and explain that Chris and I have been together for four years and that it's different, but she would act like it wasn't and . . ." She sighs, letting her voice trail off, lost to the warm evening breeze. "Anyways, I feel bad saying that but it's true."

I try to swallow, but my throat's too stiff.

Is this really how Bella feels about Mom not being here? Relieved?

I want to argue, to tell her she's wrong and she shouldn't talk about Mom like that, especially when she's not here to defend herself, but the words bottleneck in my throat, trapped there by swells of emotion I'm not sure I can get past without breaking down.

After a beat, Bella says, "I need to ask you a favor."

My brows draw together. "What?"

"I got all these old photos of Grammy and Gramps on their wedding day." She digs a manila envelope out of her crossbody bag and starts showing me old photos of Grammy in a white dress and Gramps in a tux, fifty years younger, looking at each other with adoration in their eyes.

I pick out one of Grammy feeding Gramps a piece of cake. "These are so cute. Grammy looks beautiful."

"I know, right? I was planning to make a collage to show at the vow renewal ceremony, but Jonah keeps giving me all these other tasks to do. Flowers. Catering. Music." She makes a face. "I was wondering if you could do it?"

My chest falls. Bella and Jonah are planning stuff without me? Then again, they've always been closer than I am with either of them. Probably because they have the whole doctor thing in common.

"Sure," I tell her, contorting my mouth into a smile. "Of course I can help."

She beams back at me, passing the envelope over. "Great. Thanks!"

Once she's gone, I stare at the blank document on my computer screen, hoping for inspiration to strike, but the words don't come, and sometime after midnight, I admit defeat.

When I get back to the room, Liam's already fast asleep in a makeshift bed on the floor. Despite the rhythmic sounds of his breath and the less than five feet of space between us, I feel more alone than ever.

- 14 -

Now

Larsen Family Vacation Day 2

PORT OF CALL: *Kaanapali, Maui*

ITINERARY: *hiking (hilly, steep inclines, mountainous terrain)*

ATTIRE: *athletic, dress for the elements. Don't forget sunscreen!*

When I wake up the next morning, my head is pounding and my mouth tastes like the inside of a garbage can. I haven't been this hungover since the night Liam and I celebrated my first publishing deal, and I woke up wearing nothing but his boxers.

I wince and flop back against the pillow, willing the throbbing pain in my temples to subside. But eventually my bladder gets the best of me, forcing me out of bed.

I swing both legs over the side of the mattress and onto the floor when something crunches underneath me. Not something. *Someone.*

"ARRRRRG!"

I jump in surprise and look down to find my left foot hovering over Liam's right arm. "Oh. It's you."

"Of course it's bloody me!" he cries. "Who else would be asleep on your fucking floor!"

"Sorry. I forgot you were here."

He grimaces. "Of course you did. Because while you were sound asleep in a nice, big, comfy bed, I was tossing and turning all night on the cold floor."

"You're the one who volunteered to sleep on the floor first and for your information, I didn't exactly sleep great either," I say, wincing. "I'm hungover as fuck."

I expect him to say *I told you so.* Instead, his expression softens, and he asks, in a tender voice that catches me off guard, "Are you sure you'll be able to go on the hike today?"

A groan slips out of me. I totally forgot Jonah scheduled us for a jungle hike. RIP me.

"I can't believe I used to chug Everclear in dirty frat basements," I tell him. "Now I need a precautionary ibuprofen before I leave the house."

Liam laughs. "Here. I've got some in my bag." Then, almost guiltily, he adds, "And I grabbed you some granola bars and crackers last night."

I frown, taken aback. "You did?"

Pink creeps up his neck and into his cheeks. "I figured you wouldn't feel great after drinking last night, so I picked some things up before I went to bed. I got the ones with peanut butter that you like."

I balk, taken aback by the gesture. Is he baiting me? Trying to prove that I *did* drink too much last night? But the softness behind his eyes says otherwise.

"Thanks," I finally manage. "That's nice of you."

He shrugs like it's no big deal, and I wonder why the sudden shift. Is this about what happened in the supply closet last night? Does he feel sorry for me? Or is it something else? But the question is instantly vanquished from my mind when Liam sits up and shoves the blanket off, exposing what can only be described as a very—and I can't stress this enough—*very* hot bod.

It's Liam, but dialed up. Like Da Vinci took a scalpel to Liam's chest and arms in pursuit of the Vitruvian Man.

He's not just leaner, but more defined, and now I can't seem to look away from the ladder of abs, or the ripples of muscles stretching across his shoulders and arms. And those veins in his forearms? They're a phlebotomist's dream.

I suck in a sharp breath, and Liam frowns. "What?" he asks. "What's wrong?"

"Nothing."

"Is there drool on my face or something?" He drags a hand along his chin.

"No . . ." I allow my eyes to skate up and down the length of his chest. "Have you been working out or something?"

Color floods his cheeks again. "Kevin set me up with a trainer buddy of his."

A trainer? Liam's always looked good, but he's never cared that much about his appearance.

Unless . . . My stomach opens like a sinkhole as I think back to the condoms I'd seen in his wallet. Is this about a girl? Someone he's trying to impress? *Someone he's fucking?*

I shouldn't ask. Not when I don't really want to hear the answer. But what if it makes me feel better to know? At least that way it will be out in the open and I can stop wondering, right?

I go back and forth, warring between whether to ask or not until finally I blurt out, "Are you dating?"

The blood drains from Liam's face. "What?"

"Just tell me, are you dating?" I ask again.

He shifts his weight, lips folding together. "No, not technically."

His response leaves a lot to the imagination and unfortunately my imagination is very unkind to me. "What do you mean, *not technically*?"

His mouth pinches, twin parentheses forming on either side of his jaw. "Why do you care if I'm technically dating or not? You ended it."

I wince like I've been slapped. He's right. I'm the one who asked for a divorce. I have no right to care whether he's *technically* dating or not. But it doesn't stop the tightness concentrating in my core.

For a moment I consider telling the truth. The truth that's been building inside me like a dam waiting to burst. That of course I care. That I hate that he's got condoms in his wallet. That he hasn't been wearing his ring. That he's moving to London. That he took shots with some girl named Katie. That he's gotten fucking hot!

But as bad as it feels to know Liam's utterly *fine* without me, I imagine it will only feel worse to admit how miserable I've been. How hard this all is for me. Not while he's clearly moved on. So I settle for a half-truth.

"You're right," I say quietly. "I was the one who ended things." Then in an even quieter voice, I admit, "But it's still weird to think about you with someone else."

As soon as I say it, I worry I've revealed too much, been too vulnerable, that he'll see right through me, all the way to my splintered core. But his chin dips into a nod, his eyes weighed down with understanding.

"Yeah. It's weird to think about you with someone else too." He clears his throat, dragging a hand across his jaw. "Are you, uh . . . ?" He gestures vaguely. "Dating?"

I swallow roughly. After Liam left, I tried to imagine what it might be like to date again. To have sex with someone else. I even thought about downloading an app and sleeping with a stranger I never planned to see again just to try to dull the pain, to attempt to wash away some of the *himness* that still lingered in every fiber of my being. To prove I wasn't still his. But even at my lowest, I couldn't do it.

It wasn't just that I don't know how to navigate the current climate of dating apps and hookup culture—do I tell people I'm getting divorced? Should I walk around with a scarlet *D*?—it's that I don't know how to be intimate with anyone else. How to not feel sick at the prospect of being touched by another man. Not when part of me still feels like it belongs to Liam. Like my body is for him and him alone.

I wish I could leave the past behind, the way Liam appears to. That I had Abby's confidence. That I could walk into any room with my head held high, convinced any man would be lucky to date me. But I'm not Abby. Or Liam.

And it's even harder to dig deep and find my confidence when my own husband didn't want to fight for me. When even he, the one person who was supposed to see me as *enough,* didn't.

I shake my head. "No. I'm not dating."

As soon as I say it, I search his face, looking for traces of emotion, a clue that the chaos that's broken free inside me might have also broken free inside him, but his face remains purposefully blank, any hint of expression tucked neatly away, and suddenly I wish I hadn't asked.

After slurping down cold cereal and toast at the buffet alongside a hundred other overly ambitious tourists, we're taken ashore then picked up by a too-perky-for-this-ungodly-hour private guide named Mikayla, whose chipper voice plucks at the strings of my hangover in new and torturous ways.

After telling us all about the hike and what to expect (Spiders! Snakes! Poisonous plants! Oh my!), Mikayla ushers us into a jeep that will take us over the hilly, mud-soaked terrain into the depths of the lush Maui jungle.

Liam and I are last, and by the time we climb inside, there's only one open seat, in the back beside Bella.

"I don't think there's enough room," I say.

"Just sit on Liam's lap," Bella suggests.

"Oh. Uh. That's okay," I say quickly. "I'm sure I can sit somewhere else."

Liam frowns. "Like where? The roof?"

Actually, yes. I would, in fact, rather be strapped to the roof than sit on his lap. But that doesn't appear to be an option, so I delicately place myself atop Liam's muscular thighs, trying to dissociate.

This is fine. It's just Liam, I remind myself. Boring old Liam, whose lap I've sat on a million times. Who cares that my ass is nestled against his crotch. Or that every time Liam laughs at something someone says, I can feel the sticky heat of his breath on my neck.

I attempt to focus on the lush greenery outside. The hills rising like towers in the distance. The hazy, morning pink still tracing the skyline as the jeep rattles along the dirt road. But it's hard to focus when every time the jeep hits a pothole, my ass crashes into Liam's groin with all the force of a fourteen-year-old grinding at her first middle school dance.

"Sorry, everyone," Mikayla calls from the driver's seat. "These old backroads can be pretty bumpy!"

You don't say.

"You all right?" Liam asks, his mouth brushing my earlobe.

I swallow and murmur a quick *mm-hm,* glad he can't see how flushed my face is.

"Sure? You're soaking wet."

My breath snags. "Excuse me?"

"You're really sweaty." He pulls back, practically unpeeling his chest from my back.

Right. Sweat. He's referring to sweat, and definitely not anything else. *Duh.*

But it's not just the closeness, or that I can feel *all* of him. It's the way my heart beats faster under his touch, like some kind of primal memory stored deep in my bones. A reminder that my body still belongs to him.

You're not his anymore, I remind myself.

But that's the problem. We might sign papers and legally separate. Liam might even move to London and start *technically dating.* Even so, there will always be a part of my soul that belongs to him. An invisible string between my heart and his.

- 15 -

Eight years earlier

It's a gray, rainy day when Liam and I move into our first apartment together. A one-bedroom walk-up in Seattle's Green Lake neighborhood that's close to the hospital where Liam's in residency, and the restaurant where I'm waiting tables. The apartment is old and drafty, and the puce-colored walls are *a choice*. But it's ours.

Ours. The word beats heavily against my chest with a kind of awareness that I feel all the way in the hollow of my stomach.

It's hard to believe we only met a few months ago and now we're moving in together, but things just feel right with Liam. He's kind and generous and funny and easily the smartest person I know—something I got to brag about when he graduated top of his class from med school. Mostly he makes me feel safe and loved.

You're mine, he whispers every night before we fall asleep. He doesn't say it in a possessive way, like I'm something to be owned. He says it like I'm his to be cared for, loved, cherished, protected. And I never sleep better than when I'm wrapped in his arms, lulled by the steady rhythm of my heart tapping out *his, his, his*.

And yet, despite my excitement to be taking this step forward together, I'm afraid of how things might change between us when the walls come down and Liam gets a front row seat to all my messes, both the literal and the emotional ones.

What if Liam decides he hates my laugh? Or he gets annoyed with how I load the dishwasher? Or he can't stand that I always leave too much hair in the shower drain?

Mostly, I'm afraid of losing him.

When we first got together, I was afraid of getting too close, of falling too hard. But now that I'm his, that I know what it's like to fall asleep in his arms and wake up to sleepy morning kisses, I know for sure that the pain of losing him wouldn't just be a surface-level wound, the kind that would fade and heal with time—it would be a permanent scar on my heart. One I fear I won't recover from.

I'm unpacking a box of pots and pans in the kitchen when I feel the solid warmth of Liam behind me. Hot fingers dig into my waist as he plants a kiss on my neck, a not-so-subtle clue that Liam is no longer interested in kitchen organization.

"Babe, we have to finish unpacking," I remind him.

"Five minutes?" he asks, his teeth nipping the place under my earlobe. "I can do a lot in five minutes."

I gasp at the feel of him pressed against my back, broadcasting his need, and I consider surrendering myself to his scent, his touch, the feeling of him between my legs, the way I usually do. But I know it won't ease the knot of anxiety wedged inside me, and I pull back, untangling myself from him.

"What's wrong?" he asks, brows furrowing.

"I'm just worried," I admit.

"About what?"

I gesture vaguely to the mountainous pile of boxes crowding the tiny, seventies-style kitchen. "I've never moved in with a partner before."

"Neither have I."

I chew on my bottom lip, hesitating. "What if you don't like how my skincare products crowd the bathroom counter?" I ask. "Or the sound of you chewing makes me homicidal, or you get annoyed with how much I cry when I'm on my period? Or you get bored of having sex with me?"

What if you stop loving me? I think.

There's a long beat of silence before he takes my hand, tangling his fingers with mine, and says, "First, I could never get bored of having sex with you." He gives me a heated look I feel all the way in the bottoms of my toes. "And second, I don't think it will be easy. I think there will be days when it's really hard, but I love you and I want to do this with you, and if it takes work on both of our parts, then that's worth it to me." He pauses, his eyes finding mine. "Is it worth it to you?"

He makes it sound so simple, so straightforward, and slowly I nod. "Yes," I whisper. And I mean it. I want this. I want him. I want this little life we've built together. A life of cooking together and forehead kisses and secret signals when we want to leave parties. I want as much of Liam as I can have.

"But what if I'm still scared?" I ask.

I think about all the times Mom told us to pack our belongings because things didn't work out with yet another boyfriend. All the times I never even bothered unpacking because I knew we wouldn't be there long.

I spent years learning that nothing ever lasts. Not even the good stuff. But I so badly want to believe that things with Liam are different. That this home, this relationship, this love between us is the enduring kind.

Liam's gaze holds mine as he wraps his arms around me, pulling me into the fortress of his chest. "I'm scared, too, but we're in this together," he whispers into my neck. "Me and you."

My heart swells too big for my chest. I love how certain he is. How sure of what our future holds.

I've never felt that kind of certainty before. Not as a child waking up somewhere different every other week, or even now as an adult without a plan for the next year. But when I'm with him, I feel a little more certain. A little sturdier. Like no matter what happens, our future together is something solid and firm and reliable. Something I can trust completely without hesitation or worry about what tomorrow will bring.

Liam and I stay like that, arms wrapped around each other, swallowing each other's unsteady breaths until his mouth dips to mine, drawing me in for a kiss.

As he walks us back against the wall, lips pressed to mine, hands wandering lower until they find the zipper on my jeans, I realize that home isn't just a drafty walk-up, or a kitchen full of moving boxes.

Home is a person, and he's mine.

- 16 -

Now

When we finally arrive at the trailhead, the sun is just beginning to sneak over the treetops, showering us all in a Dreamsicle filter. In the distance, looming green hillsides rise above the canopy of trees, framed in a haze of early morning mist.

We're all given a water bottle and told again to watch out for spiders (yikes), then we're off, traipsing down the muddy path as Mikayla regales us with legends about Mauian history and culture.

"Roslyn, dear," Grammy says, falling in step beside me. It's amazing what great shape she's in. All that water aerobics must be paying off. "I'm worried about Liam getting sunburnt. He has such fair skin and all. You should put some sunscreen on him."

Of course the Official Liam Fan Club is worried about his poor fair complexion.

"He's fine," I tell her.

Bella gawks. "Not wearing sunscreen? In this economy?"

All the blood instantly evaporates from my veins. There definitely isn't a good time to hear your Gen Z sister drop your and your ex's safe word. But it's absolutely not after getting hot and bothered from sitting on his lap. And *not* when you're pretending to still be together.

Liam, who is mid-drink from his water bottle, breaks into a coughing fit.

"Dear, are you okay?" Grammy asks.

Liam pounds his fist against his sternum. "Yup. All good," he adds, his face turning red.

I look away, not daring to meet his eye.

Okay, so he definitely remembers. Then again, who can forget all the times he had me pinned down, naked and breathless. Certainly not me.

"I don't know what sunscreen has to do with the economy, but Bella's right, you need to reapply sunscreen or you'll burn," Grammy says, handing me a bottle. "Make sure he gets his back, Roslyn."

I take the sunscreen and approach Liam. "Your fan club is worried about you getting sunburnt."

He looks down at the bottle then back at me, before pulling the hem of his shirt up and over his head.

I swallow tightly, forcing my eyes away from his pecs. And his abs. The V-shaped thing disappearing into his shorts suddenly feels like a personal attack.

When my gaze mercifully makes it back up to his, Liam's watching me expectantly and I realize he's waiting for me to apply the sunscreen.

"I'm not putting it on you," I whisper.

"I can't do my own back."

Ugh. This must be karma for all the lying.

"Fine," I whisper. "But I'm only doing one layer."

As I squeeze a dollop of sunscreen into my palm and begin rubbing it over his broad shoulders, I do everything I can to dissociate. I think about my next dentist appointment. If the milk I bought before I left will still be good when I get back. Anything but the terrain of familiar, warm skin stretched across broad shoulders and tightly knotted back muscles. But it's still not enough to prevent the full-body jolt when I see it. Or perhaps more accurately, I remember that it's there. The tattoo on the back of his left shoulder. The same one I have in the same place. A quote from my debut novel.

We didn't plan to get matching tattoos. But it was the night of my book release and we were celebrating with a bottle of gin, and before we knew it, we were both at Sleeve It to Me, Seattle's most popular tattoo studio.

Two hours later, we walked out with *Forever isn't long enough when it's with someone you love* inked into our shoulders.

I used to think it was romantic. A permanent symbol of our enduring love. But now it's like looking at the crumbling remains of a once powerful and mighty civilization. A reminder of everything we lost. Or maybe what we never had to begin with.

"Everything okay?" Liam asks, and I realize I've been rubbing sunscreen on the same spot over and over.

I clear my throat. "Um, yeah," I tell him. "Fine."

But he looks over his shoulder anyway, following my focus down to his tattoo then back up. Our gazes meet, and I instantly feel transparent. Like all the hurt I've tried so hard to hide is as bold and obvious as a highway billboard.

I should probably feel embarrassed. After all, I don't want him to know how hard this is for me, how painful even just looking at his tattoo is, not when he's so *fine*. But his eyes soften, an unguarded look sweeping his expression, and I can't help but wonder if he feels it too. This punch to the gut of emotion. If behind all the clenched jaws and pursed lips, he's not as fine as he seems.

The moment lasts a beat longer before he turns around and I resume applying the sunscreen. As soon as Liam's glistening like a glazed donut and Grammy is satisfied with my sunscreen application, we continue on the hike.

Of course, Bella and Chris—adventure junkies that they are—sprint off, leading the crew, while Jonah, easily the most competitive person I know, tries to keep up. But the duties of fatherhood keep him in the middle of the pack with Grammy, Gramps, Ben, and the kids.

Liam and I are last, but I know that's my fault. Because not only am I hungover as fuck, but I'm also vastly out of shape.

I've never been an active gym-goer, but since my mom passed, my exercise regimen has consisted of moving from the bed to the couch and back to the bed. So it's no surprise to me that a mere ten minutes into our ascent, I'm already a huffing, puffing, sweaty mess, while Mr. Personal Trainer isn't even breaking a sweat.

"Are you okay?" Liam asks, pausing a few paces ahead.

"Super," I wheeze.

"We can stop and take a break if you want."

"I said I'm fine," I bite back, a new kind of determination swelling inside me.

My lungs might feel like overinflated balloons right now, but I *need* to complete this hike. I *need* to prove to myself and to everyone else that I'm truly as fine as I keep saying I am. Besides, I can't let two six-year-olds beat me. Jonah will never let me hear the end of that.

The twins rush ahead, picking up sticks while their fathers yell after them to *put that down* at least three million times. Henleigh gets tired and asks Jonah to carry her because *my legs don't like this,* as she puts it.

Same girl, same.

Jonah stops and holds his backpack out to me. "Can you hold this? While I carry her?"

By the time I've got the bag and Jonah's picked up Henleigh, the rest of the crew are a few paces ahead, leaving Jonah and me in the back.

As we walk in silence, I'm increasingly aware that it's been ages since Jonah and I have been alone, and I don't know what to say to him.

Finally, I ask, "So how have you been?"

"Busy," he says gruffly. "Ben just got promoted to head of the cardiology department and is working more than ever. The twins just started soccer and Henleigh is going to school next month and Ben thought it would be great to join the PTA, as if we don't have enough on our plates right now," he adds, making a face.

I wonder if he'll say something about how hard it's been since Mom died, or even how he wishes Mom was here to see the kids get so big—*something* to acknowledge the giant gaping hole that is her absence—but he doesn't, and I wonder if he feels the same quiet relief Bella does without her here.

"Wow, school already," I say. "She's getting so big."

Henleigh's eyes are now closed, thumb shoved into her tiny mouth, and my chest aches a little bit at how the months have flown by since I saw her last. How many dance recitals and fridge-worthy crayon drawings have I missed?

"I miss the kids," I tell him. "I should come see them sometime."

"You should," he agrees. "I had to remind Henleigh that you were her aunt when she asked me who the lady with curly hair was."

"It hasn't been that long," I say, almost defensively.

Jonah gives me a look. "We've barely seen you in the last year, Roslyn. That's a long time when you're four."

Guilt spreads in my chest, heavy and achy.

"Sorry," I say quietly. "Just got a lot going on."

Jonah looks me up and down, his eyes softening ever so slightly. "Is everything okay?" he asks.

The words dangle on the tip of my tongue. *I'm not okay. I've been miserable since Mom died. I feel isolated in my grief. I hate that my niece doesn't remember me. I feel like everyone has moved on except me.*

But I don't think uptight, too-busy-for-feelings Jonah will understand, so I stow my carefully packaged grief where no one else can see it. Where I can continue to pretend I'm okay, just like everyone else seems to be.

"Just tired," I tell him. "I didn't sleep well last night." My gaze cuts ahead to Liam, now effortlessly carrying both Jackson and Riley, one in each arm. *Show-off.*

"Well, try and get some sleep tonight," Jonah says. He gives me one more look before taking the bag and zipping ahead toward the kids.

After he sets the kids down, Liam falls back in step with me. We trek along mostly in silence, avoiding each other's gaze until he nudges my elbow and asks, "Everything all right?"

"Terrific," I say tightly, wondering which Hawaiian gods I have to make a sacrifice to for people to stop asking me that.

"How's your headache? Any better?"

"Not really."

"Do you need snacks? I brought the granola bars if you're hungry."

I stop in my tracks, eyes cutting to his. "What's going on with you?"

He stops too. "What are you talking about?"

"I mean, why are you suddenly being nice?"

His eyes widen, surprised, before narrowing into a frown.

"You seem like you're having a tough morning. I'm just trying to be helpful."

I sense I've offended him in some way, but I don't care. I'm annoyed that I'm a hot mess while he's *fine*.

"I don't need your help," I say with a huff. "I'm fine."

"Yeah," he says tightly. "You keep saying that."

"Well, I am!" I say loud enough that a flock of birds takes flight from a tree nearby.

His brow scrunches. "Fine. Don't accept my help. Can I have some of your water?"

"Seriously? We just left and you already drank yours?"

He shrugs. "I got thirsty."

I retrieve my water bottle from the side pouch in my backpack. "Don't drink it all," I warn. "I need that to last the rest of the hike."

He takes the bottle and immediately starts guzzling it.

"Hey! I just told you not to drink it all!"

He wipes the excess water from his chin. "Sorry. I was thirsty."

"You always do this," I say, exasperated. "Every time we go somewhere, you don't bring your own water bottle, then you end up drinking mine!"

He gives me a look like he has no idea what I'm talking about, which only irritates me more. "I'm sure Jonah has more."

We both look ahead, only to realize my brother is no longer in front of us. In fact, no one is.

Shit.

"They're gone!"

"I'm sure they're just ahead, we can catch up to them. Come on," Liam says, ushering me to quicken my pace. But as soon as we follow the bend in the path, we're met with a fork in the road that's completely washed out by the mud.

"Great, now we're lost!" I cry.

Liam shakes his head. "We're not lost. We're just momentarily separated from the group."

"Which is the same as lost!"

Liam's mouth sets into a hard line. "I'll just text them and ask them to wait for us." He pulls out his phone and immediately frowns. "Shit. No cell service."

Great. Just fucking great.

"Now what are we supposed to do? Didn't you hear what Mikayla said about spiders? What if we get eaten alive?" I look around as though afraid a giant, man-eating spider might pop out at any moment. "And we don't even have any water, thanks to you, so we'll probably die out here!"

Liam's lips purse, his jaw clenching, his eyes shifting back and forth until finally he says, "Look, this isn't ideal, but at least we're not alone."

"Not ideal?" I repeat. "Not ideal is when your phone charger doesn't reach your bed—this is a disaster!"

"We're going to be fine," he says, his voice low like he's trying to negotiate a hostage situation. "It's a tourist hiking trail, not base camp at Everest." Though from the creases in his forehead, I can tell he's not too certain about that.

Neither Liam nor I are particularly outdoorsy. Our idea of roughing it is when Uber Eats takes more than an hour to deliver. Which means we are entirely ill-equipped for this scenario.

Panic surges through me as I imagine a series of outcomes that each end with me dying a gruesome death. Snakebite. Dehydration (thanks, Liam). Starvation. Eaten by a jaguar. Do those even live here? Now I wish I'd done more (or any) reading on the ecological habitats of Maui's North Shore.

"Do you think we're better off sleeping in the trees to avoid becoming jaguar dinner?" I ask. "Or making a lean-to?"

He raises one eyebrow. "Do you know how to make a lean-to?"

"Do *you*?"

"I grew up in London. My survival skills involve knowing how to get from Waterloo to King's Cross when there's a tube strike and which takeaway shops stay open past midnight."

A dark laugh rips out of me. "Well, in that case, you'd better start drafting your will because we're gonna die. I don't think I can drink your pee."

Liam makes a face. "Why would you have to drink my pee?"

"Isn't that what happens when you're stranded in the wilderness without water? You have to drink pee?"

"Wouldn't you drink your own pee over mine?"

"I don't know! I'm not a wilderness survival expert!" I exclaim, exasperated.

"Can you please just calm down? I don't think anyone has to drink pee."

"Easy for you to say. *You're* fully hydrated."

Liam presses the pads of his fingers to his temple as though trying to summon the patience to deal with me right now.

"Maybe we should try and walk back the way we came," he suggests, gesturing down the muddy trail. "We could find our way back to the parking lot."

"How are we going to do that?" I ask, gesturing to the dense greenery camouflaging either side of the trail. "We'll just get even more lost."

"We could wait and see if—" But I don't get to find out what Liam thinks we should wait and see about because he freezes, his eyes stretching wide. "Don't move," he whispers.

I lift my hands. "But—?"

"I said *don't move.*"

Liam creeps closer, his usually calm and cool demeanor sharpening into something that looks a lot like panic. Not that I've ever actually seen Liam panic. But if he did, this is what I imagine he'd look like.

"Roslyn, I need you to stay still," he whispers.

I blink. "Why?"

"Because . . ." He hesitates to swallow. "There's a massive spider on your shoulder."

My vision blurs, panic strumming against my chest as I catch sight of way too many legs in my peripheral vision.

"Get it off!" I cry.

"That's what I'm trying to do," he says, inching closer. "Just stay still for me."

"I'm gonna die," I whine. "This is not what I meant by *until death do us part*!"

"You're not gonna die," he says in his gentle, *Don't worry, I'm a doctor* voice. "Just breathe."

Liam breathes deeply, mimicking for me to join him, so I inhale, holding it several seconds too long before remembering to exhale.

"Good. Now just—" But just as he's reaching toward me, the spider moves. It *fucking* moves.

There's a split second where I'm frozen with fear, unable to do anything, before full-on fight or flight takes over and I do the only thing my body knows how to do right now: I run.

"Roslyn!" he calls after me, but I don't turn back, I don't stop, I just keep moving.

Liam's footsteps squelch in the mud behind me. A second later, his arms wrap around my waist and we collide, bodies suspended in the air, before we both go down, collapsing into the mud in a tangled knot of limbs.

As soon as my body hits the ground, a sharp pain that should be cause for concern shoots through my leg, but I'm too busy trying not to die via spider bite.

"Where is it?" I cry, scrambling backward on my elbows. "Is it still on me?"

Liam unwinds himself from me, his eyes darting up and down. "I think it's gone."

"Are you sure?"

He looks again. "I don't see any massive, killer spiders, but if I do, I'll be sure to mention it."

I punch his shoulder. "Not funny!"

His mouth quirks as he catches his breath. "Are you okay?" he asks.

I look down, taking stock of all vulnerable body parts. Arms. *Check*. Legs. *Check*. Head. *Check*. "I think so? Are you?"

He looks down at himself, now splattered in mud. "Dirty, but okay."

Liam stands up and holds out his hand to me. I take it, attempting to stand, but as I do, the same sharp pain I felt moments earlier returns with a vengeance.

"Ouch!"

His brows jump up with worry. "Where does it hurt?"

I chomp down on my lip, fighting back the swell of pain. "My left ankle," I tell him.

"Can I see?"

I nod and he lowers himself, gently lifting my foot to his chest. I wince.

"Does that hurt?"

"Fuck!"

"How about that?"

"Fuuuuuck!"

"It's starting to swell. I think it's twisted."

"But we need to get out of here," I protest.

Liam shakes his head. "Roslyn, I don't think you should walk on it."

I reach for the words to tell him I'm fine, the way I've been telling everyone I am. But this time I know I'm not. And before I can stop them, hot tears sting the backs of my eyes.

- 17 -

Now

It's not just that I'm injured. Or that we're stranded in the jungle without water. Though that alone is reason enough to cry. It's *everything.*

It's the confusing mix of pain and anger and longing I feel toward Liam. The pressure that sparks under my skin every time we touch, and all the ways that terrifies me.

Most of all, it's how alone I feel in all this. While I'm struggling to clean up the shards of glass where my heart once was, Liam's fine. No, better than fine. *Good. Great.*

I try to blink back the tears, to banish the evidence before Liam can see just how *not fine* I am, but I'm not quick enough to stop two fat tears from spilling down my cheek.

"Hey," Liam says, his expression softening. "We'll get your ankle taken care of. I promise it'll be okay."

He winds his arms around my shoulders, hauling me to him, and my heartbeat stumbles over itself at the gentleness in his voice. The heat of his hand. The familiar scent of sunscreen and sweat clinging to skin.

For a moment I imagine he's still a soft place to land. Somewhere safe.

But he's not. And it's not *okay*. Because nothing's been *okay* in a long time.

I pull back, untangling myself from his arms. "Just stop," I say, inching far enough away that I can't smell his cologne or the soap on his skin.

A divot forms between his eyebrows. "Stop what?"

"*This!*" I wave between us. "Stop trying to be nice to me."

"I'm trying to help."

"Well, you're not. You're making everything worse. So please just stop pretending like you care about me."

I watch as his expression absorbs my words, eyes widening, mouth parting before dipping into a frown. "Me? You think *I'm* the one pretending? *You're* the one acting like you're okay when you're clearly not."

His words feel like tiny, well-pointed arrows, sharp and accurate, and suddenly the frustration I've been trying to keep at bay is frothing to the surface, threatening to boil over.

Maybe it's because I'm covered in mud and injured. Or because I almost just died, but I pin my eyes to him and finally let the bomb inside me detonate.

"You're right, I'm not okay," I say tightly. "Not all of us are just *okay* with getting divorced."

Liam sits up, hitting me with the full force of his attention. "What are you talking about?"

A humorless laugh breaks in the back of my throat. "I'm talking about the fact that I've spent the last three months trying to be okay, to pull myself out of this dark place. But I can't. I'm fucking miserable. Some days I'm angry and other days I'm in so much pain I feel like I might break in half. But it never goes away. Meanwhile *you* seem to be doing fine. Like your life is so much better without me in it. Like you don't even care. And yes, I ended things so maybe this is what I deserve. But it still *fucking hurts,* Liam."

His jaw tightens. "You really think I'm just okay with all this? That I don't care?"

"That's what it seems like. You're in the best shape of your life. Your career is taking off. You're going to parties. You already took your ring off. You've got fucking condoms in your wallet! So yeah, you seem to be doing pretty great to me."

His face turns stony, his lips folding into a tight line. "You have no fucking clue, do you?"

I don't know what pisses me off more. The words themselves, or the way he's looking at me, like he knows something I don't—something I couldn't possibly understand. But my frustration reaches critical mass.

"No," I say, my voice loud enough that it echoes off the trees. "I guess I don't have a fucking clue. So why don't you explain it to me, because from where I'm sitting, it looks like you're perfectly okay with this whole thing. I mean, maybe I should have asked for a divorce sooner! Maybe I've been holding you back from doing shots with *Katie* and working at prestigious research institutes in London. Maybe I—"

"Roslyn. Just stop." His voice cuts through the end of my sentence, thundering between us, and I freeze.

His expression shifts, an angry current sparking from his eyes to the canyon between his brows, and I can't help the tiny, satisfied thrill that emerges inside me at the sight of him finally losing his cool.

"You know that chart at the hospital?" he asks, his voice thin, like it's taking everything in him to keep his composure. "The one where you're supposed to choose the face that corresponds with how much pain you're in on a scale from one to ten? Ten being excruciating?"

I frown, unsure where this is coming from. "Yes, but—"

"I've been at a fucking ten every day for the last three months, Roslyn. So no, I'm not *okay*."

I stare, stunned into silence.

My first reaction is disbelief. Because it doesn't make sense. All signs point toward Liam doing *fine*, great even. But the longer I look at him—the weariness in his features, the lines under his eyes, the sag in his posture—the more my sturdy case collapses like a house of cards.

"What do you mean?" I finally force out.

He swallows, slivers of sunlight catching the lines around his mouth. "I've been miserable, Roslyn. That party you heard over the phone? Kevin threw that because he saw how depressed I'd been and was trying to cheer me up. He's also the one who put condoms in my wallet." He pauses, giving me a heavy look that pulses through me. "Working out has been a way to deal with my stress and anxiety, and I took off my ring because every time I looked at it, I was reminded of everything I lost. So no, I'm not *thriving* right now, Roslyn. I'm a fucking mess."

I try to make sense of what I'm hearing. To fit it within my neatly curated picture of Liam. The one where he's already moved on. But it's like a trapdoor has opened up beneath me and I'm in free fall, my stomach climbing into my throat, no safety net to catch me.

I'm a fucking mess. His words ring in my ears, shaking me to my core, and not at all in the way I thought they would. I'd thought—*perhaps hoped*—that I'd enjoy knowing he was torn up over the divorce. That it would be validating. A relief to know that he's just as messed up and hurt by this as me. Instead, I feel there's a weight on top of my sternum pressing down, making it harder to breathe.

There's so much I want to say. So much I want to know. But the first thing that comes out is, "What about London?"

His brows pinch. "What about it?"

"I mean . . ." I shift my weight, my legs squelching in the mud. "Why London? Is it for the job? Or . . ." I swallow hard. "Do you really want to get away from me?"

His jaw clenches, his eyes dipping to the ground. "Let's not do this."

"Please," I ask, my voice fraying. "Just tell me the truth."

He shifts his weight where he's seated in the mud beside me. "I *am* trying to get away from you."

Hot, fevered panic steals my breath.

"But it's not like that." His gaze morphs into something sad, almost mournful. "I can't stay in Seattle anymore because it's too painful."

"Painful?" I repeat, my voice so hoarse I hardly recognize it.

"I can't live there when every corner of the city reminds me of us, of everything I had. Everything that's no longer mine."

It's a confession so large, so overwhelming, that for a moment I swear the ground shifts beneath me.

There's a part of me that wants to scream he didn't have to lose it. He didn't have to lose *me*. He could have stayed. He could have fought. He could have come back. But another part of me doesn't want to know why he didn't fight. Why he didn't come back. Why I wasn't enough.

"Why didn't you tell me you were feeling this way?" I whisper after a beat. "This whole time you've been so cold and indifferent with me, and I thought . . ." My chest tightens as words form in the back of my mouth. "I thought you didn't care," I finally say.

He sounds exhausted when he says, "Of course I fucking care. But what was I supposed to say? You asked for the divorce. Then you ask me to pretend that we're still together and . . ." He carves a hand through his hair. "I guess I don't know how to be around you anymore."

The admission knocks me off-balance. It's how I feel too. Like I'm orbiting in space, with no gravity to ground me.

"I don't know how to be around you either," I admit. "This has been really hard on me."

"Me too." His jaw softens, and it feels like a tiny opening in what has otherwise been a shut door between us.

"I wish you would have told me how you were feeling. Maybe we . . ." But I let the words fade away, too unsure, or maybe too afraid, to say them. "You could have said something," I force out.

"So could you."

I feel caught, like he's pulled at one of my fraying threads, and now I'm slowly unraveling in front of him.

"You're right," I say after a beat. "I could have."

He nods, his throat bobbing like he's digesting my answer.

"Would it have changed things?" he asks.

I don't know what *things* he means. If he means things now. Or things in the past.

"I . . ." I start to say, but the words melt away as I realize I don't know how to respond. I feel like I'm stuck on an impossible Jenga turn, where no matter what I do next, the entire tower will collapse.

Either I tell him he's right, there's nothing he could have done or said that would have changed anything. Which isn't necessarily true. Or I admit to the confusing part. The part dividing my brain, equal parts want and fear. The part of me that still wakes up searching for his warmth. The part that burns every time his skin meets mine. The part that wonders if maybe he'd fought for me—*for us*—if maybe he hadn't just walked away, then things might be different.

But he hadn't, I remind myself. He made his choice three months ago when he packed his bag and left. And so had I.

"I don't know," I say at last. "Things were bad. Right?"

"Right." But there's a question primed behind the tightly uttered syllable, like he's looking for confirmation. Like he, too, is wondering if in some alternate universe we'd still be happy, or if every path would have inevitably led here, to the end.

"I should tell you," Liam says after a pause, eyes shifting to the mud then back up to mine. "I've been talking to someone."

I jolt up, every internal alarm in me suddenly tripped. "You mean like dating?"

He licks his lips and swallows; something unreadable crosses his expression. "I mean like a therapist."

"Oh." The word punches out of me with a sharp exhale.

"I started seeing someone a few weeks ago." Then in a lower, more cautious voice, he adds, "It's really helped."

A rush of something—anger, hurt, confusion—swims in my chest.

If this were a game to test how reactive I am to certain topics, *Liam going to therapy* would be on the Chernobyl end of the scale.

Liam, who never shares his feelings, who spent nine years finding every excuse *not* to talk about his family, is seeing a therapist? And it's helping? With what? Our breakup? Or something else?

My thoughts zigzag back and forth, trying to unravel this new detail, until I realize Liam's watching me, clearly waiting for a response.

"What made you decide to see a therapist?" I finally force out.

"Kevin, actually," he says.

I blink. "Kevin? As in the guy who has a porno stache and thinks lining his mantel with empty liquor bottles is the height of interior decorating?"

"Kevin's actually been a good friend these past few months," Liam says, giving me a look as though to say *when I needed someone.* "But eventually he got sick of seeing me mope around and said maybe I should talk to someone. I didn't want to at first, but . . ." He hesitates before saying in a low voice, "Things got bad."

My joints tighten. "What do you mean *bad*?"

He looks away, his eyes focusing on the stump of a nearby tree, before he says, "I wasn't doing well. I was drinking a lot and calling out sick from work. I got really behind on my lab reports, and for a while, I thought we might lose our research funding. Kevin got worried and helped set up an appointment for me to talk to someone."

His words shoot through me, and I'm not sure what to focus on. That Liam, who cares more about his job than anything, started slacking at work? Or that said *slacking* is the thing that finally got him to seek out help—*not* the end of our marriage?

I draw my hand along the ground, tracing patterns in the mud. After a beat, I ask, "What do you talk about with the therapist?" His mouth parts, eyes widening like he's surprised I'd ask. "I mean, sorry, that's confidential; you don't have to tell me," I say quickly.

"You, mostly."

I feel my pulse in my throat.

Liam talks about me?

I consider pressing him on it, but to be honest, I'm not sure I want to hear the answer. I don't want to know what he tells his therapist about me. Or what they might say back. I don't want to hear why I wasn't worth fighting for.

"But we also talk about family stuff," he says. "She's helped me work through some of my *repressed feelings*, as she calls them."

A conflicting swell of emotions presses against my chest as I think about all the phone calls he never told me about, all the nights he emotionally withdrew, all the times we went to bed in silence because he didn't want to talk about something that happened with his sister.

We were together for nine years, and he never once sought professional help to work through his family trauma. But now, when we've been broken up for only three months, he's suddenly working on himself? Where was this interest in mental health three months ago? Hell, three years ago?

I want to be angry. To turn my pain into something with claws and sharp edges. And yet, as his eyes meet mine, as I watch his hand flex from his side as though stopping himself from touching me, I know that I can't. That despite the bubble of frustration and resentment concentrating in my core, there's a part of me that's glad he's getting the help he needs. Maybe it wasn't for me or our marriage, but at least he found the courage to do it for himself.

"I'm proud of you," I tell him after a pause. "For taking that step."

He looks up, his soft eyes meeting mine. "Thanks," he says quietly.

"How's it been?"

"Hard," he admits, and I see the answer written across his face. In the deep lines surrounding his mouth.

"Sometimes it feels like I'm making progress, like I'm working through some of this shit from the past. But then something happens." He gestures vaguely. "And suddenly I'm a helpless kid all over again."

His face crumples, and it breaks me apart into tiny, fragmented pieces. First for him, for the pain he's still carrying. Then for me, for all the doors that stayed closed between us. All the conversations we never had.

"I'm so glad that you're talking to someone and that it's helping." I pause, searching for the words I'm not sure how to say. "But there's a part of me that wishes you'd tried when we were together."

As soon as I say it, I'm afraid it's too much. That I've taken things too far, broken this tenuous, fragile moment between us. But his eyes widen, understanding sifting through his features like grains of sand falling through an hourglass. After a long pause, he asks, "Would it have helped?"

It's a derivative of the same question he asked me earlier. But this time the answer feels clearer.

"Yeah," I admit. "It always felt like your family stuff was this wedge between us, and I could never quite reach you. Like you didn't want to let me in. And maybe if you had . . ." I swallow, looking away, unsure how to finish that statement. Or maybe I do know, I'm just afraid to say it.

"I'm sorry," he says, his voice low, barely above a whisper.

He doesn't elaborate, but I can tell he means it, and a bristly ache emerges against my chest.

"I'm sorry too," I tell him. Though I'm not sure what exactly I'm sorry for. Sorry that it ended the way it did. Sorry that we're both hurting. Sorry he never opened up to me. Sorry that whatever we once had wasn't enough to save us.

A breeze lifts the ends of his hair. Somewhere in the distance a bird croons. His eyes catch mine, and I wonder if he feels it too. This soul-bruising crush of loss. If in some strange way we're in this together, branded by the same marks, hurt by the same wounds.

"So what are we going to do?" I ask after a beat. "Should we start rationing food? Peeing in water bottles?"

"Probably. I mean since we're going to be stuck here forever. Or at least until a lion eats us."

"There aren't lions here," I say.

"Not that we know of," he says, giving me a look.

I whack his arm and he laughs, a real one, all low and throaty, and I realize how much I've missed it. How much I've missed a lot of things.

"You know," I say, tracing a circle in the mud with my index finger. "Maybe this was actually a good thing."

"Which part?" he asks. "Getting lost in the jungle? The spider? Or the fact that we're covered in mud?"

"I thought you said we weren't lost?"

His teeth tug on his bottom lip, fighting back a grin. Yet another thing I've missed.

"I mean maybe us getting stuck together wasn't a bad thing," I say. "The whole near-death-by-spider thing sucked, but now that I've lived to tell the tale . . ." I pause, my eyes tracking to meet his. "I'm kinda glad this happened."

His mouth wavers into a smile. "Me too," he says, letting his knee bump against mine. The base of my throat warms as I bump his back.

We sit there, our knees touching probably longer than they should until he stands and holds out his hand to me. "Should we try and get out of here before we have to drink each other's pee?"

I take his hand, but as I try to stand, pain shoots through my leg once more and I stumble, straight into Liam's steadying grip.

"You can't walk on that, Roslyn."

"I'm fine," I insist.

He hits me with a hard look. "No, you're not."

The bossiness makes me want to argue, but I know he's right.

"So what do we do?" I ask.

His eyes sweep up and down the length of my body, examining. "What if I carry you?"

My mouth turns to chalk. "Oh, uh . . . You don't have to do that. It's not that bad."

"Roslyn." He says my name low and serious. "Either you let me carry you, or you'll have to wait here for me to get help. It's up to you."

I bite my lip, weighing the wisdom of letting Liam carry me. Or more precisely, letting him touch me. *Everywhere.* But then again, I don't think I have a choice. It's not like I'm going to stay here with the spiders.

"Fine," I say, exasperated. "I guess you can carry me."

"Good, because I wasn't going to leave you alone with the spiders." Then he scoops me up, hands sliding under my thighs, and presses me against his chest.

"Is this okay?" he asks.

I'm not sure if he means my ankle, or the way his arms are wrapped around my body, holding me close enough to hear the *tap tap* of his heartbeat, or something else, but I tell him, "Yes, I'm okay."

And this time I mean it.

- 18 -

Eight years earlier

"So let me get this straight," Liam says, reaching for the popcorn bowl between us. "Rachel McAdams doesn't remember that Channing Tatum is her husband, so he has to remind her?"

"Isn't that so romantic?" I say.

Liam snorts. "That's the most ridiculous thing I've ever heard. How could she not remember her own husband?"

"She was in a car accident and has amnesia," I tell him. "Which you would know if you were paying attention to the movie."

His mouth curls upward, his eyes shining in the dim half-light of the laptop screen. "I've been paying attention."

"No you haven't."

"I *am* paying attention," he whispers, his hand climbing the outside of my thigh, giving me a possessive squeeze. "I just didn't say what I was paying attention to." His gaze flares mischievously, but I can see the tired creases around his eyes. Creases that have become a permanent feature since starting residency.

We were supposed to go out tonight for a date—our first in weeks—but Liam's exhausted from twenty-four-hour shifts at the hospital in addition to the full-time master's degree in clinical research he's working toward, and my feet are killing me after a double shift at the restaurant and the extra catering gigs I've been picking up. That, and we're broke, so we decided to stay in and watch a movie on the couch instead. Not that Liam's been paying much attention to said movie.

"You know," he says, eyes flashing to mine. "If you ever forgot who I was, I'd remind you."

"Oh yeah?" I lift an eyebrow. "How?"

Liam's hand moves from my thigh to the waistband of my sweats, then lower, grazing the top of my underwear. "Like this." He plants a rough kiss on my neck that sucks all the air from my lungs. "And this." His tongue sweeps back and forth, painting velvety strokes against the hollow of my throat. "I'd always make sure you knew you were mine."

His mouth migrates upward, capturing me in a searing kiss, and I kiss him back, a fraction of a kiss, then more, want striking hot against my core. It's been over a week since the last time we were intimate and the ache between my legs is almost painful. He's pulling me onto his lap, needy hands carving into my waist, when his phone buzzes from inside his pocket.

The sound catches us off guard, but it's not enough to derail us. "I've been thinking about this all week," he rasps, his voice like sandpaper against my skin. "I've been imagining you under me, on top of me, every way possible."

"That's funny," I tell him. "Because I've been imagining that too."

We move more quickly, our desperate hands traversing skin to bring us as close as our clothes will allow.

Pressing my chest to his, I draw our mouths together and grind against where he's hard. I'm working up a rhythm that has us both gasping and panting when his phone vibrates again. And again.

A tiny, pathetic whine slips out of me when Liam pulls back.

"Sorry," he says, voice thick and groggy, like he's just been pulled from a deep sleep. "It might be the hospital."

"It's fine," I tell him, trying to hide my disappointment.

"Hopefully it's nothing big, maybe I can even be back by—" But Liam doesn't finish because he takes one look at the screen and his whole demeanor shrinks.

"What?" I ask, sitting up straighter. "What's wrong?"

"I have to take this," he mutters. And before I can ask who it is, he's rushing off into the bedroom, where he shuts the door with a tight thud. A moment later I hear the low murmured hum of his voice behind the wall. Whoever it is, they talk for nearly thirty minutes before Liam finally returns, looking exhausted, like he's been drained of his life force.

"Who was that?" I ask as he takes his spot beside me on the couch.

"No one," he says, not looking at me.

"You were in there for thirty minutes."

"Don't worry about it," he says tightly.

"So it wasn't the hospital?"

"No."

He gives me one long look like *Please, can we drop it,* before reaching for the laptop to resume the movie.

As much as I'd like to ignore what's just happened and go back to our much-needed date night, I can't pretend like Liam's guardedness doesn't bother me.

Since we've been together, Liam's avoided telling me almost anything about his past.

Sure, we talk about residency and our dreams for the future, but never about his life back in England. Nothing about his childhood, or his family. Things most couples talk about. *Should* talk about.

I've tried to ask, but he usually shuts the conversation down within the first few seconds, making it clear it's not a subject he wants to broach. At least not with me.

I understand that whatever it is, it's upsetting to him, and I want to be sensitive to that. But I hate feeling like I'm left on the outside looking in, like there are parts of himself he's not willing to share with me.

We live together. We love each other. We talk about getting married someday. Shouldn't this be something he opens up to me about? Isn't that what a relationship is all about? Confiding in each other? Being transparent? Messy parts and all?

I place my hand over his. "Liam, please. Can you just tell me what the phone call was about?"

He shifts his weight, trying and hesitating to speak before finally he says, "It was my sister."

My stomach leaps into my throat, surprise stealing my breath.

Liam has a sister?

I think of all the times he could have mentioned this. Not even a casual *Hey, I have a sister,* or *One time my sister and I . . .* ? My skin prickles, a heavy discomfort settling behind my navel.

"You have a sister?" I ask.

Slowly, he nods. "Felicity is seventeen years younger than me. Probably a last-ditch effort to save my parents' marriage," he adds with a humorless laugh.

I sit back on the couch, digesting this new particle of information. But I'm not sure where to start. With the fact that whatever his sister said is upsetting him. Or that we've been together for over a year, and this is the first time I'm hearing of said sister.

"Are you close?" I ask.

"She's eleven, so we don't exactly have a lot in common," he says. "But I try to check in when I can."

"Why did she call?" I ask. "Did something happen?"

His gaze dips into his lap, and I can feel him slipping away. The man I was about to have sex on the couch with moments earlier is somewhere else, somewhere far away, somewhere I can't reach him.

"She says my parents are fighting again and she wants me to come home," he says. "But she knows I can't."

I frown. "Why not?"

He rubs his palm down the side of his face, dragging the skin with it. "When I was eighteen, right before I left for uni, my dad and I got into a fight." He pauses, swallowing. "He told me I wasn't welcome back home. Ever."

My insides clench. "Ever?"

His eyes darken, the muscles around his mouth tightening in confirmation.

"Why? What happened?" I ask.

Liam's whole body stiffens as he draws in a long breath then pushes it back out. "My dad doesn't treat my mum well."

My chest throbs, blood pounding in my ears. "Does he—?"

"Let's not talk about this anymore." His voice is calm, even, but I can feel whatever door was momentarily opened shutting and locking between us. *This conversation is over,* his narrow eyes tell me, loud and clear.

Part of me wants to demand he let me in and that we continue this conversation whether he wants it or not. It's not fair to keep me in the dark like this. But I also don't want to push on buttons that I know are fragile, so I nod and pretend to return my attention to the movie, watching as Rachel McAdams and Channing Tatum find their way back to each other. But even later, as we brush our teeth in front of the mirror and climb into bed together, I can't shake the sense that Liam feels further away than ever.

- 19 -

Now

Does this hurt?" Liam asks, adjusting then readjusting the pillow elevating my ankle the same way he's been doing for the last hour after we eventually found our way back from the hike. "How about this?"

"You don't have to baby me," I tell Liam. "I'm fine. It barely hurts anymore. See?" I flutter my leg in the air, but Liam doesn't seem convinced.

"You twisted your ankle," he says with the same seriousness as if I had lost a limb. "You need to rest, Roslyn."

I know he's being overly dramatic, but I can't help enjoying how worried he is about me. It's kind of cute.

"Do you think we'll have to amputate?" I tease.

He gives me an exasperated look, like he's *so* over me, but not before I catch a glimpse of a twinkle behind his eye, like maybe he's secretly enjoying this.

"Just elevate your foot." Liam gestures to the pillow he's propped up under my ankle. He adjusts it, frowns, then readjusts again as if a judging panel will be here any second to assess his work. "How's that, baby?"

I stiffen, an inhale catching in my throat. Did he just—?

Liam's face instantly turns red in confirmation. "Sorry," he mutters. "Habit, I suppose." Then he turns away, busying himself with the pillows while I swallow down the lump in my throat.

It was an accident. Of course it was. But my heart doesn't seem to know the difference as it performs a series of complex acrobatics that leave my chest tight, and my breath stilted.

After a tense beat, he asks, "What about food? Are you hungry? I could order room service. Chicken nuggets?"

I snort. I'm not exactly a sophisticated eater. More of a chicken tenders and boxed mac and cheese sort of gal.

"You know, I have been known to eat a salad on occasion," I say, giving him a look.

"Which occasion?"

I roll my eyes. "Very funny."

"I don't care what you eat, you know."

"Why? Because we're getting divorced, and it doesn't matter if I die of malnutrition anymore?"

"*No.*" He gives me a sharp look. "Because you're an adult, and if you want to eat like an unsupervised thirteen-year-old boy, then go for it. Also, I'm English, so I really don't have room to talk."

I snort-laugh. "Whoever decided beans go on toast was seriously disturbed."

"Don't even get me started on atrocities like spotted dick and black pudding."

"Spotted dick?" My mouth parts into a horrified *O*. "That's a thing?"

"Unfortunately. Someone really thought to themselves, *You know what we need?* A dessert with beef fat *and* dried fruit. And while we're at it, let's give it a name that sounds like a form of genital herpes."

A wild laugh tumbles out of me, and the corners of Liam's mouth rise a fraction of an inch, like he's trying very hard to resist a smile as he pulls a granola bar out of his backpack. "Want one of these?"

My stomach growls at the sight of food, and I take the bar. "Aren't you going to have one?" I ask, biting into the chewy, peanut butter-y center.

He shakes his head.

"Oh right. Of course. A body like that isn't built on sugary processed foods," I say.

He lifts one eyebrow. "A body like what?"

My cheeks heat up. "You know what I mean."

"I'm afraid I don't," he says, his eyes flashing with amusement.

Good grief, he's enjoying this, isn't he?

"Are you really going to make me say it?" I ask.

"Say what?"

I throw the granola bar wrapper at him. "God, you're an asshole. You got hotter, okay?"

He lifts one eyebrow, his gaze flaring playfully. "Careful, Roslyn, or I'm going to think you're flirting with me."

A spark of heat travels down my spine, and I look away, not wanting him to see the way his words affect me.

"You look good too," he says after a beat.

"Now I know you're lying. The dirty dishes at the bottom of the sink look better than I do right now."

His eyes soften. "I'm serious," he says. "You're always beautiful."

There's a chance he's just being nice—probably because I'm injured—but the earnest tug of his mouth makes me think he means it, and my chest pangs, a sticky ache spreading from limb to limb.

"Okay, so if you don't want me to order food," he says after a beat, "how about a nightcap?"

I ought to tell him no, that us holing up in our stateroom as drinking buddies isn't part of the plan. But so far none of this has gone to plan. Besides, I can't help but think that after the day we've both had, a drink sounds good.

"Okay," I tell him. "One drink."

Unfortunately for me and my liver, one drink quickly becomes splitting a bottle of gin, and now I'm tipsy at sea with my ex.

Liam passes me the bottle, and I swig straight from the mouth. The gin is tangy and sweet and burns all the way down.

"I guess this is our only venue for drinking," I tell Liam, wiping my mouth and passing back the bottle. "Considering we're supposed to be trying to have a baby," I add, giving him a look.

He winces. "I hate that word, *trying*. Like, everyone knows what you really mean by that."

"You mean that they think we're boning each other's brains out?"

He shakes his head, making a face. "I don't want your family thinking about us doing *that*."

"Oh, too late. My sister definitely does."

He laughs low and deep, a throaty noise that lasts only a second before it's lost to the hum of the ship and the crash of the waves below us.

We don't have a cabin with a balcony, but the sliding glass door that opens to a barrier overlooking the crash and tumble of the Pacific is just as good, and I turn my face skyward, taking in the smattering of stars overhead.

I've never been a nature girlie. *Clearly*. But there's something almost comforting about being here under the night sky, feeling both small and big. A tiny drop in the big ol' universe.

A light breeze lifts the ends of my hair, and I shiver in the cool air.

"You cold?" he asks.

I shake my head *no,* but he shrugs his way out of his sweatshirt and hands it to me. It's his old UW Med sweatshirt. The same one I used to "borrow." And by "borrow," I mean that it lived in my side of the closet for years—my go-to lazy outfit around the house or running errands—until it disappeared along with Liam's other clothes when he moved out.

I'd hoped he'd leave it behind for no reason other than he knew I liked it, but he hadn't, and somehow the thought of him intentionally plucking it from my side of the closet hurt worse than any other material absence.

But the air does have a chill, and I can tell he's trying to be nice, so I pull the sweatshirt over my head.

Almost instantly his scent envelops me, that intoxicating mix of soap and citrus that transports me back to nights curled under his arm, my face buried against his chest as he played with my hair.

I wish I could carve out these memories, the once-sweet ones that now feel like tender bruises, and put them in a box under the bed, where I can pretend they don't exist. But I guess that's what gin is for, so I lift the bottle to my lips, relishing the burn as it slides down my throat.

We continue to pass the bottle until Liam suddenly asks, "Do you remember the night we met?"

I pull back, eyes narrowing, the question—or perhaps the memory—catching me off guard. "You mean the night we got ditched by Abby and Kevin and you lured me back to your place with lasagna?" I ask.

His mouth quirks. "I didn't lure you. You came willingly."

I'm not sure if he means it as a double entendre, but my cheeks simmer anyway.

I had indeed *come willingly.*

Liam tilts the bottle to his lips before he says, "I still consider myself lucky that you slept with me that first night we met, though I'm sure the circumstances would have been different if I'd made you spotted dick instead of lasagna."

I roll my eyes. "Please. You were charming and you knew it. You had a whole little routine."

He shifts his weight, hip bumping mine. "It wasn't a routine. I just knew what I wanted."

"To sleep with me?"

The side of his face catches the glow of the moon, revealing a glimmer in his eyes. "Yes. But I wanted more than that. A lot more."

It's all I can do to keep my cheeks from flaring as I think back to that night. How he'd kissed me soft and slow, then rushed and hungry. How after one quick plea of *bedroom*, he'd carried me there, limbs braided with mine. Mouths colliding. Warm breath and tiny, strangled moans. The weight of our bodies reaching, grasping, fumbling as need coursed through us like cars on a racetrack.

I hadn't intended to sleep with him the night we met. And even after we started hooking up, I'd fought our connection. But he'd pulled me in with that Liam spell of his. All-consuming and overpowering, like a riptide. He'd made me feel like he was someone I could trust with something as fragile as my heart. Someone for whom I could be enough.

But in the end, I hadn't been.

"I still think about that green tube top," he says, his voice whisper-light, almost like the words aren't meant for me. "You looked so fucking hot."

Still. The word burns hot against my chest, followed by a car crash of emotions, each one colliding into the next.

All I can manage is, "You remember what I was wearing?"

"Of course I do. I remember everything about that night."

A loose strand of electricity zigzags between us as our eyes collide. But I can't tell if we're flirting or reminiscing. The gin is blurring the line.

"I remember how badly I wanted you out of that top. Wanted *you,*" he adds, pinning me with a heavy look I feel right between my legs.

This conversation feels dangerous. I need to retreat.

"Well, you got what you wanted," I say diplomatically.

His tongue swipes across his bottom lip. "Didn't you?"

I take another sip from the bottle, forcing my gaze away from his. "You know, I almost didn't come out that night. I was in a slump after dropping out of med school, and I didn't want to go, but Abby made me."

"Do you regret it?" he asks.

"Regret what?"

"Coming to the bar that night."

He says it casually, like it's a throwaway question, but I can see the intensity hovering behind his eyes, the words he's not saying out loud: *Do you regret me?*

It's a question I've asked myself before. If I could go back in time to that night we'd met—or the million moments after it—and choose differently, would I?

Maybe my life would be easier. Maybe I could have avoided this world-ending hurt. But I can't help thinking that the painful part isn't that we met, or even that we loved each other. It's that we had something great, something beautiful and passionate and heart-wrenching, and we lost it.

“No,” I tell him after a long minute. “I don’t regret it.”

Maybe I imagine it, but relief flows from his eyes, down to the flat corners of his mouth.

“Do you?” I ask.

He shakes his head. “I wish I’d done things differently, but I don’t regret that any of it happened.”

I want to press him on it, to ask what exactly he wishes he had done differently, but this newfound solidarity between us feels too delicate, so instead, I murmur, “Me too,” and take another long sip.

As I hand him back the bottle, I realize how overly aware of him I am. The shape of his palm as it wraps around the glass. The stripe of moonlight painting his eyes in a warm glow. The way his hip gently brushes mine every time he shifts his weight. And how chaotic it all feels. Like I’m adrift in the ocean, helpless to the swells threatening to pull me under.

The hum of the ship’s engine fills the silence until Liam says, “Earlier, you asked me about the condoms in my wallet.”

All the air rushes out of my lungs.

“You should know that I haven’t, uh, *needed* them.”

I hate how relieved I feel.

“So you’re not *technically* seeing anyone?” I ask.

He shakes his head. “Kevin’s been trying to get me back out there. Hence the condoms,” he adds sheepishly. “But to be honest, I don’t feel ready to date.”

There’s forced levity in his voice, like he’s trying to come across unbothered by the whole thing, but I can’t help noticing the way his hand taps nervously against the railing, an anxious tic I recognize from when he was studying for his board exams.

“I’m not thrilled about dating again either,” I tell him. “The dating market isn’t exactly kind to divorced women in their thirties.”

"I'll be judged too."

"It's different for you. You're a man."

"So?"

I give him a hard look. "Liam. You're a thirty-six-year-old hot doctor with a British accent and a sob story. All you have to do is *exist* and a million women will materialize." I pause, rolling my eyes like the whole thing is silly and shallow even though I know all too well the allure of a broken, messy man. "Meanwhile I'll be seen as damaged goods. A walking red flag."

He shakes his head. "You're not damaged goods, Roslyn."

"I know I'm not, but—" The rest of the sentence dies on my tongue because maybe that's not true.

I'm not the same girl I was when Liam and I first got together. I'm no longer the cautiously hopeful romantic who desperately wanted someone to come along and prove her wrong. I've been hurt too badly. Had my heart broken one too many times. And it's hard to imagine someone wanting to take on all my baggage. Especially when my own husband didn't want to.

"Maybe I am," I say after a moment.

"That's not true."

"Isn't it? I'm a struggling writer. I'm getting divorced. My niece doesn't recognize me anymore. My family thinks I'm a joke. My mom's dead." I tick them off on my fingers, each one a bullet point on my résumé of failures. "Sounds pretty damaged to me."

"Roslyn, no," he says again, this time more determined. "You're not damaged. You're . . ."

His lips part then close, and I realize we've inched closer, close enough that I can smell the bite of gin on his breath. Close enough that I know I ought to move away. But neither of us does.

"I'm what?" I ask.

Our eyes latch. My breath hitches. A familiar swell of longing settles between my legs and for one wild moment I wonder if Liam might close the gap. *If he might*—but Liam pushes out a tired exhale, and along with it, the words, "You're going to be fine." Then he puts his hand on top of mine, giving it a squeeze.

It's a chaste gesture. Friendly, even. But I see the way his gaze drops to my lips, lingering for a beat so quick I wouldn't notice, unless I was looking for it.

I expect this new discovery to offer some kind of validation. After all, I'm not the only one affected by the closeness. That he, too, feels the ember of want that refuses to go out. Instead, I feel unzipped, vulnerable, like I'm starring in one of those dreams where I realize I'm onstage naked with nowhere to hide. Though it's possible that's just the gin.

I reach for the bottle and take another sip.

"This sucks," I say after a beat.

He frowns. "Really? I thought the gin was good."

"No. *This.*" I gesture between us. "Divorce."

He snorts. "Ah. Yeah, it sucks."

I raise the bottle as though performing a toast. "To divorce sucking," I say.

Moonlight-struck eyes catch mine. "To divorce sucking," he repeats, mimicking the gesture.

The corners of my mouth curl up into a grin, and he mirrors my expression, like we're sharing an inside joke. Perhaps it's a cruel one, but there's something cathartic about being victims of the same wound. About knowing the cuts and bruises might look different, but the pain is the same.

We pass the bottle back and forth a few more times before Liam declares he's exhausted and is going to bed.

"I'll take the floor again tonight," he says.

"But it's my turn."

"You're injured."

"I'm fine, *really*," I add, wiggling my foot for emphasis.

He gives me a heavy look. "Roslyn, I insist."

It's possible he just feels sorry for me. But I really don't want to sleep on the floor, so I climb into bed and turn off the light, submerging the room in darkness.

"Good night, Liam," I say into the black.

"Good night, Roslyn."

Maybe it's because I'm still a little drunk, or because this is the first time in months we've really talked, but as the hum of the ship's engine carries me off to sleep, I allow myself to wonder if there's something left between us, something more than just pretending for my family. If underneath all the hurt and wreckage of the past, a version of *us* still exists.

- 20 -

Now

I can see the intersection up ahead. The light is green, and I press on the gas, propelling us forward. Mom is telling a funny story about a date she went on last week. One moment I'm laughing and the next the lights blur, and I'm being thrown forward, up and out of my seat, nose nearly colliding with the dashboard. I scream, but the sound is drowned out by the earsplitting crunch of metal and the hiss of the engine. Steam pours into the air and everything goes fuzzy.

Someone's asking if I'm okay.

"Mom?" I glance around for her. She's beside me, eyes closed, but I can't reach her. I call out to her, shouting. But she doesn't hear me. I'm pleading now, begging her to look at me.

There's something wrapped around me. I try to push it off so I can get to her, but it only grips me harder. I need to get to her. I need—

"Roslyn! It's me!" Firm hands tighten around me, shaking me awake. "Wake up!"

Slowly, the voice moves from background noise to full volume, and I become more aware of my body. Of the manic thump of my racing heart. Of the strong arms winding tightly around me, rocking me back and forth as Liam's face swims into focus, his voice growing sharper against my eardrum.

"Roslyn? Can you hear me?"

The words leap inside me, pulling me out of the dream and into bed, where Liam's body is crushed to mine, holding me steady. I press a clammy palm to my forehead, already slick with sweat and matted hair.

"What's going on?" I ask. "What happened?"

"You're having a nightmare," he says, brushing a sweaty strand of hair from my forehead. "You were yelling a lot, and calling out for her."

Her.

I shut my eyes, trying to dislodge the memory, but as soon as my eyelids drop, I'm there in the car all over again, the green light up ahead, the sweet scent of my mom's perfume hanging in the air. The memory hollows me out, pain stretching like a spiderweb expanding outward from my sternum all the way to my fingertips. Before I can stop myself, I'm sobbing. Not cute little sniffles, but full-bodied, chest-heaving, throat-closing sobs.

Liam grips me tighter, wrapping his arms around me like warm protective blankets, his thumb drawing gentle circles at the base of my neck. "It's okay," he whispers into my hair. "I've got you. You're safe."

His words squeeze around my lungs, threatening to uncork all the messy feelings I've worked so hard to seal away: Longing for when he was mine, grief because he's not, then finally, embarrassment. He's not supposed to see me like this. Not again.

"I'm sorry," I tell him. "I'm sorry for falling apart like this."

"Nothing to be sorry for," he says, his hands roaming into my hair.

His voice is soft and steady, a stabilizing metronome for my racing heart. A sound I want to drown in. And yet, as good as it feels to have his voice in my ear and his hand in my hair, I'm aware that I shouldn't.

Eventually he'll move to London, and I'll return home, alone, and I don't want to get used to this or think I'll be able to call him up in the middle of the night like last time. I don't want to indulge in the luxury of his comfort when I know it's something I won't get to keep, so I jerk back, untangling myself from him.

Liam frowns. "Did I do something wrong?" he asks.

I shake my head. "No. I'm just fine, that's all."

His frown intensifies. "You're not fine, Roslyn. You're crying."

"I'm not," I insist, putting my hand to my cheek. *Oh.* It's wet. "I'm sorry, I'll stop—"

"No, that's not what I'm asking," he says, his voice gentler as he lifts his thumb to my jaw, brushing away a stray tear. "You're clearly still upset."

I should reiterate that I'm fine. That I don't need him. That there are divorce papers sitting in an envelope a few feet away and we have no business holding each other like this. But maybe it's because he's right, I *am* upset, and he feels strong and sturdy, an exact contrast to how I feel, but I allow myself—*just this once,* I think—to lean into his touch, savoring the brush of his thumb on the inside of my wrist as he alternates between soft circles and gentle pressure.

We stay like that, our chests pushing and pulling with each breath, until Liam asks, "Do you want to talk about it?"

"About the nightmare? Not really."

His hand runs along the outside of my arm, leaving goose bumps in its wake. "Does anything help?" he asks.

An unwanted image of Liam stroking my back, whispering, *It's okay. I'm here,* strikes hot across my subconscious.

"How about a distraction?" I say.

"Okay." A thoughtful divot appears between his brows. "Want to tell me about the book you're working on?"

"You mean the draft for a book that doesn't exist?"

"I thought you said you were working on something new?"

"I sort of lied," I admit. "I haven't been able to write in months. Not since Mom . . ." I gesture vaguely and Liam nods. "Now I'm scared I won't be able to write again. That the first two books were flukes and I'll be trapped in this painful, exhaustive writer's block forever."

As soon as I say it, worry strangles me once more. What if the words are just . . . *gone*?

"Roslyn." He says my name so soft, so tender it hurts. "It's okay to take breaks, especially after . . ." He trails off before starting again. "After everything that happened this year."

I shake my head. "But I can't afford any more breaks, not when the clock is ticking."

"The words will come to you."

"But how do you know?" I ask, my voice unexpectedly small.

His mouth wavers into a half smile. "Because I've heard you tell me a million times that you'll never write another book, that you're not sure you can do it again. But you always do."

"But what if this time it's different? What if—" An unforeseen crack worms its way into my voice. "What if now that she's gone, I've lost my spark?"

What if I don't believe in happily ever after anymore?

"If I know anything from watching you over the last few years, it's that creativity comes in waves, and you can't control it," he says, his hands a sturdy lifeline on my back. "But the words will still be there for you when you're ready to return to them. I know they will."

He looks so certain. Like he just knows I'll write again. If only I felt that way too.

"What's it like to be so certain about your goals and your career?" I ask, genuinely wanting to know. "To just know that you're good at something and to have everyone always affirming it for you all the time?"

His eyes widen, lips parting then closing again. "I don't feel that way at all."

I can't help the scoff that rips out of me. "Of course you do. You're good at everything, and you know it. *Everyone* knows it."

"That's definitely not true."

"Really? Because the committees that award grants and the directorial board at the Institute of Cancer Research in London seem to disagree."

Maybe I imagine it, but a soft blush creeps up his neck. "Would you believe me if I said I'm scared?"

I'm about to roll my eyes and say something like *Yeah right,* but as my gaze tracks across his features, taking stock of the tight lines bracketing his mouth, I wonder if maybe he means it.

"What are you afraid of?" I ask after a beat.

He swallows again and I watch the way his throat tightens, like there's a wedge in his esophagus. "I know this job in London is a great opportunity, and I'm thankful for it. But I worry that I won't measure up. That I'll get there and start working with all these top-notch researchers who are experts in their fields and they'll see what a fraud I am. That I'm just some kid who somehow managed to sneak his way in."

"You're not a fraud," I tell him. "You're easily the smartest, most hardworking person I know."

"But I think that's exactly what's scary about it. *Everyone* will be the smartest, most hardworking person and I won't be able to keep up."

A shadow of uncertainty lingers behind his gaze, and it makes me wonder if under the golden boy facade, he's just as insecure as I am. If maybe we all feel like frauds, at least sometimes.

"I get feeling that way," I say after a minute. "But I think you need to trust yourself. You're a great doctor who brings a lot to the table. Sure, you're young, but being young isn't a bad thing. It means fresh perspectives and new ideas, right?"

He nods, but his expression remains tight. "There are so many days when I doubt myself," he says. "When I doubt that anything I'm doing even matters."

"Of course what you're doing matters," I urge. "You're saving lives."

His mouth moves upward as though attempting to smile. But instead of the shiny, confident young man I met at the bar nine years ago, he looks tired, worn down, wrinkled, like a pair of pants that's been left on the floor too long, and I wonder if it's not really the job he's thinking about, but his mom and sister. The two people he couldn't save.

Silence swallows us until he says, "This year has been hard, but I know you'll write another book. *Really,*" he adds, reaching down to take my hand.

His fingers loop through mine and I must be more touch starved than I realize because a burst of want centralizes in my core. He's kissed and touched me everywhere. Been inside me in every conceivable way, but a simple handhold now feels painfully intimate.

My reaction must be written across my face because Liam pulls his hand back.

"Sorry. I shouldn't have—"

"No. It's okay," I tell him, taking back his hand. "And thank you," I add, my eyes finding his. "This helped."

His mouth parts, lips drawing up into a half smile. "I'm glad," he whispers, giving my hand a squeeze. Then, in a lower, almost hesitant voice, he adds, "I want you to know that just because we're ending things doesn't mean I don't still care about you."

My throat warms. "I still care about you too," I whisper.

But I realize as the words leave my lips how insufficient they are. *I can't imagine a day I won't think of you* is more accurate. Because no matter what happens, no matter how many miles between us, or how many papers we sign, there will always be a part of my soul that's entangled with his.

I'm not sure how long we stay there, hips pressed together, fingers wound tightly, but eventually he pulls back. "I should probably go back to bed."

Maybe it's that I'm still a little drunk, or that I'm not quite ready to be alone again, but I hear myself say, "Can you stay?"

He pauses, his gaze locking with mine through the darkness. "You want me to sleep with you?"

I know what he means but I can't help blushing as I nod.

Liam's brow tenses in thought. "What about the rules?"

"How about we call this bed Las Vegas?" I try.

"Las Vegas?"

"You know? What happens here stays here?"

His eyes widen. "Wh-what?"

"I don't mean like *that*. I just mean we can forget the rules for tonight," I add.

But his brow continues to furrow. "I don't think that's a good idea."

My insides deflate like a popped balloon. "Right. Of course. I understand if you don't want to."

"I do," he says quickly. "I definitely do, I just . . ." His voice trails off as his gaze jumps to the floor, his forehead creased in thought before he finally asks, "Are you sure?"

No, I'm not sure I should share a bed with my soon-to-be-ex-husband, but I really don't want him to let go, so I tell him, "Yes, I'm sure."

Liam gives me one more tentative look before he pushes back the covers and slides into bed beside me. He feels different now, harder, more sculpted, but even under all those new muscles, it's still him, a body that feels as familiar to me as my own.

"You feel good," I tell him.

His muscles turn taut beneath my touch, and I think he might pull back, remind me of the rules, that we shouldn't be touching *alone*. Instead, he releases a breath and draws me into him, his hands palming my waist.

"You feel good, too, Ros."

My heart swells, an uncontained smile slipping over my mouth. *Ros.* I'm Ros again.

As I burrow against his warm, solid chest, I allow myself to remember what it was like to have unfettered access to his body. Not just sexually, but the simple acts of intimacy I used to take for granted: A hug at the end of a long day. A gentle hand stroking my back as I fell asleep. The kinds of intimacies that said things words couldn't.

"I'm glad you're here," I tell him.

"Me too," he says. "Sleeping on the floor was shit."

"No, I mean on this trip," I clarify. "I know this is weird and honestly kind of fucked up, but I'm glad you came." Then, maybe because of the gin, or the heat of his body pressed to mine, or some combination of both, I add, "I missed you."

His lips brush against my temple, lingering. "I missed you too," he whispers, and I feel the foolish, hopeful part of my heart start to beat faster.

I want to tell him I missed this closeness, his hands, his body, the feel of him, our life together. *Everything.* Instead, I settle for resting my head on his shoulder in the crook that used to feel like it was made for me. And maybe—just for tonight—it still is.

"Why'd you let go?" he whispers.

"Of what?"

"My hand."

His voice comes out scratchy, like it's been hours, not seconds, since he last used it, and a whoosh of heat rips through me as I reach for him, lacing my fingers through his again. If this is all I get with him, I want to savor it. Before it's over. Before the gin wears off and the sun comes up. Before we go back to pretending.

"Don't let go," he whispers against my ear.

"I won't."

- 21 -

Seven years earlier

"You really didn't have to come," I tell Liam, shutting the passenger door. "Grammy understands how exhausting residency is."

Liam reaches into the back seat of his dented Ford Explorer, from where he extracts a foil-wrapped pan of lasagna. "And miss Grammy's seventieth birthday party? No way." He says it with a smile, but I can see the bags under his eyes and the heaviness of his posture, like the mere act of standing up might be too much effort.

Liam's in his second year of residency and full-time master's program, so it's a big deal that he's agreed to spend his only free Saturday for three weeks at my grandmother's birthday party when I'm sure he'd much rather be rotting on the couch.

"We don't have to stay long," I tell him, taking his hand as we make our way toward the door. "Just give me the signal and we can go."

"The signal, eh?" he says, wiggling his eyebrows. "Is that what you were giving me last night?"

I playfully roll my eyes, even though we both know it's been a while since we've given each other signals of any kind.

In between long shifts at the restaurant and trying to squeeze in writing when I can, and Liam's grueling hours at the hospital, most nights we are too tired to do anything other than eat left-overs and pass out in front of the TV.

Sometimes the sounds of late-night Tupperware infomercials wake us up long enough for a half-cognizant quickie on the couch, but that's only if Liam didn't work the night before. Or I didn't just get off a double shift.

It's not exactly the height of romance, but we both understand that this is a temporary arrangement, and it won't always be like this. In two years, Liam will be done with residency and his master's program, then he'll apply to fellowships in medical oncology, and we'll finally be able to start our life together.

Though where that life will take place, I'm not sure yet.

Liam's already been approached by fellowships all over the country. Boston. Chicago. New York. He's thrilled and so am I, but I'm also nervous about what this might mean for us.

What if Liam accepts a fellowship on the other side of the country and we have to move? What if this puts a strain on our relationship? What if my mom goes through a depressive episode after another breakup and I'm not there for her? What if. What if. What if.

I want to lean in to the excitement of this new chapter for Liam, but the worries keep stacking up until I feel like I'm suffocating under the weight of them.

Liam and I approach the stained-glass double doors and ring the bell.

As a kid, I remember getting excited anytime Mom dropped us off at Grammy and Gramps's, knowing I would get my own room and Grammy would have all the good snacks Mom usually couldn't afford. Now, twenty years later, the same house feels a lot less magical and a lot more like a graveyard littered with the ghosts of my *wasted potential,* as Gramps calls it.

The doorbell chimes and a moment later my mom appears, her hair wrapped in some complicated updo with a scarf, with massive hoop earrings to match the eclectic collection of vintage bracelets rattling on her wrist. If I didn't know any better, I might assume she's just stumbled out of Coachella or Stevie Nicks's closet.

Her eyes brighten and she pulls us into big bear hugs like we've just returned from combat.

The first thing I notice is that she smells like weed, which Grammy is probably upset about, but I take it as a good sign. When she's going through a breakup, she drinks. But when she's in love, she smokes.

"Liam! So good to see you," my mom croons, squeezing him a little tighter.

"Good to see you, too, Ms. Larsen."

She wags a finger at him. "How many times have I told you to call me Maggie?"

"I think I'll need to hear it once more, Ms. Larsen."

She beams at him, and Liam's smile stretches impossibly wider.

He might not open up to me about his own family, but it feels good to see him happy with mine, to feel like in some small way I've been able to give him the family he's been missing.

My mom leads us to the backyard, where she introduces us to Steve, a tall guy with tattoos and shoulder-length hair who is a regular at the bar Mom just started working at.

After Steve wanders off looking for a beer, she pulls me aside and tells me it's serious with him and she thinks he really could be *the one.* But she says the same thing about every single guy she's ever dated.

"Does he have a job?" I ask.

"He works at a bank."

"An apartment?"

"With an in-unit washer and dryer."

"Any baby mamas?"

She gives me a look. "You really don't trust me, do you?"

"I do, I just . . ." I glance toward Steve, who is shamelessly checking out Bella. "Don't want you to get hurt, that's all."

Her gaze softens. "I know, baby, but love is about taking risks. Sometimes that means kissing a few frogs before you find your prince."

As much as I want to protect my mom from any more frogs, I can't help but admire her fearlessness, her ability to get back up and keep looking for love time and time again.

"Just be careful," I tell her. "Please."

Her mouth spreads into a smile, the kind that says *I'll try*, before grabbing each of us one of Grammy's homemade brownies.

"How are things with Liam?" she asks.

"Good." I bite into a brownie, chewing before I add, "Liam's looking at fellowships for after residency."

Her eyes light up. "That's great. I'm sure he'll have his pick of programs."

"He does," I tell her. "Out of state."

Her brows knit together. "You're moving?"

"We don't know yet. It's just something we're talking about. But it's a definite possibility."

"And how do you feel about that?" she asks.

"Scared," I admit.

"What are you scared of?"

Everything, I think. I'm not like my mom, who can just go wherever the wind (or a man) takes her.

"The idea of moving across the country terrifies me," I tell her. "What if it puts a strain on Liam and me? And I can't imagine being away from you."

Or not being here when you need me, I think.

She squeezes my arm. "Do you think Liam is *the one*?"

Before Liam, love was something hazy and hypothetical. Something that happened to other people. But now love is something concrete and real and Liam-shaped. The way he kisses me good morning and refills my tea without being asked. How he always asks me what I'm reading and listens when I tell him. How he cares about the things that matter to me because *I* matter to him. Sometimes I think maybe my life didn't start until I loved Liam, until my heart learned to love and be loved, like maybe this was what I was made for. To spend forever cherishing and being cherished by this formidable, brilliant, caring, sweet, loving man who makes my heart swell so big, I think I might break.

"Yes," I tell her without hesitation. "I love him."

"Then everything will work out," she says, giving me a smile. "I promise."

I smile back at her, hoping she's right.

After we fill up on homemade brownies and lasagna, Liam and I catch up with everyone. Liam might be running on fumes right now, but he never lets it show. He laughs at all my brother's cringey jokes and asks the right questions about Bella's senior year science fair project. He even notices Grammy's new haircut and asks for her brownie recipe. And when Gramps tells Liam he's old friends with the chief of medicine at the university hospital and that he'd love to introduce them, Liam beams and tells him he would be honored.

It's rare to get a smile out of Gramps, but Liam manages to get three.

As much as Gramps is still disappointed in me for dropping out of med school, I can tell dating Liam has cushioned the blow. Like by virtue of a kind of transitive property, some of his sparkle has rubbed off on me.

I pretend to listen, smiling politely as they talk hospital politics until Gramps turns to me. "Roslyn, any news on the job hunt?" he asks.

I jolt, surprised to find myself the focal point of Gramps's attention. "I'm not really looking for another job right now," I tell him.

"So you plan to just work at a restaurant forever?"

He says it like I sell feet pics on the internet and not like I work at a neighborhood bar and grill that serves half-price wings every Tuesday between 3 and 6 p.m.

"Well, no," I say, my voice wavering ever so slightly. "But it's a good job while I figure out what to do next."

"And what *is* next, Roslyn?" I swallow hard, eyes jumping to Liam, who is in conversation with Jonah about applying to fellowships.

So far, all my writing has gotten me is a bunch of rejections, each one taking a jab at my already withering self-confidence, and I've started to wonder if this was all a mistake. If Gramps was right.

"I'm not sure yet," I admit, feeling myself shrink under the intensity of his gaze.

"Hmmm." That's all he says. It's not even a real word, and somehow it cuts worse than any scathing remark could.

I wish I could tell him how much I love writing, that I've begun work on a new manuscript I'm excited about, and I'm hopeful this one might be *the one*. But I already know that unless I'm announcing that I've decided to return to medical school, he won't be impressed.

Gramps looks at me a moment longer, his eyes sharpening like every fiber of my being is endlessly disappointing to him—a look I've seen directed at my mom more times than I can count—before returning his attention to Liam.

They return to talking about Liam's master's program and the kinds of research he is interested in doing while I excuse myself to grab a beer from the kitchen. I'm sticking my head in the fridge when Liam comes up behind me, his hands folding around my waist.

"Liam, you scared—" But the rest of the sentence dies on my tongue as Liam presses his lips to my neck while his hands travel down the front of my dress, fisting the fabric like it's all he can do to keep from ripping it off me right here and now.

"I have to tell you something," he murmurs into my skin.

"If you're going to tell me that we should go upstairs and lock ourselves in the guest bathroom, then yes, I agree."

"As much as I love that idea, it's something else." He pauses, nibbling on my ear. "Something your grandfather just told me."

"What's that?" I ask, my breath coming out in short gasps as his lips trail down the side of my neck, lingering just above my shoulder.

He halts his movement, then spins me around to face him. "He just told me he's friends with someone in the oncology department at the university hospital and there's a fellowship opening there if I want it."

It takes a moment to transition from thoughts of sex in the guest bathroom to a fellowship, but as I do, my hands fly to my face.

"Ohmygod! Are you serious?"

He nods, his eyes flashing with excitement. "This means we can stay here in Seattle, Ros."

I imagine there must be champagne bubbles in my belly, making me feel impossibly light.

For a moment we just stare at each other, the joy on his face a mirror of my own. But after a beat, the expression dissolves, replaced with a trio of lines in his forehead as though he's just realized something.

"What?" I ask with a nervous laugh. "Do you not want the job? Do you—"

"We should get married," he blurts out.

I blink. "What?" I ask, sure I've misheard.

"I said we should get married," he repeats, the words coming out firmer, more assured, like the last two seconds were all he needed to solidify them.

My brows narrow in confusion. "But we said we'd wait until after you finish your residency to get engaged. Right?"

"No—I mean, *yes*." He shakes his head, limbs practically vibrating with nervous energy. "We had said after residency, but I don't want to wait that long."

"I don't understand—?"

But before I can even finish the sentence, Liam's dropping to one knee in front of the fridge.

"Roslyn Larsen, I've spent the last two years wanting everything with you. From that very first night we met, I've wanted to be the reason you smile. The thought that quiets the worry in your brain. The memory that makes you blush. I want to be your easiest *I love you* and your hardest goodbye. The reason you feel safe and loved. And I want to keep doing that forever, for as long as I have the privilege of being yours." He pauses, his warm, tender eyes flashing to mine, before in a whisper of a voice he asks, "Will you be my wife?"

I swear my heart stops. No, *everything* stops.

"Are you serious?" I ask, my voice as breathless as I feel. "Are you really asking me this? Right now?"

His chin bobs up and down, excitement building behind his features. "I am. I've never been more serious about anything in my life. I love you and I want to spend forever with you."

All the air rushes out of my lungs, and I press my palm to my chest, willing my racing pulse to slow down.

I knew this would happen. Eventually. Neither of us has been shy about our desire for a future together. But this is so unexpected. So out of left field. One minute we're talking about staying in Seattle, and the next Liam is kneeling on the kitchen floor proposing. But past the shock, I know I want this. I want this life with the man that I love. The man who makes me feel braver, more certain than anything in my life ever has.

So I say the only thing I can think to say. The only thing that makes sense. "Yes!" I cry. "Of course I'll marry you."

There's a brief moment of stunned silence, then we're both crying and laughing as he pulls me into his arms and spins me around the kitchen, telling me how he's going to buy me a ring, how he just has to finish residency then we'll get married and start our life together.

You and me, he whispers into my skin. *Forever.*

I try to memorize the moment. Everything from the yellow sundress I'm wearing to the faint taste of chocolate on Liam's lips as he kisses me over and over, telling me how he can't wait to marry me. How much he loves me. And I say it all back, my mouth moving hard and fast against his.

There's no ring, no candlelit dinner, but none of that matters because tonight I have everything I could ever want.

I have *him.*

- 22 -

Now

Larsen Family Vacation Day 3

PORT OF CALL: *Kona, the Big Island*

ITINERARY: *deck yoga at 10 a.m., zip-lining at 2 p.m.*

ATTIRE: *athletic, easy to move around in*

I've dreamed about Liam before.

In the weeks after he left, I used to have the same dream over and over. Him on top of me, kissing my neck, whispering how badly he wanted me—*needed* me. Then, just when I couldn't take it anymore, I'd reach for him, begging, only to find he wasn't there, and I was alone.

There were plenty of nights I wore out my vibrator trying to soothe the ache between my thighs when I woke from yet another Liam dream/nightmare. But this isn't a dream. Liam's warm hand splayed across my abdomen is very real. As is the hardness pressed against my lower back.

Maybe it's the hazy film of sleep still clouding my judgment, or because the real thing feels much better than anything my imagination can conjure, but here, in the early morning hours, when my defenses are lower and my excuses are flimsier, I let myself sink against him, savoring the hard press of his body, of parts of him I'm no longer supposed to want.

He smells good. The way he always does—citrus and soap—and it's like flipping through the dusty pages of an old yearbook, reliving memories of what it was like to be his. His to touch and kiss and tease. His to love.

But the memory lasts only a moment before awareness of what I'm doing—of what this must look like—scatters across my skin and I jerk back, putting as much distance between Liam and me as I can. But the sudden movement jolts Liam awake, and I watch, frozen in place, as he first registers me and my totally unnatural position on the other side of the bed, followed by the boner straining against the fabric of his boxers.

"Shit," he mutters, covering his still-hard dick with his hands. "Sorry."

I force my eyes away, desperate to look anywhere but at Liam's bare chest, or his not-so-subtle hard-on.

"It's fine," I say, not meeting his gaze. "Nothing I haven't seen before."

But it's not fine, I think as the reality of how we got into this situation crashes over me.

What was I thinking? Drinking together? Asking Liam to sleep in the bed with me? Cuddling up to him like I was still his and he was still mine?

Waves of shame spread across my skin like a spiderweb.

But it was an accident, right? I was emotionally vulnerable after my nightmare. We were lured together by heightened emotions and alcohol. Besides, we've been spending more time together. *Close* time. We were probably just picking up on familiar patterns. Something to do with pheromones and ovulation cycles and science. Yes, *science,* I tell myself, like last night was nothing more than the predictable sum of a mathematical equation. But the persistent spark crackling under my skin feels anything but scientific.

My heart still galloping inside my chest, I hop off the bed and head straight to the bathroom, where I intend to take a *very* cold shower.

But the cold shower isn't quite cold enough to snuff the heat swelling between my thighs every time I think about Liam's body pressed against mine—about other *things* pressed against me. Which is precisely when I remember this ship has four pools and I've yet to dip my toe in any of them. So I throw on my bikini and race out of the cabin muttering something about needing a swim.

I probably look suspicious, but I don't care. I just needed to get out of there. Away from him. Away from the shameful embers of heat burrowing under my skin every time I catch his eye.

When I arrive on the Fiesta Deck, the pool area is crowded with mothers coaxing children into water wings and older couples with skin that looks like it has already spent several lifetimes under the sun. Overhead the sky is the brightest of blues, matching the ocean framing either side of the deck.

I plop my stuff down on an open lounge chair, peel off my cover-up, and jump right in.

The water is cool and refreshing as I push off the cement bottom and into a breaststroke, where the throb in my joints and the fire in my lungs remind me just how out of shape I am. But I keep going, finding cathartic pleasure in the burn of fatigue.

Maybe if I can focus on the fire in my lungs, I won't think about the much more formidable fire between my legs. Or the way Liam held me last night. Or how we'd woken up tangled in each other's arms, bodies wound together like ancient vines. Or how good it had all felt. And how ashamed I feel because he's no longer mine to want.

I wonder if I should tell Abby what happened, but I already know how that will go. She'll try and convince me that it's fate. That of course we fell asleep holding hands because we're meant to be. That it's some kind of sign. Which is *not* what I need to hear right now.

We're getting divorced. We're over. A decision we both made three months ago. And sure, we might have gotten friendly—*too friendly*—last night. But some drinks and a bit of emotional intimacy don't change things. It doesn't change all the nights that I cried myself to sleep while he worked longer and longer hours, or that he left with nothing more than a curt *fine*. And it certainly doesn't make us friends.

I let the thought take hold, strengthening my resolve, as I push myself harder, deepening my strokes, like maybe if I can wear myself out, I won't have enough energy to want Liam.

Everything is going well, *swimmingly*, until I come up for air and find myself face-to-face with a familiar pair of legs over the edge of the pool.

Fuck. How'd he find me? There are three other swimming pools on this ship.

"How's the water?" he asks.

He's wearing red swim trunks and—*God help me*—a backward cap. If I wasn't already in the water, I'd be wet.

"Great," I say, looking absolutely everywhere but at his strong forearms.

He lowers his Ray-Bans down the bridge of his nose. "Mind if I join?"

Yes.

"No."

His lips split into an easy grin, the kind that makes my lungs deflate in a frantic *whoosh* as he lowers himself into the pool.

"How's your foot?" he asks, swimming up beside me.

My foot? What's wrong with my—? Oh. Right. The foot I came down on wrong yesterday. Somehow, in all the drama this morning—and last night—I managed to forget all about my injury.

"I think it's fine," I say. "Hard to tell in the pool, though."

He frowns. "Can I see?"

"Here? Now?"

He gives me a look like *What's the problem?* that I don't know how to argue with, so I lift my foot high enough that he can grab it.

His brows furrow in concentration. "How's that?" he asks, his thumb brushing along the joint. "Does that hurt?"

A little shiver meets my spine when his hands wrap around my skin, and a part of me wishes it did still hurt, just so I'd have an excuse for him to keep touching me. But I swallow the flutter, forcing my gaze away from his. "No," I tell him. "It's fine."

He lowers my foot back into the water with a *plop*. "You should put some ice on it. I was going to get you some more, but you ran out of the cabin so fast this morning, I didn't have time." He gives me a knowing look that sends shivers all over my skin.

I turn away, not wanting him to see the guilt I'm sure is written all over my face.

"Can I ask you a question?" he says, swimming close enough that his strokes feel like little whirlpools drawing me in.

No.

"Sure."

His eyes lock on mine, and blood rises into my cheeks. "Are you avoiding me?"

Yes.

While yesterday's honesty had been nice—refreshing, even—that was before we crossed lines we shouldn't have crossed.

Besides, what am I supposed to say?

My soul still feels connected to yours and 10/10 would fall asleep in your arms again, but I'm not supposed to want that because we're getting divorced and now I'm kind of spiraling.

Nope. That's between me and Jesus.

"No, of course not," I say, forcing my mouth into a tight smile.

Liam's brow scrunches. "So, there isn't any particular reason you sprinted out of the room this morning?" he asks.

"I really wanted to go for a swim."

"Riiiight," he says, drawing out the word. "Because you're such an avid swimmer."

I search his expression, trying to determine what kind of game he's playing, but the sunglasses sitting on the bridge of his nose give his poker face an unmistakable edge.

When I don't respond, he drifts even closer, until I can make out the tiny, sparkling droplets of water clinging to his beard.

"By the way," he says. "After you ran off, your sister came by the room."

"Oh? What did she want?" I ask, forcing my eyes above the neck, and absolutely *not* at the bead of water sliding down his pecs.

"She asked for the photos of Grammy and Gramps. Something

about a collage? I gave her the manila envelope on top of your suitcase."

The bead of water is instantly forgotten. Instead, my breath stalls and everything goes hazy.

"You gave her the manila envelope on top of my *suitcase*?" I repeat.

His brows stitch together. "Yeah?"

My vision swims.

No. This can't be happening. He can't mean . . .

"Liam," I say, unable to keep my voice from cracking. "The collage was in my bag. You gave her the wrong envelope."

He frowns. "What do you mean, *the wrong envelope*? I only saw the one." But as soon as he says it, awareness slides across his features. "Wait . . . ?"

I nod my confirmation. "You gave my sister our divorce papers."

- 23 -

Now

Here I thought our biggest obstacle would be Liam and I getting along. Turns out we're getting along a little *too* well, and the real issue is that our divorce papers are currently in my sister's cabin.

"What are we going to do?" I ask as soon as the door to our cabin shuts behind us.

Liam runs a hand through his still-damp hair. "There must be something."

"What if we just say it's the wrong envelope and ask for it back?" I try.

"But what if she tries to check?" He shakes his head. "It's too risky."

"We could say it's a prank?"

His mouth flatlines. "Great idea. I'm sure everyone will find that *hilarious,* especially when they find out it's fucking real."

I wince, *not* appreciating his tone. "Well, why don't you come up with a plan, then."

"My plan would have been to not bring divorce papers on a trip where the explicit intention is to keep said divorce a secret." His eyes cut to mine. "But since that's not an option . . . we could steal it back," he says.

I cough out a laugh. "*Steal?* What do you mean, *steal*?"

"We sneak into their cabin and switch the envelope with the divorce papers out for the right one," he says. "She'll never know."

I cross my arms over my chest. "Okay, Nicolas Cage. You want to break into their cabin and switch the envelopes?"

"*We* will," he says matter-of-factly.

I flick one eyebrow upward. "We?"

"Yes, Ros. *We*."

This is a mistake," I say, my head snapping back and forth as I look up and down the hallway outside Bella and Chris's room. "We're totally going to get caught."

"We're not going to get caught," Liam says, sliding his black Amex in and out of the space between the door and wall. "According to Jonah's itinerary, they're at yoga on deck. By the time they get back in"—he checks the time—"thirty-seven minutes, we'll have swapped envelopes and be safely back in our room getting ready to go zip-lining, with them none the wiser."

"I can't believe I'm saying this, but I'm actually thankful for my brother's overzealous planning right now," I say, watching Liam's hands as he readjusts the credit card, trying to get just the right angle to unclasp the lock.

I know the primary area of concern should be the whole breaking-and-entering thing—and that we're moments away from getting caught in a huge fucking lie—but right now my focus is entirely diverted to the veins in Liam's arms and the inconvenient heat between my legs. Damn him and his slutty forearms.

"I'm pretty sure that only works if you're George Clooney in one of the *Ocean's* movies," I say, watching him slide the credit card back and forth.

"It'll work," he says. "I've done it a million times."

"You've done this before?"

"Not breaking into someone's stateroom," he says. "But I've jimmied a lock just like this before." When I gawk at him, he adds, "I learned it at school."

"They teach you that in medical school?" I ask, my eyes growing wide. "Because if I'd known, maybe I wouldn't have dropped out."

"Boarding school," he corrects. "My mates and I used to break into the kitchen after hours and steal food."

While I don't know much about Liam's childhood in England, I've gathered from brief mentions of boarding school and skiing in Gstaad that his family is well-off. But after his dad kicked him out and cut him off financially, most of Liam's higher education was funded by academic scholarships, part-time jobs, and loans he will be paying off for the next thirty years.

"Who knew you had a criminal history," I say. "Anything else I should know? Grand theft auto? Racketeering?"

A low laugh hums in the back of his throat, but he doesn't look up from the lock. A second later it clicks. "See?" he says, catching my eye.

I shake my head, unable to deny that I'm at least a little impressed. And aroused. Dammit. Why does Liam have to be so competent?

The door swings open to reveal Bella and Chris's mercifully empty room.

Their room is the same as ours, except messier. It looks like day three of a girls' trip to Vegas in here.

"I feel creepy," I say, my eyes dancing from the blue bra flung over the back of a chair to the crumpled pair of boxers peeking out from under the bed.

"We're just switching the envelopes and leaving, not going through their stuff," he says, looking in a drawer.

"What if we see something?" I ask.

"Like what? The envelope?"

"No, smart-ass. Like sex toys. I *so* don't want to find a pair of handcuffs," I say with a shudder.

Liam's brows draw together. "Since when are you a prude? We've used handcuffs loads of times."

Heat scorches down the back of my neck, and I'm met with the sudden urge to turn and run. Though it's unclear whether that's because he just casually brought up our sexual past like it's a brand of detergent we used to buy, or the memories it resurfaces. Memories neither of us has any business reliving while we're sneaking around my sister's cabin, looking for divorce papers.

"I'm not a prude," I say, peeking through a drawer. "I'd just prefer not to know what kind of kinky shit my sister is into."

And I definitely don't want to think about the kinky shit we used to do.

I continue digging through one of the nightstand drawers, thankful for a reason not to look at Liam, until my gaze lands on a manila envelope.

"Got it!" I cry, holding it up triumphantly.

"Great, switch the envelopes then let's get out of here before—" But Liam doesn't finish his sentence because muffled voices can be heard outside the door. We both freeze, our eyes darting between each other and the door.

"It's them!" he whispers. "They're back!"

Two beats of panic pass, then the lock clicks, followed by the smooth *whoosh* of the door opening.

We're so fucked.

But just as I'm bracing myself to be caught, Liam grabs me by the waist in a football-style tackle and rolls us both under the bed.

My first thought as the tail end of Bella's laugh floats through the room *should* be relief that we're hidden, or perhaps fear that we're probably seconds away from getting caught. Instead, all I can focus on is the centralized heat of Liam's hands on my waist, his breath hot and ragged against my neck as he pulls me flush against him.

There's probably a really good reason we're touching like this. But for the life of me, I can't think of what it is. I can't think at all.

"I'm so sorry," Bella says, her voice cutting through my horny thoughts.

"Sorry for what?" Chris asks. His voice is low and sultry, almost teasing.

"I'm sorry, but due to the outrageous costs of privatized health care, I won't be able to afford my bill, Doctor," Bella says in an exaggeratedly sexy voice. "Is there another way I can pay?"

"Wait. I thought you were the doctor this time?" Chris whispers.

"No, I was the doctor last time," Bella whispers back, dropping the sultry tone. "Now it's your turn."

Ohmygod. Are they . . . *role-playing*?

Chris clears his throat. "I think something could be arranged," he says.

Bella giggles. "What do you have in mind, Doctor?"

"Why don't you go to the bed and I'll show you."

Oh God. They are.

Maybe if I wasn't trapped under the bed with my ex's hands still wrapped around my waist, about to hear my sister have wild sex, I'd ponder the ethics questions surrounding two med school students playing doctor/patient, but I'm too busy trying to hold on to my vomit.

The air fills with the sounds of sloppy, wet kisses and short, gasping breaths before Bella says, "I'm so glad we're doing this. Can't let Liam and Roslyn have all the fun on this trip."

And just when I thought this couldn't get any worse, it has indeed gotten worse. Not only am I about to have a front row seat to my little sister having sex. It's also apparently inspired by Liam and me.

This is *not* what I meant when I said I wanted to be a role model for my little sister.

I look to Liam to see how he's handling this, but his eyes are shut tight like he's praying it will end soon. Finally something we can agree on.

"I want you to do that thing to me," Chris says, his voice low, like a roll of thunder. "The thing I like."

Oh, please God, don't let it involve fluids.

The sounds of zippers being unzipped are followed by the mattress squeaking, and all the while I wonder if this is karma for lying to everyone. Though I must have done something right because a phone chime cuts through the cacophony.

"Baby, is that yours?" Bella asks.

"It can wait," Chris murmurs.

"But what if it's your advisor?" she asks. "I thought you were waiting for a call about that internship?"

The bedframe groans, and a moment later Chris says, "Shit, it's her. I have to take this."

A beat passes, then they are off the bed, tugging on clothes, and I'm breathing a sigh of relief, thankful the worst minutes of my life are now over, until I see it. A lime green thong next to Liam's head.

I nudge Liam in the ribs and point to it.

She's gonna see us! I mouth.

What do I do? Liam mouths back, his eyes panic-stricken.

Move it!

His gaze widens, horrified. *I am* not *touching your sister's knickers!*

If you don't, she'll see us!

There's a brief moment of hesitation in which Liam looks like he's debating whether he'd rather die than touch Bella's thong, but he reaches out and flicks it away.

I hold my breath, waiting to see if Bella makes a comment about flying underwear, but they continue to dress in silence. A frenzied minute later the door shuts, and they're gone so fast, it's almost like the whole thing didn't happen. If only that were true.

"Are they gone?" Liam whispers.

"I think so."

Liam rolls out from under the bed before helping me to my feet.

"I don't think I'll ever be able to look my sister in the eye again."

"Same. I could have gone the rest of my life without knowing they're into . . ."

"Role-playing doctor?"

He winces. "I don't even want to *begin* to psychoanalyze that."

A shiver wracks my body as though trying to physically dispel the memory. "Me either. Do you think it's like a kink or—?" I pause, shaking my head. "Actually no, don't answer that. I don't want to know."

He laughs and it's not until our eyes meet that I realize he's still holding my hand. I clear my throat and pull back, remembering my earlier resolve. *We're not friends. Last night didn't change anything.*

"Come on," I say, not looking at Liam. "Let's swap the envelopes and get out of here. We're supposed to go zip-lining in a few hours."

I'm turning toward the door, ready to make a swift exit, when his hand folds around my wrist, pulling me around to face him. "Are we really not going to talk about it?"

"Liam, I *really* don't want to discuss my sister's sexual fantasies—"

"No, not that." His mouth twists. "I mean last night. And . . . this morning," he adds, a soft blush creeping into his cheeks.

My head rushes as my vision momentarily blurs, fraying around the edges.

Liam has always been the one who shies away from tough subjects, the one who wants to brush everything under the rug. But apparently New Therapy Liam likes to talk. Which was great last night—and would have been great six months ago—but isn't so great right now.

"Come on. Let's not do this," I say. "We need to get the fuck out of here in case they come back."

I turn toward the door, but Liam's feet stay rooted in place.

"I know you're pissed about what happened," he says. "And I know that's why you ran out of the room this morning." His gaze pins me down and I have the feeling of being backed into a corner with nowhere to go. "So why don't you just say it so we can talk about it. Like adults."

Maybe it's the smug implication that he's the adult here. Or the way he's looking at me, his jaw flexing with barely contained irritation, but something inside me snaps.

"Well, it shouldn't have happened," I say. "It was reckless!"

His eyes flare triumphantly. "See? I knew you were pissed!"

"Of course I'm pissed!"

And it's true. I am pissed. But mostly at myself. For getting drunk with him, for falling asleep in his arms. For getting swept up in his spell. *Again.*

"Is this about the boner?" he asks.

"No, Liam, it's not about the fucking boner," I say, exasperated. "It's about the fact that we're getting divorced and we can't . . . we can't . . . we can't get drunk together and fall asleep holding hands!" I finally bark out.

For a long moment Liam doesn't say anything. He just stares at me, a range of emotions weaving across his expression, each so finely intertwined, I can't distinguish one from the other.

I wonder if he'll yell. And a fucked-up part of me hopes he will. At least yelling would shatter this intolerable angst, or better yet, distract me from the tightly wound knot of sexual tension stewing in the pit of my stomach.

Finally, Liam says, "So, you're saying you regret it?"

"Of course I regret it," I snap. "We were drunk. I was upset after the nightmare. We had rules and we broke them."

"I wasn't that drunk," he says, eyeing me carefully. "Were you?"

My skin burns with awareness. I know what he's implying—what he's *rightfully* implying. That alcohol isn't to blame. But rather something much scarier than finding sex toys in my sister's room.

"No," I admit. "I wasn't that drunk, but it shouldn't have happened, and it can't happen again. It's . . . it's . . ." But the end of my sentence catches in my throat as I realize how close we've shifted. Close enough that the familiar spicy scent of his cologne wafts in my nostrils, trapping me in that magnetic vortex of his that I've never been good at resisting. Not nine years ago, not last night, and certainly not now.

"It's what?" Liam prompts, and fuck, I can't think when he's looking at me like that. Like he knows exactly what I'm thinking.

"It's . . ."

His eyes stay locked on mine like he's trying to coax the words out of me with the sheer potency of his gaze. I swallow hard, willing myself to focus.

"It's dangerous," I say at last.

"Why is it dangerous?"

A laugh spills from my lips. "Are you serious?"

"It's an honest question."

I pinch my mouth, dragging my gaze away before I say, "It just is."

He steps toward me, his brows drawing together, the air thick with the scent of his skin—citrus and sweet. I feel the hair on the back of my neck stiffen. "That's not a reason, Ros."

"What do you want me to say, Liam? That it *should* happen again?"

"I don't know. Should it?"

I cough out a laugh. "You're joking, right?"

He turns from me, running his fingers through his hair. When he looks back, I feel the heat of the gaze everywhere. My neck. My thighs. My mouth. There isn't an inch of my body his eyes don't reach.

I wish I could say it's one-sided, that I'm the only one who feels this pulse of need and fear and confusion hanging between us, but I can tell he feels it too. I can tell in the way his focus keeps dropping to my mouth. In the way we're finding every excuse to shift closer. In the way he's looking at me like I'm something he wants to drink down to the last drop.

"So last night meant nothing to you?" he finally asks. "It didn't change anything between us?"

Something heavy presses against my ribs at the word *us*. We've always been an *us*, but now the word means something different. Something I can't define.

I think about last night. How he held me. How he stroked my hair and talked with me. How good it all felt. How badly I wanted—*needed*—it. Needed him.

"I just . . ." I try to swallow down the tightness in my throat. "I thought maybe we could be friends," I try.

His eyes widen, then narrow. "Friends?" he repeats. "You want to be friends?"

I wish I didn't hear the rejection of the premise embedded in the question. But he's right. He knows just as well as I that we can't be friends. That there's too much history, too many feelings—some good, some not so good—for us to ever be *just friends.*

When I don't answer, he steps closer, closing the final gaps between us. "Tell me last night meant nothing, Ros. Tell me and I'll drop it."

A shiver jumps down my spine.

This is my chance, I think. My moment to set the record straight. To tell him last night doesn't change anything. It's over. It's *been* over. But the words stay trapped in my throat, lodged between the covetous way his eyes trace my lips and the proximity of his body to mine.

When I finally speak, my voice comes out choked and raw. "It wasn't nothing. It was nice."

"Nice?" he repeats.

"Yes," I force out, but I can tell he doesn't buy it, and neither do I.

"Ros." He says my name low and serious. "Nothing about this is nice. You and I both know that."

Want and something else, something a lot more dangerous, simmer between my thighs.

"You're right," I finally say.

Seconds pass. Neither of us moves. I forget to breathe. Then Liam steps closer, close enough that I can feel the tension crackling in the narrowing space between us. *Inches,* I think. *That's all that separates us.*

"Then tell me what you want, Ros," he says, his voice heavy and ruinous. "Say it."

My heartbeat pounds in my ears.

You, I think. *I've always wanted you.* And despite every warning sign and cautionary thought, I still do. I want his hands on my body and my name on his lips. I want the parts of him he puts on the highest shelf, out of sight and out of reach. I want him in every way I can have him, so I take a moment, allowing myself to see his whole face, before I finally say, "You know what I want."

His eyes flash with understanding like sparks bursting from a flame. "Ros—" he starts to say, but whatever it was, he doesn't. Instead, his gaze lowers, sharp and determined, right before he closes the gap between us, takes my head in his hands, and kisses me.

- 24 -

Now

There's still time to stop, I think. To pull back. To uncross whatever lines we've already crossed. But once his mouth is on mine, his thumb brushing my cheekbone, it feels inevitable. Like this would always happen. Like kissing him is an inescapable outcome we could have no more avoided than gravity or the need to breathe.

His knuckles trail down the side of my arm, then lower to my hips, pulling a string of moans from me. The sound invites another kiss, this time slow and deep, and I don't know what I like best. If it's the way he angles my chin, deepening the kiss, or the rush of hot air on my cheek as his body sinks against mine, taking control. All I know is that it's not enough. I need more.

And apparently he feels the same.

"God, Ros." He makes a needy sound that nearly ruins me. "You feel so fucking good."

They're the first words either of us has spoken, and I expect them to break the spell. Instead, my name on his lips is a kind of siren song, only making me more feral for him. Like his need is fueling my own in some ravenous feedback loop.

His tongue slides over mine, one hand on the back of my neck, the other cradling my chin, and a hot whoosh of want rips through me, every pulse point in my body humming at max volume. A whimper rises out of me as I tangle my hands in his hair, desperate to give him that messy, just-fucked look that used to drive me wild. *Still* drives me wild.

"We're breaking so many rules right now," I breathe, then because I can't think, can't trust myself to answer the question, I ask, "Is this a bad idea?"

He pulls back a fraction of an inch, just enough to meet my gaze. "Tell me to and I'll stop."

Perhaps if this were our first time, if I didn't already know exactly how things will play out, I'd be more hesitant, more likely to stop myself. But looking at Liam with his messy hair and bee-stung lips is like looking into a crystal ball. I can see the future. And it's *hot*.

I already know how Liam will pin me against the bed and kiss my neck. How he'll pull down my shorts and put his mouth on me, slowly at first, sucking and tasting and savoring, then hungrier, messier, until I'm squirming and begging. Until I'm coming apart.

I know how he fucks too. Slow and sensual, then rough and fast. I know all the hungry groans he'll make. And just how thoroughly it will undo me. So I skim right past any thoughts of caution or fear, and reach for the words that have been primed on my lips since the moment he kissed me.

"*Please* don't stop."

His eyes lock on mine before tilting his chin and claiming my mouth in a thorough, ruinous kiss made of fire and oil. And suddenly I'm desperate to get burned.

It's like I'm a teenager all over again, every touch, every movement bursting with a thrill of newness. But nothing about his body is new to me. I've had all of him. Seen all of him. Being with him isn't an exotic trip somewhere new. It's visiting a familiar haunt. Somewhere I know well. Somewhere I never thought I'd return to.

I bring my hand down the front of his shorts, pausing where he's hard. Liam responds with a groan as he takes a handful of my hair, pulling my head back, catching the skin under my jaw with his tongue.

"Fuck, Ros," he breathes.

"Fuck," I agree. Because yeah, *fuck*.

Fuck, I can't believe we're doing this.

Fuck, he feels incredible.

Fuck, I need more. More him. More *everything*.

"I need you inside me," I gasp.

His body stiffens, and for a moment I fear I've gone too far, said the wrong thing, mistaken whatever this is for something more. Something it's not. But when Liam draws back, eyes wide, there's only the briefest of pauses. A cursory inhale, followed by a short, breathy exhale, then he's picking me up, wrapping his arms around my thighs, guiding me toward the bed.

Thankfully I still have enough thinking faculties to cry out, "Not here!"

He freezes, his eyes narrowing in confusion, before slow seeds of understanding bloom across his expression as though he's just now remembering we're still in Bella and Chris's room. The only thing weirder than the whole doctor role-playing thing would be us doing it in their bed.

"Right. Sorry," he says in a voice so raspy, it hurts. "Thinking is sort of *hard* right now." He winces and my eyes travel down his frame, where it seems like a lot of things are *hard* right now.

"Let's go back to *our* room," I clarify.

"Right." He adjusts himself. "Good idea."

After we've successfully switched the envelopes, we race back to our cabin, barely making it through the door before Liam's mouth collides with mine. Tandem moans rise out of both of us as he walks me back against the wall, his thumb scraping my spine, his knee wedged between my thighs.

I haven't felt this kind of anticipation in years—nine to be exact. Not since we were in his kitchen, right before he kissed me for the very first time. Before he carried me to his bed and fucked me for the first time. And the second. And the third.

Back then there was nothing but possibility between us. No hurt. No pain. No bone-crushing agony of loss. But this is different, and as much as I want to give in to him the same way I did that night, to push aside any and all cautionary thoughts and let him make a mess of me the way I need him to, I know we still need to at least talk about it.

"Liam," I gasp, unwinding myself from his grasp. "Wait."

I feel his body grow rigid against mine. When I look up, his pupils are blown out, his lips pink and swollen, his chest pounding out frantic, desperate rhythms.

"What's wrong?" he asks, his voice muddled, like I've just pulled him out of a deep sleep. "Did I hurt you?"

"No. But before we . . . before we do this." I pause, my gaze hovering on his. "I think we should talk about what this is."

"It's sex, Ros. Or at least I thought that's what you meant by *I need you inside me*?" he says, giving me an electric look.

My cheeks flood with heat. "Yeah, but what kind of sex? Hate sex? Breakup sex? *I'm horny and you have a pulse* sex?"

He watches me from under a creased brow. "What kind of sex do you want it to be?"

As soon as he asks it, I realize I don't know. Then again, I haven't exactly had time to think this through. Ten minutes ago we were fighting. Now we're moments away from fucking. It's all so fast, I practically have whiplash. All I know is that I want this. I want *him*. I want him in a way that feels too big, too overwhelming to manage.

"We never had breakup sex," I say after a beat. "Maybe that's what we need. For closure." Yes, *closure*. That feels like the key word here.

"Right. Closure," he repeats, his hands trailing along the waistband of my shorts, his fingers toying with the ties. "Is that what you want? Closure?"

I press a palm to my rapidly beating heart, trying to calm down enough to think this through. Maybe this is a bad idea. Maybe we need to let each other go. If the past three months have been agony, having Liam only to lose him again will be infinitely worse. But the need for self-preservation falters as thoughts of him grow magnified. Not just him, but him and me wound around each other. Him on top of me. Him between my thighs. Him pulling my hair. *Him. Him. Him.* And I know without a doubt that, whatever this is, it won't bring me any closure, but I want it too badly to stop.

"Yes," I tell him. "This is what I want."

"Are you sure?" he asks. "Because we don't have to do anything you don't want to."

His voice is low, serious, and I know what he really means. He's not just asking if I'm sure I want to throw caution to the wind and sleep together. He's checking to see if I'm ready to have sex. With him. Like this.

I think about the months after my mom died, when my body didn't feel like my own. When I was too heavy, too choked with grief. When Liam felt so distant. But this feels different. *I* feel different. I feel alive. Electric. Overcome with something I'm not strong enough to resist. Something I don't *want* to resist.

"Yes," I tell him. "I'm sure."

There's one more tempered pause, a brief meeting of eyes, then we're crashing into each other with a mixture of hunger and restraint like we're unsure whether we want to devour each other or take our time, making this last.

My body decides for me as I reach down for his belt buckle, eager to touch him—be full of him. But he places his hand atop mine.

"Wait. Slow down," he rasps.

"I don't want to slow down," I whine. "I need you."

He pulls back and I can see the unrestrained lust etched across every hard line of his expression, the way the words *I need you* turn him feral. He wants me just as badly as I want him, but he guides my hands away from his belt and up over my head, pinning my wrists against the wall. A whimper rises out of me as he holds me there with one hand while his other slides down the front of my shorts, cupping me over my underwear.

"Are you this wet for me?" he asks, his voice low like he already knows the answer.

He slides the fabric a fraction of an inch to the side, just enough to brush his thumb over where I'm most sensitive. I clench under his touch, a tiny whine escaping me as a vein appears on the side of his forehead, like it's all he can do to control himself—and suddenly I want nothing more than to snap that restraint like a twig.

I push my hips forward, riding the pressure of his thumb. "Still want to go slow?" I ask, in a low, sultry murmur that vibrates in the narrow space between us.

He looks absolutely wrecked and a spark of pleasure races down my spine that I have that effect, but in a flash he pulls his hand away, withdrawing the heat of his touch.

"We're going to take as long as we need to take," he says. "And if that means edging you for hours, then it's hours."

Hours.

The thought of us, like this, for *hours* looms in my brain like a powder keg and a discarded match.

"But we're not rushing this," he says. "Understood?"

I nod, feeling light-headed.

"Good girl." Then he picks me up, guiding my legs around his waist as he carries me to the bed.

His breath is hot against my neck as he lowers me down onto the mattress. "Lift your hips," he murmurs.

I do as I'm told, and he slides my shorts down my legs.

His mouth curls up. "Nice knickers."

I look down just in time to remember the very unsexy pair of gray cotton underwear I hastily threw on before going to Bella's room. "I was dressing with espionage in mind," I say. "Not *this*."

"And this is how you usually dress for espionage?"

"No, but I was all out of camo, and I tragically left my black latex at home."

"That's too bad," he says, hooking his thumbs in the waistband. "You always looked sexy in black."

"Everyone looks good in black," I point out.

"But not everyone is you," he says, his heated eyes catching mine. Then, with a flourish, he tugs my underwear off and stows them in the pocket of his shorts.

"A souvenir?"

"It was this or a Hawaiian T-shirt I saw in the gift shop," he says with a smirk before dipping his gaze between my legs. "Fuck," he whispers, looking utterly wrecked at the sight of me.

"You act like you've never seen me naked before," I tease.

"Yeah well . . ." His throat bounces as he swallows. "It's not exactly something I tire of."

Dark eyes trail up and over me, pausing, lingering, then starting over like he's attempting to memorize every inch of me, a different kind of souvenir. But he only lets himself savor the view a moment longer before he's right there, on top of me, chest to chest, kissing down the length of my neck, pausing only to pull my shirt up and over my head before continuing south.

I arch my back, pushing my hips upward. "Please."

"Please *what*?"

"Please take your pants off." I reach for his belt buckle, desperate for him, but he brushes my hands aside.

"Slow down," he commands.

I sit up on my elbows. "Are you purposely trying to torture me? Because it's working. What do you want? Government secrets?"

His lips quirk with amusement. "Do you know any government secrets?"

"No, but trust me, if I did, I'd give them up right now."

"As thankful as I am to know you're not the one with the nuke codes, I'm taking my time with you, Ros."

He positions himself right between my legs, his beard scratching my inner thighs as he draws slow, agonizing circles with his tongue. I squirm, thrusting my hips to meet the pressure of his mouth, now delirious with want, but he continues to make good on his promise—or threat—to take his time.

When finally—*finally*—his mouth is on me, the strokes of his tongue are slow, drawn out, and painfully restrained as he eases back and forth, in and out, keeping my orgasm within sight but just—*just*—out of reach. A skill that is as delicious as it is frustrating.

"I forgot how good this felt," I pant, gripping a fistful of sheets.

"I didn't."

I let out a string of moans interspersed with breathless pleas of *yes* and *more* until he nudges my legs far enough apart that he can slide one long finger inside me. A low, whiny sob breaks in my throat.

"I know, baby." His voice rumbles across my skin, rewriting my DNA with each breath. "You needed this, didn't you?"

All I can do is moan my response. I'm so close. Embarrassingly close. And he can tell.

"That's it," he praises. "Come hard for me." So I do, crying out low, trembling whines as my orgasm rips through me.

It's been so long since I've come from anything other than my vibrator or my hand, and it's so perfect, exactly what I needed and how I needed it. Not just the orgasm itself, but *him*. Him touching me the way only he knows how. Him, pulling me apart and putting me back together again. Him, taking control.

After the last shock waves of orgasm have subsided, I open my eyes to find Liam looking up at me from between my thighs, eyes wide and worshipful, and suddenly I can't wait another minute. I need him inside me.

"Please," I beg, and this time he obliges.

His weight settles on top of me and my hands slide under his shirt, desperate and possessive.

Mine, I think with feral instinct as I trace the lines on his chest, but the thought is quickly replaced with *no, not mine*. But *mine* for tonight. *Mine* for the next hour. *Mine* for however long this moment lasts.

It's this thought that slows me down, undoing his belt and tugging down his boxers with careful precision. If this is all I get, I don't plan on wasting it.

But my carefulness lasts only a beat before I'm pressed against the mattress, his hands curling around the nape of my neck, his mouth beckoning mine open in a maneuver he knows I used to like. Still likc.

"Is this still what you want, Ros?" He takes my bottom lip between his teeth, biting hard enough to send a sting of pleasure and pain through my body.

"Yes," I gasp, needing him so badly, literal tears prick my eyes. "Fuck me, Liam. *Please.*"

I'm so desperate, so eager, that it's not until he's right there that a realization strikes hot against my core.

I jerk back. "Wait."

Liam's body stiffens. "What's wrong?"

Something swells at the base of my throat, acutely aware that this isn't an easy topic to navigate.

The last time we talked about condoms was nine years ago. We used them until becoming exclusive, after which they hadn't seemed necessary anymore. I was on the pill, and we weren't seeing other people. But now everything is different. Now there's no longer a safety net of commitment and exclusivity between us. Liam might have said he hasn't needed the condoms in his wallet, but I don't want to make assumptions about what that does or doesn't mean.

I lick my lips, swallowing a tentative breath before I finally ask, "Should you wear a condom?"

For a string of seconds, he just blinks at me, then slowly comprehension ripples through his features. "I haven't been with anyone else." Then in a choked voice, he asks, "Have you?"

All my organs switch places.

"I haven't either."

Our eyes meet, a silent accord passing between us, but what it means, I'm not sure, only that everything in me is suddenly wound tight.

"You're still on birth control?" he asks.

I nod. It's such a clinical question. And yet here with him, it feels heavy, laden with subtext.

"I can wear one if you want," he says.

"You don't have to. Unless you want to," I add quickly.

"Not really," he says, blushing like he's embarrassed to admit what we both know, that it feels much better without.

He blinks. I swallow. Another beat of silence passes. Then finally, he's right there and I'm saying his name over and over in a string of whiny, trembling pleas.

It's better than I remember. Not just the feeling of him thrusting inside me, smooth and strong, pausing, then doing it again, but the way we move together with a kind of practiced fluency, a language we've spent years learning and mastering.

We breathe in tandem, our foreheads pressed together as he grips my hips, angling deeper, sweat dripping down his neck, his chest.

Liam might be more of the strong-and-silent type elsewhere, but in bed he coaches me through everything. *Open your legs wider for me, baby, that's it. Good girl. Can you take me deeper? Yes. Just like that. Keep making those pretty sounds for me.* But the closer he gets, the less he talks, until his movement is punctuated only by a score of muffled moans, thrusts losing all sense of consistency as our bodies crash into each other with needy, desperate force.

My own exhales come in shallow, tempered bursts, senses narrowing to the points where our bodies meet. Where our limbs are so intertwined, it's impossible to tell where I end, and he begins.

Closure, I tell myself. *You're getting closure. That's all this is.* But the mantra dulls under the weight of his body, the way my blood hums with a singular rhythm.

Him, him, him, it chants, like little electric currents firing off between us, pulling us closer, deeper.

His pace picks up, losing any semblance of tempo or structure, and it's suddenly too much. Too soon. All of it. The slick wetness coating the inside of my thighs. His scorched breath on my neck. The decadent pressure of him inside me.

There's one more strangled moan, one more collective gasp, then his eyes claim mine, blown-out pupils holding me captive as we unravel together.

- 25 -

Two years earlier

"We should paint that wall," Liam says, using the wooden spoon in his hand to gesture to the wall behind the dining table. "What do you think about green?"

I tilt my head to get a better look from behind the kitchen island.

I've never lived anywhere permanent before. I've spent most of my life in a constant state of transience, packing up and leaving as soon as a lease or one of my mom's relationships was over. But this was the first place that was really mine—*ours*. Somewhere we planned to stay forever. And I wanted Liam and I to leave as many fingerprints on it as we could.

"I like green. Or yellow," I tell him. "We can paint it next weekend," I add, adjusting the volume on the kitchen speaker system, where smooth jazz plays in the background.

"I'll be in Chicago, remember?" he says over the music.

Last night we found out that Liam's team is being awarded a prestigious research grant, and that Liam is the youngest recipient ever. I'd say I'm shocked, but I'm not. Ever since Liam's first research publication on HPV and cervical cancer captured the attention of the broader oncology community, his star has been on the rise.

He flies out to Chicago next weekend to present his research, so tonight we're celebrating at home with Liam's lasagna and a forty-dollar bottle of wine.

Glass in hand, I come up behind Liam where he's studiously mincing garlic with that damn towel over his shoulder, just like the night we met.

"Have I told you how proud of you I am," I whisper in his ear.

"Several times last night," he says, giving me a heated look that sets my insides to a simmer. "But I wouldn't hate to be reminded again."

"Oh, I intend to, Dr. Woods," I say, matching his heated look as I lift my glass. "Cheers, baby."

He leans into me, gently kissing the side of my temple before setting his cutting knife down and swapping it out for his own glass of wine.

"Since we're toasting," he says, holding up his glass. "To your rave review in *Entertainment Weekly*. '*The perfect dose of charm and heat*,'" he recites.

Blood rises in my cheeks. "It's not as big a deal as your grant," I tell him. "I mean, it's not saving lives."

Liam shakes his head. "It's a huge fucking deal, Ros. And I'm so proud of you too."

I know he means it, and I'm thankful for Liam's encouragement, but it doesn't quite quell the sting from when I'd told my family my debut novel was going to be published, and Gramps had responded with nothing more than a curt nod and a dismissive *well done*.

There's always been a part of me that hoped if I succeeded, Gramps would come around. But apparently, a published novel and rave review in a major news outlet still aren't enough to bolster his opinion of me.

But this is Liam's moment, so I push down the thought. "Thanks, babe," I tell him.

Liam responds by planting a kiss that tastes like tangy tomato sauce and red wine. When he pulls away, his eyes are shining like he's just heard a secret.

"What?" I ask, voice cracking with a laugh.

"Do you hear that?"

"Hear what—?" I ask just as he turns up the volume on the radio and Cass Elliot's crooning voice fills the kitchen, telling us to dream a little dream.

It's the song we danced to at our wedding three years ago. A night that still makes my heart swell, two sizes too big for my chest.

The ceremony was small, just my immediate family, followed by an intimate reception in Grammy and Gramps's lakefront backyard, where we'd danced under the stars, full of champagne and so much joy I thought I might burst. At the end of the night, we got drive-thru French fries and made giggly, high-off-each-other love for the first time as husband and wife in our bed at home.

There wasn't a honeymoon, since Liam had just started his fellowship at the hospital, but it didn't matter. We were in love. We had each other. There was nothing more we wanted. And tonight, three years later, I feel the same way.

"We should dance," Liam says, setting his wineglass down and taking my hand.

"What about the food?" I ask.

"It can wait," he says, his hand curving around the small of my back, drawing me closer. "I want to dance with my wife."

My wife. We've been married nearly three years, but those two little words still send a shiver of pleasure down my spine.

Unsurprisingly, Liam, in addition to being a superstar doctor and an amazing chef, is also a terrific dancer. If I wasn't in love with him, I'd probably hate him.

"God has favorites, doesn't he?" I ask, letting him spin me in a little circle.

"Hmm. Why do you say that?"

"Because you're good at everything."

He leans into me, his breath warming the tip of my nose. "That's not true."

"Oh yeah? What are you bad at?"

He frowns, considering. "Figure skating," he finally says.

I laugh. "Have you even been figure skating before?"

"No, which is why I imagine I'd be very bad at it. I also don't think I'd look good in those little outfits."

"I don't know," I say, straightening the collar on his shirt. "If anyone could rock a skintight sequined unitard, it's you."

A slow, cocky smile spreads from one side of his mouth to the other as his hands skim my waist, then lower, fingering the hem of my dress. "Speaking of outfits, I got you something."

"Me? We're supposed to be celebrating you tonight."

"One thing is for you, and the other is for both of us."

I frown as he pulls away then returns a moment later with a carrier bag in hand.

"Open it," he says excitedly.

I reach inside the bag and pull out a gorgeous leather Smythson journal. "Liam," I gasp. "It's beautiful."

He beams back at me. "So you have somewhere to put all your story ideas."

I press the journal to my chest. "I love it. Thank you."

"There's something else in there too," he says.

I dig around in the bag before pulling out something black and lacy.

I blush. Liam loves buying me lingerie, and I love receiving it. There's something deeply sexy about imagining him deliberating between silky negligées and lace sets, trying to decide which he most wants to take off me.

"It's gorgeous," I tell him.

His hands find my waist, his mouth dropping to my ear. "Why don't you go upstairs while I put the lasagna in the oven."

"Yes, Chef."

Liam gives me a light slap on the ass and tells me he wants to find me wearing nothing but his gift. "Just the knickers," he calls after me.

"They're called underwear, weirdo," I call back.

"Call them whatever you like, but I better not find you wearing anything else."

I do a little wiggle in response before disappearing down the hall.

Upstairs, I slip into Liam's gift then attempt to arrange myself on the bed, anticipation rushing through me like a fast-acting drug. But a full five minutes pass and still no Liam.

"Liam?" I call.

When he doesn't answer, I shrug on a robe and head back downstairs. "You know it's rude to keep a lady waiting—" I start to say until Liam's voice echoes into the hall.

"I don't know what you want me to do. I told you I'd send money if she wants to leave him, but there's nothing else I can do if she doesn't want to see me."

I pause in the kitchen doorway, my eyes zipping between the phone pressed against his ear and the scowl lines bracketing his mouth.

As soon as he registers my presence, his entire body jolts. "Listen, I have to go," he says into the phone. Whoever is on the other line responds because he nods and says, "Okay. Love you too," before ending the call.

"Who was that?" I ask even though I'm fairly certain I know.

He doesn't meet my eyes when he says, "Felicity."

"Did something happen?"

"She's just upset."

I hover in the doorway, unsure whether to come closer or not. "Is there anything I can do to help?" I ask after a beat.

His attention shifts toward the door, and I feel him slipping away, like he's somewhere else. Somewhere I can't reach him.

"I think I'm gonna get some air," he says, his voice totally devoid of his earlier flirty-ness.

"Do you want me to go with you?" I ask.

He shakes his head. "No. I'll be back later, okay?"

"What about dinner?"

"Lasagna is in the oven," he says. "Should be ready in an hour." And before I can protest, he's reaching for his keys, then out the door, and I'm left standing in the kitchen feeling like a tornado blew past me.

What the fuck just happened?

But I know exactly what happened. It's the same thing that always happens.

I've tried not to let it bother me, since his family stuff is clearly hard for him. But we're married. I'm his wife. If there's anyone he can open up to about this, it's supposed to be me. And now, I can't help but wonder if it's not just that the past is painful for him to talk about, but if there are parts of his life that he doesn't want to let me into. Parts of himself he doesn't trust me with.

In the romance novels my mom and I read, the love interest is always so right, so good, so *enough*, that the main character allows their walls to fall, to be raw and authentic and vulnerable just for them. I'm aware that real life doesn't always work that way, that it's not that simple, but even still, I wonder what I'm doing wrong, why I can't be that for Liam. Why I'm not enough.

It's past midnight when I hear Liam's car pull into the driveway, followed by his keys in the front door and footsteps on the stairs.

When he opens the bedroom door, he looks tired, like he hasn't slept in weeks.

"You're still up."

"Of course. You left like a bat out of hell. I was worried."

The rigid line of his mouth catches the half-light of the bedside lamp. Gone is the flirty man who just hours ago danced with me in the kitchen, instead replaced by someone with sunken eyes and deflated shoulders.

"Where did you go?" I ask.

"For a drive."

He doesn't elaborate as he undresses down to his boxers and slides into bed beside me. His hands and feet feel like ice.

"You know you can talk to me, right?" I say, trying to catch his eye.

He rakes his fingers through his hair, gaze skittering away. "I don't want to talk about it."

"But maybe it will help if—"

"I'm fine," he interrupts, rolling onto his side, facing away from me.

My pulse jumps with frustration. "You raced out of the house and were gone for hours. That hardly screams *fine* to me."

When he doesn't say anything, I swallow an exasperated sound. "I'm your wife, Liam. Why can't you talk to me?"

I watch his profile, waiting for him to explain, to offer me something, *anything,* but apparently that's all I'm going to get from him because he reaches for the light and plunges the room into darkness, leaving me with the increasingly uncomfortable thought that Liam's all too happy to dance in the kitchen and buy me lingerie. But as soon as things get too real, too messy, he shuts me out.

- 26 -

Now

My eyes blink open with a jolt.

The cream ceiling and the subtle vibrations of the floor are as unfamiliar as the stiff sheets wrapped around me. The only thing that's not immediately unfamiliar is the hard chest pressed against my back—a chest I could draw from memory.

His *naked* chest. Because we're both naked. Because we had *sex.*

Oh.

Memories of our fevered hookup return in hazy snapshots of lips and sweat and skin and thrusting. God, *so much thrusting.*

I look at Liam, still sound asleep beside me, checking for signs that whatever came over us has passed—if I've found *closure.* But the sheet's slipped off, exposing a sliver of tattoo along his shoulder blade, and my mouth waters. God, he looks good, painfully good. The kind of good that makes me ache with want all over again.

Okay, so definitely no closure.

But what did I expect?

Before the accident, sex was always easy for us. Even when Liam was closed off, even when things were hard, the bedroom was a place where our walls could come down. Where no matter what, we belonged to each other.

Maybe that's all this was. Two bodies being lulled into a familiar pattern.

But then I think about the way he looked at me, touched me. That heavy beat that passed between us when it became clear neither of us had slept with anyone else. Sure, maybe it was just lust and familiarity. But maybe it wasn't.

And now I feel increasingly foolish for thinking sex with Liam would give me any kind of closure. For thinking we could do *that* and it wouldn't ensnare me in a web of dangerous, complicated feelings. But that's precisely the problem. I *hadn't* been thinking. No, I'd been lusting, wanting, needing, *fucking*. Anything but thinking.

For months I've tried to get over him, to be okay, to move on, to protect my heart. And now? I walked straight into the line of fire, naively expecting not to get burned.

It was foolish and reckless.

And yet the one thing that's even more foolish and reckless is the part of me desperately hoping it will happen again.

The thought burns against my chest and suddenly it's too hot in here, and I can't stand to be in this bed—*naked*—with Liam a second longer.

I wrap myself in a sheet, slide out of bed, and proceed to hobble around the cabin collecting discarded apparel.

I'm thinking ahead to the zip-lining excursion this afternoon and how I'll probably have to use concealer to hide the slight beard burn between my thighs, when Liam says, "Please, for the love of God, don't put that back on."

I freeze, looking down at the crumpled shirt in my hand, then up at Liam, whose mouth is stretched into a lazy smirk, his eyes roaming across me with unfettered heat. "Why are you wearing a bedsheet?" he asks.

"Because I'm naked."

He cocks one eyebrow. "Don't you think it's a bit late for modesty, considering I was just inside you?"

Unwanted heat settles in my cheeks, and I look away, anywhere but at his bare chest. Or his bee-stung lips. Or the hickey on his neck I have no memory of leaving.

When I don't move, he says, "Why don't you drop the sheet and come back to bed."

My eyes skip from his rumpled hair to the very tempting spot beside him, and it takes everything in me to not immediately do as he says. *Reckless and rash,* I remind myself. *It can't happen again.*

"We have to go zip-lining, remember?" I say, grateful for Jonah's activities schedule.

Liam checks the time. "We still have a few minutes. And there's a lot we can do in a few minutes," he says, giving me an unscrupulous look that feels like a third-degree sunburn.

I tighten my grip on the sheet, pulling my only form of armor closer. "That was a one-time thing. For closure," I add.

The muscles in his jaw leap, the flirty twinkle dissolving from his eyes. "I thought we . . ." He pauses, scrubbing a hand over his beard. "I thought you had fun."

Of course it was fun. It was the best sex we've had in a long time. Possibly ever. But I don't want him to get the wrong idea. I don't want him to think that this changes anything between us. Or that it's going to happen again.

"Fun has nothing to do with it," I say stiffly. "It's a bad idea. It's . . ." I twirl my wrist, searching for the right words. I'm about to say *dangerous,* but I think we both remember what happened the last time I called this thing between us dangerous.

"It's *messy,*" I finish. But he doesn't look convinced.

"Ros, I don't know if you know this, but things are already messy between us."

He's going to make this hard, isn't he?

"It's a bad idea," I repeat, halfway hoping that maybe if I say it enough times, it will curb the swell of want expanding inside me.

His eyes drop to my mouth. "Why is it a bad idea?" he asks.

"Because we're getting divorced," I tell him. "And divorced people don't fuck."

"Maybe they should," he says, his gaze taking a hungry lap over my exposed skin.

I pull the sheet closer to my body. "Stop looking at me like that."

"I'm not looking at you any particular way."

"Yes, you are. You've got your horny eyes on."

"I *am* horny, Ros."

"Well, stop. Think about something else!"

"Like?"

I look around the room, searching for inspiration. "Like climate change. Or the rising cost of housing. Or—"

"*Or . . .*" His eyes cut to mine. "You could stop pretending you don't want this, too, and come back to bed."

I swallow down a groan, unsure whether I'm more irritated by his presumptuousness or the fact that he's right. I *do* want this. I want nothing more than to fall back into a pattern my body knows so well. To turn off the part of my brain that's worried about what's next or what this means and let Liam take control, the way he used to, the way I still want him to. But I also want to eat cake for breakfast and never wear real pants, so no, *want* isn't enough.

"You don't know what I want," I tell him.

Liam gives me an impertinent look. "I've been married to you for five years, Ros. I know—"

"No, you—"

"—the way your cheeks flush when you're turned on and all the little moans you make when you're coming on my tongue, and"—he goes on, his eyes trapping mine—"I know when you need me to fuck you and how you want me to do it. I know when you want me to go slow with lots of eye contact, and when you need me to bend you over and tell you how good you are for me."

Arousal joins the tornado of emotions spiraling inside me, obscuring the line between frustration and want, and I'm not sure what's worse—that he's right, or that he *knows* he's right.

"I know how to make you come whenever and however you need, Ros." His voice drops, low and hoarse. "And that's what I want to do. I want to give you everything you need, just how you need it." He shakes his head, tearing his gaze away. "But I'm not going to touch you again until you tell me you want me to. Until you ask for it."

The words hang in the air between us, a warning or maybe an invitation. Then he climbs out of bed, naked, and walks toward the bathroom, providing me with an unobstructed view of exactly what I want.

- 27 -

Now

Everybody got your helmets strapped on?" Our guide, Eduardo, asks, giving us a thumbs-up.

I check the straps on my helmet, disassociating from the fact that I'm fifty feet off the ground, hovering over the jungle somewhere outside Kona on the Big Island, until I catch sight of the looming treetops swaying underneath me. I wince and drag my gaze back up to where Eduardo is explaining the safety protocol for zip-lining.

I'm sure the words he's saying have meaning—important meaning—but I'm having trouble paying attention. And not just because we're *way* too far off the ground right now. But because Liam is standing close enough that I can't look anywhere without catching a glimpse of his toned butt in shorts that can only be described as *European length.*

If he's trying to torture me, it's working.

"Psssst," Bella hisses from behind me.

"What?" I ask, strategically avoiding eye contact. Since *the incident,* I haven't been able to look at my sister. Or Chris, for that matter.

"How come you guys weren't at yoga?" she whispers. "If I have to suffer through an hour of Jonah in short shorts, then so do you."

"We were, uh . . ." I glance at Liam, who is—Lord, help me—bending over to tie his shoe. "Busy," I tell her.

She gives me a look. "Really taking that baby making seriously, I see?"

My cheeks flush. I want to tell her off, but I should probably at least attempt to keep up this insufferable lie.

"You know how it is when you're ovulating," I tell her.

I'd say I'm going to hell for this, but given how good Liam looks in those shorts, I think I'm already there.

"Did Liam start working out?" Bella asks. "His arms are massive."

Ugh. As if I needed any reminders.

"Yeah, he got a trainer," I say, commanding myself not to look at said arms. Arms that pinned my wrists over my head and—*no, do not go there!*

"Is it the person who trains Marvel actors?" she asks. "Because daaaaaamn."

My mouth pinches into a grimace. "Can you please go back to the phase where you were too nervous to talk in front of him? I think I liked that better."

She puts her hands up in a sign of surrender. "Hey, I'm just congratulating you on having a hot husband."

Hmph. Lucky me.

"I bet he'd totally kill someone for you," she goes on. "Like if he had to, he would."

I give her a look. "What the hell are you talking about?"

"It was in this Mafia romance I read," she says with a shrug. "Her ex made her cry, so he just offed the guy. It was surprisingly hot."

"Since when do you read romance?" I ask, distinctly aware that in all the years my mom and I spent swapping mass-market paperbacks, my sister never once took any interest. She was always much more into self-help and *Gray's Anatomy* (the textbook, not the Shonda Rhimes masterpiece).

"I sort of started getting into them lately," she says slowly, her eyes shifting away like she's embarrassed.

My chest clenches with little pangs. "Really?"

She nods, still avoiding eye contact, and I can't help but wonder if maybe this has something to do with Mom. I'm about to ask when Jonah turns around, giving us both evil eyes.

"Will you two shut up?" he hisses. "I had to wake up at five a.m. two months ago to book this, so if you could be present, that'd be great."

Bella rolls her eyes, and we redirect our attention to Eduardo as he explains how to properly hold on to the harness.

"Any questions?" Eduardo asks when he's finished. "No? All right, so for this first platform we're going to need partners." He claps his gloved hands together. "Everyone, buddy up!"

Before I've so much as turned around, Liam's beside me. "Hey, *buddy*."

"We're not buddies," I snap.

"Come on, the two of us, strung up together in a harness?" His eyes shimmer deviously. "Could be fun."

I glare at him. "You're enjoying this, aren't you?"

"I was enjoying whatever happened this morning."

"Don't get used to it. That was a lapse in judgment, and you know it."

But even as I say it, I know he can see right through my flimsy defenses. And honestly, I can too. I'm a romance author. I know better than anyone that when two people agree to bang under the pretense of *getting something out of their system*, they inevitably won't. But I need to stay strong here, romance tropes be damned.

"I told you," I say stiffly. "That was one time. For closure."

"Right." He bows his head, lips barely grazing my earlobe when he whispers, "And when exactly did you find closure, Roslyn? When you were dripping all over my hand? Or when I was inside you? Fucking you like you begged me to?"

Ribbons of heat coil around my skin and I step back, turning away from him before he can see the telltale blush working its way up my neck, but his fingers wrap around my hip, pulling my body flush against his like he's a paddle and I'm the Ping-Pong ball at the end of the string.

"Careful," Liam whispers, his lips hot against my ear. "Your family is watching us. You wouldn't want them to think we're fighting, do you?"

I swallow an unsteady breath, desperately trying to block out the scents of cologne and sweat and pheromones, all of which feel like emotional assault weapons right now.

"What do you want from me?" I force out.

"The same thing you want. The only difference is I'm willing to admit it."

But perhaps that's the problem. I don't know if we want the same thing. Of course I want sex. But I want more than that. I've always wanted more than that. I want him to be vulnerable and honest and raw. I want him to trust me with his broken, messy parts and to know I can trust him with mine. I want something he's never been able to give me. And that terrifies me.

"All right, everyone have a buddy?" Eduardo asks, clapping his hands to gain our attention. "Now you and your buddy are going to be harnessed in together for this one, so don't be afraid to get cozy."

Great. Cozy is the last thing I need to be getting with Liam.

I'm still roiling as Eduardo helps us get strapped in, but as soon as we near the edge of the platform, where nothing stands between us and a fifty-foot drop to the ground, I forget all about Liam.

My vision blurs, my body growing sticky with panic as I peer over the edge, following the line of the cable across the ravine and into the abyss.

Heights didn't used to bother me, but since the accident, the same thoughts that were once nothing more than uncomfortable niggles now feel like full-blown terror. Without warning, I'm hit with flashes of memory. The green traffic light up ahead. The crash of the car, followed by ringing in my ears and muffled cries.

I shut my eyes and pull away from the edge just as Liam leans in close enough so that only I can hear and whispers, "You okay?"

"I'm fine," I lie, not meeting his eye.

"You don't look fine. You're pale." The flirty, mocking timbre is gone from his voice, instead replaced with concern. "Is it the height?"

I nod, losing my angry edge.

"Do you want to hold my hand?" he asks.

I search his face, looking for the trap, how this might be one more piece in the game he's playing with me. But his face is serious, full of concern, and so against any vague notions of pride, I take his hand. As soon as his fingers wind through mine, my breathing changes. Like despite everything, my body still knows that he's someone safe.

"How about a distraction?" Liam whispers.

Another Liam-shaped distraction is *not* what I (or my vagina) need, but the treetops start to zoom in and out of focus, so I tell him *okay*.

"Do you remember the night we got tattoos?" he asks.

I frown, unsure why he'd bring that up, of all things. "Some of it," I admit. "We were pretty drunk."

His mouth quirks. "I honestly don't know why they let us get them. We were clearly inebriated."

"I guess we're just lucky we didn't end up with the Chinese symbol for water or *live laugh love*," I say.

He lets out a low, buttery laugh, which vibrates against my rib cage. "I would have gotten *live laugh love* for you. I would have gotten any tattoo you wanted if it made you happy, Ros."

A painful lump emerges in my throat. I think about the words *Forever isn't long enough when it's with someone you love*, and how they feel like a cruel joke. Apparently forever was too long for both of us.

"Do you think you'll keep it?" I ask after a beat. "The tattoo, I mean."

His eyes move back and forth across my face, searching. "I don't have plans to get it removed if that's what you're asking."

It *is* what I'm asking. But there's something else I want to know too. Something I'm still too afraid to ask.

The question strums my internal nervous system until Eduardo asks if we're ready.

"It's okay if you don't want to do this," Liam whispers. "I can tell him no. Just say so." But I shake my head. I want to do this.

"I'm good," I whisper. "I can do it."

"You sure?" His voice is like gravity. A heavy pulse that centers me, a reminder that I'm okay. Or at least I will be.

"Just don't let go."

He squeezes my hand, reassuring fingers looped through mine like I'm something precious, something he wants to be careful with. "I promise," he whispers.

Liam gives Eduardo a thumbs-up, then I'm strapped into Liam's lap, my back pressed against his chest. Liam squeezes my hand one more time and then we're off.

My belly swoops up into my throat and I shut my eyes, bracing myself. But the steady drumbeat of Liam's voice appears in my ears.

"Open your eyes," he says, his fingers still intertwined with mine. "You have to see this."

Tentatively, I open my eyes, waiting for the precipitous lurch in my stomach, the breach of panic. Instead, the jungle comes into view and my breath is stolen for a different reason.

It's majestic.

Not just the swirl of green. The layer of mist and fog hovering like crowns around the base of hills in the distance. But the feeling of flying. Of being weightless.

For so much of the past year I've felt heavy, like I could feel the physical weight of pain and grief in my bones. But here, flying over dense jungle and ravines so deep we can't see the ground, Liam's and my shrieks vibrating against our bones, I feel something I haven't felt in a long time. I feel alive. Present. *Here.* There's no pain of the past, no agony of the future. Only here. Only now. Only weightlessness.

The whole journey lasts about thirty seconds, then, just as quickly as it starts, we're landing on the platform, blood pumping like my body is a flame, newly ignited with oxygen. But it's hard to say if that's because of the adrenaline rush, or the lingering sensation of Liam's body pressed against mine. Of his hand, still tightly wound with mine.

In that moment I feel my body and my heart and my mind warring against one another. One desperate for him, one too afraid to act, and another arguing, perhaps most rationally, that wanting him is casting myself in a role I know is destined for a painful third act.

It's a bad idea. One that will burn me in the end. But I like the heat too much to stop dancing near the flames.

Now

Liam and I don't talk again until we're back on the ship, but I can feel the shift between us. And so can he.

That's the problem with trying to hide your feelings from someone you've been with for nine years. Liam knows me better than anyone. He probably knows what I'm thinking right now. Which is probably why he's looking at me like that, with that insufferably indulgent look on his face. It almost makes me want to change my mind about what I'm about to say. Almost.

As soon as the cabin door shuts behind us, I turn to face him. "So, I've been thinking . . ."

His full attention settles on me.

"We clearly want each other, right?"

He tilts his chin, studying me. "I thought you said you didn't want to sleep together again?"

"I changed my mind," I tell him.

"About?"

Great. He's going to make this hard.

"About us fucking," I say.

A slow, knowing smile unfurls across his mouth, but I press on, trying to get the words out before I change my mind again. "What if we keep doing this?"

"You mean keep sleeping together?"

"Maybe *this*"—I wiggle my index finger between us—"could be good for us."

Liam's eyebrows scrunch together. "A few hours ago you were telling me it was messy and complicated. Is that no longer the case?"

"No, it's still messy," I say. "We're exes pretending to still be together who want to fuck. It's a dumpster fire."

"But . . . ?" he prompts.

"*But* we're both consenting adults. And if we want to fuck, then it would be a waste to not at least explore this. Right?"

He nods, conceding the point.

"Besides," I go on, "fucking is better than fighting. Right?"

Again, he nods, and I feel a little burst of confidence. Look at us being mature adults.

"But if we're going to do this," I continue, "then I think we should agree it's only until we get back to Seattle."

He frowns. "Why?"

"Because by putting a parameter around the arrangement, we can mitigate potential emotional fallout."

"Hmm. Yes. Mitigate emotional fallout," he repeats. "You know, I always loved it when you talked dirty to me, Ros."

"I'm serious," I chide him. "We're getting divorced. I think it's best if we at least come up with some kind of boundaries. Right?"

Liam shifts his weight, eyes dropping to the floor then back to mine. When our gazes meet, the flirty flare is gone from his expression. "Why do we have to put parameters around it?" he asks, his voice turning serious. "Why is us having sex something we should be afraid of?"

The question, or perhaps the genuinely curious tone with which he asks it, knocks all my carefully curated logic out of place once more.

Our bedroom once felt like a refuge. A place where I could give in and fall apart and unravel, knowing I was safe and loved. Sex wasn't just a manifestation of our passion, it was a source of stability. Somewhere Liam could be in charge and I could let go. But after the accident, intimacy became a wedge between us—both a symptom and a cause of the fractures in our marriage.

So *of course* sex is something we should be afraid of.

Which is why I know that doing this without rules, without parameters, would be like going eighty on the highway with no seat belt. And to be quite frank, I don't trust myself. Not when the lines between real and fake, between *just sex* and *more,* are already blurred. Not when he's kissed and touched every inch of my skin, but it's my heart where his fingerprints are most prominent. Where his touch still weighs heaviest.

"Because . . ." I swallow a long, tempered breath, my eyes meeting his. "I don't want to get hurt again."

I watch as Liam's expression absorbs my words. His shoulders drop with the corners of his mouth, and a furrow appears between his brows—a tiny clue that despite his big talk earlier, he's just as fragile as I am. And maybe just as scared.

"Roslyn, I know I hurt you in the past. And I don't want to hurt you again. I just . . ." He pushes a hand through his hair. "I want to be clear that I don't take what happened this morning, or anything you're willing to give me, for granted. I want you—all of you." His eyes flash, hard and determined. "But I'll respect whatever boundaries you need if it means getting to have a part of you, even if it's just for a little while," he adds.

Blood pounds in my ears. *I want you, too,* I think. *All of you.* But that's exactly the problem, because I know that whatever he can offer me won't be enough. I'll want more—more intimacy, more vulnerability, more transparency, more *him*—and he won't be able to give it to me because he's never been able to give it to me. Not nine years ago, not on our wedding day, not when I was broken with grief and heartache, and certainly not now. Which is why I need to protect myself.

"I want you, too," I admit. "I probably want more than you're willing to give me." The admission feels almost too vulnerable. Like I've just shown Liam all my cards. The ones I've been so careful to keep close to my chest.

His expression wobbles, like maybe he might argue, tell me I'm wrong. He *is* willing. But he blinks and it's like wet concrete hardening into place.

"Which is why we need parameters," I go on before I lose my resolve. "So no matter what happens between now and when this ship docks, we both understand that this comes with an end date. Okay?"

For a long moment he's silent, his gaze narrowed in contemplation. "Okay," he finally says.

My throat thickens, a knot pressing low in my trachea. I feel like we've just entered into some kind of Faustian bargain. But I want this. I want *him*.

So I pull myself up, trying to appear braver than I feel, and say it back. "Okay."

Silence follows, and for a moment I wonder if that's it, if whatever spell we've been cast under has finally broken, if maybe we have, in fact, gotten closure, but then our eyes lock and what happens next occurs in a split, almost unidentifiable, second. So fast that I'm not totally sure who makes the first move. Maybe it's him. Maybe it's me. But from one moment to the next, our fingers are interlaced, our mouths crashing into each other with a ferocity that nearly knocks me over.

In a flash, he's peeling my shirt over my head, desperate fingers scraping against the clasp on my bra. The thin lace falls away, and everything in me turns wobbly and pliable against his touch.

"Aren't you going to say it?" I gasp into his mouth.

"Say what?"

A breathy laugh tangles in the back of my throat. "*I told you so.*"

I feel the corners of his mouth tilt up against mine. "I don't need to be right," he whispers. "I just need you."

- 29 -

One year earlier

Everything hurts. I can't eat. I can't sleep. I feel like I've lost a vital organ and am now being told I'll have to figure out how to live the rest of my life without it.

Logically, I know she's gone. I know she died from internal bleeding after the accident. I know I was driving but it wasn't my fault, that we were hit by a drunk driver. And I know by the time we got to the emergency room, it was too late.

I know all of that, but it still doesn't feel real. A part of me is still halfway expecting a text about the last Tessa Dare novel she consumed. Or a phone call in which she tells me about the cute guy she flirted with last night.

But she won't.

And somewhere past the initial shock waves of hurt and grief is fear. I've lived my whole life without a dad, but I've always had my mom. She's been there through everything. She is—*was*—my best friend, my confidant, my cheerleader. The person who bought me my first Beverly Jenkins novel and stroked my hair when I found out David G. was asking Amanda P. to the spring fling, not me. She was the one who FaceTimed me with tears in her eyes after finishing my first book to tell me how proud of me she was. And now that she's gone, I don't know how to do life without her. I don't know how to live without my vital organ.

I expect myself to mourn the big things. That she'll never meet Liam's and my children. That she won't get to see Bella graduate from med school. That she'll never see Henleigh, Jackson, or Riley grow up.

Instead, I find myself focused on the smaller things. Like that I'll never hear her laugh again or drink overpriced iced coffees while we peruse stacks of romance novels in our local independent bookstore. I'll never get to call her with good news or gossip over glasses of boxed wine on the porch.

Even just the other day I logged into Netflix to see that my mom had finally started watching *Gilmore Girls* on our account, and now I have to contend with the strange (almost comforting) reality that at least she'll never get to see what a spoiled asshole Rory turns into.

It's these fractured realizations that have me doubled over with the weight of the loss. Each one emerging with fresh pain, like finding out she's gone all over again.

Liam's grieving too. But instead of fragile emotions that can so easily tip from *okay* to *not okay,* Liam's thrown himself into his work, spending nearly every night at the hospital or the research center. And when he is home, he gives me space. *Lots* of space.

He'd been on shift when the accident happened, so he was the first one to the emergency room. The first one to hold me as I sobbed uncontrollably into his chest. The one who took me home from the hospital and immediately put the kettle on—the English equivalent of therapy. But since then, he's been distant.

Perhaps naively, I thought that the death of my mom might bring us closer together. That we would lean on each other in new and deeper ways. I even wondered if maybe Liam would finally open up about his own family. If tragedy might finally be the thing that broke the ice. But in the weeks since her death, I feel even more disconnected from him, like we're cohabitating strangers rather than husband and wife.

I can't even remember the last time we had sex. Though it's hard to say if that's because he's working so much, because grief has stifled my libido, or something else—something more permanent.

It's just past midnight when Liam comes home from the research center to find me sitting in the living room with a book in my lap. Since her death I've been trying to reread her favorite authors, Lisa Kleypas and Judith McNaught, trying to find her somewhere in the pages of the stories she loved.

"I thought you'd be in bed," Liam says, his tall frame casting a long shadow across the living room floor.

"Couldn't sleep," I tell him. "How was work?"

"It was okay." Through the dim half-light of the hall, I see how tired he looks, like he's being held together by a single thread. "How was your day?"

I think about my day spent roaming from the bed to the couch then back to bed in a depressive haze. How I ate stale cereal for dinner because I didn't have the energy to cook.

"Not great," I say honestly. "It's been really hard."

A dozen emotions scatter across his face: Concern. Pain. Fatigue. Then finally resignation. "Maybe you should talk to someone," he says. "A therapist."

I blink through the darkness, taken aback by his response. Or lack thereof.

I try to remind myself that these conversations are hard for Liam, that it's not his fault, that he's grieving too. That he's probably right. I *should* talk to someone. But I wish it were he who would talk with me. I wish it were he who could sit with me in this pain, not a stranger paid for by insurance.

"What about you?" I ask. "Can you talk with me?"

The muscles around his jaw tighten as he scratches the back of his neck. "I don't think I'm good at talking about that kind of stuff."

"Can you try?" I ask, my voice dipping into a plea.

He swallows, his eyes jumping away then finally back to me. "It's really late," he says. "I just got off a twenty-four-hour shift at the hospital and I'm not really in the headspace for that kind of conversation."

My chest sinks. I want to be sympathetic and understanding of the fact that he likely spent all day working with patients who don't have long to live, and he probably doesn't want to talk about death right now. That he's exhausted and this has nothing to do with me. But I can't help the swell of disappointment rising in my throat, because it's not just tonight that he's not in the right headspace. It's that he's *never* in the right headspace. And now I wish I hadn't asked.

When I don't respond, he turns and heads upstairs, leaving me in a silence so deafening, I can hear its echo in the increasing space between us.

- 30 -

Now

Larsen Family Vacation Day 4

PORT OF CALL: *Kona, the Big Island*

ITINERARY: *snorkeling excursion at 12*

ATTIRE: *swimsuits, clothing optional*

The day after zip-lining, Liam and I tell the rest of the family that we're too seasick to go on the snorkeling excursion, but as soon as they've disembarked the ship, we spend the day getting reacquainted.

We reacquaint ourselves in bed. Against the wall. On the floor. In front of the mirror. We even reacquaint ourselves in the tiny shower that's definitely not made for two people.

We fuck and fuck and fuck. Then, when we're sore and bruised and out of breath, we fuck some more.

I'm not sure whether it's the prolonged celibacy, or the forbidden allure of fucking an ex, but it's like we're addicted to each other. One touch, one taste, one whiff is enough to send us both spiraling into a lust-induced craze.

Sometimes it's frantic and rushed, like we're competing in a timed activity. But other times it's slowed down, every movement like pulling taffy as we take our time exploring, lingering, pausing, then losing track and starting all over.

But just because we've swapped out fighting for fucking, and hostile silences for muffled moans, doesn't mean we've let our guards down. There's still a lingering undercurrent of tension running between us. I can feel it in the way he holds me. In the way we catch each other's gaze a beat too long before looking away.

It's a muted awareness that we're currently in no-man's-land. A borderless, undefined wilderness that neither of us knows how to navigate. That the time between us is fragile and in a couple of days this whole thing will be over. I'll go back to my cold, empty house and Liam will move to London.

I just need to be careful, I warn myself. *I can't get attached or want more than this.* And yet, a part of me already knows it's too late. Wanting more is a tune I never forgot, steps to a dance my heart still remembers.

Sometime after midnight, I untangle myself from Liam's naked body to pee, but not before he grabs my wrist and pulls me back onto the bed.

"Don't go," he murmurs against my neck.

"I need to pee," I whine. "You don't want me to get a UTI, do you?"

Joke's on me. After the last twenty-four hours, nothing short of divine intervention would prevent me from getting a UTI.

Liam's mouth twists upward, his grip loosening around my wrist. "Be quick," he says, giving me a heated look. "I'm not done with you yet."

I laugh. "Aren't you tired?"

"Never felt better." His hands drop to my hips, fingers tracing the hickeys he left there earlier. "Besides, I think we've got some lost time to make up for."

I survey the sheets, now tangled into ropes, evidence of the messes we've been making, both in bed and of each other. "You know, we don't have to make up for a year of celibacy all in one day, right?"

"Is that a challenge?" he asks, lifting one eyebrow. "Because if so, I accept."

"Careful, Liam," I say, parroting the tone he used the other night. "You don't want me to think you're flirting with me."

His eyes flash. "I am flirting with you, Ros."

Sparks that have nothing to do with our exertions flare against my ribs all the way to the bathroom.

Once the door shuts behind me, I look in the mirror, surveying the flush in my cheeks and the wild curls framing my face.

Gone are the bags under my eyes and the gray pallor in my skin. For the first time in months, I look and feel healthy. Or maybe that's just because I'm getting laid.

After I pee, I check my phone to see that I have a few new messages from Abby.

ABBY: Helloooooo?

ABBY: Are you dead? Is Liam dead??

ABBY: Do you need an alibi???

I type back: **No casualties yet.**

ABBY: So how are things going?????

I think about telling Abby that Liam and I are hooking up, but I can already hear the chorus of *I told you so*s all the way from New Jersey. She'll tell me that of course we couldn't keep our hands off each other. That clearly this means we're getting back together. That we're fated mates or whatever. But this isn't one of her smutty books. And the only happy ending we'll get is the one where we both climax, so I type back: **Liam and I are actually getting along.** Which isn't a total lie.

Abby responds instantly. **Getting along??? Like getting back together????**

I'm about to type back **No** when I hear Liam's muffled voice on the other side of the door.

"What happened?" he asks, followed by, "Are you sure?"

I put down my phone and shift toward the door. I probably shouldn't eavesdrop on his private conversation, but then again, the cabin is a whopping total of one hundred and fifty square feet, so it's not like I have a choice.

Liam responds to whoever he's speaking to with a few *hmm-mms* and *okays* before finally ending the call with a not-so-cheery *Ring me if anything changes.*

I count to ten before I open the bathroom door, so he doesn't suspect I was listening, but as soon as I do, I see how pale he is.

"What's wrong?" I ask.

His eyes drop to his lap. "Nothing."

A familiar churn of anxiety rolls inside me.

I know that *nothing*. It's the same *nothing* I've heard for years every time his family comes up.

Liam stands up, his gaze focused on the door as he reaches for his discarded boxers. "I'm, uh, going to get some air."

Maybe it's the illusion of honesty still hanging over us, or the fact that we're both naked, but I feel brave enough to say, "Wait."

But as tense eyes meet mine, I realize that I don't know what to say next. I know better than to press him on it. I'm also aware that he was never open with me about his family while we were married, so why would he be now when we're getting divorced? But the past few days have felt like a crack in the door between us, one I can't help but try to push open a bit further.

"I understand if you don't want to talk about it." I pause, searching for the words I'm not sure how to say. "But I just want you to know that if you do, I'm here to listen."

He looks away, and I brace myself for this to be the end of the conversation, the way it usually is. But after a long beat, he turns back to face me. "It's my mum," he says, his voice low like the words have been pulled from somewhere deep. "She's been in an accident."

I jerk up, my body jumping to attention. "What kind of accident? Is she hurt?" The words all come out in a breathless rush of syllables as my mind scatters from one worst-case scenario to the next.

He sits back down on the bed. "My sister says it's a broken leg. That she fell down the stairs. Other than that, she's okay. I guess it could have been worse, but still."

I search his face, trying to piece together what he's still not saying, but he looks away and my chest lurches.

"Is that . . . ?" I pause, trying to find the best way to word this. "Do you think that's really what happened?"

He scrubs a hand down the side of his face. "That's the thing. I don't know what happened because I'm not fucking there."

His eyes flash with something heavy, and I don't know what to say. Only that an ache starts to build behind my ribs and my head rushes, like I've stood up too fast.

I sit beside him on the bed. "Is there anything we can do to help?" I ask.

Part of me knows it's a silly question. Of course there's nothing we can do. That's the entire point of why he's upset in the first place. But I feel the need to let him know I'm here for him, that I want to help, even if I can't.

"No," he says, pushing out a long exhale. "Which is exactly how my dad wants it. He likes keeping me out of it and making me feel powerless." Then, in a lower, almost cracked voice, he adds, "It's part of why I want to take this job in London. So I can be closer. Just in case."

It's that last sentence that sends shivers down my spine. He doesn't say just in case of *what,* but I can guess.

Maybe it's the wrong thing to do. Maybe I'm misunderstanding this uncharacteristic display of vulnerability. But I take his hand and give it a squeeze, hoping the small gesture can fill in the gaps for the words I don't have.

He looks down at our knuckles clamped together, his eyes widening, and I immediately draw back my hand.

"Sorry," I say quickly. "I know we're just—"

"No. It's okay," he says, taking back my hand. "And thank you," he adds.

There's a sincerity behind his gaze, an earnestness that brings a new kind of ache to my chest. He's here. He's present. He isn't trying to push me away.

"Thank you," I say after a beat. "For telling me."

The muscles around his mouth tighten. "You were right, what you said in the jungle. I should have been more open with you."

A lump emerges in my throat that I can't quite swallow down.

When he first confessed to going to therapy, it brought up a lot of complicated feelings of anger and resentment. Why hadn't he gotten help when we were together? When our marriage was falling apart? When I needed him? Why had he waited until we were broken up? But now, as I search the deep lines of his face—ones I wish I could reach out and smooth away—I wonder if the only thing Liam getting help proves is that the breakup was just as cataclysmic for him as it was for me.

For a long moment we stay like that, our fingers knotted together, currents of electricity passing between us like flesh and blood semiconductors until finally I ask, "What do you need?"

His brows pull together. "What do you mean?"

"I mean, I know this is a horrible situation and there isn't a lot either of us can do, but what do you need right now to make this suck less? And how can I help?"

He blows out a breath. "Do you want to go for a swim?"

My brows furrow with confusion. "A swim?"

"You know? The act of moving one's body under the water so as to not drown?" He mimes the act, his cheeks puffed, his arms stretching out in front of him.

I give his arm a playful whack. "Okay, smart-ass. You want to go now?" I ask, still confused.

"Why not? We've been cooped up in bed all day."

"I wouldn't exactly call what we've been doing being *cooped up*. Would you?"

He looks me up and down and my skin burns everywhere his gaze lingers. "No, I wouldn't. But I'm sure we could afford to get some fresh air."

"It's the middle of the night."

"We're on a giant cruise ship with four swimming pools."

A nervous laugh bubbles in the back of my throat. "They're all closed."

Liam's fingers tangle loosely with mine, his thumb mindlessly drawing shapes on the inside of my wrist. "So?"

"So? We'll get in trouble!"

"Only if we get caught."

The pool deck is eerily empty, a far contrast from the hordes of swimmers and screaming children who occupy it during the day.

A breeze floats through our hair, and goose bumps rise across my skin. Though I'm not sure if that's from the chill or nerves. Or the fact that Liam hasn't dropped my hand since leaving the room.

Moonlight spills all around us, drenching the pool water in a ghostly glow. I look around, searching for some kind of security or patrol, someone to stop us from doing this, but we're all alone.

"What if we have to walk the plank?" I whisper as Liam holds the gate open.

"Come on," he says. "It'll be fun. I promise."

I promise. Two dangerous words I should never listen to. Especially from him. And yet, *Hello, masochism, my old friend,* because as soon as Liam lifts the hem of his T-shirt, revealing his tanned, toned stomach, every cautionary thought instantly vaporizes.

I, too, pull my T-shirt over my head and shimmy out of my jean shorts, leaving me in my white bikini, which somehow makes me feel more exposed than when we were in bed, actually naked.

"Ready?" he asks, holding out his hand to me.

I take it, lacing my fingers with his.

"One . . . two . . ." But we don't make it to three because in a flash Liam lets go of my hand and flattens his palm against my back, sending me into the pool with a splash.

I come up, gasping and sputtering. "Ohmygod! Did you just—"

But he doesn't let me finish before he dives in—*show-off.* A second later Liam's head bobs beside me, his eyes glowing in the underwater lights.

I don't give him a second to catch his breath before I hurl back a retaliatory splash.

Shock reverberates across his face, but the look only lasts a beat before he's lunging toward me.

I try to swim away, but he's too fast, and banded muscles fold around my waist, drawing me back to him. Even underwater my skin burns at his touch.

"*Stoppppp!*" I whine, my voice crackling with laughter.

He laughs, too, deep and throaty, his hips rocking against mine as he pushes me below the waterline. But this time I get my footing and push off the bottom, bouncing toward the surface. I have one second to suck in a breath before I'm throwing all my weight at his chest, pushing him underwater.

I think I've been triumphant, until he pops back up, his fingertips digging into my thighs as he hoists me over his shoulder caveman-style.

"Put me down!" I laugh, pounding my fists against the solid wall of back muscle as he tosses me back-first into the pool, where I land with a loud smack. Water crowds my nostrils, and when I come back up, I'm gasping and coughing.

"You're an ass!"

"Name-calling? Really, Ros?"

His grip tightens around my waist, pulling my body flush against his. I struggle to break away from him, but my resolve loses out against the press of his body, until we're chest to chest. Until I can feel the rhythmic *tap, tap, tap* of his heart pounding against mine, a sound that's as familiar to me as my own pulse.

We've stopped moving now. We're just floating, caught in the ebb and flow of the gentle lap of water, our chests rising and falling together.

In the still, my gaze travels over his wet, moonlight-soaked skin, all the way up to his eyes. Eyes that are already on me, bursting with heat and hunger and something soft.

He's so beautiful like this. *Shiny,* I think.

"What?" he asks.

"Nothing," I say, looking away.

"Nothing, huh?" he whispers, his thumb tracing my jawline. The touch is light, barely more than a brush of skin, but it sends a rush of awareness to the spot right behind my navel.

The barest hint of a smile curls across his mouth, and I don't know what I hate more: The effect he still has on me. Or the fact that he knows it.

His thumb moves upward, arching across my cheek before finally landing on a stray piece of hair, which he gently tucks behind my ear.

"Do you remember when we house-sat for Grammy and Gramps?" he asks.

Heat floods my sternum. Liam had just started his new job at the hospital when Grammy and Gramps asked us to stay over while they were out of town. We made a blanket fort in the living room and shared a joint under the stars, before eventually ending up in the pool at 3 a.m., naked.

"Of course I remember," I tell him. "How could I forget the neighbors almost catching us having sex in the pool."

Liam laughs, his eyes flaring. "Maybe we should do a reenactment," he murmurs. "For old times' sake."

The words flare across my chest, lighting up like a sign over a freeway overpass. **Warning,** it reads. **Do not marinate in a cocktail**

of nostalgia and past memories with your ex. Not when you don't have a future.

I pull back an inch. "I don't know what people do in England," I tell him. "But if you think breaking and entering isn't a big deal, wait until I tell you about public indecency."

"It's only public indecency if we get caught."

"Is that like the tree in the woods? The one that only makes a sound if someone is there to hear it?"

Liam pulls me closer, his hands sliding down to cup my ass. "Should we find out?"

Light reflects off the water, bouncing across his eyes in a way that makes him appear to be glowing from within.

We shouldn't.

It's a bad idea.

But I'm tipsy off the gleam in Liam's eyes. The way he's playing with the ties on my bikini.

So I drag my knuckles down the side of his face, tracing the outline of his beard, and whisper, "Kiss me," against the hollow of his throat.

There's no hesitation as his mouth catches mine, amplifying from want to need to something more intense, something nearly indecent.

Mingled gasps rise into the night air as his hot tongue circles mine, melting me one vertebra at a time. His mouth is an ocean I want to drown in, waves I want to be swept away by. And just when I think I might liquefy right then and there, Liam picks me up, hooking my legs around his hips, and props me against the wall of the pool.

His name slips out of me, a string of needy pleas as his hands travel between my legs, his mouth still hard and fast against mine.

I'm so lost in the hard press of him rocking against me, I barely hear the creak of the gate followed by a patter of footsteps. It's not until I see the long beam of a flashlight across the deck that I realize someone is there.

"Hello?" calls out a deep voice.

We both freeze, our panicked eyes meeting through the darkness.

Shit.

"What do we do?" I whisper, but Liam holds one finger to his lips, and motions for me to follow his lead.

In one fluid motion he hoists himself out of the pool and holds his hand out to me. I have no idea what he's up to, but it's not like I have a lot of choices right now, so I take his hand and allow myself to be hauled out.

Together, we dart across the deck, our wet feet slapping on the concrete.

"Hey!" calls the voice just as Liam drags me behind the wall of the lifeguard hut, narrowly avoiding the flashlight's glare.

"Liam, what—"

"Shhhh." With one hand, Liam covers my mouth while his other pulls my body flush against his right as the flashlight's beam hovers over the ground, mere feet away. I know the primary concern *should* be getting caught, but suddenly I'm a lot more distracted by the taste of chlorine and salt on Liam's fingers, and the steady push and pull of his breath on my cheek.

"I know you're there," the voice calls. "Come out."

The flashlight darts back and forth feet from where we're standing. Fortunately, our little splash fight soaked the concrete, obscuring any footprints, which should buy us a few more minutes.

I knew this was a bad idea.

"This is your last chance before I call the captain!"

I look to Liam, wondering if maybe we ought to just give ourselves up, but he shakes his head, and a handful of seconds later, the sounds of the person's footsteps fade in the opposite direction.

We stay slotted together, flat against the wall for two, three more beats until Liam whispers, "I think they're gone."

"Are you sure?"

Liam's grip on my waist tightens as he peers past me, his eyes narrowed through the darkness. "I don't see the torch anymore. But maybe we should wait until we're sure."

When it's obvious that whoever was there is now gone and we're in the clear, we collect our clothes and run the whole way back to our cabin.

As soon as the door shuts behind us, we both burst into wild, full-on, can't breathe, wheezing laughter.

"I can't. Believe. That. Just. Happened," I gasp.

"You should see your face right now."

"If I look horrified, it's because I am. I thought we were going to have to spend the night in the brig!"

I bend over, trying to regain control of my breathing, but then I look at Liam, and I burst into another round of deranged laughter, which makes Liam laugh even harder.

His eyes catch mine, mouth open mid-laugh, and my chest aches with a kind of homesickness. *God, I missed this.* Making him laugh. Having fun together. It feels like finding a favorite sweater I thought I'd lost and realizing it still fits perfectly.

Maybe it's that, or a desire to hold on to this moment—to hold on to *him*—but I reach out, tracing the line of his jaw with my thumb.

Our eyes meet. "Thank you," he whispers.

"For what?"

"For the distraction."

We're close. Close enough that I can count the water droplets still clinging to the hollow of his throat. He swallows. I inhale. My world narrows to the shrinking space between us.

"Did it work?" I ask.

He doesn't answer; instead he catches my wrist, pulling me against his chest.

Time bends, everything slowing down. Everything except my racing heart.

Maybe it's because I want to finish what we started in the pool, or because I sense he still needs to be distracted, but I step back, letting my gaze linger on his before I drop to my knees in front of him.

"Ros—" A sharp gasp escapes him. "You don't have to."

"I know," I tell him, pushing his swim trunks down and taking him long and hard in my hand. "I want to."

And I mean it. I want to hear all the sounds he makes. The sharp inhales. The guttural moans. I want to feel him shake as he comes in my mouth. Mostly, I want to make him forget all the things he can't control, if even for a moment.

As my mouth curls around him, taking him inch by inch, he rocks into me, slowly at first, like he's trying to be careful.

"Can you take more?" he asks, voice thin and frayed like he's already on edge.

I nod and he thrusts deeper, rougher, his grip tightening in my hair until I'm no longer controlling the depth or speed—he is.

"That's it, baby," he whispers as he moves his hand to the back of my neck, holding me in place. "You always took me so well."

This is supposed to be for him, but somehow it feels like it's for me too. Like he knows that I need this just as much as he does.

He tilts my chin, his other hand twisting in my hair. His thighs clench, breath coming out in short, trembling bursts. I can feel how close he is. I can see it too.

Part of me wants to turn away, close my eyes, anything to avoid the friction of his gaze, the way he's watching me as I take him—how reverent he looks—but another part of me wants to see it. The flush in his neck, the pink in his lips. How undone he looks right now.

He's not shiny anymore, I think. He's something else, something real. Something that makes my heart want to break free of the barricade I've built around it.

"Fuck," he gasps, his eyes closing. "I'm going to come." Then he does, and we both moan as he spills hot and fast on my tongue.

When the last echoes of his orgasm have faded, his eyes find mine, tender and wide, as he brings his thumb to my lips, gently wiping across them. "I like you like this," he whispers.

"On my knees?" I tease.

He shakes his head. "No, *messy.*"

A shiver runs down my spine and I don't know what I like more, the certainty with which he says it, or the way he's looking at me, a perfect kaleidoscope of need and desire across his face. Like he doesn't just *like* my mess, he wants it. *Needs it.*

The thought unravels me as he helps me to my feet, cups my jaw, and kisses me.

It's not the frantic, rushed kind of kissing we've been doing. The kind that's eager to turn into more. This kiss is slow, searching, like he's taking his time with me. Exploring, lingering, memorizing. Like he's desperate to stretch out the limited timeline as far as he can.

There's a part of me that wants to cling to this moment, to the swells of *more* gathering between us, to tell him that sex isn't enough for me, that I want more. I've *always* wanted more. But another part of me is terrified to want that, to ask for something I can't have.

I think about what Liam said the other day. *I want you. All of you.* But that's exactly the problem. He didn't want all of me. Not when it mattered. He hadn't wanted my grief or the sharpest edges of my pain. And I have no reason to believe that he does now.

So when he presses me into the mattress, his mouth claiming mine, I try to lose myself in the moment. In the familiar shapes of his body. In this liminal space where I don't need to think about London or divorce papers or what happens next. Where I don't have to think at all.

- 31 -

Now

Larsen Family Vacation Day 5

PORT OF CALL: Kauai

ITINERARY: *shuffleboard on top deck*

It's midafternoon the next day when Liam and I join my family on the top deck for a far-too-competitive game of shuffleboard.

Liam claims he's never played before, but either he's an expert hustler, or he really is good at everything.

"Of course you're good at shuffleboard," I say, brushing a windswept curl from my eyes as Liam adds another three points to his already overwhelming lead.

"You say that like it's a bad thing," Liam says, not taking his eye off the puck as he lines up his next shot with mathematical precision.

"I'm just glad you've put all your energy into curing cancer," I tell him. "Otherwise, you'd probably be in a jungle leading a cult somewhere."

He nods sagely. "True. It was either oncology or cult leadership. Bit of a toss-up really."

I snort out a laugh, watching as he earns a whopping seven points, solidifying his already massive lead over Jonah.

Liam shoots me a look as he pretends to blow smoke from the tip of his cue like it's a smoking gun and I full-on giggle.

Oh God.

I have a crush, I think. *I have a crush on my husband.*

"Is there anything he's bad at?" Jonah asks, eyes narrowed with frustration. I haven't seen him look this pissed since he found out the florist got the wrong shade of peonies at his and Ben's wedding.

I scrunch up my face in thought. "I've heard figure skating isn't his strong suit. Oh, and one time he put too much garlic in his lasagna."

Jonah's face drops, looking genuinely disappointed. "God. That's it?"

Liam takes his next shot, but this time he misses.

"Don't tell me you did that on purpose for Jonah's fragile ego?" I whisper.

Liam's eyes sparkle, catching a column of sunlight. "You know I like winning too much for that."

"So you have no excuse?"

"Actually, I do. I was distracted."

"By?"

He looks me up and down with unguarded want.

"Me?" I press a palm to my chest in mock shock. "Whatever did I do?"

"You had the audacity of having *those* legs in *those* shorts." Then he leans in close enough that only I can hear him say, "If I wasn't about to crush your brother in this game, I'd already have taken you back to the room and had you show me how good you are at handling *my* shuffleboard stick."

I smirk. "It's called a shuffleboard cue, but nice try. I guess you can't really be good at everything."

"I'm good at the important things."

"Like?"

His index finger slips inside my belt loop, pulling me close. "You know which things," he whispers, giving me a lingering look before turning his attention back to the game.

Don't get sucked into his Liam Spell, I remind myself. After all, this is temporary. A vacation fling. One that will eventually wash away like the sand between my toes, and I need to be able to let it go when the time comes.

But that's the problem. I went into this thinking that I could sleep with Liam and control the outcome. That I could control my feelings. But I can't. And maybe there's a part of him that can't either.

I think about last night. The warm, searching press of his mouth as he'd opened me up, unbuttoning me with his lips, then his tongue, then later his hands. How good it had felt. And how badly I wish it hadn't.

I wish the kiss hadn't been so tender.

If it had been desperate and rushed—like how we've been fucking—I could chalk the whole thing up to lust. To two people with a sexual history being lulled into a familiar pattern. Something to do with pheromones and mutual dry spells and *closure.*

But that's not what it was.

The kiss had been consuming. Utterly romantic. The kind of kiss that undoubtedly meant something. The kind of kiss that will hurt me in the end.

* * *

My ovaries are doing inconvenient little flip-flops as Liam shows Henleigh how to use her cue to aim when my phone rings from inside my pocket. I pull it out and see Abby is calling.

This time it's my stomach that flips. Shit. I forgot to text her back.

I excuse myself to the other side of the deck, far enough away that I can't be overheard, and answer the call.

"Hey," I say, leaning against the railing, slightly breathless.

"Finally!" comes Abby's familiar voice. "I was worried you fell overboard. Or maybe you and Liam fed each other to the sharks."

"Nope," I say with forced levity. "No shark casualties yet."

There's a brief pause.

"What's wrong?" she asks. "You sound freaked out."

Damn. She's good.

"I'm not," I lie.

"Roslyn, where are you? Is he there? Find a way to use the word pizza casually so I know you're alright."

I bite back a laugh at the use of our old code word, briefly wondering if I can get away with lying to her, just to keep the secret a little while longer, at least until I can figure out my own feelings, but Abby knows me too well to fall for that.

"I'm fine," I tell her. "Actually . . ." I grip the railing like I'm afraid I might fall overboard, then say in my most *please do not freak out* voice, "I'm sleeping with Liam."

Silence follows. An uncomfortably long silence.

"You're *what*?" she finally cries.

"We're having sex," I say, the irony not lost on me that we had a very similar conversation nine years ago.

"Is this what you meant when you said *we're getting along*?

Because I'm getting along with my accountant, but it doesn't mean we're fucking."

"We *have* been getting along," I insist.

"Clearly," she says with a laugh. "How did this happen?"

"I don't know, we just like started kissing? I guess?" I think back on the day we'd snuck into Bella's cabin, but suddenly the details are hazy. A collection of blurry moments all frayed around the edges. "It was only supposed to happen once, for closure," I add.

"And did you get closure?" she asks.

I look over my shoulder at Liam, now carrying one of the twins on his shoulders, the breeze lifting the ends of his hair. My heart flutters in my throat.

"Not exactly," I say.

She hums affirmatively. "To be honest, I'm surprised it took you so long."

"You are?"

"I mean I knew you would eventually get back together. There's no way you two were just over each other," she says. "But I expected this call days ago."

The view of turquoise ocean in front of me is suddenly indistinguishable from the blue sky on the horizon and I have to lean against the railing to stay upright.

"We're not back together," I say, shaking my head as though physically trying to dislodge the words.

"So you're still figuring things out?" she asks, and I hate the hopeful lilt in her voice, the one clearly itching for me to tell her that everything is going to be okay.

"There's nothing to figure out," I say stiffly. "We're just having sex."

"Right," she says, and I can hear the hollow note of disbelief in her voice.

"We are," I insist. "I need to get laid."

"And the only available person was your soon-to-be-ex-husband?"

"I mean, yeah. Sort of."

She sighs. "Honey, if you need to get off, I'm happy for you, but is that really what this is about? Getting laid?"

I try to reach for one of the excuses I've been storing up. *It's just until the ship docks. We're getting closure. It's just sex.* But the words sound as hollow as they are weak.

When I don't answer, she gently asks, "Do you still have feelings for him?"

My limbs tighten, skin feeling hot and prickly in the midday sun.

That's the problem, I think. I thought if I just made enough rules, built enough boundaries, I could protect myself from my feelings, from getting hurt. That it won't crush me when this comes to its inevitable conclusion.

But I know, now more than ever, that's not true.

And yet I feel trapped. Stuck between wanting more—wanting *him*—and knowing that good sex and a few meaningful conversations aren't enough. They don't fix our problems or guarantee that things will be any better in the future. Or even if there will be a future.

It's not like Liam's asked to get back together, or begged for a second chance.

Which is probably for the best.

I think about all the second chances my mom gave. How she let the same men who broke her heart back in over and over again, claiming they'd changed, that love was nothing without second chances and forgiveness. But they never did change. Sure, maybe they bought roses the day after a fight, or showed up in the middle of the night with tearful promises to be better, but then a week or two later they were always back to repeating the same behavior, leaving my mom more brokenhearted than the first time.

I've always blamed and resented the men she dated for the

instability in our lives. For breaking her heart, for being the reason we were always moving and never had any money. But now, as I think back on all the nights I spent holding my mom while she cried over men who didn't care that she would have burned down the world for them, I wonder if maybe it was just as much my mom's fault as it was theirs. If maybe she broke her own heart by repeatedly trusting men who never deserved her trust. Who never changed. Who never did better.

I watched it happen time and time again. And I won't make the same mistake.

"What does it matter if I still have feelings for him?" I say with renewed stiffness. "It's too late for us."

"But why?" Abby asks, a beat of desperation coursing through her voice. "Why does it have to be too late? I mean it's not like you've told anyone or filed. There's nothing stopping you from—"

"Abs," I interrupt, a hard edge to my voice. "It's over. This isn't a romance novel. There isn't going to be a grovel or a grand gesture. My life isn't like yours. Our marriage fell apart, and we didn't save it. That's that. So just stop, okay?"

As soon as I hear the words, I know I'm being unfair. Abby's been nothing but a supportive friend to me and she doesn't deserve to be on the receiving end of my frustration.

"I'm sorry. That wasn't fair of me," I say, tone softening. "But I need you to know that it's over. He hurt me and I hurt him and a few days of hot vacation sex doesn't change that."

A heavy beat passes, and I worry I've upset her. Finally, she says, "Okay. I trust you. I just . . ." She pauses and I can hear the hesitancy in her voice. "I don't want you to get hurt."

"Me either," I say, almost mournfully.

But it's too late. I'm already hurt. And I'm only going to get hurt again.

- 32 -

Now

Larsen Family Vacation Day 6

PORT OF CALL: *Wailea, Maui*

ITINERARY: *beach day*

ATTIRE: *swimsuits*

The golden stretch of beach nestled between crashing surf and lush hillside on Maui's western coast is the perfect place to be buried alive.

"More sand!" the twins yell as they dump another bucket over my splayed-out limbs.

I'll probably be scraping grains out of my ass for at least three weeks, but it's worth it for the delighted shrieks of my niece and nephews as they perform my burial.

Liam scoops the pail into a wet stretch of sand and hands it to Riley. "Here, don't forget to cover her toes," he suggests.

"Don't encourage them," I say through broken laughter. "I'm going to be in the shower until Tuesday scrubbing all this off."

His eyes flare playfully before he lowers his voice so only I can hear. "Don't worry," he whispers. "I'll join you."

"You take showers together?" Jackson asks, his little brow scrunched with confusion.

My face burns. So much for trying to be discreet.

But Liam, as usual, doesn't miss a beat. "Sometimes Auntie Roslyn needs help scrubbing all that sand off," he says matter-of-factly.

I can see Jackson's little brain trying to work out the logistics of this before he says, "I don't need help in the shower. I'm big enough to do it myself," and goes back to digging in the sand, unperturbed.

Liam's eyes catch mine, and I do my best to suppress a laugh just as Jonah appears. "Please don't tell me you're corrupting my children?" he says.

"You mean you don't want us telling them about nipple rings and ball gags?" I ask. "You really should have said something sooner, Jonah."

Jackson's face scrunches in thought. "What's a ball gag, Daddy?"

Jonah scowls at us. "Not funny."

"That's because you have no sense of humor," Bella says, appearing by his side in an orange bikini with a water bottle I'm almost certain doesn't have water in it.

"Trust me," he says with a heavy sigh. "You have to have a sense of humor when you have three kids under seven."

"Don't be such a downer all the time," Bella says, giving him a jab in the ribs. "You're gonna scare Roslyn and Liam off. And I, for one, don't want to be deprived of Liam's adorable offspring because you're a grouch."

"Liam's offspring?" I ask. "Don't you mean *our* offspring?"

"Have you seen Liam?" she jokes. "You better *hope* they take after him."

"Bella!" I reprimand her, wishing my arms weren't buried by my side.

"What?" She shrugs. "We're all thinking it."

"No, we aren't," Jonah and Ben say in unison.

Liam chuckles, his cheeks red. "Actually, as much as I appreciate your faith in my genes, I'm hoping our kids get Ros's eyes," he says, fixing his gaze on mine. "They look just like Maggie's."

Heat ripples down the length of my spine, all the way to my sandy toes.

This is all pretend, I remind myself. He's playing along with the charade. *Just like we agreed.* But the way he's looking at me makes me feel like a damned liar.

Bella rolls her eyes. "Just stop it already. What do you two want? A tiara and a sash for being the cutest couple ever? You're making the rest of us look bad."

"Excuse me," Jonah says, wrapping his arm around his husband. "How come Ben and I aren't in the running?"

"When either of you looks at each other the way Liam looks at Roslyn, then you can be in the running," Bella says, fixing them both with pointed looks.

Something hot and sticky blossoms in my gut. I look to Liam to see how he's responding to this, but Jonah kicks up sand in Bella's direction and she squeals, darting out of the way just as a clump lands right in my face.

"Hey, watch it!" I cry. "That almost went in my eyes!"

She laughs. "That's just payback for the one time at the park when you told me the sand in the sandbox tasted like Cinnamon Toast Crunch."

"Well, that's your fault for believing me," I say.

"I was five!"

As she pours more sand on top of my stomach and the twins shriek with glee, Jonah stands to the side, a divot forming between his brows.

"The park off Roosevelt?" he asks. "With the tunnel slide?"

Bella's expression twists with effort, like she's trying to extract a long-buried memory. "I think so?"

"I drive by there all the time," Jonah says, the levity now gone from his voice. "It's next to the kids' school. But I never let them play there."

"Why not?" I ask.

A shadow crosses his face. "Bad memories, I guess."

I frown, trying to figure out what he's talking about. "What do you mean?"

His brows knit together. "You don't remember?"

I shake my head, confused.

He digs his foot in the sand, his eyes downcast, before he says, "That's the park where Mom left us to go meet up with some guy and I thought we were going to have to sleep in the tunnel slide." He winces like it's something he'd rather not think about.

A strange new weight presses against my chest that doesn't have anything to do with the sand. "Mom would never leave us anywhere," I say.

Jonah gives me a look. "She used to do it all the time. Take us to the park, tell us she had to run an errand, then go meet up with her boyfriend. One time it got so late, I had to ask some lady to borrow her cell phone so I could call Grammy to come pick us up. You don't remember?" he asks again.

The tightness in my chest expands, turning sharper, more like an ache. Sure, she had lots of boyfriends, but she would never leave us alone for hours at a public park. Right?

"You're exaggerating," I say. "I'm sure she was just grocery shopping or something. Right?" I look to Bella, hoping she'll back me up, but she just shrugs.

"I was too little to remember," she says. "But it sounds like something Mom would do."

She and Jonah share knowing looks, and I have the feeling this is something they've discussed before.

The usual pangs of feeling left out are there, but this time they're joined by frustration. How can they talk about her like this?

"Mom wouldn't do that," I say again, this time more determined.

Jonah's gaze sweeps over me before hitting me with a hard look. "She would, but you only remember what you want to remember about Mom."

Suddenly the sand atop my chest might as well be cinder blocks. I try to sit up, but the sand is too thick, too heavy. Panic presses against my sternum, blocking my airflow, and I struggle to break free, to catch a breath.

Almost instantly, Liam kneels beside me. "You all right?" he asks.

"Just get me out of here," I gasp.

He shovels the sand off and pulls me to my feet.

His eyes strain with worry, but he doesn't ask questions, or say anything at all; he just takes my hand and leads me to the shore.

All around us, children play in the sand and teenagers bob in the waves, but I don't see any of them. All I feel are Liam's hands on my thighs. The cool water hitting my skin as he washes the sand off me. The unrelenting tightness in my chest.

After a beat, Liam finally asks, "Are you okay?"

I twist my mom's bracelet around my wrist, reaching for the words to tell him I'm fine, the way I'm used to doing, but they don't come. Instead, Jonah's words dance in my mind. *You only remember what you want to remember about Mom.*

He was wrong. Right? But suddenly, I'm no longer sure.

"Do you think she was a bad mom?" I ask.

Liam swallows. "Maggie was a wonderful person; you know I think that."

"But was she a bad mom?" I ask again.

His brows draw together, his outstretched hand hovering over my sandy knee. "Do *you* think she was a bad mum?" he asks.

"I don't know. I mean, yeah she had a lot of boyfriends, and we moved a lot, but I always felt like she was just doing her best with the shitty hand she was dealt." I pause, collecting my breath, a breath that now feels heavy in my lungs. "But now I'm not sure."

"What do you mean?" he asks, using cupped palms to wash away the sand from my back and neck.

I look out at the ocean, hesitating before I say, "I always felt it was her shitty boyfriends' fault that we didn't have money or that we had to move or that she was always getting her heart broken. But maybe it wasn't always them." My eyes drop to my lap. "Maybe she just made bad choices."

As soon as I say it, I want to swallow the words back. To shove them deep down inside myself, where no one can hear them, not even me.

"I'm sorry," I say. "I shouldn't have said that. I shouldn't talk about her like that."

Liam pauses, his hands outstretched over the tide rushing across the sand. "Just because she's gone doesn't mean your feelings aren't valid," he says. "Grief brings up all kinds of memories."

"I know, I just . . ." But my voice tapers off, lost to the increasing tightness in my chest, like there's a crank inside me, winding my feelings tighter and tighter.

As much as I want to defend Mom's memory, to insist she was

the wonderful woman I remember her as, I know Jonah has a point. That tangled up in good memories of playing dress-up in Mom's closet and gossiping over iced coffees are memories of moving from apartment to apartment after she lost yet another job or broke up with yet another boyfriend. Memories of never having any money because she was always writing checks for her boyfriend's latest start-up or maxing out credit cards she couldn't repay. Memories I wish I could silo off in my mind where I don't have to think about them. Where I can pretend they don't exist. Where I've *been* pretending they don't exist.

"But what if my brother's right?" I ask, dragging my focus back to Liam. "What if I've only been remembering her the way I want to remember her? Because it's easier?"

Liam looks at me with tender eyes as glassy and transparent as the ocean in front of us. "Of course it's easier that way," he says, looping reassuring fingers through mine. "Grief is hard, and not all the emotions are easy to digest, so we find ways to make the pain at least a little more tolerable."

My heart clenches like a fist.

He's looking at me like he gets it, like he understands what I've been through, and a hot burst of anger pulses in my throat. Because he doesn't get it. He doesn't understand what it was like to suffocate under mountains of grief, to feel weighed down with a kind of unbearable heaviness that wouldn't go away. Maybe if he did, he would have been there for me when I needed him. Maybe our marriage wouldn't have fallen apart.

The thought cuts through me, sharp and painful, a reopened wound. I look away.

"Let's not talk about this anymore," I say.

His spine stiffens in response. "What do you need?"

A time machine, I think.

"I don't know . . . maybe . . ." But I let the words trail off. "How about a distraction?" I say instead.

His eyes skip past me to the shoreline. "We could go for a swim? Or a walk on the beach?"

I bite my lip, giving him a heated look. "How about a different kind of distraction?"

His expression shifts; understanding stretches across his features. "You want me to fuck you? Here?"

Static heat curls down the length of my spine. "Please?" I stick my bottom lip out. "I don't want to think. I just want to forget about what happened."

It's true. I want a distraction. Something to lose myself in like I did last night. But it's more than that. It's that I can feel myself needing him. Wanting things from him that I know I can't have. Which is why I need to reestablish what this is. That it's about sex. *Just sex*. The way I told Abby it was.

"There's a public restroom over there," I tell him, pointing to the bathroom facility on the other side of the beach. "We haven't had bathroom sex in a while. Or I bet those palm trees are—"

Liam puts up a hand. "Ros, stop."

"What? Do you think the palm trees would be too painful?"

"No. It's not about the palm trees." He scrapes a sandy hand through his beard. "I know you're upset right now, and I don't want to just gloss over it with sex."

"But I thought that's what we agreed to?" I say. "Just sex."

He winces, but when he speaks his voice is gentle. "Ros. I'm not going to fuck you when you're upset."

Part of me wants to demand that he do it anyway, that he take me to the bathroom and bend me over the dirty sink and make me come so hard that the lines between hurt and pleasure start to blur, that I forget what Jonah said, that I forget *everything*. But it feels a bit like grasping at the fraying edges of an unraveling stitch: much too late.

He pushes out a heavy breath, his eyes shifting to the sand then back to me. "I know I wasn't good at talking about . . ." His mouth tenses, and he gestures between us. "*Stuff*. But I'm here if you want to talk about your mum, if it would help," he adds, voice softening.

Blood roars in my ears. The sand in my toes suddenly feels like lead.

"It's too late," I whisper. "If you wanted to talk, the time was months ago, when I needed you. Not now, Liam."

His eyes take a determined shape. "You're right. I fucked up," he says. "But I want to try. If you'll let me."

I want to hold on to my anger. To tell him it's too late for that. It's *been* too late. That it's not fair of him to do this to me, not now, not when the end is so close. But as I search the hollowness of his eyes, the deep lines bracketing his mouth, the collision of shame and regret and determination colliding across his face, I lose my edge.

I think about how he was vulnerable with me the other night, how honest and transparent he was, and I wonder if maybe it's only fair to give us one last chance to have this conversation. Not just for him, but for me, because I deserve to talk about my mom with someone who is willing to listen.

I fix my gaze on the rise and fall of the tide as it runs up and over my feet.

"I miss her every day," I tell him, my voice so small it barely comes out.

"What do you miss about her?"

I don't have to think about my answer. "How resilient she was. Even when life hadn't been great to her, when people talked about her behind her back, when she got pregnant and the men never stuck around, she always kept her head high. She kept believing in love. She never stopped seeing the best in people." Tears spike my eyes, but I press on. "And her laugh. God, I miss her laugh. I wish I had a recording of it."

"She had a great laugh," Liam agrees. "I think that's the thing I first remember about her."

"It wasn't her weird jewelry?"

"That too," he says, eyes catching the light bouncing off the water. "I remember the first time I met her at your family's Christmas. She was wearing a pendant with a naked woman on it."

I reach for her bracelet like it might anchor me to her.

"It's funny," I tell him. "I used to be embarrassed by the clothes and the jewelry. But now I'd give anything to hear the jangle of her bracelets, announcing her presence from a mile away. She never cared what anyone thought of her."

A lump catches in my throat as I think about the time she yelled at another mom in the school parking lot when she found out they wouldn't let Jonah come over because he was gay. And the time she made my homecoming dress by hand even though no one asked me to go because she wanted me to have *something that sparkles*.

She was a passionate woman, someone who loved fully and deeply. Who lit up every room she entered. But she was also rash and impulsive, and often very selfish. And I hate that her death is forcing me to grapple with the duality of a woman who was both my best friend and my hero, but also painfully flawed.

"I wish I could only remember the good parts," I say, trying to swallow down the ache in my throat. "But I can't untangle those memories from the not-so-great ones. All the times she chose boyfriends over us. All the times we moved because of some new guy. All the times she broke promises."

Liam leans toward me, taking my hand in his. A part of me wants to fight it, to not need his comfort, to not need *him*. But as his fingers tangle with mine, gripping just a little too tightly, I wonder if maybe he needs this too. If maybe he needs me as much as I wish I didn't need him.

"You think you get older, and this stuff won't matter anymore," I tell him. "But I guess you never forget the time your mom disappeared from your tenth birthday party and came back two hours later smelling like rubbing alcohol. Or all the times we had cereal for dinner because she was giving half her paycheck to the guy she was dating." I shake my head, biting back the painful slew of memories now coursing through me like a dam's broken loose. "I know she loved us and was trying her hardest, but . . ." My voice cracks with an unexpected sob as a tear breaks free.

Liam lifts his hand to brush it away. "Hey," he says, his voice so soft it hurts. "It's okay."

And I know he doesn't mean it's okay that she's dead, or even that it will be okay, but that it's okay for me to cry, to fall apart.

So I do.

I lean into his damp chest, where he's warm and solid and sturdy, and I cry. I cry until my throat is sore and my eyes are raw. I cry until I'm no longer sure what I'm even crying for.

Maybe it's for my mom. Or Liam and me. Or maybe it's the rapidly approaching deadline between us. That in four days we'll fly back to Seattle, and this will be over. No more midnight swims. No more flirting. No more sex. No more *this*.

I try to tell myself it's okay, this is for the best.

It has to end like this. I always knew that.

But it doesn't stop the sting of loss. Or the ache in my bones. It doesn't stop the unbearable crush of want clawing at the walls of my heart.

- 33 -

Ten months earlier

Liam's keys jangle in the door, followed by footsteps on the hardwood. A moment later he appears in the kitchen, his hair damp from the rain, plastic bags of Chinese takeout in hand. The room fills with the scent of fried noodles and egg rolls.

"Hi, baby. I got takeaway for dinner," he says, his voice a little breathless as he leans in to peck me on the cheek. He smells of disinfectant and latex gloves—the way he always does when he gets home from the hospital.

Lately, he hasn't been getting home until after midnight, which means we've barely seen each other, nothing more than passing *hello*s and *goodbye*s and the creak of our mattress when he slides into bed after 2 a.m. But he's got the first evening off in weeks, so we're planning to eat takeout and watch a movie for a much-needed date night. The first since my mom passed.

"How was work?" I ask, taking the bags and setting the Styrofoam boxes on the counter.

He rubs his eyes—red and bleary with fatigue. "Fine. Long. We're finally starting to make some progress on our model."

I don't really know much about his research—most of it is way over my head—but I know the model has something to do with new radiation technology and that, if all goes well, it could save lots of lives.

"That's great," I tell him.

He tries to smile, but it's strained, weary. The way he looks most nights.

"I'm glad you're home tonight. I feel like I've hardly seen you," I say, reaching for a bottle of white wine I picked up. "I was thinking we could pop this open and pick a movie while we eat?"

"Actually . . ." Liam rubs the back of his neck. "Kevin's having some people over and I thought it would be fun to go."

I pause, my hands freezing over the stack of napkins. "Tonight?"

Liam nods and my throat tightens.

"I thought we were going to hang out just us?" I ask.

"What if we pop by for just one drink?"

"I don't know," I say, putting out the napkins. "I was looking forward to staying in."

"But it's been ages since we've seen any friends or gone out, and I thought it might be good for us to get out of the house." His eyes fill with a kind of heat I haven't seen in a while. "Remember the last party?"

Blood rises in my cheeks. Last year at Kevin's birthday, Liam and I spontaneously had sex in the bathroom with most of our clothes still on. But that version of myself feels nearly unrecognizable. I don't feel sexy or spontaneous or fun. And this just feels like a reminder of all the ways I'm no longer myself.

"My mom just died," I say tightly. "I don't really feel like going to a party tonight."

"Maybe if we just went out for a bit—"

Disappointment bleeds into frustration.

"You're not listening," I interrupt. "I said I want to stay in tonight. Okay?"

He swallows. "I know, but—"

"No, you *don't* know," I snap, my anger feeling like an overboiled pot. "You don't know because you haven't been around, Liam."

His shoulders drop with his mouth. "I've been busy with work; you know that."

I try to force down my feelings. He's right. He's been busy saving lives, and it feels silly and petulant to demand his attention. To need him. But I can't help the rising swell of disappointment, the feeling of watching him drift further and further away while I'm powerless to stop it.

"But you're working more than normal and you're never home," I say after a pause. "Sometimes it feels like . . ." A choke steals my breath, and a sudden, unexpected rush of hot, stinging tears pricks the backs of my eyes.

It's been like this since the accident. All my emotions feel so fragile, one strong gust tipping the scales from *okay* into very much *not okay* real fast. Every disappointment, every inconvenience, every broken promise feels like an unbearable pain I'll never recover from.

But this feels like more than just an inconvenience. This feels like we're speeding toward an inevitable tipping point. One we've been moving closer to for weeks.

Liam and I have gone through rough patches before. The first two years of Liam's residency. The months leading up to board exams when he would study ten hours a day. Times when we hardly saw each other and tensions ran high. But living in the aftermath of my mom's death is different. It's not a test or a training program. There's no deadline or an end date. It's just endless days of hurt so potent, it feels like my stomach is corroding, and I've started to worry that this distance between Liam and me, like the grief, isn't just temporary.

"Like what?" he asks, his eyes flashing to mine.

I look down at the kitchen floor, away from him. "Like you're avoiding me," I say at last.

Liam's frame stiffens. "I'm not," he says, sounding almost hurt. "Which is why I thought going to a party would be good for us. We could have some fun, blow off some steam, like we used to," he adds hopefully.

Used to. It's those two words that hit me the hardest. The admission that he misses the way things used to be. Before grief chewed me up and spit me out. And now he doesn't like this new version of me. The broken version.

It's a fear that's long lived in the back of my mind. That I was never enough for someone like Liam, someone so shiny. It just took grief and the total collapse of my life for him to see it, to see that I'm not the fun, sexy girl he took home from the bar nine years ago, that there's a part of me that's messy and broken and utterly disappointing. That's simply not enough.

"Sorry, I'm not much fun right now. Like I used to be," I add, an edge to my voice.

Liam rakes a hand through his hair, eyes slanting away. "Come on, Ros. I'm not saying that. I just thought that maybe—" But he doesn't finish. Instead, he rubs his temples and says, "Okay. We can stay in tonight."

But he doesn't say it like he wants to. He says it like he's trying to avoid a fight by appeasing the angry troll under the bridge. Which makes the whole thing worse.

"You should just go without me," I say coolly. "I'm sure you'll have much more fun with your friends."

The line of Liam's mouth hardens. "That's not . . ." But his words trail off, swallowed by a tight-lipped grimace. "Fine. If that's what you want."

It's not what I want. What I want is to tell him to stay. That I need him. That I want him to cuddle with me on the couch and tell me he's there. He's got me. That he's not going anywhere. But I can't bring myself to beg for his attention right now. Not when he seems so unwilling to give it.

"Fine," I say. "Have a good time."

Liam gives me one last look before reaching for his keys and disappearing out the door, letting it shut with a tight thud, which echoes in my chest long after he's gone.

- 34 -

Now

Larsen Family Vacation Day 7

PORT OF CALL: *Wailea, Maui*

ITINERARY: *ocean kayaking at 12, followed by luau in evening*

ATTIRE: *swimsuits, resort casual*

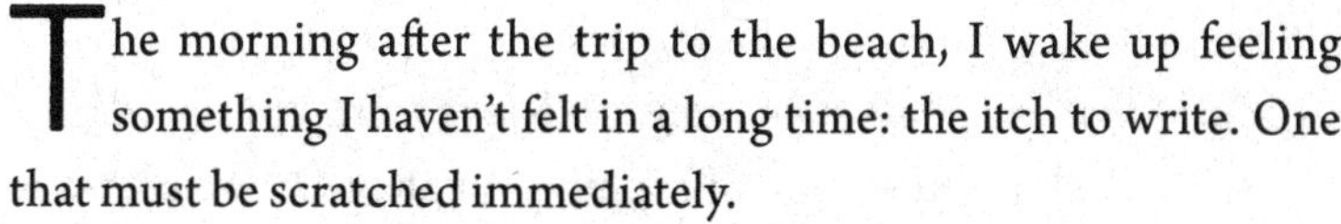

The morning after the trip to the beach, I wake up feeling something I haven't felt in a long time: the itch to write. One that must be scratched immediately.

I untangle myself from Liam, who is still fast asleep beside me, grab my laptop, and settle at the edge of the bed, ready to word-vomit all over the page.

I don't know where exactly the idea comes from, or at what point it enters my consciousness. But from one moment to the next, it's just *there*. And once it is, everything changes.

I wonder if it's been there all along, hiding in the back of my mind, waiting to be found. Or if it just fell into my lap, almost out of thin air. Or perhaps yesterday's conversation with Liam unclogged the jammed drain of my brain. But either way, my fingers glide across the keyboard with a kind of fevered urgency I haven't felt in months.

I can't say for sure who I'm writing for. Maybe it's for my mom, for the stories she loved so much, for the hope they gave her. Or for Liam and me, for the happily ever after we didn't get. Or maybe it's just for me, to prove I can still do this. That I still have stories inside me. That even after death and tragedy and pain, there can still be joy and love and hope.

I write furiously for the next two hours, letting the story pour out of me until I can feel a headache coming on from too much screen time, so I shut the laptop and hop into the shower.

As the hot water pours over my head and shoulders, I think about my character, a young widow grieving her late husband while trying to remain open to the possibility of finding love again, and I can't help but feel a rush of affection for her. For her story. For the inconvenient chemistry building between her and the curmudgeonly love interest with a secret soft, molten center. For the hopefulness that continues to burn bright inside her despite everything bad that's happened.

Maybe that's what my mom clung to all those years, I think. Maybe it wasn't a Hollywood version of happily ever after. Or foolish optimism. Maybe it was hope. Hope that in spite of a cold, callous world full of heartache and disappointment, she could continue to believe in things like true love and happy endings. Maybe she was right. Maybe the bravest thing we can be is hopeful.

When I get out of the shower, we are already running late for today's kayaking excursion, so Liam and I both scramble to get dressed and out of the cabin without exchanging more than a few words.

It's not until later when we are out on the water, hugging the shoreline, several strokes behind the rest of the family, that Liam asks what I was doing up so early this morning.

"Don't tell me you actually got up for sunrise yoga with Jonah?" he teases me, paddling his kayak close enough to mine that we keep playing bumper boats.

I drag my gaze from the jagged hulk of black volcanic rock jetting out from shore. "Actually, I was writing," I admit.

His eyes widen, catching the glare of the light feathering across the water's surface. "Really?"

I bite my bottom lip and nod, twin pangs of pride and excitement coursing through me. "I woke up and it was like my brain just knew what it wanted to write."

His mouth kicks into a smile. "I knew you'd do it. What changed?"

I think about our talk at the beach, how it was the first real conversation I've had about my mom since her death, the first time I'd felt like my grief was seen. Like *I* was seen.

"I think it really helped talking about my mom yesterday," I say, pulling my paddle in and out of the water. "I feel like it released something inside me, something that had been stuck since she died." I lick my lips, tasting salt and sweat before I quietly add, "And since you left."

His shoulders drop a notch, a kind of reckoning passing behind his eyes. After a beat, he says, "I'm proud of you."

Something warm balloons in my chest. "Thank you," I tell him. "I'm proud too."

But there's something else I want to know. Something that's been tugging at the back of my mind.

"How come you never supported my writing?" It comes out in a rush, like if I don't say it fast, I'll swallow the words back down.

He squints against the sun's rays. "What do you mean? I've always supported you. I have a tattoo to prove it," he adds, pointing to his shoulder.

The words aren't exactly accusatory, but there's a stiffness behind them that tells me I've struck some kind of nerve.

I wonder if I should drop it. After all, things have been good between us, and I don't want to ruin that. But the question continues to pull at my chest, and I realize I need to know. I need to know why he's willing to tell me he's proud of me, but he can't do it in front of my family.

"I know. And I appreciate that." I hesitate, mulling over my next words. "But when it came to my family, you never spoke up. You never defended me. You always just sat by while they questioned my work and acted like it was this big mistake. And I guess over time I started to believe you agreed with them."

Liam sets his paddle across the mouth of his kayak and runs a hand through his sandy hair. He looks frustrated, but it's hard to tell if that's with me or himself.

"I've always believed in your work," he says after a moment. "I didn't realize you *wanted* me to say something."

"Of course I did," I say, a little exasperated. "You're my husband."

His jaw stiffens, tight and square, his eyes pinned ahead, and I wonder if it was a mistake bringing this up, if our relationship is too fragile for this kind of reckoning. If maybe we shouldn't have *any* kind of reckoning. Not when the end of this arrangement is so near.

"I'm sorry," he says after a beat. "You're right. I should have stood up for you."

My mouth turns dry. I hadn't actually expected an apology from him, but now that I have one, I'm not sure what to do with it.

"Why didn't you?" I ask.

He swallows, his gaze shifting to the shoreline, then back to me. "I suppose I didn't want to upset your grandparents. They've done so much for me, and I was worried what they would think of me if I argued with them."

A part of me feels vindicated. A part that wants to say, *I told you so* or even *I knew it! You love being their favorite more than you loved me!* But even as the accusation hovers on my lips, I can see from the look on his face that this would be neither helpful nor true. Liam seems genuinely apologetic.

"It's okay," I say, the words a reflex. "It's water under the bridge now, I guess."

His brows draw together. "No, it's not. And I want you to know that I'm *so fucking proud* of you, Ros. No matter what happens between us, I'm always going to support you." His voice is hardened, determined, like he isn't just making a promise to me, he's making one to himself. "And for the record, your family were assholes to you at dinner the first night."

I look ahead to where Grammy and Gramps are pointing out something underwater to the twins while they shriek with delight. "I thought you loved them," I say.

"I do." He hesitates, tilting his chin to catch the sun's rays. "But sometimes the people you love act like assholes."

The way he's looking at me—sharp and intense—makes me wonder if there's another meaning there.

"Well, thanks," I say after a pause. "That actually means a lot."

"That I called your family assholes?" he asks.

I laugh. "That you're validating my feelings."

"I'm really sorry for not defending you before," he says again. "I should have done better. I *will* do better," he adds.

As much as I want to tell myself it's an empty promise, one that comes with the same expiration date this arrangement does, I know it's not. It's a genuine apology, one said with weight and purpose, like he wants me to know he means it.

It's still too late, I tell myself. But the reminder fades against the warmth of his eyes and the ache in my chest.

We paddle ahead in a silence broken only by the gentle lap of waves against the plastic kayak and the wispy breath of the ocean's breeze in our ears, until we reach a reef made of black volcanic rock and Bella announces she's going to do a backflip.

Jonah, Grammy, and Gramps all tell her not to, that she doesn't know how deep it is, but to the delighted cheers of Henleigh, Jackson, and Riley, she swims to shore, and climbs the reef.

"You better not get yourself killed and give my children lifelong trauma that will cost me thousands in therapy bills," Jonah warns from his kayak.

Bella pretends to scratch her head, giving him the middle finger, before turning and flipping into the water with a splash.

When she reemerges grinning, Liam turns to me. "Want to jump in?" he asks, his eyes catching the light of the sun reflecting off the water.

"You know I can't do a backflip," I tell him. "Well, I can, but we'll spend the night in the ER. It's up to you."

He laughs. "Last I checked, Jonah's itinerary doesn't leave room for any ER visits, so how about a regular jump? Feetfirst?"

We carefully climb out of our kayaks, then swim to the rocks, which are much rougher and sharper than they appear from the water.

When we're standing on top, warm from the day's sun, Liam holds out his hand to me.

"Ready?" he asks.

I look back over my shoulder at the beach dotted with beach blankets and palm trees swaying in the afternoon breeze, then ahead to the ocean stretching toward the horizon like an infinite expanse of Cool Blue Gatorade. I know I just saw Bella leap in. But I'm still afraid. Afraid of jumping into the unknown. What if I land on a rock? Or smack my head? What if one careless moment lands me in excruciating pain, or worse?

But then I glance up at Liam, the sweep of his mouth, the warm press of his eyes, the way he looks both boyish and manly, a nexus of the young man I first met nine years ago and the sturdy one he's grown into, the one I've been through so much with, and I can't help but feel a little braver knowing that he's by my side. That I'm not alone.

"Yes," I tell him. "I'm ready."

Then I grasp his hand, and we take the plunge together.

- 35 -

Now

After the kayaking excursion, we head to a traditional "cowboy luau," where we listen to ukulele music and eat our body weight in kālua pork, huli-huli chicken, fresh tuna poke, and Spam musubi under the shade of hundred-year-old palm trees.

I try to focus on the performers on the stage, on the gasps of glee and delight from my niece and nephews as the dancers swing fire around their heads and move their hips in inconceivable ways, but my thoughts stay stuck on Liam. Or more precisely his hand on my thigh under the table. The heat of his skin burns through the smooth material of my dress, and for a brief moment it's easy to imagine there was no fight. No breakup. No earth-shattering heartache. That this is how it's always been and will always be with us.

It's not, I tell myself. But at least through dessert, I'll allow myself to pretend.

I'm picking at my purple ube pie when Grammy turns to me. "So, Roslyn, will you and Liam find out the gender? Or are you planning to be surprised?"

I nearly choke on my pie. "Grammy, I'm not even pregnant. We haven't talked about it."

"You should," she says, her eyes catching the glow of a nearby tiki torch. "Babies require a lot of planning. You'll need to start thinking about the nursery. And a registry."

"We have lots of time to think about that," I tell her.

"And once you're no longer writing, you'll have even more time to plan."

Now I really do choke. "What?" I ask.

"You'll have to pick out a color for the nursery and—"

"No, not the nursery," I interrupt. "What you said about my writing. I'm not giving that up. It's really important to me."

Her brows draw together with confusion. "But, dear, you can't do both. Babies are a lot of work. Besides, it's not like you need the extra income," she adds, glancing at Liam.

"Your grandmother is right," Gramps says, turning in his seat to face me. "It'll be best to put the writing on hold for a while."

Indignation burns in my chest at their presumptuousness. Would they be saying this if I were a doctor? Suggesting I quit my practice to stay home with a baby? But it's not worth the upset, so I go back to my pie, expecting that to be the end of it until I feel Liam's grip on my thigh tighten.

"Roslyn's writing career *is* very important, to both of us," Liam says. "And when the time comes, we'll figure out a way for Roslyn to do whatever she wants." He pauses, his eyes finding mine before he says, "Whether she decides to continue working or not, I support her no matter what."

"Yes, but—" Gramps starts to say, but Liam cuts him off.

"Thank you for your input, Gramps," he says tightly. "But this is a decision Roslyn and I will be making on our own."

A hush falls over the table. Eyes bulge. Brows raise. If I didn't know any better, I would have thought a ghost had just floated by. I wait for Gramps to give Liam one of his signature disappointed grimaces, the way he usually does when someone dares to disagree with him. Instead, he just looks surprised. And honestly, same.

After a beat of awkward silence, Liam turns to me. "Want to go for a walk?" he whispers.

My gaze drifts upward, where the clouds have started to congeal, forming one long stretch of darkness on the horizon. It's probably going to rain soon. But I don't want to be at this table anymore, and judging by the look on his face, neither does Liam, so I stand up and take his hand.

Together, we excuse ourselves, then wander down a narrow sandy path to the public beach. It's mostly deserted save for a few lone photographers trying to capture what's left of the sunset, now obscured by the clouds shifting across the horizon, where a storm seems to be gathering.

When we reach the sand, we both bend down to remove our shoes.

"Thank you," I tell him. "That was . . ." I struggle for the words. *Amazing? Overdue? Hot?* "I appreciate it," I say instead.

His hand flexes by his side as though unsure what to do with it. "I told you I was going to do better."

I study the hard lines of his face, trying to determine what he means.

If it's another apology. Or a promise.

Or maybe this is a goodbye of sorts. One final calm before the storm—figuratively and literally.

I look from the whitecaps rushing the shoreline to the long stretch of sand disappearing into a jagged formation of black volcanic rocks in the distance.

If it is goodbye, this isn't a bad place to do it.

"Thank you," I say after a beat.

He turns to me, his eyes pinning mine. "You already said that."

"I know . . . I just . . ." I stop, digging my toes into the sand. "I mean for earlier and yesterday. For talking with me about my mom, for being so present, for . . ." But my voice cracks and I look away. It feels like we've come to a kind of bridge. One I'm not sure how to cross.

I didn't want to have this conversation. I didn't want to ask why he wasn't there for me after my mom died. Why my grief was too much. Why *I* was too much. I told myself it was better to keep things simple, easy, so that when the vacation ends, it wouldn't be so painful to let go.

But now, after the last few days, after everything we've said and still haven't said, I know that's not true. Nothing about this is simple, and I realize I need to know. Maybe it will bring me closure, or maybe it won't, but I need to hear it. He at least owes me that.

"Liam," I say, trying to manage the shake in my voice, "I know we agreed that we would only do this until the ship docks, so maybe it doesn't matter . . ." He steps toward me, his gaze weighing me down, the scent of sweet cologne heavy in the air, and I have to force the next words out. "Why couldn't you talk to me about the hard stuff when we were together? Why couldn't you talk with me about my mom until this week?"

I watch as the question reverberates across his face.

"I—" He scrapes a hand through his windswept hair. "I didn't know how."

"It felt like you never even tried. Why not?"

His eyes drop to the sand then back to me. "It might be too late to tell you this . . ."

Maybe it *is* too late. Or maybe I'm just terrified to hear why he was never open with me, why he couldn't sit with me in my pain. Why I hadn't been enough to make him stay, to fight for us. But I need to know, even if it will hurt.

"It's not," I say over the crash of the surf in the distance. "It's not too late."

His gaze roams past me, out to sea. When he finally speaks, his voice comes out rough, like the words are stripped from somewhere deep inside.

"My family used to go to Cornwall in the summers. We'd stay at this little cottage by the seaside where we'd watch the surf for hours."

He gestures to the long stretch of sand separating us from the endless line of ocean.

"I remember I used to love going there. My father would read on the deck, and my mum made this amazing Sunday roast with all the fixings. It was the only place where my parents seemed genuinely happy. Like maybe they weren't just pretending." His voice breaks and he looks away. "I'm sorry," he says. "I've been in fucking therapy for months, and this is still really hard for me to talk about."

The raw emotion in his voice hits me with a force that nearly knocks me over, and I realize I'm scared. Not just to finally hear the truth, but because I know that any piece of himself he offers won't be something I'll be able to keep. That when the vacation ends, so will this thing between us. But then I think about how he stood up for me. How he's gone to therapy and opened up about his mom. How he's been brave with me. And I think maybe I can be brave too. So I take his hand, letting him know I'm here and I'm listening.

"Don't apologize," I tell him. "I'm here, okay?"

He swallows twice.

"On the outside, my family looked perfect. Perfect house. Perfect kids. Perfect marriage. But behind closed doors, my father was controlling and cruel. Problems weren't dealt with in the open—instead, everything was brushed aside, ignored, like it had never happened. I learned to hide my emotions, to pack them away. If my father couldn't see how I felt, then he couldn't use it against me the way he did my mum."

His expression darkens, and it's like watching a solar eclipse pass over his face, features turning sharp and shadowy.

"I was eight years old the first time I saw my father with another woman. He knew I'd seen him, so he pulled me aside and said it was going to be our secret. The first of many.

"One night when I was about fifteen, I heard my parents fighting through the walls. I don't know what it was about, but the next day my dad left, and I remember feeling this overwhelming sense of relief. Like, finally, he was gone, and we would be okay. But my mum wasn't okay. She stopped eating, stopped taking care of herself. It felt like a part of her was just gone, and I didn't know what to do. I tried to be there for her, to show her we were going to be okay without him. That we didn't need my dad. But everything I did only pushed her further away." He flinches like the memory still torments him. "I felt helpless."

I hear the ache in his voice, the pain of childhood wounds that are still raw and bloody, and I want to wrap my arms around him, bury my face in his chest. I want to take his pain and pour it into the cracks of my own skin, anything to make him hurt a little less.

"Eventually, my father came back and Mum pretended like it never happened, and I was expected to do the same," he says. "So I did. Mostly because I was afraid that things would get bad again.

"For a while things were good. My mum got pregnant with Felicity, and I thought maybe another baby would finally make my father happy. Maybe we'd be okay. But shortly after she was born my father started up another affair." He hesitates, jaw clenching. "One night I heard a crash and came into the kitchen to find broken glass all over the floor and my mum kneeling, her shaking hands covered in blood. I knew my father had been the one to throw it and she was cleaning up the mess the way she always did, the way she was expected to, and something in me just sort of snapped. I couldn't keep pretending."

There's a pang in my chest, hurt and indignation clashing together inside me. "What happened?"

"I told my dad that if he ever touched her again, I'd kill him. I was seventeen and hotheaded, but I was so angry, I thought maybe I really could." His mouth pulls down, like the memory still haunts him.

"After he kicked me out, I expected my mum and sister to leave with me. I figured we'd go and start somewhere new, together. That it would be a relief to my mum that someone had finally stood up to him." He hesitates, swallowing a long, shaky breath before he says, "But she didn't want to."

I frown, trying to gather his meaning. "But why?"

"She told me I'd made a mistake in confronting him, that I should have kept it to myself. That I'd made everything worse. She told me I should have pretended I hadn't seen anything. That it was *better* that way."

He rubs his face, eyes dark and ashy. "I know it's hard to leave an abusive relationship. It's something I've talked about with my therapist. And eventually, someday if I can, I'd like to reconcile with my mum, but it's still difficult to get past the fact that she chose to stay and pretend everything was fine over her kids."

My stomach—no, everything—sinks, like the sand is dragging me down. It's not just the confession; it's the carved-out meaning behind it. The way everything slides into place like dominos falling in perfect order.

I think back to all the times Liam didn't stand up to my family about my writing because he was afraid to rock the boat, all the times he walked out and shut down when hard topics came up. But this time I see it all through a new lens. A lens in which Liam was afraid to confront conflict because the last time he had, his whole world fell apart and he'd been blamed for it. Because he'd spent his whole life being told to brush things under the rug, *to pretend.*

Suddenly the word *pretend*—the very thing we've been doing this whole time—takes on a new, sour meaning, one laced with bad memories and broken relationships.

I think about the perennial advice splashed across dating columns and social media, *If he wanted to, he would.* But the same advice that once felt bloated with righteous indignation and empowerment now feels flimsy, toxic even.

Maybe he wanted to but *couldn't.* Because Liam's guardedness was never about me. It was about him. About old wounds that were still bloody and raw. Wounds that he was too afraid to share lest I see him as he saw himself—not a brilliant doctor or esteemed researcher or responsible husband, but a scared, uncertain boy who couldn't protect the people he loved. Someone whom his own mother hadn't even been able to choose.

"I'm so sorry," I whisper. "I wish she chose you. But it's not your fault, Liam."

"I could have done more," he says, his voice stretching thin. "I could have protected my mum. I could have applied for custody of my sister when I turned eighteen. I could have told someone. I could have . . ." But he doesn't finish. Instead, he drops my hand and looks away. "I just left like a fucking coward," he says.

I shake my head. "You're not a coward. You were a kid. What were you supposed to do? Take care of an infant all on your own? You can't blame yourself. You did what you could."

He nods, but I can feel the tension winding him tight.

"There are so many days I still wake up with this guilt in my chest, this feeling of *what if.* Sometimes it's, *What if I'd told someone? What if I'd been the older brother my sister needed?* And other times, it's *What if I hadn't said anything? What if I'd kept their secrets?*"

His eyes meet mine and the lump in my throat grows.

"I think that's why it meant so much to be included in your family," he says. "I remember when you first brought me home for Christmas and there was this funny ache in my chest, this realization that you can have a family who isn't trying to hide anything. Who you don't have to hide your emotions from. I didn't realize how badly I wanted something like that until I met you. Until the funny ache in my chest started to go away. Until I felt a little less fucked up."

I lift my thumb to trace the creases along his jaw, lines formed by years of anger and hurt and fear. "You're not fucked up," I whisper. "But you *did* have some fucked-up stuff happen to you. Stuff that wasn't your fault."

"But it doesn't mean I haven't hurt people along the way," he says, sounding tired. "It's taken therapy to finally see just how much of my behavior was a trauma response and how much I hurt people as a result." He pauses, bringing his forehead to mine, our mouths only inches apart. "I'm sorry I wasn't there for you the way you needed me to be after your mum died," he whispers. "I'm sorry I shut you out when I should have let you in. I'm sorry that I hurt you."

His voice cracks on the last syllable, and my heart breaks in a thousand different ways. For him. For me. For us. For our marriage, sacrificed at the altar of hurt and grief and loss.

"I'm sorry too," I whisper. "I'm sorry you went through that alone."

"I should have opened up a long time ago," he says. "But every time I thought about it, I felt helpless all over again. Even saying that makes me feel like a failure, like I let you down." He brings his thumb to my chin, commanding my gaze. "But I want you to know that I didn't keep things from you because I didn't love you or because I didn't trust you. It was because I was afraid to show you a version of myself I didn't like very much." Then lower, almost a whisper, "A version I didn't think you'd want."

He looks the way he did the other night. Not shiny, perfect, everyone's favorite golden boy Liam. But someone raw and scrubbed down. Someone he's worked hard to put out of reach. And suddenly I feel greedy for him. All of him. Every sharp corner and jagged edge. Every version I haven't had the privilege of knowing.

"I would have wanted it," I whisper, looping my fingers through his. "I wanted every version of you. Even the ones you didn't like."

For a moment he just looks at me, gaze awash in the dying light, then he wraps his arms around me, pulling me into his chest where I rest my head, fingers fisting the back of his shirt, heartbeats echoing, breath synchronized.

When I brought up this conversation, I'd thought it was for me—for some kind of closure. But as his grip tightens, hands carving into my back like he's afraid the tide might rush up and sweep me away, I wonder if maybe this wasn't for me at all. If this was something he needed—has needed for a long time.

I'm not sure how long we stay like that, bodies bending into each other, rib cages expanding and contracting, but eventually I pull back, making myself do it before I can no longer come up with a reason not to.

"We should probably go back," I say, my voice coming out thick. "It's going to start to rain." As soon as I've said it, two fat raindrops plop on my head, followed by three, four more.

I squeal, throwing my hands up for cover, but it's no use as the rain falls harder, soaking us both.

"Come on," I shout over the downpour. "Let's go!" But Liam's feet stay rooted in the sand.

"Want to go for a swim?" he asks.

I blink. "It's raining."

"I can see that," he says, droplets coming down in droves around us.

My gaze travels beyond him to the ocean, now wrinkled with raindrops.

It's the kind of thing that would happen in a rom-com. Something witty and classic starring Julia Roberts or Jennifer Aniston. Something where one of them would look up at the sky and start laughing, all while their makeup and hair remain flawless.

It's a fantasy. A trope. Certainly not something that happens in real life. And yet here I am, on a beach, in the pouring rain, with a man who makes my heart swell too big for my chest, being given an opportunity to dance in the rain.

"Okay," I say, looking back at him. "Let's swim."

He takes my hand, and I don't pause to question it, or to tell myself no. I just fall into him, letting his firm fingers thread through mine, as we rush the ocean, still fully dressed. His laughter echoes in my eardrums, my pulse, my blood as we wade out, shrieking every time a wave breaks against our thighs. When we get out to our waists, Liam scoops me up into a fireman's carry, and I cry out with surprised, happy laughter.

One arm curls under my thighs, while his other catches my lower back, pressing me against him just as a wave crashes over us, dragging us into the ocean in a tumble of limbs and salty spray.

When we bob to the surface, our lungs burning, waterlogged

clothes sticking to our skin, his face cracks into a wide, open-mouthed grin, like I've just caught him mid-laugh.

A moment earlier, I was aware of the ocean lapping against my skin, the sand between my toes, the taste of salt on my tongue. But all of that melts away under the warm press of his hand on my back and the rhythmic hammer of my pulse, now narrowed to everywhere his eyes fall.

He reaches out, thumb tracing the soft pathway of my jawline, and my heart patters in my chest, the same tune it composed for him nine years ago.

His, his, his.

There's want behind his gaze. But it's more than that. There's regret. And need. And longing. And hope. And a dozen other emotions so finely intertwined, I can't quite distinguish one from another.

I want to tell him he shouldn't look at me like that, that it's not fair to either of us, not when the end is so near, but I can't manage the words, so I shut my eyes and look away.

"Ros." He tips my chin with his thumb. "Look at me."

I open my eyes, and I wish I didn't. I wish I didn't have to see the tenderness of his gaze. Or the softness of his mouth. Or the tiny flecks of water clinging to his hair and eyelashes.

Mostly, I wish I didn't have to see the way he's looking at me.

Like he still loves me, I think.

Like I'm still his.

And in that moment, in between the rush of rain on my face and the heat of his thumb on my chin, I desperately want it to be true.

- 36 -

Six months earlier

The glowing red numbers on the digital clock tell me it's just past 1 a.m. when I hear Liam's car in the driveway.

After his keys jangle in the door, I wait for the sound of the living room TV. Lately, Liam's been watching TV instead of coming to bed when he gets home late from the research center. I can't say for certain, but I think he's avoiding me. That, or he's got a newfound obsession with late-night infomercials. But instead of the usual static hum of the TV, I hear Liam's feet on the stairs. A second later he appears in the bedroom, a shopping bag in hand.

"Hey," he says, looking exhausted as usual.

"Hey," I say back, realizing it's the first word I've said all day.

"You're up."

"Couldn't sleep."

Which is true. I've barely been sleeping. Time just keeps moving forward with no discernible beginning or end to each day.

Liam steps toward the bed, then pauses, like he's reconsidering. A protracted silence follows until finally he says, "I got you something."

I look down at the brightly colored shopping bag in his hands, then back at him, questioning. He hands it over, and after an encouraging nod from him, I push past the tissue paper until I find something soft and feathery at the bottom. Frowning, I pull out a sheer nightgown.

"What's this?" I ask, holding it up.

He rubs the back of his neck, looking uncharacteristically nervous. "You always loved when I bought you lingerie, and things have been . . . weird with us, so I thought maybe it would . . ." He swallows. "I thought maybe you'd like it," he says at last.

Everything in me pulls tight; my skin instantly feels too hot, too heavy.

Since the night of Kevin's party, things have indeed been weird between us. I figured we'd both apologize and the whole thing would blow over, but he got home late, then went into the research center early the next morning, which felt intentional. Like he was purposefully trying to avoid talking about it.

Since then, everything has felt strained. Including our sex life.

Liam's tried to initiate a few times—a hand on the inside of my thigh, a kiss on the back of my neck, even a few dirty words whispered in the dark—but instead of the usual pangs of want and need racing through me like a drug, my body feels heavy as though physically weighed down by the pain of grief.

Now it's been six months since we've slept together.

Liam says he understands, but I can feel the carved-out tension between us. The way every interaction is just a little off, like a painting that won't quite hang straight.

It's not just that grief is a bitch, and I haven't exactly been in the mood; it's also the increasing emotional distance between Liam and me, distance that makes it hard for me to have an intimate connection with him when we don't seem to have any kind of emotional connection lately. When Liam has started to feel less like my husband and more like a ghost that slips in and out of the house at odd hours.

"Thank you," I say, looking down at the gift. "But I'm just not ready yet."

His hands fidget at his sides. "I understand," he says, wrapping his mouth carefully around each syllable. "When do you think you're going to be ready?"

His tone is calm, gentle even, but I can see the disappointment lurking behind his gaze, and a thick layer of shame instantly washes over me. For not being ready to have sex again. For not meeting my husband's needs. For not being *fine* again.

"I don't know," I admit.

And it's the truth. The scary truth hanging over both of us. I have no idea when I'll feel okay again—if ever.

Liam runs a hand through his hair, mouth flatlining. I can feel him trying and hesitating to speak. Finally he says, "I want to help, Ros, but I don't know how."

There's a part of me that wants—*needs*—to believe he means it. That he genuinely is just trying to help, but another part of me, a deeper, more resentful part, is hurt.

I'm hurt that he keeps avoiding my pain. That he hasn't even tried to talk to me about it. That instead of showing up for me when I need him most, he's become distant. And now he thinks he can buy me some frilly lingerie and that will fix the ever-widening cracks between us? That it'll make up for the past few months?

"You want to help?" I repeat, my voice fraying. "Then why won't you sit and talk with me?"

His features widen with surprise, but just as quickly his jaw stiffens like a mask being put back into place. "I told you, I—"

I shake my head, and the frustration I've tried to push down rises up the back of my throat, unbidden. "Don't tell me you're not good at these types of conversations, Liam. You're always working late or coming up with some excuse to not spend time with me."

"I'm not," he says.

"Okay. Great. Thanks. I guess that's cleared up."

Liam sighs. "Ros, I've been trying to give you space. I thought that's what you needed."

I push out a *pfft* noise. "Yeah. I've noticed."

His eyes narrow. "What does that mean?"

I wish I could believe him, that he's just trying to give me space, that he doesn't know how to talk about my grief. But what if this isn't about any of that? What if it's me? What if I'm too broken? What if he opened all my doors, saw all my layers, and now that he's gotten to the messiest one, he's decided he doesn't want it? He doesn't want me.

I swallow down a stilted breath. "It means that ever since my mom died, you've been acting distant and I just feel like . . ." My voice cracks as the fear that's been swimming in the back of my mind for months now finally worms its way to the surface. "Like you don't like being around me anymore," I finally say.

Liam's shoulders drop as though absorbing the weight of my words. "Of course I like you. *I love you,* Ros." He rubs week-old scruff on his jaw, voice dropping off before he says, "But the past few months have been hard for both of us, and I don't know what to do, and I thought maybe this . . ." His gaze drifts to the lingerie curled under my fist. "Would help."

His tone tips toward pleading, desperate even, and if I wasn't so emotionally wounded, I might be able to see that he really is trying to help, that he's just as hurt and confused as I am, but instead his words land like well-aimed darts, hitting each one of my insecurities with impeccable precision.

"Well, it's not helping," I say stiffly, dropping the lingerie back into the bag. "And buying me underwear isn't an excuse to avoid talking about my feelings."

Liam steps back like he's been burned. "I'm not trying to avoid anything, Ros. That's not—" But his voice breaks with frustration, and he turns away.

For a moment I think he's going to yell, and a part of me hopes he will. At least that way we can scream it out and finally have the fight we've been needing to have. The fight that will break us out of this miserable rut. Instead, he says, "I've had a long day and I really don't want to fight about this, Ros."

Then he turns and leaves the room. A few minutes later I hear the hum of the TV downstairs.

- 37 -

Now

Larsen Family Vacation Day 8

PORT OF CALL: *at sea*

ITINERARY: *vow renewal ceremony at 5 on back deck*

ATTIRE: *formal*

The night of the vow renewal, the back deck of the ship is set up with white chairs and an arch draped in lilies, orchids, and jasmine. Overhead, a string of twinkle lights shimmer in the final embers of the sun's blaze.

Jonah, Ben, Chris, Bella, the kids, and I are all seated while my grandparents and Liam take their spots under the arch.

The unwritten rule is that no one is supposed to look better than the bride, but apparently Liam, looking dashing in a bow tie and a crisp white shirt that's tight in all the right places, didn't get that memo.

"Welcome, everyone," Liam says, giving a little nod. "It is a pleasure to be here today with all of you." A murmur of agreement rises up in response before he turns to Grammy and Gramps. "I'm honored to play a role in celebrating the vow renewal of Kathleen and Harrold Larsen."

Grammy and Gramps join hands, both of them beaming like a pair of lovesick teenagers.

"Before we begin with the exchange of vows, I'd like to say a few words. I think we can all agree that Maggie would have loved to be here, not just because it's a beautiful day in paradise"—he gestures to the perfect stretch of blue ocean behind us—"but because she was the biggest fan of love."

My heart swells. Somehow, impossibly, I feel like she's here. Like I can feel her in the sunlight feathering across my face. In the gentle lick of wind tousling my curls. In the echoes of Liam's voice bouncing like beams of light across the deck. Like maybe her presence isn't something physical, but something much greater, more permanent than that.

"She believed that love was one of the best parts of life, something worth sacrificing for," Liam goes on. "And even though her presence is sorely missed, she's still here in spirit, reminding us that always choosing love is one of the bravest things anyone can do."

He pauses, allowing a meditative silence to fall over us before he says, "I remember on our wedding day, Maggie figured I might be nervous. Which I was," Liam adds to a smattering of chuckles. "So she pulled me aside and showed me the bracelet she was wearing—silver with blue stones."

My eyes drift down to my left wrist, where the same bracelet now sits.

"She asked me how old I thought it was, and I told her it looked brand-new," Liam says. "She shared it was actually over a hundred years old, but when you take care of things, they can last forever. Then she told me that relationships are the same. That when you work hard and take care of them, they'll last."

Liam's gaze lingers on me, and a shiver that has nothing to do with the ocean breeze scatters across my skin.

"Every day since that moment, I've learned that relationships are hard," he continues. "That the easiest part of loving someone is the falling, and everything after that takes hard work. But I don't mean long hours at a job you hate. I mean the kind of work that lights your soul on fire, that's worth every long night and early morning. Every up and down. Every sacrifice. The kind of work that fulfills you and challenges you every day. The kind that makes you want to show up and build something that lasts because it's worth it."

His eyes flick back to Grammy and Gramps. "I could say it's luck or good fortune or fate even that we're standing here today celebrating fifty years of marriage, but it's not. We're here because Grammy and Gramps have done the hard work to build and maintain their relationship. They are proof that when we take care of each other, our love can stand the test of time."

When Liam finishes, everyone claps. I join in, too; all the while my heartbeat is slamming against my ribs, breath coming out choppy and uneven.

It's just a speech, I tell myself. One I'd known all along that he would make. I just hadn't known he would say *all that*. Nor had I known he would keep looking at me, like the words were meant for me, and only me.

Was it all part of the roles we're playing? Him the perfect, shiny husband and me the supportive, loving wife? Or did he mean it?

The question fans the flames of the emotional fire raging inside me even as I do my best to smile and clap as well, playing it off like of course Liam believes every word of what he just said.

Like he still wants this to last.

After the ceremony, there's a reception with cake and dancing on the deck overlooking the ocean, as the sun finishes its descent in fiery bursts of pink and orange and lavender.

Jonah and Ben show off some salsa moves from a class they took, and Grammy and Gramps dance with Jackson, Riley, and Henleigh while everyone *oohs* and *awws* over how cute it is.

I try to muster up the enthusiasm to join in, but not even the millennial siren call of "Peace up, A-town down" can get me out on the dance floor, and I hang off to the side of the deck, nursing a seltzer and lime, still caught up in Liam's speech.

What he said was beautiful. Thoughtful. *Romantic.* But why did he say this now?

Where was this big speech about making things last when I told him it was over? When he walked out? When I cried myself to sleep night after night? When the crush of loneliness was unbearable?

Why now? Why tonight?

I wish I could tell myself the answer doesn't matter. That in two days we'll go back to real life, and there's no point wondering about *what ifs* and *could haves*. I wish I could shut off the gravitational pull of him. The feeling of my heart wrapping around his once more.

But I can't.

Not after the past few days. Not when I can still picture the way he'd looked at me last night—like we still belonged to each other. Like I was his.

I'm wondering if I could get away with retreating to our cabin by claiming I'm seasick when Liam appears beside me.

"Hey," he says, his hip brushing mine. The touch is light, barely there, but my lungs, my pulse—*everything*—jumps.

"Hey," I say back.

He leans against the railing, studying me. "Is everything all right? You ran away so quickly after the ceremony."

"I'm fine. I just . . ." But I let my voice trail off, lost to the ocean breeze, mostly because I don't know how to explain everything that I'm feeling right now. Or even if it's a good idea to try. "I'm fine," I say again.

Silence ensues, and his eyes drop to my mouth, lingering. There's heat behind his gaze. A final flame of want that won't go out. And suddenly I'm angry.

"Don't look at me like that," I tell him.

His mouth turns down. "Like what?"

Like you still love me.

"Like you meant what you said back there." I gesture to the spot where the ceremony took place.

His brow stiffens against the twinkle lights overhead. "I *did* mean what I said."

He says it like it's obvious. Like I was supposed to know that.

"You could have warned me, you know."

"Warned you about what?"

"That you were going to say all *that,*" I say, waving my hand vaguely.

He frowns, dragging his hand through his beard. "What was wrong with what I said?"

"Nothing, I just . . ." But my voice fades and I turn from him, afraid that if I look at him a second longer, all the thoughts I've tried so hard to tamp down, to pretend aren't there, will rush to the surface in one frothing *whoosh,* and I won't be able to control what happens next.

"I can't do this," I say.

"Do what, Ros?"

I look back at him—at his arched brow and the slight downturn of his lips and the way the ocean breeze lifts the ends of his hair, making him look so handsome, it hurts—and that's all it takes for the thin strand of composure that's been holding me together to finally snap.

"*This.*" I gesture between us. "This push and pull. One minute we're hooking up with an expiration date, and the next you're . . ." I scramble for the words. "You're looking at me like *that* saying all *that*!"

His mouth parts in surprise. "Ros," he says in a quiet rasp.

But I keep going, a boiling pot finally frothing over.

"If you really meant it, why couldn't you have said all that stuff three months ago when our marriage was falling apart? Maybe if you had, then things would be different, maybe we'd . . ." But I stop, afraid to say what's next.

Liam inches closer, close enough that I can feel the heat of his skin, smell the sharp scent of his cologne. "Maybe we'd what?" he asks.

"Maybe . . ." I choke, my voice broken by a sob. "Maybe things wouldn't be like this . . ."

"Ros." He places a tender hand on my arm, but I brush him away.

"Stop," I say, pushing past the wedge in my throat. "You were supposed to be there for me when I needed you. You were supposed to be the one person in my life I could lean on, who would be there for me when I was at my lowest, and you weren't. So you don't get to come here and say a few nice words and act like that fixes things. It's too late."

Liam's face falls like a balloon that's lost its air. "That's not—" He stops himself, shaking his head. "You're right. I fucked up and I lost you for it. But it's not too late for—"

But I don't let him finish. I don't want to hear what it's not too late for. I don't want to be held captive by any more false promises and pretty-sounding words. I made that mistake once before and I won't do it again.

"I've tried to control my feelings, to not need you anymore, to be okay with saying goodbye when this trip ends," I tell him. "But you're only making it harder. So just stop. Okay?"

"Ros," he says again, this time coming out low and strained. A plea. "You're the one who wanted an expiration date. And you're the one who asked for the divorce. Not me."

"I know but . . ." My voice trails off as the hurt and confusion I've been shoving down for months finally bob to the surface.

I told myself we didn't need to have this conversation because the answer doesn't matter. Because it doesn't change anything between us. Because when I said it was over, he left and neither of us tried to save it. But now, the sturdy ground I've laid my arguments on feels shaky and off-balance, one point on the Richter scale from tipping over entirely. Now I need to know the truth.

"Why didn't you fight for us?" I ask. "Why did you just give up?"

Recognition ripples through his eyes.

"You told me you were done," he says. "You said it was over."

"But what if I *wanted* you to fight for me?"

His jaw tightens, features sharpening under the glow of the lights. "What are you saying? That it was some kind of test? That I didn't pass?"

"No," I say, pushing out an exasperated breath. "But I think it says a lot about our marriage that you quit so easily. That you didn't even try."

"I thought I was giving you the space you wanted."

Old hurt rears its head at the familiar words. "So you left?"

His mouth twists, his eyes narrowing. "You pushed me away, too, Ros."

"I was grieving!"

"I didn't know how to help you," he says, his voice turning frayed and thin. "You wouldn't get help. I told you to see a therapist, I—"

I grip the railing, frustration and hurt colliding inside me. "It wasn't about the therapist, Liam. It was that I wanted *you* to talk with me. I wanted *you* to be there for me."

I just wanted you, my brain screams.

He moves closer, his eyes dark and pleading. "I wanted to, but I didn't know how to handle my own grief or how to be the person you needed me to be, and every time I tried to fix it, it only pushed you away further and made everything worse."

"So it's my fault you weren't there for me after my mom died?"

He shakes his head. "No. I'm not saying that."

"Then why wasn't . . ." My lungs squeeze out a slow stream of air. "Why wasn't I enough to make you stay and fight for me?" I finally force out.

"'Enough'?" he repeats like he doesn't know the meaning. "You think you weren't enough for me?" He runs a hand through his hair, gaze flashing with something wild and raw, and for a moment I think he's angry, that he's going to yell. But when he speaks again his voice is fragile, so low I barely hear him.

"Do you know how fucking hard this week has been?" he asks. "To touch you and taste you and just be *near* you again, knowing that I wasn't going to get to keep you? To know that when it was all over, we wouldn't be going home together, to our house, our life, our bed?" He winces, his hands flexing at his sides as though trying to keep himself from reaching out to me. "This week has been *agony* for me, but I knew I would rather leave this ship in excruciating pain having accepted whatever you were willing to offer me than not get to have you at all." He swallows down a shaky breath before he says, "You're more than enough, Roslyn. You're *everything*."

His words rush through me like a tornado on a prairie, turning everything upside down, but it's that one word, *everything*, that cracks me down the center, splitting me wide.

"Then why did you leave?" I whisper.

Heavy eyes look up to meet mine, and I don't just see the pain in his eyes, I feel it. The raw hurt buried under every hard line and edge of his expression.

"My whole life I've never been able to fix anything. I was told to ignore the problems at home and pretend they weren't there. I spent most of my childhood and teenage years feeling helpless." He drops his gaze, a deep breath rattling in his throat. "Then I became a doctor and suddenly I *could* fix things. I could find answers. I could help people. And then I met you and I felt like I could give you what you needed, I could be safe and reliable and sturdy for you. I could give you the stability we both wanted." He pins me down with a heavy look. "But when your mum died, I didn't know what to do. I didn't know how to deal with that kind of grief, and every time I tried to make things better, I only made everything worse.

"I hated watching you suffer. It was like I was that helpless fifteen-year-old boy watching my mum lose herself to grief and heartache all over again without a clue how to fix it or make it better. I was so afraid of losing you the same way I lost my mum. But I also hated myself for not knowing how to be the partner you needed, for not being able to take away your pain, for throwing myself into my work because that's the only thing I've ever had any control over. For letting my own shit keep me from being who you needed me to be." His voice breaks, the dampness in his eyes catching the lights overhead.

"I felt like the only place I could really be steady for you—where I wouldn't mess things up—was in bed. But then we stopped having sex and I felt like maybe there wasn't anything else I could give you."

His words slide down my back like a block of ice.

"Then you said it was over, and there was this part of me that wondered if maybe you were right to walk away. If maybe you were better off without me. If I was just too fucked up to be what you needed."

He steps closer and I see it all, the hurt and regret. All the anguish he's kept locked inside himself for so long now bleeding across his face like spilled paint on a canvas.

"After I left, there wasn't a day I didn't spend thinking about you, about what would happen if I called, if I came after you, if I told you everything. But I was in such a bad place. I was so fucking broken, Ros, and it didn't feel fair to beg you for another chance when I couldn't give you what you needed."

I feel my pulse in my ears.

"Then you asked me to come on this trip. And I knew it would fucking break me all over again to be so close to you and know it wasn't real, that you didn't want me back. But I could see that you needed my help, and it felt like one small thing I could do, one thing I could try to fix.

"But as soon as I saw you standing in the driveway in that fucking dress"—his hand flexes by his side—"I could hardly *breathe*, much less act normal around you, so I tried to keep my distance, if only to make the trip more tolerable. But then things got . . ." He gestures between us. "We started sleeping together and I thought maybe we still had a chance. That *I* still had a chance," he adds, giving me a meaningful look.

You always had a chance, my heart thunders. *Always.*

"But it also felt like a confirmation of everything I'd worried about, that sex was all I could offer you, all you wanted from me, and I knew it would destroy me to have you only to lose you again. But I was also desperate enough to take whatever crumb you'd give me, for however long you'd give it to me because . . ." His breathing slows, heavy eyes lifting to mine. "Because you're all I want, all I've *ever* wanted." He chokes back a sound. "And I know it's not an excuse and it doesn't fix everything that happened, but it's the truth, and it kills me every fucking day, and probably will for the rest of my life."

His words send shock waves down my spine, straight into my splintered core, and suddenly my dress is too tight, my breath too short, my vision too blurred.

I can't do this, I think. Not here. Not now. Not with my family a few feet away.

"Let's not talk about this anymore," I tell him. "We're supposed to be acting like everything is fine."

His shoulders slump, his eyes blinking away in defeat. "Right. *Acting*," he repeats. "Because that's all this is."

"No, that's—" I start to say just as Bella appears. We both jump apart like we've accidentally touched an electric fence.

Bella frowns. "Oh, sorry. Am I interrupting something?"

"No," Liam and I say in unison.

Her brows stay furrowed, and I can tell she doesn't quite believe us. "Okay, well, I was just coming to tell you it's your song."

Our *what*?

Then I hear it. "Dream a Little Dream of Me" is playing over the speakers.

- 38 -

Now

We went back and forth trying to decide what should be our first dance song. Liam wanted an eighties ballad, while I wanted something more classic. *What's more classic than Bonnie Tyler?* Liam argued. We debated it until one night we were over at my mom's for dinner and she started singing along to the Mamas & the Papas' soulful version of "Dream a Little Dream of Me." Liam and I looked at each other and just knew. It was the song that played at the bar the night we met and we couldn't think of anything more perfect to dance to. But tonight, not so much.

My first instinct is to make an excuse, some reason why Liam and I can't dance right now, but before I can come up with anything, Liam's taking me by the hand and leading me out onto the dance floor.

"What are you doing?" I whisper.

"What does it look like I'm doing? I'm *acting*." Then he puts his hands on my waist, pulling me into his chest. "Is this okay?" he asks brusquely.

No. It's not fucking okay. None of this is, I want to scream, but what choice do we have when my entire family is watching, so I nod and wind my hands around his neck.

As we sway back and forth like a pendulum, I try to hold on to my anger, to remind myself of all the ways he let me down and that overdue explanations don't fix things. But Liam's words pinwheel inside my brain. *Every time I tried to make things better, I only made everything worse,* and I can't help the collision of regret and loss surging inside me. The realization that our marriage didn't fail because he didn't care. Or because he didn't love me enough.

He always loved me—maybe even still does—he just didn't know how to show it. And maybe I didn't know how to either. Maybe we both hurt each other in different ways because we were scarred by old wounds that still haven't healed. Because we were both broken.

I think about what he'd said. *It felt like a confirmation of everything I'd worried about, that sex was all I could offer you, all you wanted from me.*

The words cut like jagged glass against my ribs. But hadn't that been exactly what I'd worried about too? That he couldn't give me anything more than just sex? And hadn't I confirmed that for him by telling him I wanted an expiration date? By not telling him how I felt because I, too, was afraid I wasn't worthy of more? Because I was afraid of the exact same thing he was?

The realization pulls me apart and pins me down until I'm suffocating, crushed by the weight of it. Liam must feel it, too, because our dancing turns less angry rocking and more mournful swaying as he draws me closer, until we're body to body, and it's all I can do to fight the rush of tears swarming my eyes.

"I'm sorry," I choke. "I'm sorry for pushing you away, for expecting you to be the one to fix the problems between us when they were mine to fix too. I know I hurt you and I'm sorry."

The tears are falling now, hot and fast. "I wanted so much more than sex from you, Liam. I always have. I still do. But I thought I was asking you for something you didn't want to give me because . . ." My bottom lip quivers, the avalanche of feelings inside me finally breaking loose. "Because I wasn't worth it to you."

"Ros," he whispers, his voice so tender, it's like he's found a way to crawl inside me and peel back every last protective layer surrounding my heart. "You were always worth it. Every day. Every moment. Even when I didn't know how to show it. You will always be worth it to me."

As he gathers me into his chest, I feel like I'm being untangled, thread by thread. All my poorly stitched wounds unraveling before him.

"I never wanted space," I tell him. "I didn't want you to go. I didn't want it to be over. But I was broken and hurting, and I felt like I was losing you, like I wasn't yours anymore." Tears blur my vision, breath clogging in my throat. "We were supposed to make it," I choke. "I was supposed to be yours. I *wanted* to be yours."

He cups my chin, commanding my gaze. "You *are* mine," he says, his voice gritty with fresh determination. "Still mine. *Always* mine." Then he leans down, angling his mouth, and kisses me, rough and possessive, like he's trying to prove what he just said. That I'm still his.

"Mine," he whispers into my mouth, the word puncturing my skin, all the way to the deepest parts of my soul. He says it again and again. *Mine,* as his hands mold around my hips, pulling our bodies flush. *Mine. Mine. Mine.*

Salty tears mix with hot breath and wet lips as he kisses me over and over, needy and seeking.

When my tears turn to inelegant sobs, Liam takes my hand and leads me off the dance floor, out of the view of my family.

In the shadows, under the glare of the moon, our bodies slot together, close enough that I can feel the *tap, tap, tap* of his heart beating in time with mine.

We're two misshapen, jagged-edged shards of glass. We've cut each other before. But here, in his arms, I feel my sharpest edges dull.

"Do you think there's a world where we get it right?" I ask. "Where we're okay?"

His eyes catch mine, heavy and determined. "This one, baby," he says, tilting his mouth to mine. "I promise, it's this one." He kisses me harder, fingers digging into my waist. "We're okay."

Want sears in my chest, but it's more than just physical. I'm greedy for this moment, to make it last, to lock it in the safe house of my mind where I can remember what it feels like to be in his arms, safe and warm. Where I can remember the feeling of being his. Of being okay.

His mouth chases mine, tongue parting my lips, and my spine bends, arching into him, desperate to ruin him, to be ruined by him. The only thing keeping me from climbing him here and now is the knowledge that my family is right around the corner.

"Take me back to the room," I gasp.

He pulls back, tongue swiping across his swollen lips. "Let me tell the family you aren't feeling well and turning in for the night, okay?"

I nod and he gives my hand a squeeze.

When he returns, we move like we're in a trance, drifting through space like thick taffy. By the time we shut the door to our room behind us, we're both on edge.

Liam flattens me against the wall and I let out a sharp gasp.

"Is this what you want?" he murmurs, planting rough, greedy kisses along my neck.

I don't know what *this* is. If it's sex, or him, or all of it, but the answer's *yes*. I want it all.

"Yes," I say in a voice empty of air. "I want this."

I want you.

He pushes one strap of my dress off my shoulder, then the other, letting the bodice fall to my waist. "The dress," he whispers, his mouth hot and fast on my neck. "The one you wore to the airport. Was it for me?"

"Yes," I tell him, my voice straining as my hips press forward, arching into his touch.

It was for you, all for you.

"What about the beard?" I ask, running my fingers through the coarse bristles. "Was it for me?"

He cups my face, his gaze stripping me down to skin and bones. "Yes," he whispers. "Everything was for you."

"Even the—?"

"Yes," he answers, swallowing the end of my question with a kiss. "All of it was for you."

His mouth sinks against mine, his hands roaming the length of my spine. *Mine, mine, mine,* the staccato of his breath whispers against my lips. *Yours, yours, yours,* my tongue says back as he walks us toward the bed.

He peels the rest of my clothes away until we're both naked and bare. Until there are no more walls. No more rules. No more pretending. No more secrets. No more distractions. It's just us. Him and me. Stripped down, exposed.

"God, Ros." His voice is a soft hum against my throat. "You fucking ruin me. You always have."

And in that moment, looking like the fraying end of a tapestry, I believe him.

In the nine years I've known Liam, he's always been the calm and collected one. The one who holds his emotions close to his chest, away from scrutiny. Who thought his hurt was something to hide. But here, with his breath turning ragged, hands firmly on my waist like he's afraid I might slip out from under him, I feel like I'm looking into a room whose doors were previously locked. Like I'm seeing all of him. Every sharp corner and broken edge.

Parts that are already familiar, ones I know as well as my own, and ones he's hidden away, out of reach. Parts I want to spend the rest of my life learning, memorizing, knowing.

Loving, I think with a jolt.

The thought unravels me as I reach out, tracing the lines of his jaw with the pad of my thumb. His gaze travels from my eyes to my mouth, then back again, expression drawn with need.

When he speaks, the sound is ripped from his chest. "Ros, I—" He pauses, a shallow breath pulsing between us. "I love you." Then lower, firmer, more determined, "I've always loved you, Ros. I never stopped."

Everything around us blurs. Every sound. Every sensation. Even the ever-present hum of the ship's engine fades away until all that's left are those three little words. Three little words that change everything.

I try to remember when I first knew I loved him.

Was it the night we met? When I tried so very hard not to fall for him? Or maybe the first time he took care of me when I was sick? Or was it that first Christmas when he met my family and I saw how well he fit in, how much they loved him, and it made me love him too? Or was it a million small moments in between, each one so indistinguishable from the next that I can't quite pull them apart?

Or maybe, in some impossible-to-understand sort of way, I've *always* loved him. Maybe in every world, every timeline, every version of this life, there was space in my heart carved out for him and only him.

Maybe there always would be.

"I love you too," I breathe back.

Our eyes catch and my nerve endings flare. It's an accord, an acknowledgment that we mean what we've said. It wasn't a mistake or a slip of the tongue. It wasn't pretend or words spoken in the heat of passion. They were real and we meant them.

A heavy, pulse-pounding beat passes, then his hands are cupping my cheeks, drawing his forehead to mine, our shaky breaths comingling in the narrow space between my mouth and his.

When he kisses me, it's like being swept up in the ocean. I'm powerless against the waves of his touch, the swell of his mouth on mine. He's a force so intense, so profound, I fear I might drown right here in his arms.

His hands travel up my back and into my hair, pulling me into the familiar scaffolding of his body. A body I was made for. To love and be loved by.

"Mine," he says as his teeth sink into the delicate skin of my neck, hard enough that I know he'll leave a mark.

"Yours," I whisper back as he hoists me up, wrapping my legs around his waist, and carries me to the bed.

Normally Liam would take his time, teasing me until I beg, but we're both too needy, too desperate, and he spreads my thighs, entering me with a long, drawn-out thrust that wrenches a quiet sob out of me. He moves slowly at first—a deliberate exercise in restraint—then faster, like he can't quite help himself, until his hands brace against my thighs, sweat dripping down his neck and onto my throat. Until we're both unraveling at the seams.

"Don't let go," he whispers, his fingers tangling with mine, hips rolling in perfect synchronization.

"I won't, I promise," I choke out, something between a gasp and a sob. "I'm here."

I'm yours.

His mouth slants over mine, his spine arching to bring himself deeper, both of us moving together, performing choreography we both know by heart.

I love you, his fingers whisper as they comb through my hair.

I need you, my teeth say back as they nip at his earlobe.

Don't let go, we say together as we tip toward the edge, falling apart slowly, then all at once.

Tomorrow, we'll have to talk. About what it means. About what's next. About everything. But for now, in between tender kisses and whispered chants of *I love you,* I lose myself in him. In the curves and ridges of his body. In this moment with the man I've always loved.

- 39 -

Three months earlier

Pass the salt?"

Liam looks up, blinking, as though surprised to see me on the other side of the kitchen table, before passing the saltshaker and returning his gaze to his phone.

We rarely eat together anymore. When we do, it's like this. Silent.

I can't even remember the last time we had a real conversation, one more substantive than if the dishes in the dishwasher are clean or dirty, or if the other can pick up milk on the way home.

Every interaction feels like we're on edge, one misstep from starting a fight. Though frankly I wish we would fight—at least that would be better than painful cycles of silence and avoidance. But anytime it feels like we're on the brink of a real fight, Liam ends the conversation, or makes an excuse, and we go right back to avoiding each other, reminding me that whatever we used to have has crumbled under the weight of grief and anger and resentment and all the things we're not talking about.

We continue to eat in silence until finally Liam says, "So, I'm going out of town tomorrow."

I jerk my head up, frowning. "Where?"

"Portland, for a few weeks. There's this lab and—"

"A few *weeks*?"

He nods and suddenly everything goes out of focus.

Are things so irreparably broken between us that he didn't think this was something I needed to know?

"Why didn't you tell me?" I ask, sitting up straighter.

He pauses, his fork hovering over his plate of leftovers. "Things haven't exactly been good between us lately. We haven't even slept in the same bed in ages." His eyes dip below the table's surface before he adds, "I figured it wasn't a big deal if I was gone for a while."

A hot whoosh of unease slams against my chest. He's right. We're barely talking, haven't slept together in months. It's not like his absence will be missed. But something about this feels final. Proof of the sneaking suspicion that's lived in the back of my mind for months. That it's over—*has been over*—and our marriage has become nothing more than a holding pattern.

"So you just weren't going to tell me?" I ask.

"I'm telling you right now," he says, his features sagging with a kind of bone-deep weariness, like this conversation has already drained him. "But if you don't want me to go, I'll see if I can get a colleague to go in my place."

"It's not about Portland," I say tightly. "It's about the fact that our marriage has fallen apart, and you don't seem to care."

"Of course I care." He licks his lips, his gaze shooting down then back to me before he says in a quieter voice, "I've been trying. But you keep pushing me away."

The same frustration that's been simmering below the surface for months creeps up the back of my throat, hot and potent.

"You're trying?" I repeat. "When? When you sleep at the research center three nights a week? When you're gone all the time?

When you come up with excuses to avoid being with me? Or when you tell me to see a therapist so they can fix me?"

He scrapes a palm across his cheek, hurt flashing behind his eyes. "I'm not trying to get someone to fix you. I just don't see why you won't talk to a professional."

"I can talk to a professional, Liam. But that's not the point. Why won't *you* talk with me?"

We're back to the same fight we've had over and over. But it's like poking a bruise to see if it's still sore.

His lips fold together, the skin around his eyes creasing as he looks to the door then back to me. "I told you, I'm not good at these conversations."

There's a flash of regret in his eyes, like maybe it's not just an excuse. But I'm too hurt, too angry to hear his words as anything other than merciless blades, unyielding and precise, knowing just where to target for maximum impact, and whatever thinly veiled composure I've been operating under snaps like a toothpick.

I stand up, shoving my chair back with enough force that it scrapes the wood floor. "You never even *tried*! Where were you the last few months? When I needed you? When my mom died? *Where the fuck were you, Liam?*"

I'm crying now, but I don't bother to wipe the tears away. My words thunder between us, and I wait, almost feverishly, wondering if this is the moment his composure will break and the mask will finally fall.

He lowers his head to his hands, and my heart skips a beat. *This is it,* I think. I've finally gotten through to him. We're going to fight. He's going to tell me he loves me. That he's here for me. That he's sorry. I'll say it too. Then he'll gather me in his arms and take me upstairs and make love to me. The way he's supposed to.

Instead, he stands up, his expression weathered and worn

down, like stone that's spent too much time in the elements, and moves toward the door.

"Where are you going?" I ask, my voice drawn like a weapon.

He pauses, but he doesn't turn around. "To Kevin's. I have a long drive tomorrow, and I need to get some sleep."

Everything in me clenches.

"You're just leaving?" I call after him. "Again? Like you always do?"

He hangs his head, his back still to me. "Maybe we need some space, Roslyn."

Rage and something deeper, more painful, rises inside me like volcanic lava, ready to spew everywhere.

It's not just about Portland. Or the fact that he's running away. Again.

It's everything.

It's every night I went to bed alone, every night he wasn't there for me. Every night he let us slide further and further apart as I tried to convince myself things would get better. That this was just a rough patch. But it's not and it never was, the reality now washing over me in thick, painful waves.

"The last nine months of space haven't been enough?" I ask.

I wait for an answer, for him to turn around. To show me the chinks in his armor. To show me something, *anything*. But the longer we stand there, the more aware I am of the truth. That the cracks between us aren't just cracks anymore. They're gaping, bloody wounds. Deeper than perhaps either of us has recognized.

Suddenly, I'm furious. Not just with him, but with myself. For trusting him with something as fragile as my heart. For lowering my walls. For needing him. For fruitlessly hoping things would change when over and over again he's proven to me that my grief is too much. That *I'm* too much and whatever glue used to hold us together has splintered, flaking into a flimsy, crumbling mess, unable to withstand the weight of the last year.

When I speak, my voice comes out stronger, more confident than I feel. "If you're going to leave, then don't bother coming back."

Liam turns back to face me, his dark eyes narrowed. "What's that supposed to mean?"

"I mean that we're done."

For a long minute, Liam just stares at me, a range of emotions crossing his face. First, confusion, then hurt. Finally, exhaustion. Not just tired, but worn down, stripped of his life force, like it's taking everything in him to even look at me.

"Is there someone else?" he finally asks.

Bile rises in my throat. Tears sting my eyes.

"I know you don't think much of me right now, but if you seriously believe I would cheat on you, then we have much bigger problems than I thought."

He rakes a frustrated hand through his hair. "I didn't say that."

"But you asked."

"Of course I'm asking," he says, exasperated. "We haven't slept together in months. Everything I do only seems to push you further away, then you say it's over. What the fuck am I supposed to think?"

I shake my head, anger and buried hurt colliding like cars on a speedway. "I'm unhappy, Liam! We both are!"

As I stand there, tears now flowing freely down my face, I silently plead for him to fight with me. To tell me he doesn't want it to end. That he'll do anything to prove he loves me, that I'm *his*, the way he used to. But he doesn't. And with each passing minute, the words hovering in the back of my throat grow firmer. More resolute. Shifting from hazy and improbable to sharp and immediate.

When I first met Liam, I was a cautiously hopeful romantic. I was afraid of heartache, of giving myself to someone who would break me. Afraid of ending up in a relationship like one of the dozens I'd seen my mom in, so I protected myself with tall walls. But little by little, Liam broke down those walls. He made me feel safe, wanted, *enough*.

He made me believe that not only was happily ever after real, but it was something I could have. With him.

But the man standing in front of me is no longer that man. He's not the man who danced with me in the kitchen, who asked me to marry him with tears in his eyes, promising he'd always be there for me. He hasn't been that man for a while, and maybe I haven't been that woman either, but I can't do this anymore.

I can't wait for things to get better.

I can't keep lying to myself.

I can't end up like my mom.

So I take a shaky breath and tell Liam the truth: "I want a divorce."

For a long moment he holds my gaze, my words reverberating across his features like ripples in still water.

When finally he speaks, my heart is thundering so loud against my ribs, I'm surprised I even hear his terse response.

"Fine."

That's it. *Fine.* A single syllable that breaks me with one swift, precise blow.

Suffocating silence follows. My ears ring. My pulse pounds. Every muscle clenches.

I wait for one of us to take it back, to confess we didn't mean it, that this is a mistake. But either that's not true, or neither of us is brave enough to say it, because the silent seconds stretch into a painful minute before he finally turns and goes upstairs.

Ten minutes later, I watch him walk out the front door. The lock clicks, followed by the rumble of his car in the driveway, then I drop to my knees, throat raw, chest tight, body crushed in unimaginable pain.

Ten minutes, I think. Ten awful minutes is all it took to wipe away nine years with the ease of an Etch A Sketch. For Liam to leave with just a duffel bag, like he's taken everything he wanted, and it didn't include me.

- 40 -

Now

Larsen Family Vacation Day 9

PORT OF CALL: Honolulu, Oahu

ITINERARY: *family breakfast in main dining room followed by a pool day*

ATTIRE: *casual, swimwear*

When I wake up the next morning, Liam's arm is slung over my waist, the rhythmic push and pull of his warm, sleepy breathing feathering across my cheek. An ache sweeps through me as memories of last night come back to me like grains of sand falling through an hourglass.

Liam's speech.

The fight.

Dancing under the stars.

I love you.

Everything else filters away as those three little words burst through my mind in blinding Technicolor.

He still loves me. And I still love him.

No, not still, I think. *Always. I always loved him and always will.*

I keep my eyes closed, replaying last night over and over. The way we kissed and touched, writing love notes with our fingers, our hands, our tongues. The way our bodies moved together, performing choreography only the two of us knew.

It was raw. Messy. *Real.* But was it enough? Enough to survive the catalog of hard conversations we still have to have? Enough for whatever is next?

I should probably wake him so we can talk about last night, about where we go from here. But he looks so peaceful with his face smooshed against the pillow, and I'm not ready for this perfect moment—this liminal space before reality comes rushing back in—to end, so I curl against him, relishing his warmth, his sturdiness.

I'm not sure how long we lie there, drifting in and out of sleep, but eventually the furious red glow of the clock tells us we're now five minutes late for breakfast. I shake Liam awake.

"We should get up," I tell him. "Everyone will be wondering where we are."

"Let them," Liam says, his lips grazing my bare shoulder.

Heat stirs in my belly. I desperately want to give in. To lie here. To make this moment last as long as we can. But my phone buzzes with a text from Jonah asking where we are. I can feel reality clawing its way into our bubble, so I climb out of bed and put on a bikini and cover-up in preparation for a day at the pool.

When we arrive at the breakfast table in the main dining room, everyone else has already gone through the buffet and finished eating.

"Well, well, well," Bella says, eyeing us over the rim of her coffee mug. "Look who decided to join us."

"Sorry," Liam says, offering everyone apologetic smiles. "We slept late."

"Suuuuure," Bella sings. "And is that why you two snuck off last night? So you could get some extra *rest*?"

Maybe I imagine it, but her eyes zip to the bite mark Liam left on my neck.

"We were tired," I tell her.

"Very," Liam agrees, planting a quick kiss on my temple as he pulls out my chair.

We take our seats, and the rest of the family goes back to talking about some medical conference in Boston. It's the type of thing Liam would typically join in on, but he remains quiet, his hand placed firmly on my inner thigh.

The gesture feels heavy, laden with meaning, and I can't help but feel like I'm in the waiting room, anxiously anticipating the results to a biopsy. Are we going to make it? Or is it terminal?

I know what I want. I want him to come home. I want to try again. I want everything we promised each other five years ago. But I also know there's still a lot more to talk about. That it's not as simple as that.

After breakfast, Liam gets a phone call that he says he has to take. *My sister,* he adds when I give him a questioning look. He says he'll meet me back at the room with a glance that says, *We should talk*, then he disappears onto the deck while I hang back to play with the kids.

Twenty minutes and three extremely humbling crayon drawings of my face later, I head back to the cabin.

When I open the door, Liam's hunched over his suitcase, packing up his things. His back is to me, but I immediately sense something is wrong.

"Liam? What are you doing?"

He jerks around, revealing hard lines around his mouth and eyes.

"It's my mum," he says, his voice so low, I can feel it putting down roots in my belly. "She's in the hospital."

My vision swims, everything going hazy around the edges as I rush to his side.

"Is she okay? Did something happen?"

"She's okay," he says quickly. "Or at least she will be."

Panic strums my nerves. "What happened?" I ask.

He sits on the bed, his head dipping toward his knees like he's trying to decide whether he might throw up or not. "I don't know," he says to the floor. "But she left him."

I sit beside him and I reach for his hand, lacing my fingers through his. "Can you tell me what Felicity said?"

He blows out a steadying breath as I stroke the inside of his wrist with my thumb. "She said there was a fight, and Mum was trying to leave him." He winces like the words taste bad. "Felicity didn't give many details. She knew I'd panic."

He holds his eyes shut and I can tell the not-knowing is worse for him. I squeeze his hand tighter, my other moving to his back, where I rub in slow circles.

"Is Felicity there with her?" I ask.

Slowly he nods. "She's there. Which makes me feel better. At least Mum's not alone."

My palm pauses at the base of his neck, damp with sweat. "How do you feel about her leaving him?"

"I don't know," he says, his voice a cracked whisper. "I've

thought about this for years, and now that it's actually happening, I don't know how I'm supposed to feel. Scared that she's in the hospital? Relieved that she finally got out?"

I cup his jaw, drawing his forehead to mine. "Hey," I say softly. "It's okay to be scared. This is a lot all at once."

His gaze meets mine, wide and vulnerable. "She's asking for me," he whispers. "My mum wants to see me."

I pull back enough to search the worry lines bracketing his mouth and eyes. "Is that what you want?" I ask. "To see her?"

He swallows, his eyes distant like he's already gone, thousands of miles from here. "I don't even know how to process this. It's been fifteen years. It's all happening so fast." He drags his knuckles over his forehead. "But I think this is something I need to do."

An uneven breath cracks against my chest, unfurling inside me as I look to his hastily packed suitcase, then back to him, understanding washing over me in swift waves.

"So you're going to London?" I ask.

Hollowed-out eyes meet mine in confirmation, and my blood turns thick.

He needs to do this. I *want* him to do this. But all I can think is, *He's leaving before we've even had a chance to talk.*

I chew on my bottom lip, hesitating before I finally ask, "Do you have to go right now?"

"I think so," he says hoarsely. "She's finally left him, and it feels like I should be there. It feels like something I need to do, for them and for me."

The realization that he's already made this decision weighs like a band across my chest, binding my breath.

"I understand, and I support you," I say, choosing my words carefully. "But what about us?"

He takes my hand in his, slanting his forehead against mine. "I want you to come with me, Ros."

The words jolt inside me, reshuffling all my thoughts.

"What?"

"I want you to come with me," he says again, this time stronger, firmer. "To London."

My heart pounds in my throat. "Now?"

He nods, a kind of nervous energy coursing through his movements, exaggerating each feature. "I know that I haven't done a good job of letting you into the messy parts of my life, that I should have opened up to you, been more vulnerable, more honest. But I want to, if you let me, starting now."

My mind races. *Everything* races.

I think about last night, this morning. How we touched and tasted and had all of each other. How we said words I never thought I'd hear again. And how intense it all felt. But we haven't even talked about our marriage, about what we want, what's next. And now suddenly he's asking me to travel across the world with him at a moment's notice?

This feels like too much, too fast.

"But we haven't talked yet," I say, trying to coax the panic out of my voice. "Shouldn't we talk first?"

"The travel time from here to London is twenty hours. We'll have plenty of time to talk," he says.

I stand up, feeling light-headed. "This is so fast, Liam. I need time to think."

Liam checks his watch. "The flight leaves in a couple hours, which means we need to leave for the airport . . ." He frowns at the face on his watch. "Now."

"Now?"

"Now," he confirms.

My ears ring. Blood pounds in my skull.

He's not exactly asking me to decide what I want right now, but it feels like it. Like the future of our marriage hangs in the fragile balance of a decision I have to make in the next handful of minutes.

I start to pace the length of the cabin. "How long do you think you'll be gone for?"

"I don't know. Weeks? Maybe months?"

Months?

"What about work?" I ask.

"I'll ask for a sabbatical."

I glance at his hastily packed suitcase.

"What about the job in London?"

"I won't take it."

My vision frays as the implication becomes clear.

He's choosing me.

It's what I've always wanted. But I feel like I'm spinning out with no time to gather my thoughts.

"I want to be there for you," I tell him, pushing past the wedge in my throat. Then in a smaller voice, I ask, "But what does this mean?"

He drags a hand through his messy hair, his eyes lifting to mine. "It means I want you back, Ros."

He blurs in front of me, a fuzzy, Liam-shaped blob.

It's exactly what I hoped he'd say. What I've dreamed about for months. And yet all I feel is stomach-churning fear.

Liam's about to do one of the hardest things he's probably ever had to do, something that would be challenging even if our relationship was rock-solid. But it's not.

We've only just begun to sift through our issues. Only just started to heal the deep wounds between us. And I'm terrified that my going with him is too much, too fast. That whatever foundation we've only just started to repair will crumble under the pressure.

"I want that too. I want *you*." I swallow around the heaviness in my throat. "But I'm scared of rushing back into this only for things to fall apart again."

He grips my hands tighter. "I'm scared too. So let's be scared together."

He makes it sound so easy, so simple. But it's not. The last few days have been on vacation. What happens when we return to reality? What if he shuts me out again? What if three, six, ten months from now we're fighting again, and everything is right back to where it was?

What if we crash and burn again, only this time I don't survive the landing?

"But we don't know what's going to happen. The last year almost broke me, Liam. What if we hurt each other again?"

"I'm not going to hurt you," he says, drawing his hand along the side of my cheek.

I shake my head, my vision blurring behind the glassy layer of tears. "You can't promise me that," I tell him.

He gently brushes a tear from my chin with the pad of his thumb.

"You're right. I can't." His gaze is equal parts tender and determined. "But I *can* promise that things will be different this time. I can promise to love you, to be there, to let you in. I can promise to show you all my broken parts, and hope you'll trust me with yours."

"I want that." *I want you*, my heart screams. "I just . . ." My voice breaks as a tear runs down my cheek. "There's just so much we haven't talked about, and I wish that didn't matter, that I could just say yes, but . . ." The lump in my throat expands. "But I want us to work, Liam, and I think the best chance we have at that is to be careful. Right?"

Slowly his face transforms, wide eyes focusing, jaw setting with resolve. "You're right. There's still a lot we haven't talked about. And we owe it to each other to be honest. So I want to lay my cards on the table, cards I should have laid out a long time ago."

He takes my hands in his. "I don't want a divorce. I didn't then, and I don't now. I love you, Roslyn. You're the beginning and end of everything for me, and no matter what happens next, no matter where we go from here, there will never be a time that I don't love you. Not now. Not a decade from now. Not forty fucking years from now."

His voice starts to waver, but his eyes stay planted on me. "I want to kiss you good night and wipe away your tears and hold you at the end of a long day. I want to grow old together and witness each other's lives. I want that to be us up there someday celebrating our fiftieth wedding anniversary with our children and grandchildren and great-grandchildren. I want all of that with you and only you, Ros. Forever."

He lets one of my hands go to bring his palm up, gently cradling my cheek, moving closer until his forehead is resting against mine.

"I'm sorry I wasn't the husband you needed me to be. I'm sorry I hurt you. I'm sorry I didn't let you into the hard parts of my life. I'm sorry I let my past dictate our future. I'm sorry I wasn't there to help carry your burdens. But I don't want to lose you again. I *can't* lose you again," he adds, his voice splintering.

"I know I didn't fight for you three months ago, but I want you to know where I stand now. I'm here, and I will fight for you. I'm all in, and I always was, even when I didn't know how to show it."

Desperation and something like hope threads through his

voice, and my throat fills, pangs of want and despair crashing together.

If this were a book, the choice would be easy, the warm embrace of a well-deserved happily ever after only a few pages away. But this is real life and happily ever after isn't guaranteed. It never was.

I think about my mom. About all the packed bags and moving boxes. All the times she had her heart broken. How she remained hopeful nonetheless. If she were here, she'd urge me to go with him. She'd tell me that love is about taking chances. About being brave.

But that's exactly the problem. I was never brave like her.

"I'm so sorry. I wish I could say yes," I tell him, my tears falling hot and fast. "I wish I could be brave enough to do this with you."

His gaze is heavy with a kind of sadness that I feel against my chest, a pressure that makes it hard to breathe. "So what does this mean for us?"

I press my palm to his cheek, forcing his gaze to mine. "I want to be with you. I want to try again." My voice starts to shake. "But we've only just started to work through our issues, and this is such a big conversation that I think deserves more time. From both of us."

His shoulders slump, but slowly he nods. "I understand." Heavy eyes flick up to mine. "We can talk again when I get back."

My heart splinters, realizing I have no idea when that might be. And neither does he.

"But before I go." He cups my cheek again, his gaze roaming the terrain of my face like he's trying to memorize it. "I want you to know that no matter what happens next, we'll figure it out together. You and me." Then he leans in and kisses my temple, letting his lips linger. "I love you, Roslyn," he whispers against my skin.

"I love you, too," I tell him. But it's different than when I said it last night. Last night it had felt like a dam breaking loose, like coming home again, full of hope and longing and possibility. But this time it feels more like coming to the end of a long path only to find a crossroads.

When he finally pulls away and walks toward the door, suitcase in hand, I don't turn around. I can't watch him leave. Not again.

- 41 -

Now

Not wanting—or perhaps not being able—to be in the room a second longer, I slip out the door and start to run. I'm not sure where I'm going, or what I'm going to do when I get there, only that I need to move, to breathe, to think, anything but stand there.

I make it all the way to A Deck before hot tears sting my eyes, vision blurring as I lean over the railing, wondering if I'm going to be sick.

Liam said all the right things. Beautiful, heart-wrenching things. But I still couldn't do it. I couldn't go with him.

I've spent my whole life scared. As a child, it was the constant volatility in my life. Of not knowing where we'd live or if my mom had a job or if we would make rent that month. When I got older, it was fear of being hurt, of going through the same heartbreak I saw my mom go through.

Then I met Liam, and loving him felt like balm on a burn, and the anxiety morphed into a fear of losing him, of losing the stability I'd spent my whole life yearning for.

It's a fear I was able to push to the back of my mind for most of our relationship, but it was always there, hovering around the periphery, until my mom died and it reemerged, sharper, more painful than ever.

It's not just that Liam wasn't there for me when I needed him. It's that he'd seen all my broken pieces, felt the weight of my heaviest burdens, and decided he didn't want them. That the sum of my parts didn't amount to something Liam was willing to fight for. And in the end, when it mattered most, I wasn't enough to make him stay.

And I realized it wasn't instability, or a man, or even heartbreak I was most afraid of, but that I wasn't enough. That deep down, at my core, I wasn't worth it.

Perhaps it's the same part of myself that's never felt I measured up for my own family. That was always terrified of disappointing everyone. That's been pretending to be *fine,* covering up my hurt, so I don't have to burden those around me with my grief.

Now, despite everything that's happened the past few days, every pretty word and beautiful promise, there's a part of me that's still afraid it's not enough. That's terrified to take this plunge into the same waters that nearly drowned me the first time.

Maybe we'd float to the surface, unscathed. But maybe we wouldn't.

I don't know how long I stay there, letting the ocean breeze dry my face until my phone buzzes inside my purse. My heart leaps into my throat, wondering if it's Liam, but it's a string of messages from my sister.

Come to Grammy and Gramp's cabin!

We have a surprise.

Come now!!

Where are you??

I shove my phone back in my purse. I don't want to see them. Or hear about whatever surprise they have. I want to be alone. I want to cry until my throat is raw and my eyes burn. But the insistent buzzing inside my purse is relentless, so I wipe my eyes and tell myself I'll stay for a minute, act surprised for whatever it is, then make some kind of excuse to leave.

But as soon as I arrive outside Grammy and Gramps's stateroom and hear the excited chatter through the door, my visions of a quick exit begin to dim.

I knock, and a moment later the door opens. Bella appears, champagne flute in hand.

"Finally! You're here! I've been texting you!" She looks past me. "Where's Liam?"

"Oh, uh . . ." Before I can figure out what to tell my family, Bella cuts me off, pulling me into the room.

"It's fine, we can tell him the news when he gets here!"

My gaze snaps between a positively giddy Bella and everyone else, already holding drinks. "What news?" I ask.

A smile ripens across Bella's mouth before she flings her left hand out at me. My eyes widen when I see the massive diamond.

I gasp. "You're engaged?"

Her eyes fill with tears as Chris pulls her into his side and recounts how he was planning it for weeks and was so worried Bella would figure it out. Then Bella jumps in to say she had no idea and was shocked when they'd returned to their cabin this morning to find rose petals all over the bed.

They go back and forth, correcting small details like if she gasped or screamed, and whether Chris kneeled then asked or asked then kneeled.

I try to smile and laugh at all the right parts of the story, but a deep-seated sadness festers in my belly.

All I can think is how my mom would have loved to be here. To see Bella beaming with a sparkling diamond on her finger. How excited she would have been for them. And how painful it is that she won't see Bella and Chris get married.

I search their happy, smiling faces, wondering if they feel it too. If anyone will mention her. Or say how much they miss her. How badly they wish she were here right now.

But the conversation transitions to the pros and cons of a spring wedding in Seattle, and my sadness morphs into something else, something that pulses in the back of my throat.

Are we really going to stand here and laugh and smile and pretend like her absence isn't this giant elephant in the room? Like no one cares that she isn't here?

But maybe that's it. Maybe they don't care.

I try to push down the thought, to lock it away with all the messy feelings I've tried so hard to pretend aren't there, but I can't—I can't pretend anymore—and before I can stop them, hot tears sting my eyes.

Bella stops in the middle of describing what kind of venue they'd like. "Roslyn? What's wrong? Are you okay?"

I twist my mouth into a smile, trying to mask the sharp edges of grief tearing me open. "Fine," I tell her. "I'm so happy for you. Really . . ." I open my mouth, hoping something like *Congrats* or a celebratory scream comes out, but it's as though I've stepped onstage and suddenly forgotten my lines.

"Roslyn?" Grammy asks, putting a hand on my arm. "What is it, dear?"

I reach for the words to tell her I'm okay. After all, this is Bella and Chris's special moment, and I can't ruin it. I can't be the family fuckup again. But the tears begin to fall and my throat burns, my tongue tasting like copper and salt.

"I'm sorry," I gasp. "I'm so sorry. I'm really happy for you and Chris and I—" I wipe my eyes, determined to pull it together. "I'm fine," I finally force out, but Bella doesn't look convinced, and frankly, neither does anyone else.

"Hey," Bella says, voice softening. "Whatever it is, you can tell us."

That's exactly the problem, I think. *I can't tell you. That's why I've spent the last year pretending to be fine, because you don't get it. Because none of you miss Mom the way I do.*

"I think I should go," I say. "I don't want to ruin your moment."

I run out the door, hoping I can get back to my cabin before I make an even bigger mess of things. But I only make it three feet down the hall before I'm doubled over, lungs burning, eyes wet with tears.

I've been trying so hard to keep it together, to be fine, even while on the inside I was falling apart, but I can't do it anymore. Not now. Not after everything that's happened. So there, in the hallway, I finally fall apart. I give in to the hot press of tension corkscrewing in my chest, the heaviness in my bones, the bruising crush of hurt in my lungs. I let myself feel every ounce of shame and guilt and hurt and fear until all my emotions are bleeding together. I let myself feel all the grief and sadness I've tried to push down.

I'm crying so hard, I barely hear the door to Grammy and Gramps's room open until Bella is standing in front of me.

"I'm sorry I'm ruining your engagement," I choke, hating myself.

She shakes her head, her eyes wide with concern. "Roslyn, can you please just tell me what's going on? Are you okay?"

I look down the hall then back at her. There's still time to leave. To tell another lie. To keep the truth buried inside me just a little longer. To accommodate and appease. But as I wipe under my eyes, trying to stabilize my breathing, I realize that I'm exhausted. Not just from pretending, but from the pain itself, from the effort of holding it in, of trying to make my grief more palatable.

Maybe she'll hate me. Maybe I'll just solidify myself as the family disappointment. But I can't keep pretending.

"I'm not okay," I finally say. "This past year has been the hardest of my life and I've been trying to keep it together, to be fine, the way everyone else seems to be, but I miss Mom so much." A sob splinters through my voice, but I keep going. "Maybe you guys don't miss her or care that she's not here, maybe you don't need her, but I do. And it's been so fucking hard without her." The words are tumbling out of my mouth, rushing out now that I'm finally letting them free. "While you guys have all been moving on, relieved that she's not around, I've been grieving alone, going through a fucking divorce and—"

Bella steps back, her expression clouding over with confusion. "What do you mean, *going through a divorce*?"

I wait for feelings of panic, to feel like the walls are caving in around me. Instead, I just feel angry. Angry that *this* is what she cares about. Not me. Not Mom.

"Yeah," I say, not meeting her eye. "Liam and I split up three months ago."

Her brow furrows. "Split up? As in . . . ?"

I draw a choppy breath, the words that I know will bring everything crashing down around me hovering in the back of my throat. "I asked him for a divorce," I finally force out.

"You *what*?" I turn toward the door, where the entire family has gathered, and judging by the looks on their faces, they've all heard.

Fuck. This isn't how I wanted it to happen. Especially now that Liam and I are figuring things out. But I don't see a way to keep lying, nor do I want to. I have to tell the truth.

"I asked him for a divorce," I repeat. "We've been living apart for months."

I watch, almost in slow motion, as their faces shift from perplexed to shocked to horrified. All the stages of grief in a span of seconds. It's exactly what I worried would happen.

"But . . . but I don't understand," Grammy says. "I thought you two were trying to have a baby."

"And last night you two seemed so happy," Jonah says.

"You were kissing on the dance floor," Bella adds.

"We've been pretending."

I know that's not entirely true. There were moments that were real. Or maybe they were all real, and in the end the only people we were fooling were ourselves.

"But *why*? What happened? Where is he?" Grammy looks up and down the hallway like she's half expecting Liam to pop out from somewhere.

"He got off the ship. He had to leave for London because of a family emergency." Then, more urgently, I add, "But we've been figuring things out. We're going to talk when he gets back."

Grammy's mouth parts. "But when will he be back?" she asks.

I think of the moment we shared before he left. The way he'd cradled my chin as he told me he loved me. The tears in my eyes as I'd looked away, unable to watch him leave.

"I . . ." A crack catches the end of my voice. "I don't know," I admit.

Eyes widen, brows furrow.

I catch Bella's eyes, hoping she can forgive me for being such a shitty sister, for ruining her special day, but she just stares at me, shocked.

"So, you've been lying this whole time?" Gramps finally asks.

"Liam and I didn't want to hurt you all or ruin the trip," I say, swallowing around the wedge in my esophagus. "And I was afraid of disappointing you again."

"What do you mean, disappointing us *again*?" Grammy asks. "Why would you think that?"

A wave of frustration climbs up my throat as the words I've long held on to bob to the surface.

"Of course I think that," I say, exasperated. "You're constantly making me feel like I'm this huge failure because I didn't make the life choices you wanted me to. You were disappointed in me for dropping out of med school. You were disappointed when I waited tables instead of getting a *good job*. You're disappointed in me for not being a successful, bestselling author of *serious* fiction. You've always treated me like I was a failure. Like Liam was the only thing I ever did right. How could I not be worried about that? How could I—"

"That's enough," Gramps cuts me off. "You're not going to come in here after lying to us all for months and talk to your grandmother and me like this." He shakes his head, narrowed eyes focusing on me. "You're just like your mother. Always playing the victim, acting like the whole world was out to wrong her, when she was the one who threw opportunities away and made poor choices. Never realizing how good she had something until it was gone. Now you're doing the same thing with Liam." His voice is controlled, but I can hear the barely contained intensity hovering behind every word. "I don't know what's happened between you two, but you need to fix this, Roslyn."

Anger vibrates through my bones. I've always played it safe, first confiding in my mom, then keeping my feelings to myself where they couldn't burden anyone. But she's not here to confide in or stand up for me. Now I have to stand up for myself.

"You're right," I say, my voice coming out a lot stronger than I feel. "You don't know what happened between Liam and me. You don't know that Mom's death tore us apart or that I've spent the last year crying myself to sleep every night. You don't know anything about me or what I want. You never have." I look at Bella. "I'm so sorry for ruining this. I hope you can forgive me."

Then, my heart still pounding in my chest, I turn and leave.

- 42 -

Now

As soon as I'm back in my own cabin, I let the tears race down my cheeks in thick, hot waves. I'm crying so hard, I barely hear the knock on the door until Jonah calls my name.

"Roslyn, open up! It's us."

I swallow my breath before opening the door, where Bella and Jonah are both standing, red-faced and sheepish.

"If you've come to tell me I'm making a mistake—"

"That's not why we're here," Jonah says. "We just want to talk."

My eyes dart between them, unsure if this is some kind of ambush to tell me how awful I am for breaking up with Liam and lying about it. Or possibly to tell me off for wrecking Bella and Chris's moment—which I definitely deserve—but the concern etched across their faces brings my defenses down and I step aside, letting them in.

"Are you okay?" Bella asks as soon as the door shuts with a thud behind them.

I frown. "Aren't you mad? I just ruined your engagement."

She chews on her bottom lip. "I mean, I have a lot of questions, but the first thing is whether you're okay?"

Part of me considers one more lie, just to get them off my back, something to smooth out the crinkle between Bella's brows, to fix the mess I've made, but I've already been this honest, I might as well go all the way.

"No," I admit. Then in a lower voice, I add, "I haven't been okay for a while."

Bella's expression softens. "Want to tell us about it?"

My first thought is that I don't know how to. I don't know how to talk about Liam. About everything that happened. About the swell of hurt that's taken up permanent residence inside me for the past year. But I think I owe them this, so I find my breath and start from the beginning.

I tell them about how things got bad after Mom's death. How we grew distant and Liam started sleeping at work. I tell them about when he left. The three months without him. How ashamed and hurt and broken I felt.

Then I tell them about the plan. How we decided it was better to pretend to still be together than ruin the trip. How the family would be so upset. How they'd blame me for ending my marriage. I tell them how he and I were fighting until we weren't. How things got better. How we opened up and were honest with each other. Then I tell them he's gone and now I don't know what will happen next.

When I'm done, they don't say anything, Bella just pulls me into a hug and squeezes me tight.

"I'm sorry you've been carrying this alone," she says into my neck.

"You're not mad at me for lying to you all?" I ask again.

She shakes her head. "Of course not. Breakups suck. We saw Mom go through enough of them to know that." She glances at Jonah, who nods in agreement. "But I wish you could have told us what you were going through," she says.

“I know how much you all love Liam.” I pause, choosing my words carefully. “I guess I was scared that you’d all hate me, that you’d choose him over me.”

Bella’s face softens. “We do love Liam, and I know we haven’t always been super close, but you’re our sister. We’d never choose anyone over you.”

My heart stretches against the confines of my rib cage.

“I get how you’re feeling and why you didn’t feel comfortable telling anyone,” Jonah chimes in. He presses his lips together before he says, “A few years ago, Ben and I actually considered divorce.”

A sonic boom goes off in my chest. “What?”

Slowly he nods. “Thankfully we were able to work through it, but I couldn’t sleep for months because I was terrified to tell anyone,” he admits. “It felt like this huge personal failure. There was a lot of shame involved. So trust me when I say that I get not wanting to tell people.”

My lungs expand and contract with a mix of shock and hurt that Jonah went through that alone, just like I did. That I had no idea.

“I’m sorry you and Ben went through that,” I say after a beat. “I can’t imagine how hard that must have been, especially with the kids.”

“It was rough.” He pauses, hesitating before he says, “Ben and I are here if you ever need anything. Somewhere to crash, a hot meal.”

Typical Jonah to offer practical resources like food and shelter.

“Thanks,” I tell him. “I appreciate that.”

The corners of his mouth creak out an uneven grin, and I don’t realize I’m crying again until I look down and see the blotches on my cover-up. I sniff and wipe the snot from under my nose.

“I’m sorry,” I say to Bella. “You just got engaged and I totally ruined it. We should be popping champagne and celebrating. I'm the worst sister ever."

"Hey, it's okay," Bella says, putting a hand on my shoulder. "You're going through something really hard right now and we're here for you. We can always celebrate later."

I feel my heart expand, stretching to make room for the mix of hope and love and relief all crashing together inside me.

"Thank you," I whisper. "I know I don't deserve that."

Bella shakes her head. "Yes, you do. Everyone deserves some grace."

I push out a shaky breath, allowing myself to soak up her words.

"I know I should have been honest earlier," I say after a pause. "But ever since Mom died, I've been in a bad place." My throat clogs, my eyes stinging with tears, but I press on, needing to get the words out. "And the further I sank into the bad place, the harder it was to reach out, to ask for help. Especially when it seemed like everyone else was moving on and getting over her, while everything in my life was getting worse."

Bella reaches for my hand, and I let her take it. She tangles her fingers with mine and gives them a squeeze. "We didn't just get over Mom's death," she says, her voice quiet, barely above a whisper. "Why would you think that?"

I look between my brother and my sister, unsure where to even begin.

"It seems like you did, like you don't even miss her," I say. "I mean, you even said you were relieved she wasn't here."

Bella's mouth parts then closes to form a tight line. I feel her trying and hesitating to speak. "Of course I miss her. She was our mom. I just . . ." She pauses, combing a hand through her hair. "My feelings towards her are complicated," she finally says.

"What do you mean?"

"Mom was . . ." She gestures vaguely. "A lot," she says at last. "And after she died, there was a lot of anger and resentment to unpack."

My skin tightens, awareness pressing against the walls of my chest.

"You and Mom had so much in common that I never had with her, and I always felt left out," she admits. "Even when I got into med school, it was like she didn't really care. She was always more interested in you and your romance books. You two were so similar, and I could always tell she liked you better."

The words hit me in the center of my chest. I had no idea Bella felt that way. Or that it hurt her.

I never thought my siblings cared that Mom and I were closer, considering how much praise and validation they received from Gramps and Grammy—approval I never got. But now I can see that's not true, and the realization twists inside me like a scalpel.

I grip her hands tighter. "She was always proud of you," I tell her. "And she loved you so much, even if you two were different."

"I know, but . . ." She hesitates, her eyes flashing with something timid. "I just never felt close to her. And even after she died, there were reminders of it." She swallows, her gaze dropping to the bracelet on my wrist.

"I know I pushed Mom away when I was younger, but I also resented that she didn't show more interest in me." Then, lower, in a voice close to a whisper, she says, "I've been angry and hurt for a long time."

I think about what Liam said at the beach. That grief is complicated, and not all the emotions make sense or are easy to digest. Words that feel truer than ever.

"But even though I was angry, I still missed her," Bella goes on.

"It's why I started reading romance novels. I guess I wanted to try to connect with that part of her."

Understanding pings inside me. Bella isn't over Mom, or relieved she's gone. She's just grieving differently. Perhaps we all are.

I turn to Jonah. "Is that how you felt too?"

His eyes dip away, then back to me. "After it happened, I just felt, I don't know . . ." His mouth migrates to the corner of his jaw. "Empty inside. Like this huge part of my life, someone who was both a source of joy and frustration, was suddenly just gone, and I didn't know what to do with those emotions, or how to respond to that, so I guess I just didn't. I filled up the schedule with more activities and work obligations, so I wouldn't have to think about it," he admits. "The last year has been so busy with the kids and work and everything that I feel like I haven't yet had time to process her death."

My insides corkscrew with awareness. My siblings and I have all been struggling with her death, but in different ways. And if only we'd leaned on and confided in each other, it might have made the burden of grief a little easier to bear. Maybe the last year wouldn't have been so hard, or so isolating. Because maybe grief isn't meant to be handled alone. Maybe it's meant to be shared.

"For what it's worth, I've been unpacking resentment and confusing feelings towards her too," I admit.

Bella's eyes dart up to meet mine. "You have?"

"She was my best friend, and I miss her more than anything," I say. "But I think you were right the other day, Jonah." I look at my brother. "I only wanted to remember a certain version of her, because it was easier that way." I pause, gathering the next words. "But the truth is she wasn't always a good mom. That's been a hard reality to accept."

As soon as I say it, I feel stricken by the same guilt I had when I told Liam, but almost instantly it's swallowed by the look of understanding slipping across both Bella's and Jonah's features.

"Yeah," Jonah agrees, so quiet it's almost a whisper. "It has been hard."

We don't have to say it; I know what we're all thinking about. The times she didn't come home until well past midnight. When she quit her job and went to Paris with a man she'd only just met because *he might be the one*. All the birthdays we didn't have cake because she had lost yet another job.

I hate that I still remember, but I also know that part of grieving her is accepting the totality of who she was, both an effervescent, free-spirited woman who stood up for me and supported the people she loved, and a very imperfect mother. Because like Liam said, sometimes the people we love act like assholes. But it doesn't mean we can't continue to love them or forgive them.

Then again, maybe forgiveness isn't for my mom; maybe it's for me. So I can step into the next chapter of my life, free from the pressure of having to remember my mom as perfect, and instead remember her as a complex human being, flaws and all, the way we all are.

I slide Mom's bracelet off my wrist and clasp it around Bella's. "I want you to have this," I tell her.

Bella's eyes widen. "But you love that bracelet."

"I know, but Mom would want you to have it, especially today," I add. "She would be so happy for you and Chris."

Bella's lips fold together and I think she might refuse, but then she lets out a tremulous smile. "Thank you," she says. Then in a whisper, she adds, "Maybe I'll wear it on my wedding day."

Bella's eyes fill with tears, and I allow myself to feel the full force of my mom's absence. Of all the milestones and moments she'll miss and how each one will come with fresh waves of heartache. And then I let myself feel a surge of hope because even though she won't be there, we will still be able to carry pieces of her with us.

"I'm still wrestling with a lot of complicated feelings towards her," Bella says, wiping her eyes. "But I've been talking to a therapist and it's really helped me." She pauses, her eyes dipping to the floor before she says, "I think for a long time, I thought I could handle it on my own, but then my grades started slipping. It was really hard, but Chris encouraged me to get help and I did."

"How has it been?" I ask. "Seeing someone, I mean?"

"Some days are harder than others, but if I've learned anything, it's that the pain doesn't go away; it just feels more manageable." She hesitates before she says, "And that it's okay to ask for help. You don't have to bear this burden all on your own."

Her words tighten around me like a too-small belt, constricting my flow of blood. All this time I've been silently struggling, trying to manage the pain of grief on my own, pretending I'm fine. But I'm not. I haven't been for a while. And maybe Bella's right; maybe it's okay to ask for help. The same way Liam did.

That thought gives me a quiet burst of hope.

"We should talk about Mom sometime," I say after a minute. "The good. The bad. All of it. Just the three of us."

Bella bobs her head in agreement. "We could go to that pho place on Aurora that she always liked."

"That's a great idea," I say.

"I'd like that," Jonah agrees.

We haven't had a conversation like this in a long time, maybe ever, and I'm not sure we know what to do next. But then Bella lunges forward, wrapping us in a big bear hug, squeezing us tight.

"I'm glad we talked about this," she says, pressing the top of her head against my neck. "I'm glad we have each other."

"Me too," I tell her, and I mean it. We haven't worked through the mountains of grief and distance between us, but it's a start, and maybe for right now, that's all we need.

We hug a beat longer until Jonah declares, "Okay, okay, that's enough," and we break away, laughing.

"So," Bella says, turning to me, "are you gonna spill the tea on you and Liam?"

"What tea? I already told you everything."

"Not everything." Bella exchanged a look with Jonah. "You said things were getting better, so what happened? Why did he leave?"

I shift my weight. It feels weird to open up to my brother and my sister about the nuances of my marriage, but I guess if we're going to be more open and honest with each other, now is a good time to start.

"Things *were* good," I tell them. "But this morning he got a call that he needs to go to London for a family emergency. He asked me to go with him, but it felt so fast. We were just starting to work things out, and rushing off to the other side of the world together felt like a massive step. I couldn't do it."

"So where does that leave you now?" Jonah asks.

"I want to be together," I admit. "But I'm also scared to jump back in so quickly. What if nothing's different? What if we fall into old patterns again? What if I'm just doing what Mom always did?"

"I get that you're scared, and those feelings are totally valid," Bella says, choosing her words carefully. "But do you still love him?"

My breath snatches like I've missed a step. "I can't think of a time I won't," I tell her. "But what if loving each other isn't enough? I mean, Mom loved a lot of different men, and it broke her heart every single time. I'm not resilient like her. I can't just jump headfirst and potentially get hurt again and again and again."

Bella nods, considering. "I understand where you're coming

from, but do you really think Liam is like one of Mom's shitty boyfriends?"

Her eyes catch mine, and it feels like there's a giant bowling ball in my stomach, weighing me down.

I think back to when Liam and I first got together nine years ago, how resistant I'd been to falling for him because I was afraid of getting hurt, of replicating the same relationship patterns I'd seen with my mom, but Liam had shown me he was different, that our relationship was different.

Yes, things fell apart in the aftermath of my mom's death. And yes, Liam hadn't shown up for me when I needed him. But had there also been a part of me that had anticipated, perhaps even expected, that Liam would hurt me? That he was no different than my mom's shitty boyfriends? Because that's what I always believed would happen? Because that's the pattern I'd come to learn, the same way Liam had come to learn that it was better to bury the hard stuff and not talk about it?

That thought shoots through me, straight down to my splintered center, gripping me with a force I don't expect when I hear a soft rap at the door. My insides lurch.

Is it Liam? Did I somehow conjure his existence just by thinking about him?

Almost trancelike, I move past my siblings toward the door, my heart tapping out hopeful currents. But when I open the door, it's not Liam standing there. It's Gramps.

"Roslyn. Can we talk?"

- 43 -

Now

There's an instinctual part of me that wants to tell Gramps to go away, that I'm not in the mood for another verbal laceration. But there's an uncharacteristic discomfort to the way he's looking at me that catches me off guard, so I open the door wider and gesture for him to come inside.

Bella and Jonah swap uneasy looks, but I give them a nod that says, *It's okay,* and they both shuffle out of the room to give us some privacy.

As soon as they're gone, Gramps clears his throat. "How are you?" he asks.

My eyes narrow. "Not great."

"Right, right." He scratches the back of his head.

"If you're here to criticize me again and—"

He shakes his head. "No. Actually." He coughs into his fist. "I wanted to tell you that I'm sorry for what I said earlier."

I step back, shocked. Gramps, whom I've never heard admit fault once, is apologizing? To me?

He licks his lips, pushing out a breath before he says, "I realize that my response to you ending your marriage with Liam was . . ." Gramps hesitates, his eyes dipping to the ground then back up to me. "Inappropriate of me," he says at last. "You're right. I don't know what happened between you two, and it was wrong of me to tell you what to do."

His voice comes out almost mechanical, and I wonder if Grammy pushed him to come talk to me the way she so often did when it was my mom he needed to smooth things over with. But the flash of regret behind his usually stoic expression makes me feel like he means it.

"Thanks, Gramps," I tell him. "I appreciate it."

He presses his lips together. "Your grandmother and I love Liam very much, and this is obviously hard on all of us. But *you're* our grandchild, and we will be there for you."

My heart kicks against my ribs. It's everything I ever wanted to hear from him. I should be elated. Instead, my whole body feels tight, like all my internal organs have been smooshed together.

For a long minute, he doesn't speak, and I wonder if that's the end of the conversation, until Gramps says, "You're so much like your mother."

"I know, you told me," I say tightly.

His expression falls, but he picks it back up to say, "I think you're even more alike than I expected."

My tongues swipes across my bottom lip. "What do you mean?"

"She was passionate about the things that mattered to her. The people too," he adds, giving me a long look. "She always knew how to stand up and say what she thought, a quality I admired, even when she was standing up to me, and I think I saw that in you today too. It reminded me so much of her, it was a bit like seeing a ghost." He shakes his head, eyes turning glassy before he says, "I miss your mother every single day."

Pressure builds in my chest. A hot press of air, weighing down my sternum.

"You do?" I ask, my voice small, fragile.

He nods. "You never expect to outlive your child. You think you'll always have them, that you'll be the one to go first, that you'll have more time. But there wasn't enough time with her and there's so much I regret." His voice falters before he continues, "I made a lot of mistakes with your mother. Most of which are things it's too late for me to fix."

An ache builds behind my ribs. In all my life I've never once seen Gramps get emotional, but his usually stiff face softens, giving way to something pliable. Something weighed down by the pain and grief of losing his only child.

"I know I put a lot of pressure on you and your siblings to achieve what your mother never did," he goes on. "But I want you to know that I'm proud of you for what you have accomplished, and I'm sorry for not listening to you. For not supporting your choices, especially your writing." His jaw sets with determination. "You were right about what you said, that I don't know you as well as I should. But that's my fault, and I'm going to try to do better."

A thorny knot appears in my throat. "That means a lot, Gramps," I force out.

He makes a strangled little coughing sound before he says, "The other night Liam told me I should read one of your books."

My chest feels tight all over again, but this time for a different reason.

"He did?" I ask.

Gramps's chin dips into a nod. "The first night we arrived, actually. You'd gone off and he and I were talking after dinner. He told me I should read the one on the island. About the man and woman who meet at the couples' retreat and pretend to date."

He frowns like he's not sure he's gotten that right, and my skin flares with heat because that one is quite spicy—like sex-on-the-beach, face-sitting spicy.

"It's not my usual reading material," he goes on. "But Liam told me that you're a terrific writer who works harder than anyone he knows. Then he told me I was an idiot to not give your work the chance it deserves."

"Liam said that?"

"He's very proud of you, you know."

A dull throb spreads across my sternum.

I think about the past ten days, all the ways he's fought for me, both in words and actions. How he's listened and been honest and let me in. How he's gone to therapy and stood up for me, the way I always wanted him to. Most importantly, how brave he's been.

But what about me?

I picture Liam on his way to the airport, about to go do one of the scariest things of his life, alone, because I was afraid. Because despite wanting him to fight for me, I haven't done the same for him. I haven't been brave.

My whole life I've been scared. Of heartache. Of not being enough to make someone stay. And maybe so has Liam. But while he's gone to therapy and worked to break the patterns of trauma, I've been fearfully barricading my heart, afraid to truly give him a second chance. To give us *both* a second chance. The one we each deserve.

The realization scatters inside me, breaking off into a million tiny pieces, which work their way into every cell, every particle, until I know without a doubt what I need to do.

Maybe things won't work out with us. Maybe we'll lose each

other again. Maybe it will hurt like hell. But I don't want it to be because I didn't fight for us. Because I couldn't be brave. Because this time I'm the one who wasn't there when he needed me.

I turn to Gramps. "Gramps, I really appreciate you coming here and saying all this, but I have to go. There's somewhere I need to be."

Two months earlier

I sit up in bed, screams ringing in my ears. It takes me a moment to realize that the screams aren't in my dreams, they're real and they're mine.

My pulse thumps against my ribs, followed by a painful tightness that makes it hard to breathe.

I wonder if I'm having a heart attack. If I'm going to die here, alone, in my bed. Then I wonder how long it will take someone to find me. Days? Weeks?

I reach for my phone and dial the only person I can think to call.

He answers immediately, and when I tell him about the pain in my chest and the tightness in my throat, he says he's coming over.

I don't know how long it takes, but when Liam arrives, he finds me curled up on the edge of the bed, clutching my chest, crying.

Am I dying? I ask him.

You had a panic attack, he says.

But am I dying?

No, he says. *You're going to be okay. I'm here.*

Then Liam pulls me into his chest, his hand on my spine, his pulse synchronizing with mine.

I'm sure in the morning I'll be embarrassed about calling him, about asking for help, about falling apart in front of the absolute last person I want to see me like this, but right now, with his fingers in my hair and his arm tucking me into his warm, solid frame, I allow myself to sink into him. To forget, even if for a moment, that everything between us is broken. That I'm not his and he isn't mine.

I don't remember falling asleep, but when I wake up the next morning, I'm tucked into bed and there's no trace of Liam.

I half wonder if I dreamed the whole thing. If Liam was nothing more than a fevered extension of my nightmare. But when I drag myself out of bed and downstairs, I find that the fridge is stocked, the laundry is folded, and the pile of dirty dishes that cluttered the sink before I went to bed is washed and put away.

There's no note, no other evidence he was there, almost as if the chores were performed by ghostly apparitions. But it was him. And a foolish, naive part of my heart hopes that maybe, just maybe, he still cares.

- 45 -

Now

I don't stop running until I'm off the ship and in an Uber to Daniel K. Inouye International Airport.

"No luggage?" the driver asks when he pulls up outside the cruise ship terminal at Honolulu Harbor.

I look down at my hot pink swimsuit cover-up and flip-flops.

I was so singularly focused on getting off the ship and to the airport that I hadn't thought to grab anything besides my phone and passport, much less change.

I suppose close-toed shoes and real underwear would have been a good idea. But I'm here now, and either Liam still wants to give us another chance—bikini and all—or he doesn't.

"No, no luggage," I tell him. *Just me and a whole lot of baggage.*

I spend the entire journey oscillating between hope and fear.

What if Liam is angry at me for showing up unannounced? What if he no longer wants me to go with him and this is all a huge mistake? But this feels like the first right thing I've done in a long time. The first truly brave choice.

Sure, I could wait for Liam to come home, for the timing to be better, for me to feel less scared, but this moment right now is when he needs me to be there for him.

Maybe bravery isn't about waiting for the absence of fear, but about doing it anyway. About doing it scared.

As we take the freeway exit toward the departures terminal, I pull out my phone and fire off a quick text to my siblings to let them know where I went.

ME: Hey, so I'm going to London. Surprise!

BELLA: are you going after Liam???

ME: I am

BELLA: eeeeeeeeeeek!

Because Jonah is a sociopath, he just gives the message a thumbs-up.

BELLA: keep us posted! good luck!

BELLA: mom would be so proud

I smile down at my screen because she's right. My mom would be proud. I can practically hear her say, *It's so romantic, you going after him at the airport. Just like a Nora Ephron movie.*

And maybe it is a little bit. But this isn't a movie. The credits won't roll. The screen won't fade to black after the final kiss. The audience won't get up and leave, their cheeks sore from smiling, satisfied that all is right with the world. Because real-life happily ever afters don't look like the ones we see on-screen or in the pages of our favorite books. In real life, the credits never roll. The last page never gets turned. There's always another scene. Another day. Another heartache. Another challenge.

Maybe real-life happily ever afters don't mean never getting hurt or messing up or being scared. Maybe they mean forgiveness and hope and trying again. Maybe real-life happily ever afters look like going to therapy and asking for help. Being honest with each other. Choosing to stay together even when it's hard. Maybe *happily ever after* means running to the airport in flip-flops and a bikini to tell the man you love that you're not giving up on your marriage. That you want to be there for him, messy parts and all.

By the time the car comes to a stop, I'm so pumped up with adrenaline that I'm ready to sprint to security. That is until I realize in all my excitement to get here, I forgot about things like logistics.

What airline is he flying? What flight?

I pull out my phone, ready to fire off a quick text to see where he's at, when I spot a familiar head of dirty blond hair on the other side of the terminal.

It's an accident that I even see him at all. Surely in a crowded airport full of hundreds of people, he would be easy to miss. But maybe he was looking for me too. Or maybe we were drawn to each other by a gravitational pull, the way we've always been.

From across the room, our eyes lock, and a painful ache emerges inside me. The feeling of wanting something so badly, it hurts.

Maybe I move first or maybe he does, but somehow we're standing in front of each other, chests rising and falling like we've crossed an invisible finish line.

"Ros?" he asks, his voice stretched thin with disbelief. "What are you doing here?"

I step toward him, my blood pounding loud and hard in my veins. "I'm coming with you," I tell him. "To London."

He blinks. "What?"

The narrowing space between us suddenly feels cavernous, and it takes everything in me not to reach out, to touch him, to feel his skin on mine.

"When you asked me to go, I was scared," I tell him. "I was scared that maybe we were rushing into things. That we'd make the same mistakes again. I was scared that I couldn't be the partner you needed me to be. But then I realized there was something even scarier. And that was losing you again."

His eyes widen and I swallow down the wedge in my throat.

"This past week you've been brave with me," I tell him. "You've gone to therapy. You've been honest and real. You've let me into the messy parts of your life. You've shown me that you're willing to fight for us, and now I want to do the same. I want to show up for you and love you and fight for you and forgive you and be brave with you, because I want us to last. Because I want *you*, Liam, messy parts and all."

For a long moment he doesn't speak. His brow tenses, his mouth parting then closing again, and I hold my breath. Finally, he says, "I want that too."

My heart—no, *everything*—lifts.

"I asked you to marry me in your grandparents' kitchen seven years ago because I wanted to spend forever with you, Ros. That never changed. Not today, not three months ago, not ever."

He eyes the remaining gap between us before stepping toward me and taking my hand, lacing his fingers with mine like he's afraid I might float away. "But we can slow down. We can just date for a while. I can give you space if that's what you need."

I shake my head, tears blurring my vision. "I don't need space. I never did. What I want is all of you. As much of you as I can have. If you'll still have me."

His knuckles squeeze against mine. "Of course I want you, Ros. I want all of you." His hands move to my neck, fingers twisting in my hair. "Forever."

Forever. The word slithers past my last protective barrier, wrapping its way around my heart. It's a promise, a reminder, maybe both.

I launch myself at him, winding my arms around his neck. He laughs, and I feel the sound like lightning in my veins.

"We don't have to have it all figured out, or know what comes next, or how we'll deal with it," he says, his forehead pressed to mine. "I just want to do it together."

"That's what I want too," I tell him, my breath hitching as my eyes flood with tears. "And I'm sorry. I'm sorry for pushing you away, for not understanding that you were struggling too. I'm sorry for not giving us the chance we deserved." I swallow down the emerging lump in my throat. "I wish we could go back and do it all over."

"I'm sorry too." He tucks a loose strand of hair behind my ear and his gaze drops, his dark eyes finding mine and holding them tight. "But I don't want to start over."

I frown. "What do you mean? I thought . . . ?"

"There are a million ways we could rewrite our story, Ros," he says, fingers twitching as he cups my face. "But I want our story just the way it is. I want this life we've built and torn down and will build again. I want the good and the bad. The fights we had, and the fights we should have had. All of it. No editing."

My heart cracks, a long, wide fissure right down the center.

"I don't know if you remember the night we met—"

"I remember everything," I tell him.

His mouth wavers into a smile. "—I told you that the risk was what made loving someone meaningful. That you might get hurt, but it was worth it for the chance to love someone and to be loved in return." The full force of his focus settles on me. "I want you to know that it was all worth it. Everything. *You* are worth it."

I don't have to think; the words just tumble out of me. "You're worth it too."

Liam is brilliant, infuriatingly good at so many things. But the parts I love most aren't the shiny, peer-reviewed parts. They're the messy parts. The real ones. The parts I want to spend the rest of my life learning and knowing and loving.

Liam's brow softens, his lips parting, then his arms close around me, pulling me into an embrace that whittles me down to my core. "I don't want to pretend like it never happened," he says into my hair. "In fact, I don't want to do any more pretending at all."

My heart squeezes, a force so intense, so powerful, I feel like it might split me apart.

"I don't want to pretend either," I tell him. Then, in a lower, sturdier voice, I say, "Which is why I've decided to ask for help."

He pulls back, his brows drawing together. "What do you mean?"

I lick my lips, not realizing I've started to cry until I taste the salt. "I mean that I've been pretending to be fine since my mom died. But I'm not, and I can't carry this alone anymore. So here I am, asking for help."

As soon as I say it, I feel a rush of awareness across my skin, the feeling of being exposed, vulnerable. But instead of afraid or ashamed, I feel brave.

Liam brushes the pad of his thumb across my jaw, flicking away a stray tear. "I want to carry this with you," he whispers. "I want to do everything with you."

Hope ruffles its feathers against my chest. There's still so much work to do—hard, painful work—but just like Liam said in his speech, it's the kind of work that's worth it, that I want to do with him.

"I want to carry your burdens too," I tell him. "I want to carry the parts that are too heavy to carry alone."

"We'll do it together," he says. Then he takes my jaw in his hands, angling my face to his, and kisses me, a slow, bottomless kiss that turns me boneless.

"I love you, Ros," he whispers, his lips brushing mine, and suddenly we're no longer in a crowded airport, surrounded by hundreds of travelers. It's just us as his hands spread across my back, hauling me to him. Just us as my arms tighten around his neck, savoring our closeness. Just us as he crashes his lips to mine, sending sparks scattering over my skin.

"I love you too," I tell him. And in that moment, my love for him is overwhelming. Something too big, too powerful for my body to contain.

This thing, this love between us, isn't simple—it never has been. It's the hardest, scariest thing I've ever done, but it's worth it. Worth it in the way a difficult hike is worth the sore legs and depleted oxygen for the view. And this moment with him is the best damn view in the whole world.

We stay like that, holding each other, trading kisses like we're the only people in the airport, the only people anywhere, until finally Liam pulls back, his eyes damp, his lips swollen. "As grateful as I am to have you going to London with me, I have one question." His mischievous gaze travels up and down my frame. "Are you really planning to meet your mother-in-law for the first time in a bikini and flip-flops?"

I look down, remembering how I'm dressed. "Yes, and?"

A chuckle breaks in the back of his throat. "She'll love you no matter what, but, uh, maybe we should get you some proper clothes."

"And a toothbrush," I add.

"You didn't bring a toothbrush?"

"Nope. Just the clothes on my back," I say, gesturing to the pink cover-up. "Well, and my passport," I add, holding it up.

His mouth splits into a grin. "Wow, you must have really been in a hurry."

"What can I say? I needed to chase down my man. There wasn't time for things like real clothes."

He laughs, then leans in, gripping my waist, and kisses me. "Good," he whispers. "I like you better without real clothes anyways."

As his lips meet mine once more, I feel the same rush of anticipation that I did nine years ago in his kitchen, back when I had no idea who he would become to me, or what would happen. When the future felt as vast and limitless as the ocean. And even now, nine years and a million hurts and joys later, the future still has that open-ended feeling to it.

I don't know what will happen next. Where we'll go from here. All that's still to come in our lives—the good, the bad, the messy. But I feel a kind of sturdiness coursing through me. Like the axis that has been continually spinning under my feet has finally come to a standstill. Or perhaps like returning to dry land after too much time at sea.

Maybe it comes from Liam, from the weight of his hand in mine as we walk toward the counter to buy me a ticket to London. Or maybe it comes from me, from feeling brave. But a quiet certainty thrums inside me, a certainty that whatever comes next, whatever challenges we'll face, it will be together.

Maybe that's all happily ever after is and always was, I think. Maybe it's facing an unpredictable future together, knowing that no matter what, you won't be alone.

Epilogue

Two months later

"Go on, open it," Liam urges from his spot beside me on the sofa.

His mother rattles the box as though trying to guess what it is. "It's not that pasta maker we saw the other day at the shops, is it?"

Liam's mouth widens into a grin. "You'll have to open it and find out."

Dianne unwraps the Christmas paper I spent all yesterday wrapping and beams as she pulls out a brand-new pasta maker.

"Liam! I told you it was too much!" she cries. "You shouldn't have!"

"Well, now that you're here in Seattle, you need your own pasta maker so you can make homemade lasagna," he says, clearly pleased with himself.

"Is this your way of telling me you want me to move out?" she asks, and we all laugh.

After Liam and I landed in London, we spent a couple weeks helping Dianne arrange her affairs before we all decided it would be best if she and Liam's sister, Felicity, came back to Seattle with us.

While the house is crowded, and Liam and I really wish we had more than two bathrooms, it's nice to hear Liam and Felicity laughing in the living room, or find Dianne in the kitchen, whipping up a batch of her famous blueberry scones, and I know I'll miss them when they eventually find their own place nearby.

Liam and his mom have been taking things slowly, getting reacquainted little by little, piece by piece, trying to rebuild their relationship after years of neglect. Some days are hard, while others feel like massive breakthroughs, but I can see they're both trying, that they want to repair what's been broken, the same way Liam and I do.

In addition to seeing a therapist on my own, we've started seeing a marriage counselor together. The first few sessions were hard, and we both spent most of the hour in tears, but with each session, we've found new, healthy ways to communicate with each other and build trust and intimacy back into our marriage. There's still a lot of work to be done—a lifetime of work, in fact—but we're doing it together, day by day.

"Roslyn, pass the scones," Bella says from her spot curled up on Chris's lap by the Christmas tree Felicity and I spent hours decorating last weekend.

I pass her the plate, and she takes one before handing it to Abby, who is in town for the holidays. Last night Abby told me that she and Jake are expecting, and she mouths *eating for two* as she takes three scones.

Ben, Jonah, and the kids are far too interested in the laser tag set they opened this morning to pay attention to Grammy and Gramps, who keep trying to get photos of them in their matching reindeer jammies.

Even Kevin is here with his new girlfriend. It must be serious, because Kevin shaved the porno stache, and for once he doesn't smell like weed.

On the other side of Liam, Bella and Felicity have begun poring over a bridal magazine, pointing out dresses they each like.

The only person missing is my mom. But I feel her presence even when she's not here. She's in the photographs on the walls. And the stacks of romance novels lining the bookshelves. Mostly, I feel her in every crack of laughter and infectious smile.

She'd love this, I think as I look from the bracelet on Bella's wrist to the glow in Jonah's eyes as he and Ben share a quick peck under the mistletoe Liam insisted on hanging in the entryway. She'd love the way Jake whispers something in Abby's ear that makes her laugh, and how tenderly Gramps wraps a blanket over Grammy's shoulders because she looks cold. She'd love seeing how happy everyone is, and maybe, even though she's not here, this is as much her happily ever after as it is ours.

After Dianne finishes opening her gifts, she turns to me. "All right, Roslyn's turn. You should open your present from Liam."

When I look at Liam, he's already standing with his hand outstretched.

"If you want your gift, you'll have to come to the kitchen," he says.

A nervous laugh rattles out of me. "The kitchen? It's not lasagna, is it?"

Liam shakes his head, laughing. "Better."

Frowning, I take his hand as he leads me through the hall, past the photos of us on our wedding day now back on the wall, and into the kitchen.

"What's going on?" I whisper. But Liam doesn't answer. Instead, he digs in his pocket and pulls out a small velvet box before he drops to one knee.

A breath charges out of me. "Liam, what are you doing?"

"What does it look like? I'm proposing."

"But we're already married, and I already have a ring." I point to the diamond on my left hand he gave me seven years ago.

Liam shakes his head, eyes shining in the fluorescent kitchen lighting. "When I asked you to be my wife seven years ago, I didn't have a ring, or a plan—all I knew was that I wanted to be with you. But this time I want to do it right." He pops open the box to reveal a gold wedding band.

"Not just the proposal," he says. "But the marriage. All of it. I know I'm going to make mistakes, that I might hurt you and you might hurt me, that we'll both say and do things we wish we hadn't, but I promise to keep loving you and fighting for you. For us." He stands up, taking my hands in his. "I want to make lasagna for you and watch rom-coms and celebrate your latest book and get matching tattoos and go on holidays with your family and grow old together. I want to keep building a life, you and me. Whatever that takes, I'm all in. I'm yours."

Tears prick the backs of my eyes. It's been a hard year. The hardest of our lives. But standing here with Liam, knowing that no matter what's next, it will be with him by my side, makes me feel brave.

"Yes," I tell him through the curtain of now-falling tears. "I'm yours."

He collects me in his arms, his mouth meeting mine in a desperate rush.

"I love you," he whispers.

"I love you too." My fingers rope through his hair, tugging him closer. *His, his, his.*

After nine years, it's a tune my heart knows well.

We stay there, wound around each other, our mouths colliding in a steady rush of kisses that would probably escalate to more if our entire family weren't in the other room, until Felicity calls, "Well, did she say *yes*?"

Liam's laugh vibrates against my chest. "I love our families, but I can't wait until we have the place to ourselves again."

"You have no idea," I grumble as Liam leads me back into the main room.

"She said yes!" he cries, raising my hand over our heads in triumph.

Everyone cheers, and even Gramps has what could be mistaken for a smile on his face.

"Good," Dianne says with a curt nod and that famous British stiff upper lip. "Now you two can take a honeymoon and finally get some time to yourselves."

Liam frowns. "But I thought you liked being here with us, Mum."

"I do. But you need your own space." She gives us a knowing look. "Besides, I'm getting a bit tired of being woken up in the middle of the night by you two."

"Mum!" Liam cries, his face turning bright red.

She arches a brow. "What? You think I can't hear you both? You're not exactly quiet."

Bella and Abby descend into laughter while Liam and I exchange guilty looks.

Since we have a full house, sex usually happens in the middle of the night when we think everyone else is asleep. But apparently, we haven't been as sneaky as we thought.

After we finish opening gifts, we drink tea and eat chocolate biscuits that Dianne brought from M&S while Gramps asks me about the book I just turned in to my editor and whether I think I could get him an advance copy since he's already devoured my backlist. Then we watch *Die Hard*, which Liam still insists is a

Christmas movie. When it's over, he suggests we go for a walk around the neighborhood, and we slip out unnoticed. Outside the sky is gray, and a layer of fog hangs over the quiet street.

"I'm sorry about Mum," Liam says. "I really thought we were being quiet."

I sigh, feigning exasperation. "It's your fault anyways. You know I have trouble staying quiet when you do that thing with your tongue."

He grins, taking my hand. "But I think she's right."

"About what?" I ask.

"That we should get away. Just the two of us." His fingers loop through mine, giving my hand a squeeze. Even though we're both wearing gloves, I can feel the heat of his palm through the wool. "We never did have a honeymoon, you know."

"Where did you have in mind?"

"How about a cruise? I've heard they can be quite . . ." He wiggles his eyebrows. "Amorous."

I laugh. "As long as we're together, I'm happy. But maybe somewhere on dry land with more than a hundred and fifty square feet this time?"

He stops in the middle of the sidewalk, taking both my hands. "I'll go anywhere with you. London. Paris. Hawaii. The fucking moon. Just name it."

My entire body hums, my heart rising and whirring like a carnival ride.

Loving Liam is a kind of time machine. I'm here in this moment with him, but I'm also nine years in the past, blushing from across a sticky table, and a night five years ago, being kissed under a sea of fairy lights. I'm ten years from now, watching our children play in the backyard, wondering how we'll ever get those grass stains out. Even forty-five years from now when it's our turn to stand in front of our children and grandchildren and tell them that we're still choosing forever.

All of it stretches out between us, one endless expanse of memories and dreams and moments, and I feel an overwhelming sense of gratitude that in every timeline, every version of forever, it's him and I.

"How about home?" I say after a beat.

"You mean you don't want to go anywhere?"

"You're my home. Wherever you are is where I want to be."

Liam's thumb tracks along my cheek, up toward my ear, where he tucks a piece of hair back. "You're my home too," he whispers. Then he leans in and kisses me, slow and steady, a kiss that says, *No need to rush; we have forever,* and I kiss him back, using my whole body to answer.

Forever isn't long enough when it's with you.

Acknowledgments

I can't believe how lucky I am to get to do this again.

When I first started working on this book I felt like I was staring up at a mountain, overwhelmed by the journey I was embarking on, and now three years later, here I am at the summit with boundless gratitude for all the people who helped me get here.

First, thank you to my dream editor and creative partner, Sareer Khader. I feel like you truly held my hand through this book and I am endlessly grateful, not only for all the brainstorming phone calls and editorial notes that are always spot-on, but also for believing in and championing this story every step of the way. From our very first email about Ros and Liam, you got the heart of this story (I remember reading your first edit letter and whispering to myself, "She's so smart!!!") and I am overwhelmed with gratitude to have you as my brilliant creative partner.

Thank you to my agent, Kim Lionetti. I am so grateful for your guidance and advocacy on this journey.

Thank you to my critique partners and early readers, Amy Buchanan, Amanda Hopkins, Kjersten Piper Gresk, Megan Oliver, London Sperry, Katie Naymon, and Kelli Moon. It is an honor to have your fingerprints on this book. It is so much better because of you.

To anyone who has ever beta read or CP-ed for me, you know that it's a very, uh, *involved* experience, so thank you to everyone who fielded endless voice notes and phone calls and texts about plot and characters and whatever menty-b du jour I was having. Thank you for holding my hand and reading a million different rewrites of the same scene and walking me off countless ledges. I'm sorry for being annoying. It will probably happen again.

Thank you to my pookies, GG's, and plebs for always being a text (or frantic eight-minute voice note) away when I needed to vent, cry, scream, spiral, or all of the above. Writing is a solitary endeavor but I'm so grateful to have people who make it feel like we're in this together. See you on The Needle.

Thank you to the whole team at Berkley for all their support. Special thank-you to Kim-Salina I, Daché Rogers, Kaila Mundell-Hill, Erin Galloway, Jin Yu, Orli Moscowitz, and Theresa Tran.

Thank you to Vikki Chu for another superb cover. You absolutely nailed this one. Thank you, Kristin del Rosario, for the gorgeous book design.

Thank you to Noreen Nanja for donning your doctor hat to make sure I accurately portrayed Liam's professional and educational journey. Any mistakes are my own.

Thank you to those who blurbed *Wedding Dashers*: Annabel Monaghan, Sarah Adler, Lynn Painter, Jenna Levine, Jo Segura, Naina Kumar, Courtney Priess, and Meredith Schorr. I am so grateful that you not only took the time to read but also said nice things! I'm incredibly appreciative of your support.

Thank you to everyone who has read, reviewed, posted about, or recommended *Wedding Dashers*. As a baby debut there's no certainty that anyone will read, much less like, the book, but your support has been one of the greatest gifts, and I am endlessly thankful for all the wonderful readers and fellow writers I've had the pleasure of befriending along the way. Let's keep screaming about kissing books for a long time, okay?

Thank you to my mom. This story isn't about you (don't worry!!!!), but the anecdote about Roslyn's mother asking if she liked the end of a book, and if she said no, she would ask her what she would change, is. You've asked me that same question about nearly every story since long before I could read, a question that not only taught me to think critically about storytelling, but to think of story as something malleable, something I could bend and shift and mold. Something whose architecture I could deconstruct and rebuild. That, ultimately, I could tell my own stories. So now, twenty-five years later, that's exactly what I'm doing. Thank you for being my biggest cheerleader and always encouraging my creativity.

Thank you to my husband, Alex, for always championing my dreams. This book isn't about us (don't worry!!!!) but it's probably the most personal thing I've ever written. I hope you like it, messy parts and all.

Thank you to my in-laws, Susan and David, for always being so invested in and excited about my work and for being my British accuracy consultants.

Thank you to my best friend, Demi, for being the most supportive friend a gal could ask for. It brings me so much joy to know that we are both living out our creative dreams. I just know our eight-year-old selves would be so proud.

And finally, thank you, dear reader, for going on another adventure with me.

Sunk in Love

HEATHER McBREEN

READERS GUIDE

Behind the Book

I like to think of *Sunk in Love* as the continuation of my first book. While *Wedding Dashers* was the journey both literally and metaphorically *to* the wedding, *Sunk in Love* is the journey *after* the wedding. The story of what comes next. The story of forever.

So often in romance we don't get to see the forever. We see the buildup. The pining. The longing. The tension. The will-they-or-won't-they. The struggle, after which comes the admission of feelings. The grovel, the grand gesture, and then finally the big kiss where we get to walk away with the impression that everything works out. That all is right with the world and will remain so. Our characters will stay frozen in a perpetual state of happily ever after.

It's one of the things that keeps readers returning to the pages of romance. The guaranteed scaffolding of a happy ending, the satisfaction of knowing that by the end, everything will be okay. It's also what makes romance such a safe place to explore heavy topics like divorce and death and grief, because we know that, no matter what, there will be a soft landing. No matter what, everything will end up all right.

But we know real life doesn't work that way. In real life there's no guaranteed safety net of a happy ending to catch us when we fall, no warm embrace of a final kiss and the knowledge that everything will work out. In real life, things fall apart, and sometimes love isn't enough to save them.

This was the question that sparked the idea for *Sunk in Love*. What happens in the aftermath of happily ever after? When love isn't enough to hold us together? What if forever doesn't last, well . . . *forever*?

Sunk in Love is ultimately a story of two happily ever afters. The first where they fall for each other and eventually say *I do*. The one that looks like butterflies and first kisses and allowing the walls you've built around your heart to fall. And the second that comes after *I do*. The one that looks like growth and healing and forgiveness and taking risks and asking for help and learning to trust each other with their ugliest, messiest parts. The one that looks like choosing each other all over again.

Because, as Roslyn learns, real-life happily ever afters don't end with *I do*.

In real life, the credits never roll, the last chapter never comes, the final page never gets turned. There's always another day, another hardship, another challenge. In real life, forever isn't a singular commitment, but a continuous one that must be made over and over, even when it's hard, even when it's scary. A choice to stay together, to show up, to do the work required to make something last. A choice to choose each other, messy parts and all.

I think that's why I like to write about travel, about stories that take my characters out of their ordinary lives and plop them somewhere new, somewhere exciting, somewhere different than what they are used to. Because it's in those experiences that we find growth and discover what we want and perhaps what we don't want. Where we can rediscover ourselves and each other.

In a lot of ways relationships mirror physical journeys. They don't stay frozen in time, forever immortalized in the final moments of an epilogue or last chapter. They change and grow and adapt—the same way people do. They take us to new and different and often challenging places where we might meet the messiest, least polished versions of ourselves and each other. Where we might even discover new versions. Sometimes we might lose our way or travel alone for a while. But we can always find our way back.

Perhaps that's what happily ever after is. It's not a finish line or a destination, or even a beginning. It's an ongoing journey, taken together.

Discussion Questions

1. Roslyn's family isn't accepting of her decision to drop out of medical school and pursue creative writing. Have you ever made a decision that your family wasn't supportive of? How did you handle that?

2. Liam tells Roslyn that he agreed to come on the trip and pretend to still be together because he felt like it was something he could try to fix for her, even if he couldn't fix anything else. How else has Liam's life been shaped by his desire to try and fix things and help others?

3. Roslyn's mother's relationships with men shape Roslyn's fears about love and trust. How does this change over the course of the novel and how does it impact her relationship with Liam?

4. Jonah accuses Roslyn of only remembering their mom as she wants to remember her. How do you think grief impacts Roslyn's ability to remember her mom? Do you think Jonah's right? Do you think sometimes we suppress certain memories in order to maintain an image of a loved one after they are gone?

5. Roslyn is afraid to tell her family the truth about her marriage, which is what leads her and Liam to pretend to still be together. Have you ever told a lie in order to avoid upsetting or disappointing someone you love? How did it work out?

6. Liam and Roslyn are both grieving different kinds of familial wounds. How do their wounds mirror each other? And how do they impact their relationship?

7. When Roslyn's on her way to the airport to find Liam, she remarks that real-life happily ever afters don't always look like the ones we see in the pages of our favorite books or on-screen in our favorite movies. How do you think real-life happily ever afters differ from those presented in media?

8. At the start of the novel Roslyn thinks she is the only one grieving her mother, but later she finds out that the whole family has been grieving, just differently. What are some ways grief can manifest and how do you think those different manifestations can affect our relationships with others?

9. In Liam's speech, he tells the story of Roslyn's mother's bracelet and how when we take care of things, they can last. Do you agree that relationships are like the bracelet and require consistent hard work and care to make them last? What kinds of things can we do to maintain a relationship?

10. Both Liam and Roslyn fear that they aren't enough for the other person, a fear that inhibits them from being truly honest about what they want and need from each other. Have you ever struggled to communicate your needs in a relationship with a loved one?

Heather's Poolside Reading

The Co-op by Tarah DeWitt
The Summers Between Us by Noreen Nanja
Happy Place by Emily Henry
Seven Days in June by Tia Williams
How to End a Love Story by Yulin Kuang
This Summer Will Be Different by Carley Fortune
32 Days in May by Betty Corrello
Flirting with Disaster by Naina Kumar
Temple of Swoon by Jo Segura
Expiration Dates by Rebecca Serle
A Love Like the Sun by Riss M. Neilson

Photo courtesy of the author

HEATHER McBREEN lives and writes in Seattle, Washington. When she's not writing or reading books about kissing, she can be found on a Plot Girl Walk, begging her husband to get a sweet treat with her, and surfing the web for trips she's probably too tired to take.

VISIT HEATHER McBREEN ONLINE

HeatherMcBreen.com

HeatherMcBreenWrites